CW00921664

"An interesting and important look a
African history. The story of indenture
fracted through the prism of gender and
— SIPHIWE GLORIA NDLOVU, AUTHOR, FILMMAKER AND ACADEMIC

"Joanne Joseph has written a novel of the old kind: one which brings to life different and simultaneous worlds – India, South Africa, Madras, Port Natal – of the nineteenth century, which incorporates stories of love and murder, the court and the plantation, treason and new kinds of loyalty. The narrative is a real contribution to the writing of both countries." – IMRAAN COOVADIA, NOVELIST, ESSAYIST AND ACADEMIC

"*Children of Sugarcane* is an extraordinary novel with compelling characters that draws vivid attention to the tragic heroism of indentured Indian women on the British-owned plantations of Port Natal in the nineteenth century. One of South Africa's most accomplished journalists, Joanne Joseph nevertheless writes with the finely honed skills of an academic historian, the literary authority of a seasoned novelist, and the pedagogical fluency of a great teacher. Spanning two continents and four generations, this remarkable account of human lives reveals how Indian South Africans live(d) out those troubled, intertwined identities of race, class, caste and gender under the burden of Empire. In the process, the author opens up fresh insights into our wretched colonial past and, perhaps inevitably, its lingering shadows in the present. If the decolonisation moment needed an engaging, educative text for schools and universities, this book would be required reading." – PROFESSOR JONATHAN JANSEN, DISTINGUISHED PROFESSOR AND AUTHOR

Children
of Sugarcane

JOANNE JOSEPH

Jonathan Ball Publishers
Johannesburg · Cape Town · London

All rights reserved.
No part of this publication may be reproduced or transmitted,
in any form or by any means, without prior permission
from the publisher or copyright holder.

© Text Joanne Joseph 2021
© Published edition Jonathan Ball Publishers 2021

Originally published in South Africa in 2021 by
JONATHAN BALL PUBLISHERS
A division of Media24 (Pty) Ltd
PO Box 33977
Jeppestown
2043

Reprinted in 2022 (twice)

ISBN 978-1-77619-171-0
ebook ISBN 978-1-77619-172-7

Every effort has been made to trace the copyright holders and to obtain
their permission for the use of copyright material. The publishers
apologise for any errors or omissions and would be grateful to be
notified of any corrections that should be incorporated in future
editions of this book.

www.jonathanball.co.za
www.twitter.com/JonathanBallPub
www.facebook.com/JonathanBallPublishers

Cover by publicide
Cover images by Shutterstock and Alamy
Design and typesetting by Catherine Coetzer
Printed and bound by CTP Printers, Cape Town
Set in ITC Berkeley Oldstyle

Athilatchmy   Mary-Anne Bakium

Elizabeth   Grace

May,

thank you for paving the way.

Jade,

now all is possible.

AUTHOR'S NOTE

ALTHOUGH *CHILDREN OF SUGARCANE* IS A WORK OF FICTION, I have drawn strongly on historical record and fact to recreate the period of Indian indenture in the Colony of Natal, and the narratives of the human beings caught up in it. In the course of folding history into this story, I have taken some liberties, changing the names of key players, and fictionalising certain geographic locations, names of ships on which the indentured travelled, and the plantations where they worked.

The text also contains references to the Indian caste system, a stratified social pyramid of power relations centring on "purity", in which people are ranked according to heredity, religious practice and ritual, language and occupation, among other factors. Although outlawed in India, we still witness vestiges of caste practices continuing to play out through social association and even marriage in the modern Indian diaspora.

In order to ensure that the text remains authentic and true to the period in which indenture occurred (the late-nineteenth and early-twentieth centuries, a time of significant racial subjugation), the characters employ racially offensive language and slurs in common use at the time, circulated by the British. This is in no way intended to offend, but to reproduce a sense of the racialised hierarchies and brutality of the time.

PART 1

MADRAS PRESIDENCY

India 1916

SHANTI RISES IN THE DARK, feeling it knit around her, crackling like dry wool. She shuffles out of the small house, not wanting to wake her dreaming daughter. Her heart begins to batter against her ribs. But she only presses forward more deliberately, slightly out of breath, placing one shrivelled foot before the other, until she crosses the threshold to feel the dew moisten her face.

Thick dark stains the skies over the Madras Presidency. The scent of jasmine floats, while birds invoke the morning light. Shanti's eyes moisten at the thought of how far her silences have driven her only child from her. *How cruel I have become in my old age*, she thinks.

She is a small, stubborn blot on the night now, the scratch of sand between her ginger-gnarled toes. Day will soon bleach the horizon. And she will face the coming dawn, despite the fear she has carried for more than thirty summers. Dawn has always brought loss.

And yet this sunrise feels restorative. The charred sky catches its new flame. She reaches for its warmth, its peace, whatever forgiveness it might offer. And as the first surge of daylight spills across the sky, Shanti stands beneath it with the eyes of a child, drinking it in. Port Natal is suddenly with her – the same gash of sky, the smell of cut cane at daybreak, the hands, the faces, the voices that have lived inside her for decades.

Memory lives in light, she thinks. Benevolence and redemption, too. But light illuminates all – even the darkened hollows. The sundials' mad circles have slowed, and the time for concealment has run out. Secrets are wild birds. They cannot be held captive forever.

Lying awake, Raksha hears the tiny sounds of her mother's distress, and rises to go to her and lead her indoors.

"What is the matter, *Ama*?" She speaks softly. "Why were you standing outside crying?"

Shanti is silent.

"You never rise so early. What is wrong?"

Shanti shakes her head and mutters an apology for waking her daughter, but Raksha sleeps only fitfully, as she has every night for nearly two years now.

Raksha's obsession has set her adrift from Shanti. But it is life's way. Children grow and separate from their parents. Shanti must accept that Raksha is no longer that effusive little girl running home to spill the day's news. And yet she treasures the memory of the almighty leap into her mother's lap for storytime: anticipating the poems Shanti set dancing in her little ears, the resonance of songs her mother had brought back from across the ocean. Sometimes Raksha still hears the echo of their boisterous laughter at silly jokes, or the splash of her swimming lessons at the lake. How silent their home has become.

But Raksha cannot trade that silence for the battlefield her home will become if she shares her secret. These days, Shanti is prone to fits of temper or withdrawal into isolation. Her mind swings between lucidity and forgetfulness. This is the way of growing old. And when one's parent strays, it is a daughter's duty to guide her back, stay and care for her, be a mother to a mother, if needs be.

And so Raksha deals with her inner conflict alone. How could she possibly explain to her mother how unexpectedly it happened? How he had flowed into her life and crystallised there. Raksha often recalls that blistering afternoon near the lake, that first fateful meeting. She had raised her *pallu*, the edge of her sari sash, to dab her face, and when she dropped the cloth, there he was in front of her. He'd offered her a glass of water, tried to make conversation. She'd shaken her head and refused, even though she was parched. One did not accept charity from the British.

But in the ensuing days, she'd found herself passing his house again, glancing into his garden. And he was always there in the sunshine, often reading a book, seated at a simple table with two chairs. He would get up and walk to the fence to smile and greet her each time.

She should never have gone swimming in the lake. Possessed by something other than good sense, she'd dropped her basket at the shore one day, unravelling her sari in the shimmering heat while dipping first one foot, then the other, ever deeper in the water. The burning sun on her back drove her further in until she was almost submerged. She turned to look at the swathe of fabric, lying serpentine at the water's edge, while the lake enveloped her, cajoling, rippling around her form. And then she'd felt his eyes on her body as she'd waded deeper. After a few minutes, he'd called out to ask if he might enter the water. She'd laughed. "Do as you please," she had said. "The water is yours, as the land is yours." He had flushed

5

and lowered his head, then slowly begun removing his shirt.

He entered the water tentatively, paddling until the lake swallowed him and spat him out closer to her. "I am David," he said. She swam away. But the water conspired to stir up a current that drew them closer. And she soon became aware of his proximity, the poetry of their bodies as they swam. It was forbidden, audacious and playful, limbs arcing, then outstretched, glazed water splintering then reconstituting, rushing and alert in their wake, their quiet laughter ricocheting off the banks.

Raksha felt herself coming undone. She turned, swam to the lake's edge and bounded out of the water, hastily winding her sari around her, wringing her hair, then running breathlessly for home. What had she done?

Yet since then, she had retraced her steps a hundred times to the lake. To his door, and in the end, to his bed.

A great deal is expected of Raksha as head teacher at the village school. She had succeeded her mother at the small institution Shanti had founded on their return from Port Natal – her mother a new widow, she a babe-in-arms, then a toddler scratching around in the ant-infested soil while one plank was patiently laid on top of another. The structure went up in flames more than once for fear that the villagers' children would be bewitched. But Shanti rebuilt each time, begging the men's indulgence, and in time, she proved that educating just one child could change the fortunes of a family.

If Shanti is revered as "Teacher", what might Raksha's legacy be? Will she be remembered as the turncoat who abandoned her mother for a British man?

And yet she cannot deny that she loves him. She adores the contours of his gently lined face, his hair the colour of the overcast sky, his eyes that throw back a deep vulnerability – the brokenness she has begun to repair.

She has tried to end it so often. She has told him many times that she cannot ever see him again. But her body rebels against separation from him. So she allows herself the luxury of one more act of deceit, which sees her paint the lightest kiss on her mother's forehead, promising to return with flowers from the lake's shore after her swim. Then her feet grow wings and soon she is in his arms, the guilt draining from her, his face shining, his mouth hot on her neck. There is fierceness in their love, but infinite tenderness too, the line between them bending, blurring as he takes her to his bed.

Since the letters started arriving, Shanti has lived in two places, in two times. Her body is a slowly cracking husk, gradually unfurling from the inside, wrenching her muscles from dormancy. Murmurs of the past have come alive in her, a dense path in her memory being retrodden.

The first letter was from Selvaraj – the little boy from Vākkuṟuti with whose family Shanti had travelled to the Colony all those decades ago. He stayed in touch with Shanti sporadically over the years, keeping her abreast of developments in Port Natal where he and his parents remained. She looked forward to these updates, but had not heard from him for quite some time.

My dearest Shanti,

I hope this letter finds you and Raksha in good health!

I do apologise for not being able to write as often as I used to. My business takes up much of my time these days. The fishing industry in Natal is, thankfully, thriving but leaves little time for leisure or correspondence. My sister and parents constantly complain that they see too little of me! I am glad to report that apart from a few aches and pains, the elderly ones are generally in good health and spend many hours entertaining my sons while Maliga runs the home. They all send you their fondest love and greetings.

I have something to ask of you which I hope will not be too much of an imposition. As I have neared my forty-fifth year, I have begun to wonder more about the place I came from. Having left Vākkuṟuti as a young child, I have almost no recollection of our time there. I listen to my parents' accounts of their lives in the village and I have a strong desire to know more. It was only a few nights ago that I recounted this to Maliga, and she agreed that I would never be at peace unless I visited my first home. How fortunate I am to be blessed with such an understanding wife.

I would dearly love to see what has become of our village in the last forty years or so. But that is not the only reason I hope to return. While I know that the past has caused you great pain, I also know it devastated you to leave Port Natal without Aunty Devi all those years ago. I believe it may be time to reunite the both of you in the only way I can – I wish to bring her with me.

I should like to take you up on your kind offer of accommodation for three weeks, if that will not cause too much disruption. As soon as I have heard back from you, I hope to book my passage. If all goes well, I should arrive in Madras about three months after you receive this letter. I will make my journey to Vākkuṟuti from there. I so look forward to seeing you again and meeting Raksha face to face for the first time.

With love and respect,
Selva

Shanti only realised her tears had fallen on the paper when the ink began to run. She dragged her hand across her face to dry it, but a sob, raw and strident, rose up in her, hunching her over the table. Thirty-eight summers had passed without Devi, but not a single day without the thought of her. She had loved Devi more than her blood sisters. Yet now that Selvaraj was bringing Devi here, Shanti found she was not ready. She grappled with the thought for days. But there was nothing to be done. Time was short. Selvaraj would finalise his most pressing business, and set off soon, arriving in just two sightings of the full moon.

In the days that followed, Shanti worked hard at convincing herself that since the past could not be altered, it would have to be overcome. In truth, she longed to see the man she'd once treated as a little brother during that voyage. And his presence would force Shanti to find the courage to tell Raksha the truth of what had really happened all those years ago.

She was still coming to terms with this when the second letter came, just a few days later. Rama, the barmy postman, who always arrived whistling tunelessly, thrust the envelope into Shanti's hand. It was crumpled and slightly damp from the sweat of his palm. She put it down for the moment, and almost forgot about it because there were so many chores to do. But when evening fell, Shanti re-tired early to examine the envelope more closely. It was addressed to her in a childish scrawl, much like the handwriting of one of the schoolchildren. But as she turned the envelope over, she noticed the postmark: Sindh Province – a region far off, to the north. She had never received a letter from there before. But she had once known someone who came from there.

She scrutinised the writing again, and slowly it began to take on an old familiarity. It was unmistakeable, really – the distinctive slant to the left, the haphazard spacing of letters. It could not be. Why now? After all these years? She forced her eyes shut and

9

swam in the darkness, trying to slow her heart and fill her lungs with air. Her mind began to journey to that place beyond the outskirts of charted memory, bathed in dim light. And when she opened her eyes, there was no doubt in her mind as to who the author was.

She caressed the envelope a moment longer before ripping it open, running her hands over its creases as if to decipher some small clue as to what stirred the writer's heart when quill touched paper. And when her eye fell upon the words, Shanti found herself not reading, but reciting them.

> Although I conquer all the earth,
> Yet for me there is only one city.
> In that city there is for me only one house;
> And in that house, one room only;
> And in that room a bed.
> And one woman sleeps there,
> The shining joy and jewel of all my kingdom.

The words from *Subhāṣitāvalī*, by Vallabhadeva, had been written centuries ago. But they had once come alive for her in Port Natal. More than mere verse, they had been a promise – one still unfulfilled. But perhaps, like love, promises could not be bound by the limitations of time. It was time to confess all to Raksha – to tell her that the one man Shanti had never forgotten had somehow found her after all these years – and he was coming.

David observes the bonfire he has made, hears the ping of brass buttons launching themselves into the flames and melting like tears. He can't find his cap, or he'd have added it to the flames

– and that British flag he owned when he arrived. He's not sure why he didn't think to burn his uniform before. All these months, Raksha has lain in his arms, mere feet from these remnants of his past, and he'd never thought to destroy them before, knowing what they symbolised for her.

It has been three full weeks since she last came to him, and her absence has grown tentacles that curl into his temples, take a firm grip on the inside of his head and neck, then travel with alarming malice through the rest of his body. He has sat paralysed, day after day on his verandah, waiting. It isn't the first time she has cut contact. But there was a resoluteness about her when she left this time.

Once he could have surmounted this kind of loss. He is a rational man after all – a scientist by training – who has survived failed relationships before, not least with Annabel, the aristocrat's daughter. He'd been an awful husband to her – callous, dismissive – and a yet more disgraceful father to Matthew. David is ashamed to admit he leapt upon the Vākkuṛuti posting to escape them both. He hopes Annabel has told the boy he is dead.

When first married, David had tried to cultivate an affection for Annabel. But night after night lying next to her, he felt only the curse of bloodlines and lineage, the portraits of his ancestors intruding on them like stern anaphrodisiacs. He had only ever procreated with her because it was expected of him as a man. And on every occasion his flesh touched Annabel's, he had been unyielding as an automaton, often apologising afterwards. The pregnancy had come as a relief – a sort of honourable discharge.

Coming a few years later, the posting abroad had rescued him from the emptiness of Annabel's despair and Matthew's unfulfilled yearning for a father. India had been kind to him. It turned his face to the sun and thawed the blood in his veins. He developed a fondness for the people, the textured grit of life in India – its simultaneous beauty and ugliness. But nothing had shaken him as forcefully as Raksha. From the day he first saw her at the lake, when he had offered her water to touch to her parched lips, he had been intrigued. She refused his kindness, despite her obvious thirst. Mildly offended, he'd almost pressed her to take just one sip – until he saw that glint of pride in her eye, and withdrew his offering. But he was already caught in her undertow. And as she returned and he came to know her, he began to realise that he had never before been this close to someone; more importantly, he was capable of love, after all. He learnt she was bright and fierce, more unafraid to challenge him than any woman he had ever known. He loved her mind as she grew to love his. They began to laugh, debate and dream together.

In those early days, as her passion for him grew, so she tested him, too. "What did you do to my people? Tell me!" she would ask in that quiet voice straddling investigation and accusation. "How many did you kill?" He refused to answer until one day he broke down and admitted he was a coward – that from the moment he arrived in his ill-fitting uniform, he had been too afraid to do the work of a soldier in this appropriated land. He recalled that childhood feeling of stealing his friend's toy and joylessly playing with it for hours, knowing it wasn't his. But he understood this was no toy. This geography he had been taught to read as a nebulous shape on a map was a land full of people.

Yes, he went out on the village raids. But he closed his eyes when his colleagues raised their guns. He heard the shots ring out and sometimes opened his eyes in time to see the shock in a man's face before he fell, to witness his child screaming for his father to wake up. And yes, he heard the cries of the women dragged into the bushes, their saris ripped from their bodies, while the men cheered each other on. And he ran from that horror into small homes, making a show of destroying the villagers' meagre possessions, smashing them to pieces, because a soldier too afraid to shoot and rape still had to show his loyalty to the Crown.

But those villagers, dead and alive, have never left him. They dance demonically behind his eyes at night, bleed into his dreams, haunt his waking hours. Raksha first brought the memory of them into his house, then exorcised them. She has been his confessor, his judge and his penance. He stutters. He swallows hard. He sweats. His voice breaks. He yells. He weeps. But her eyes stay on him, watchful and intense, never releasing their lock until he has spoken, until he has found catharsis. She sees his regret and contrition. And in that moment, she allows herself to love him yet more.

Raksha has saved him. Since the day he unlatched his gate and stood watching her from the side of the lake, he has known he could drown in the depths of her. There is comfort in this. It would be a pleasant way to die.

Gazing into the glowing ashes now, David finds new courage. He bathes, puts on his best suit and a pair of shoes so highly shined, his face is almost reflected in them. There is one more battle he must fight and win.

My dear Selva,

It is my fervent hope that this letter reaches you as swiftly as possible, for Raksha and I await your visit with eagerness. How wonderful to think that in just a few months, you will be here at my side! I rushed to the school to tell Raksha the good news and she, too, was overcome. I thank you sincerely for the offer of bringing Devi with you.

You have indeed married a wise woman! I have come to believe that the knowledge of where we come from is part of our birthright. No matter how far we are scattered from the mother tree, there remains a kernel of her within us, bearing the mark of our origins.

Nonetheless, I thought it worth preparing you somewhat for what you will likely experience as you rediscover the village of your birth. Upon receiving your letter, I walked through Vākkuṟuti for many hours, attempting to see her through the fresh eyes of one who left as a child. There was a delicious zest in the air of spices waking in their pods. The young villagers were warm in their greetings. "Teacher, please share our morning meal," or "May we interest you in a cup of strong *chai*?" they asked. They are kind, but quite unlike us, Selva. There was something of a restlessness – a rebellion, even – in us as we burst into the streets to play each morning. The young ones of today are quieter. They walk, shoulders slightly stooped, their eyes deadened. Perhaps, in their generation, the acceptance of subjugation is now complete. I sometimes wonder whether this is also true of the Africans in the Colony of Natal. Does their freedom remain folklore, or is there still some small spark of rebellion in them?

I must not pretend that I know liberty intimately, dear Selva. To be fair, we were all born into the Madras Presidency and the very air we first breathed belonged to the British Raj that placed shackles in lieu of bangles around our chubby wrists. Yet I played, oblivious, as a child every day in the streets of this garrison town. To me, Vākkuṟuti was all deep lakes, wild monkeys and monsoons. It was a long time before I thought to ask why the British were here. My mother had warned me not to approach them, but she never explained why, and I was much older when I noticed the flicker of hatred in my father's eye as he passed them in the village.

But after living at Port Natal, my memories of life in Vākkuṟuti took on new meaning. I remembered in striking detail the stone fort where the British soldiers revelled – the strains of their drunken songs filling the night air. I recalled the vast amounts of food and drink delivered to their fort while many of us starved.

Their mark is still very much here. Not far away, there remains a British hospital, an ordnance depot, a pretty church, and even an orphan asylum for the children of deceased British fighters who have deserted the realm of sanity. Some soldiers grew so enamoured of Vākkuṟuti, they chose to stay on after their service ended. They are still to be seen pottering around, planting and watering their very own little swathe of India.

Dear Selva, I hope you do not arrive to find me too soured or resentful. The older I grow, the more I demand the right to my bitterness. Though I feel I have made the best of my life here, Victoria's presence remains as tight as an executioner's noose, and I wish for just one breath without its constraint. The only difference I have attempted to make within the walls of my small school is to remind the children of how, when we stepped off the ships in Port Natal, the British saw only a horde of uncivilised *coolies*, but were blinded to the six thousand years of civilisation in our wake. If this lesson sows in the youngsters some minute sense of pride in themselves, I will go to my pyre a happier woman.

I am afraid, my dear Selva, the light is fading and I must now curtail my writing. For all her faults, Vākkuṟuti will always be your first home and mine, and I am sure she will welcome you as fondly as Raksha and I.

Safe travels until we meet on this shore,
Your friend,
Shanti

Raksha makes her way home from the school room, thoughts of her young charges fresh in her mind. She would dearly love to indulge them with decorative stationery and fancy ink just once, to fuel their dreams of one day also becoming head teacher. Of course, thoughts of David are never far away. But the sounds of commotion rupture them as Raksha nears her house. Perhaps Shanti, in a fit of bad temper, has got into a skirmish with one of the neighbours. Raksha drops her satchel as she sees the small crowd that has gathered outside her house. Emanating from inside are two unmistakeable voices. They are raised, as if in argument.

Raksha pushes past the neighbours and storms in as Shanti turns to her daughter in shock. She opens her mouth to speak, but instead clamps her hand to her chest and crumples to the ground. Raksha tries to break her fall, screaming at David, "What have you done? What have you bloody done?"

She slams her knees to the ground, shaking her mother. "*Ama*, wake up! Open your eyes! Open your eyes, *Ama*!" Shanti groans. David grabs Shanti's wrist, feeling only a faint pulse. He throws off his jacket and tosses it aside, reaches under Shanti, lifting her and straining to his feet. "Where are you …" he hears Raksha's urgent voice as he dashes out the door, Raksha right behind him. "Out of the way!" he shouts at the neighbours.

He is running now. "We need to get her to Jairam, the temple healer," Raksha shouts. David picks up speed, Shanti's limp arms dangling. "You run ahead – tell him I'm bringing her," he gasps. Raksha takes off, praying breathlessly, sobbing, her tears blurring the road ahead. She has run this distance what feels like hundreds of times, but it has never felt this long or arduous. She trips over stones in the road, but gets up and keeps running until she finally catches sight of Jairam in the distance standing outside the temple.

"My mother – she has collapsed—" she cries, heaving. He races inside to prepare for Shanti's arrival. By the time David reaches them, a pallid Shanti in his arms, her breathing is shallow, her hands and feet cold. David lays her on a slab lined with linen. Jairam turns to Raksha and David. "Leave us," he says.

"No – I want to be with my mother," Raksha protests.

But Jairam is resolute. "Now is not the right time. Let me tend to her. I will call you when the time is right."

Raksha nods, defeated.

Raksha and David catch their breath, standing outside the imposing temple in silence. David's shirt is plastered to his body, and he wishes for just one cool sip of the offerings that devotees are carrying into the temple.

"I'm sorry," he says. "You must know it was never my intention to …"

"You know why I left, David," she says softly. "You have known my reservations … my limitations, all along. I told you she was frail – that she couldn't stand the shock of finding out. My mother may die because of you!"

"Raksha, I thought that if I could just speak to her, plead with her … convince her that I love you … that—"

"That what, David? That she would sanction this relationship, and give us her blessing? You do not know my mother at all! Even I know only the parts of her she will show me! But if you could see the scars on her back, if you saw the grief that sometimes takes hold of her for days, you would know how much she has suffered. Whatever these secrets … they are thorns in her heart. And I left you because I did not want to drive them any deeper."

Jairam emerges as Raksha is wiping her face. He pretends to have heard nothing. "Raksha, you may see her," he says.

Shanti lies inert in the cool room behind the shrines. A look of peace has come over her, as though she is having pleasant dreams.

"She is resting now but her heart is weak, possibly because she is anxious," Jairam says. "I will continue with my treatment and prayers, but I must take my lead from her soul, Raksha. If it is meant to remain in this body, she will heal, even if it takes some time. But if it is her time to move on, you must be prepared to let her go. We cannot detain our loved ones longer than they are destined to be here. You may sit here now, but let her rest."

Raksha nods obediently, though her heart tells her this is not the way Shanti's life is meant to come to a close. She kneels quietly next to her mother, touching her forehead, holding her hand, stroking her hair, while Jairam hums his incantations.

She leaves at sunset, relieved to find David gone. "Her life is in the hands of the gods now," Jairam whispers as Raksha sets off for home in the falling dusk.

Raksha knows Jairam and trusts him. He has been known to work miracles. Yet she does not feel comfortable leaving her mother's side. But perhaps Shanti will heal faster without the hand of her betrayer intertwined with her own.

It is dark by the time she reaches home. Raksha lights a candle as she enters. The neighbours have had their taste of spectacle, and have returned to their homes. The house is achingly empty. The only vestige of the battle of wills her mother lost today is David's discarded grey jacket. She can't bear to touch it. But then she notices a book lying on the floor, one she has never seen before.

Raksha picks it up and runs her hands over it. It is worn but beautiful, the cover adorned with a peacock feather. She reaches for the candle and pulls it closer. She opens the first page.

CHAPTER 1

Durban Gaol, Port Natal, September 1878

THE SUN TIPTOES TOWARD TWILIGHT until the dark settles, suffocating the last light of day. The air is damp. It matts my hair to my face. I cannot be bothered to brush it away. The sweat of a labourer fills my nostrils – the stench of my own body. My palms and feet are calloused, this body I inhabit a constellation of scars. I cannot quite tell if it is still my body; whether I have surrendered it, or had it stolen from me.

On nights like this, the mosquitoes will not let us sleep. People fear this prison, but I have made peace with its four walls. This is my last home in this life. I can now say, 'I am a prisoner. I am a criminal. I am sentenced to die,' and those words no longer stick in my throat.

It is never silent here. Some sleep, some howl at night. I reflect and try to reconcile myself to the fate I have chosen. Strangely, I find myself fortified by these stone walls. I have spent hours curled against them, and in their crude assembly, I see the cornerstones of my destiny. I am determined to find the strength to face my end with dignity.

I have quickly grown used to the weight of chains. I'm no different, really, from the hardened men here who dig ditches with shackles round their ankles. Sometimes I try to glimpse faces beneath the arcs of their backs while I imagine what blood and gore brought them here. They work closely, their bodies almost touching, yet they are forbidden to speak. Words are dangerous. They are both gifts and weapons.

In the colonial prison, there are divisions between British, Indian and African inmates, male and female, young offenders and adults, those who have been tried and found guilty, and those who have yet to stand in the dock. Prisoners accused of monetary crimes are kept apart from those who spilt blood. In this wordless world, we eye each other as suspiciously as our gaolers. I often glance over my shoulder to see another prisoner's eyes burrowing into me. I imagine them all to be murderers and rapists.

Despair hangs like a fog here. But I do not let it swallow me. I give my gaolers no trouble. I dig trenches, plough soil and scrub prison floors unquestioningly. I am rarely beaten here. There are moments when news of a hanging frightens me. But I sponge my eyes and continue with my work. I seek courage as if she were a friend who would go to the gallows with me. I do not wish to die a coward.

There is despondency in the eyes of women here, but I take no notice. I cannot carry their pain along with my own. I go meekly into confinement at sunset. I am deaf to my gaolers' shoving – their lewd remarks about how they would like to have their way with me. They must think me feeble-minded and docile because I never answer back. They are deaf to my silent curses.

But as the lock clangs behind me and their footsteps grow faint, there is a part of me that unlatches from this body, cleaves through its broken skin and hovers unfettered, leaping these jagged stone walls, gliding between past and present as I search for the answers that will lead me back to myself.

I am a migrant, connected to my home by fragile threads that stretch across continents. They are too frayed now to hoist me back to the life I knew, to the girl I once was. Yet sometimes a longing for the place of my birth takes hold of me, and it pains me to be torn from all that was familiar to me – all whom I loved in India.

It is not that I dislike the Colony of Natal. Even with its trials, I have grown fond of the landscape, of many of the good people who reside here. I have thought of re-rooting myself here, never to return to India. But I also do not want my memories devoured. In time, it all fades – the voices of my sisters, the blemish on my mother's cheek, my father's scar from rescuing me from the neighbour's bull. My parents have become mere silhouettes. I imagine their slowing steps, the trickle from their eyes, or the reeds that have grown into savage bushes in my absence. And it knocks me off balance, like the rocking of the ship that carried us here and spewed us onto the land like waste.

And yet something quite miraculous happened as I was led away from the plantation. It prompted me to snap my head around to see who was watching, who was whispering, even as the policeman handcuffed me. I saw no one but the other labourers looking on in silence. But that night, as I lay on the stone floor of the gaol, I sensed it again – a rip in time's canvas through which small fragments escaped. I saw etchings on faces. Ridges on hands. A lock. A tress of flowing hair – all with great clarity.

I found myself swept backwards to a day when I stood bowed on that plantation with a scythe in my hands. I remembered how I had slowly tried to orientate my face towards Vākkuṟuti in the hope that it was all still there – the magnificent rock-cut temples of the Pallava dynasty on the river banks, the pillared halls and shrines that rose up in worship of the great Shiva in

Mahabalipuram, the Sanskrit writings that endured wars and the destruction of empires. And I stood a little more erect, even when the lash of the whip met my back.

I sat up in my cell and stared into the dark. If time was conspiring to unravel my bonds, I would ask it to carry me back to that child, Shanti: ebullient and unspoilt by the world.

"I am waiting," I said. "Come and take me."

CHAPTER 2

Vākkuṟuti, Madras Presidency, India, late 1860s

VĀKKUṞUTI WAS A VILLAGE SO small, so insignificant, it would be much too generous to describe it as a dot on the map. It sat near the coastal town of Madras, in the Madras Presidency. The Bay of Bengal was close enough to caress it with its breezes, but held back from swallowing Vākkuṟuti when angered. Yet come monsoon season, we always holed up in our hovels while the rain flogged our dwellings, often sweeping our few precious possessions into the streets.

Come spring, the town exploded into colour. Birdsong was a portent that it was time to rise. We children ran barefoot in the paths, shouting, playing with abandon while our parents thanked the gods for this relief. The sky flooded our lakes, and plants jostled for the sun. It was not long before the trees began to strain under the burden of their fruit. We climbed them all, the branches creaking from our weight, plucking and slurping fruit till the juice ran off our chins. Sometimes we annoyed the pixie-like monkeys by stealing their share. I loved to perch on a branch above my best friend, Thirnavelli, and squeeze a stream of mango juice into her hair until her bouncing curls hardened into stiff rings.

There were twin lakes nearby where Thirna and I splashed and dived to escape the sun's stare. We were inseparable despite a minor language barrier – she was Telegu-speaking and I Tamil, but our languages were similar, so we were able to understand each other. We spent entire days frolicking and parted sadly every evening. My elder sisters were mildly irritated that I led such a carefree life while theirs were bursting with chores.

My mother raised us and looked after the house. She spent all day cooking, cleaning and planting and tending to her vegetables. My father was a washerman who travelled some distance to work, returning exhausted each evening, the skin on his hands peeling. Sometimes, he would bring a sweetmeat home and break it into pieces for us to share.

I was loved, but my mother often complained to the neighbours, "Shanti is such a handful!" It didn't help that I accepted all Thirna's dares, including one to ride Maharajah, the neighbour's bull. I imagined it would be much like riding a horse, although I had no experience of that either. Maharajah catapulted me from his back with such force that I had a moment to take in several of Vākkuṟuti's sights from the air before I crashed into the ground and began to bawl. For good measure, Maharajah took a swipe at my father too, grazing him across the face before I was carried off for a smacking. "You're a disgrace, Shanti! You behave like a boy. No one will want to marry you!" my mother admonished. My sisters dried my tears: "Shanti, you are getting older now. These games are dangerous and much too childish for you. You must stop this now."

Their words hurt me, and I might have ignored them had I not met an unusual woman who set me on an entirely different path, at a time when I was only nine or ten summers old.

She approached me one day while Thirna and I were playing

near the temple at the centre of our village. I was caught up in the delicate operation of inventing a mud paste we could roll in like elephants to keep the mosquitoes at bay, when she cast a shadow over me. I squinted into the sun. "Good afternoon, Aunty," I said, standing up quickly and brushing at the muddy slick oozing from me. I'd seen this lady at the temple often, where her husband was a priest.

She smiled at me. "What's your name again, girl?"

"Shanti, Aunty."

"Ah, yes. You are Manickam and Meena's child?"

"Yes, Aunty ..." I hid my muddy hands behind my back.

"Why were you elbow-deep in mud a moment ago?"

"Well, Aunty – the elephants do it to keep insects off them. I thought it might work for children too. My friend is always badly bitten by the mosquitoes."

"How thoughtful," she smiled. "I see you here often with your friends. Why do you play near the temple?"

"For the blessings, Aunty."

She laughed. "And this is your friend?"

"Yes, Aunty."

Thirna shot to her feet. "I am Thirnavelli."

"Thirnavelli – a favour, please. Would you kindly go into the temple and find out for me if the prayers have started?"

Thirna was only too happy to oblige. The woman waited till Thirna was out of earshot.

"Shanti, I'm not quite sure if ... if you would be keen to ..."

"... to work in your house? No, Aunty, my mother will not allow it. She always says there's too much work to do in our house."

"Oh no," she shook her head. "I am not looking for a cleaner, Shanti. I've watched you and your friends. You are a very clever girl. And I think ... if you had the chance to learn more, you would do very well in life."

"Learn more?" I asked. "I know how to clean the house. I can't cook very well, but I am good with weaving grass mats and ..."

"Shanti," she interjected. "I'm sure you're very good at those things. But there are other things to learn too, you know." She leaned in. "Imagine what it must be like to read and write, for example," she whispered.

"Never, Aunty!" I gasped. "My father would be so unhappy. He doesn't believe girls should read and write."

"Ah, perhaps your father doesn't think it's *necessary*. But surely he can't mean it's not allowed? I am sure writing the odd letter or reading a newspaper could be very useful. That wouldn't stop a girl from doing her chores, would it?"

I had to think about that for a moment. "No – I don't think it would ..."

"Shanti," – she leaned down and held me by both shoulders – "Thirnavelli will be back soon, so I must speak quickly. You are a special girl who seems very curious about the world. I'd like you to come to my house. Let us just drink tea and talk."

"Come to your house?"

"Yes – and not to clean," she added. "But please don't breathe a word to Thirnavelli or any of your other friends, understand?"

I nodded. I was good at keeping secrets.

"Do you know where I live?"

"Oh yes, Aunty – with the rich people at the lakes."

She raised an eyebrow. "Well, come to my house between the lakes before the sun sets tomorrow. There's something special I want to share with you. But come alone, all right?"

"Yes, Aunty. Thank you. I'll try."

"I am Saras. You may call me Aunty Saras," she said, the hem of her silver-tinged sari sweeping the ground as she left.

Thirna pestered me on her return: "What did she want with you? She never speaks to any of us."

"She was just asking about my family, Thirna," I shot back.

"But how does she know your name? And who your parents are?"

"It's a small village. It's not that hard to work out."

"Careful, Shanti. Rich people are never friendly to us. They always want something in return."

I changed the subject as we walked back.

That night, I pondered why this stranger wanted me in her home. I'd heard my mother and sisters speak of people who abducted young girls to keep as slaves. But I wasn't afraid of that – my mother said anyone who abducted me would beg her to take me back the very next day before sunrise. Anyway, this lady – Aunty Saras – didn't seem like a child snatcher. She seemed kind. And of all the children in the village, she had picked me and called me clever – not childish, not a handful, but *clever*.

I decided to be brave. The next day, I dressed in my finest clothes and was about to slip out of the house when my mother saw me.

"And where are you off to dressed like that?"

"Uh … to the temple to pray, *Ama*."

"What, you are suddenly a devotee now? You will ruin your good clothes, Shanti!" she shouted as I ran off.

"I will take care not to spoil them, *Ama*," I shouted back. But she shook her head in disbelief.

Aunty Saras's house was situated in the most beautiful part of the village, slightly secluded, on a large plot of land. I looked around in awe. Her house seemed so sturdy. I was quite sure it had never collapsed in the monsoons like ours did, and had to be rebuilt.

Aunty Saras welcomed me warmly. She was short and fair-skinned, and her long hair was wound into a large bun that sat on top of her head. The light danced in the sequins on her sari, almost enough to blind me.

People in the village called her snobbish. But she put me at ease with her chatter. She questioned me as I sat drinking tea at her feet, and I was only too happy to answer. I had never set foot, let alone drunk tea in a proper cup and saucer, in the house of a *Brahmin*. I did not know how to hold the cup properly, but she actually touched my hands, guiding my fingers to show how I should embrace the cup. I loved the warmth of it in my hands and the steamy aroma of *chai* in my nostrils.

Aunty Saras listened to my stories with interest, and asked me if I'd ever wished I could go to school. "No," I said. "A girl's place is not at school." I reminded her of what my father had said.

"But Shanti," she said. "I am a woman. And I have learnt how to read and write."

"*Hare!*" I almost dropped the cup. She was like a man! "How? How did you do this, Aunty? Did you go to school?"

"No, not formally," she said, amused. "But, as you know, my husband is a priest. All priests in our village know how to read and write because they have to study the holy texts and teach them. Now, when I was newly married, Shanti, I used to go to the temple every day – just for devotional purposes. And my husband was always busy teaching the young men to read and write so they could enter the priesthood."

"Ah, so you asked him to teach you?"

"No, definitely not. Like your father, he would have refused. But while I was polishing the brass and arranging the flowers into garlands, I listened carefully and I slowly started to learn. I worked out how to watch and listen to them without actually seeming interested …"

"Ha! You spied on them!"

"I wouldn't call it spying, Shanti. It happened by accident. I came home from the temple one day and realised everything I had heard and seen them learn was stuck in my head. It was like my mind was just waiting for it – and it wanted more."

"How long did it take you to learn all these things?"

"Oh … years, Shanti. For a long time, I could only read a few short words, I struggled to write, I could only count up to twenty. But then I realised my husband also had many books here at home. So when I came back from the temple, I sat with his books for hours. I read, I memorised, I even practised my writing outside in the sand with a stick, and I tried to count further and further. And I began to make good progress."

"What kinds of books have you read, Aunty Saras?"

"Well, I started with basic readers. But when I grew more confident, I read a few pages of our holy book, the *Bhagavad Gita*. And after many years, I was able to read newspapers, religious writings, some cultural, historical, philosophy and poetry books, too. It took me a long time to understand them, though, Shanti. But when I began to make sense of them, I felt so delighted! I realised something important had been missing in my life for so long. All these people whose writings I've read – they have touched me in this small corner of India, without even knowing I exist."

"That is nice," I said. "That you could learn all this without leaving our village. I love Vākkuruti. I never want to leave."

She smiled at me. "You say that because you are young, Shanti. When you start reading and asking questions, and you find there are very few answers here, you may feel differently."

"What questions did you have, Aunty?"

"Oh, all sorts of questions – why does nature work the way she does? Where is India in relation to other countries? How many seas must we sail to reach another country? What do these sums add up to? Why did the British come to take over our country when they have their own?"

"I wouldn't mind learning some of those things, Aunty Saras."

"Well, that is why I called you here today. If you really want, I can teach you whatever I know, Shanti. Look, my knowledge is limited, and there is not much I can change about this village – the rules are strict. But I can bend this one rule as long as you never tell anyone. If you do, it will come at a serious cost to us both. You are a bright girl, Shanti! You already see things that others do not. This is your chance, if you are willing."

I was eager, but there was so much to consider, and she must have seen something of this in my face.

"Just give it some thought, Shanti. I will make sure I finish my chores in the morning so I am free in the afternoons to teach you. If you are keen, you can come when you can. Now, it's getting late – you must go. The sun is setting."

I put my hands together, thanked her sincerely for the tea, and ran home so fast, my legs ached. I felt desperate to learn, but I wanted to be a good daughter. I had no wish to lie to my parents, my sisters or my friends. And yet none of them would understand why I wanted to do this. I had lain awake so many nights wondering who lit the stars before dark, or why the body of a tiger was so powerful compared to mine, or why my father always walked three paces ahead of my mother in public. And when I had asked my parents or my sisters these questions, they either looked at me strangely, or laughed at me until I stopped asking.

Aunty Saras had not thought anything I'd said that afternoon was stupid or strange. She'd listened to me and seemed interested in all I'd told her. And then I remembered what my mother had taught me about the goddess Saraswati – the deity of knowledge and art. Aunty Saras was named after her – the goddess of enlightenment. What if it was no coincidence? Perhaps the gods had sent me my very own incarnation of Saraswati to open my eyes and awaken my soul.

CHAPTER 3

I EVENTUALLY ACCEPTED AUNTY SARAS's generous offer of her time and knowledge. It took me a while to come around to the idea, but I saw it as a unique gift for which I should be grateful. Aunty Saras and I decided that I should tell my parents she was looking for a cleaner in the afternoons, and ask their permission to work in her house as an excuse for us to meet. At first, my father was reluctant, but my mother convinced him that it was a sign that I was maturing and that any goods I brought home as payment would benefit the family. I was relieved that they had agreed, but keeping the truth from my parents made me feel horribly guilty. My lessons with Aunty Saras began gently, but grew more intense with time. I grappled with written Tamil, Hindi and English, all of which I found difficult. But she was wise and patient, always able to keep my full attention. While I sat at her feet, she funnelled language, history, poetry, mathematics, science and philosophy into my head. It was all at a very basic level, but still challenging to my young mind.

My world began to expand. I found new words to describe my

daily existence. I saw my village differently, and began to understand some of the complexities of living here.

But Thirna was upset that I hardly spent time with her any more. "Do you have to go and clean her house every afternoon?"

"My sisters told me to stop my childish ways, Thirna. It was really troubling my parents, so it's better that I spend time working to prove to them that I am becoming more responsible," I lied.

I felt awful about this, but telling Thirna the truth would amount to telling the whole village. Although irritated at first, she grew used to my absence. "I am really happy for you, Shanti," she said one day. "Who knows, if you are really good at this, perhaps they will choose you as a temple cleaner one day."

I hugged her, but said nothing. How could I explain my ambitions had grown beyond that? And yet I had to keep them in check. The society in which we lived demanded servitude of us as women. And it was much worse if, like my family, you sat on the lower rungs of the caste system.

Aunty Saras addressed this one day. "Why do you sit so far from me when I am teaching you?" she asked.

I felt embarrassed to say it aloud. "You know why, Aunty Saras – if my shadow falls across you, it may contaminate you."

"Do you really believe that, my girl? Let us try it! Cast your shadow over me, and let us see what happens."

I edged slightly closer to her, but found I could not go any further. She got up, walked around me and stood in my shadow. I gasped.

"Look, Shanti – has your shadow sullied me?" She surveyed her body. "I am the same as when I sat in front of you." She sat down again. "Now, come closer to me."

It was such a simple request, but difficult to grant, although I got used to it in time. I was mystified by this system. I knew only that the fair-skinned and dark-skinned should not mix, that we should do the menial chores and never retaliate when the high-caste children spat at us or told us to get away because we would disturb their spirits.

"Shanti, there is always a cup of tea waiting for you when you arrive, and yet you still look at that cup as if it were poisoned. In my house, you will always drink from the same china as me. You will get nowhere if you continue to believe yourself inferior. I once believed it too, because I was born a girl. But now I refuse to think like this. We are both human, flesh and blood. You have caught a little more sun than me, that's all."

"Why do you not believe in this? Everyone else in this village does," I said.

She sighed. "Shanti, the first boy I ever loved was a Christian. His name was Anboo. He was charcoal-skinned – the handsomest boy you ever laid eyes on. He used to work out in the fields where I often went to dry the glorious mane of hair I once had. I made a point of going there often. We became close friends. Our conversations stretched for hours. And before long, I lost my heart to him. I even thought of a betrothal and marriage to him."

"But that could never happen, Aunty Saras."

"No – you're right, it couldn't. But I loved how free he was. He didn't believe in the caste system. He didn't think he was better or worse than anyone else. He taught me about people who worshipped other gods, sang strange music, practised different rituals, and held celebrations quite unlike ours. We were very different. And it made me question, if we both believed so fervently in our gods, which one was real. He'd say, 'Saras, calm yourself. You have your beliefs and I have mine. Who knows which one is real? I follow Christ because he says all people are equal. That makes life easier for me because I do not have what you were born with.'"

I thought about this. "I wish you and I were also that free," I told Aunty Saras.

In her house, I felt special. But in the streets of Vākkuṟuti, we only greeted one another, never stopping to speak. Our lessons always took place in secret, and Aunty Saras warned me that if her husband ever found me there, I should make a show of having come to clean the house.

In time, Aunty Saras began to treat me as her daughter. I grew to love her as another mother. When my menstrual blood flowed for the first time, it broke my heart that she could not attend my ceremony. And although my mother brought me a cloth and showed me how to use it, I was only prepared for what lay ahead because my "secret" mother had held me close, and welcomed me into womanhood.

"Your cycle is connected to the moon and the waves that roll to the shore at the Bay of Bengal," she said. "That is powerful. And one day, you will use your power to become a vessel for a child."

"Why do you not have children, Aunty Saras?" I asked.

"Oh, the time for that has long passed, my dear. But I have you now," she said with a smile.

When I walked home that day, I felt sad for her, thinking of all the gossip I'd overheard in the village – about her barrenness, how she had been shamed by other women because she couldn't have children. They said she'd disgraced her husband and the poor man was cursed when he married her. I began to wonder how much she had lost in the course of her life. She must have been a girl like me once, with a head full of dreams. But how few had come true. She could have been more than a *Brahmin*'s wife. She could have been a woman of letters.

Years later, when Aunty Saras lay unmoving on a pyre licked by flames, I wept as if my own mother had died. People wondered why I was so overcome. I was weeping not just for her, but for all the unfulfilled dreams that had stayed so tightly knotted inside her. I watched them unfurl and take flight in the smoke around her body. And I said a silent prayer to steer her to an afterlife where her dreams could breathe and take form. "Go to a place where you can be what you were meant to be, Aunty Saras," I whispered. Then I turned my back on the fire devouring her, and walked home in the darkness.

CHAPTER 4

IN THE SUMMERS BEFORE I left Vākkuṟuti, our household was infused with the promise of love. First, my eldest sister, Vani, who was already fourteen years old, was married off to a young man from a neighbouring village. In the summer that followed, it was Asa's turn. Neighbours and relatives converged, filling our home with jubilation. My parents must have struggled to assemble dowries for both of them, but no one would have known. We rejoiced with song and dance, attired in finery of red and gold. The feasting lasted for days, and my sisters left home eager to begin their new lives.

But I missed them. A quietude settled in the house that made the corners echo. My parents forgot their talkative ways. They began to shuffle about mutely, except for a word here and there. I saw how much they were both ageing. My mother looked pale and wrinkled. Her steps were slowing, and she struggled to finish each day's household chores.

I began to withdraw from my parents. After my chores were done and I'd returned from lessons, I spent many hours in the small space I'd always shared with my sisters. Only some treasured books Aunty Saras had given me offered some solace, but I could not bring them into the house in case my mother found them. I hid them in a bush behind the house and tried to commit some of their poetry to memory so I could recite it to myself for comfort when I woke in the middle of the night missing Vani and Asa.

In time, my parents began to speak of marriage again. There was no question of whose future they were discussing. I had hoped a shortage of money would put them off. But I was fourteen now, and if I wasn't married off soon, outsiders might begin to suspect something was wrong with me. I began to panic. I imagined having to accept a complete stranger as my husband. The marriage negotiations would betray little. Your family might know his family. Your fathers might be friends. But no one knew what would happen once you left your home for his, far away. There were marriages in which women thrived, and those in which they suffered bitterly.

More than this, I still saw myself as a child. I was not ready to be separated from my parents or Aunty Saras. I had so much more to learn from her. What would become of my education if I were married off now? I could not imagine a life without my lessons, or access to the books that had become my lifeblood.

On the day my parents called me, I approached them nervously. I sat on the floor, hands in my lap, not wanting to look them in the eye. My father stroked his greying beard and asked my mother to speak.

"Shanti," she began, "remember when you were so small, running about, causing trouble, getting one hiding after another? You were so naughty, but so sweet! I have been going to the temple recently with one prayer in my heart, and that prayer has been answered, my child."

She looked at my father for approval. He nodded for her to

continue. "My brother, Uncle Vythelingum, has a wonderful son called Muthan. You were still very small when they came here. But Muthan – oh, he's such a handsome boy, and so clever! He's planning to get a job on the railways soon. He's ready to get married and he remembers you because he's a bit older than you. He wants you to become his wife, Shanti!"

A broad smile engulfed her face. But I sat there, frozen. My mother looked at me and waited for some reaction. I opened my mouth, but words failed me. Her smile knitted into a blend of concern and confusion.

My father spoke up. "What is wrong, Shanti?"

They were looking at each other.

"*Apa*, I … uh …" I shook my head. "*Apa, Ama*, this is a big … surprise." I forced a smile. "I did not expect this so soon …"

"But Shanti – you are fourteen! In the name of Shiva, girl, what were you expecting? Both your sisters were married off by this age."

"*Apa* …" My voice was breaking. "I do not mean to be ungrateful. Thank you and *Ama* for all your efforts. I only thought that because I am not as mature as my sisters … I thought you might wait a little longer before you found a husband for me. I still have much to learn. I do not want to disgrace you in someone else's household."

My mother was growing irritated. "Shanti, this is stupid! I can't believe this! You turn fourteen and when the moment arrives, instead of giving thanks to God for this boy who is willing to take you, all you can say is you are not ready for marriage? Mature or immature, you are of marriageable age!"

"Your mother is right, Shanti. You are not like the other girls who have carried themselves with grace and charm. You have behaved like a boy – running, climbing trees, playing in the mud. How many times have I had to rescue you? And yet this boy still wants to marry you! Can't you see how fortunate you are? You are already older than many girls in this village who were betrothed at birth and married at eleven!"

I opened my mouth to speak, but my mother cut in. "What will our neighbours and friends say when we tell them you don't want to get married, Shanti? What will they think of us? They'll say we haven't got any money. They'll say there's something wrong with you. They'll make up all kinds of things about us. Everyone in this village will be gossiping. And you … you will just get older and older until you die alone without anyone to look after you!"

My mother put her hand to her mouth. She had not meant to be so harsh.

"Shanti, you can't just carry on being a burden to us," my father said. "We feed you. We clothe you. You've had a roof over your head all these years. You have only now started bringing a little bit of food into the household. I go out to work every day, as I have for years. I wash rich people's dirty underclothes so I can save every coin to give you a happy future. Now you're telling us you don't want it?"

I shook my head.

My father's face twisted with rage. He stood up. "Shanti, look here!" he shouted.

I could not look at him. I was trembling.

He grabbed me by the shoulders. "Look at me, I said!"

I had no choice but to look him in the eye. He appeared distorted through my tears.

"I am not asking you! I'm telling you that this is my final word! The wedding party's coming here in four weeks to finalise this, and when they come, you are going to show Muthan and his parents respect. You are going to welcome them into this home, and you are going to marry him, no question! Do you understand?"

I nodded.

"Now go outside and finish your housework! I don't want to see your ungrateful face here!" he spat.

I pulled myself up and went outside. The tears came, but I did my housework quietly. And in the days that followed, I worked harder than before, and kept to myself. My parents barely spoke to me, but I could see our altercation had really affected them, especially my mother. She would rub her chest and sometimes clasp it. At times, she would gasp for breath. The housework seemed to exhaust her, and for the first time, I saw her stealing a few moments now and again to lie down and catch her breath. At times, she fell into a deep sleep while I took over the housework. It was the least I could do after the trouble I had caused.

Nevertheless, I was unmoved by my father's demands that I marry this faceless Muthan. Thirna and I had recently visited our friend, Sanisha – a cheerful, generous girl we had grown up with. She'd been married off to a much older man after her father drank too much and incurred a massive gambling debt he could not repay. His debtor had one demand: "Give me your daughter" – and he had agreed. Sanisha's mother had cried for weeks, but there was no undoing it.

When we went to visit Sanisha a few weeks after the wedding, we were told she could not receive us. Suspicious, Thirna and I walked around the house peering in until we saw her lying in a corner. We pulled the cloth aside.

"Hey, Sanisha, get up!" Thirna said. "Aren't you happy to see us?"

Sanisha seemed disorientated, like she'd been woken from an intense dream. She forced a smile.

"Are you sick?" I asked her. At first, she remained silent.

"What is wrong with you?" Thirna asked. "Have you been to see the healer?"

"No. This is not something the healer can treat," she said.

"Are you mad, Sanisha?" I asked. "Everyone knows the healer can cure anything, unless you are a very old person who is about to die. Ask your mother-in-law to take you ..."

"Shanti!" she replied sharply, motioning for me to lower my voice. "Don't you understand? My mother-in-law would not want the healer to see this ..."

She parted her sari to show us purple bruises beneath. Thirna and I gasped. "Who did this to you?" I asked.

"My husband," she said bitterly. "He gets drunk. He comes home and makes new marks on me every night." She looked away. "Then he forces his snake into me until I bleed."

We only stayed a few more moments, telling Sanisha we'd come back to help. Thirna and I walked home in shock and silence, remembering the dark clotted ruby hanging off her lip, the purple islands dotting the rest of her body. I almost choked on my anger. But it was worth nothing. When I pleaded with my mother to intervene, she shook her head. "Sanisha's a lovely girl, Shanti. But these are private matters between a man and his wife. It's not our place to say anything."

I was furious. I wanted to save Sanisha, but it was beyond me. I thought of Muthan, and wondered what I would do if he hurt me. My parents loved me, but I could never run back to them. Sanisha's mother must have known what was happening. But no matter how sad she was, she would leave Sanisha there because there were rules that said a roll of the dice and family honour were more important than protecting your daughter.

When Aunty Saras and I met again, she sensed something was wrong. "Shanti, your mind is far away. Is everything all right?"

"No, Aunty Saras," I admitted. "I have been so anxious the last few days. My parents want me to marry my cousin, Muthan."

She drew in a sharp breath. "Shanti, why didn't you say something before?"

41

"Because I can't quite believe it's happening to me! It will change my whole life, my future. I am not ready for this, Aunty Saras. I had dreams of doing something … of becoming someone. I tried to tell my parents it's too early, but they are adamant it must happen now."

She furrowed her brow.

"I've not only angered my parents, Aunty Saras. I think I've made my mother ill. She cannot work as before. She seems to suffer these severe chest pains. I know it's all related to the business of this wedding."

"Shanti, it doesn't help for you to be this anxious. You must calm yourself so you and I can think rationally about this. We'll come up with some solution."

"Aunty Saras, how can I tell them what I am really thinking? That I do not only want to be a married woman who will cook and clean and wash and bow low before my husband, and bear his children. There is more I can do with my life. Perhaps when I grow older, there will be a place in the world for a woman of letters. If I am married off to a man now, how will I ever become a scholar? How will my life be different to my mother's?"

Aunty Saras squeezed my hand in hers. "Shanti, it is not all bad. I am married to a man who is fairly conservative, and I have my duties, but I still have a good life."

"But it is what you chose, Aunty Saras. I do not choose this for myself. I wish to choose my husband when I am ready."

"Your parents are only repeating what they know, Shanti. Their spouses were chosen for them, and they are simply following in that tradition. They will never allow you to choose the man you will marry. You must accept that, Shanti. I can only think of a temporary solution."

"Tell me, Aunty Saras – I am desperate!"

She sighed. "I have heard via my husband that your mother has visited the temple healer, and she is unwell. She requires rest, Shanti. Go to her for her softness of heart. Tell her you will look after her and manage the household while her health is weak. Promise her that once she has fully recovered, she can return to her role – and you will marry this boy."

I considered it for a moment. "It will not be easy, Aunty Saras. Neither of my parents will agree willingly."

"But you are persuasive, Shanti. Use your words to convince her."

"I will do as you say, Aunty Saras – thank you."

"Shanti, it is still wise to remember that the greatest poets and writers ever to have walked the soil of India were human, too. They knew love's ecstasy and its bitter disappointments. Many learnt that for all their greatness, life was not worth living without love. Your brilliance matters little if there is no one to hold your hand while you lie on your death bed, or to scatter your ashes when you are gone. That cannot be what you want, my child. Once you have learnt all I can teach you, you must marry and live the life destined for you."

I held her fast and thanked her.

"Go now," she said. "You must speak to your mother urgently."

CHAPTER 5

I AM STRUCK BY MY MOTHER'S FRAILTY, her shrivelling hands and feet, by the lightness she exerts on the dung floors. I stand next to her doing the washing. I am taller, stronger. Her body is spent from years of servitude, her skin stretched like taut canvas over protruding bone. The healer says her heart is failing. Now I must ask something more of her. It will require her to stand up to my father and go against his wishes.

"*Ama*," I say to her softly. "*Ama*, may I please speak to you?"

She is surprised by my tone, which contains nothing of the defiance she has come to expect.

"Have you changed your mind about Muthan?" she asks hopefully.

I shake my head. "But it has to do with him. Please sit, *Ama*."

I sit next to her and take her hand. She is surprised. She looks at me with intense tenderness.

"*Ama*," I start, "I know you are sick. I am truly sorry I have made the last few days so trying for you and *Apa*. I hear you cry at night, and my heart breaks because I know I am to blame for it."

"Shanti," she says, "when your father and I are ready to leave this life, we want to be sure we have not left our baby to fend for herself. The world is cruel. People will take advantage unless you've got a husband to love and protect you."

"I know, *Ama*. But I am not ready." I walk over to the cracked looking glass and see how curiously it distorts my reflection. My mother's eyes follow me as I remove my sari and undergarments.

"What are you doing?" she asks as I stand in front of her, almost naked. "Cover yourself!" she says, averting her gaze.

"No, *Ama*, look at me," I say, looking down at my half-formed breasts, the downy layer of hair under my arms. My hips are narrow, my stomach flat. "I am not ready to feel a grown man pressed against me or feed a baby with these breasts. I am only half a woman, *Ama*. Please. I beg you not to take these last days of my childhood from me. I have thought about this, and I have found a way that you and I can help each other. I know you are sick. Your body is weak, and you need to rest and heal."

"How do you know this, Shanti? I have kept this from …"

"*Ama*, the villagers have been talking. They know you went to see the healer recently. What did he say, *Ama*? Tell me, please."

She begins to cry. "It's my heart, Shanti. He says it is weak. That I must stop tending the vegetables and hoeing the garden. I must try to do less in the household until I am stronger, but …"

"*Ama*, please! Allow me to take over your tasks for a while. I have learnt to do most of these chores, and where I am unsure, you can guide me. I will do everything to your liking. I will treat it as an act of love and appreciation for all you have done over the years."

"But what about your marriage, Shanti?"

"All I need is a bit more time. I beg you to tell Muthan's parents that I will marry him, but that it cannot happen now because you need my help to recover. As long as he is willing to wait for me, I

45

promise to marry him when you are well."

"Your father will never agree! He will blame me for delaying your marriage."

"*Ama*, this solution will help us both. Please try to persuade him. I beg you."

She thinks about it for a moment, and nods. "I will try. He is stubborn. But I will try to convince him. Now put on your clothes, my child."

My mother broaches the conversation several nights later, by which time I've begun to believe she has either forgotten about our agreement or changed her mind. I am almost on the verge of falling asleep when I hear the sound of muffled voices drifting across to me. I pretend I am sleeping, but my interest is piqued.

"Manickam," my mother is saying, "You know how much I respect you. You are the head of this household. But I have something to ask of you. I ask with respect and shame."

I can hear my father's weight shifting. "I'm very tired, Meena. I just want one peaceful night of sleep. Why are you bothering me now?"

"Sorry, Manickam. I don't want to bother you, but I have to talk to you. This is very important. If I wait, who knows what will happen?"

I hear my father grunt and sigh. "Carry on then. Talk."

"You know how badly I want Shanti to marry Muthan. He's my brother's son, after all. But my health is bad, Manickam. I've been working so hard for many years in this house. But now it is too much for me. My heart is not strong any more. The healer says I can only recover if I rest. But where will I get time to rest? I do one chore after another from before sunrise ..."

"What are you saying, Meena? You want to stop working, or what? And what's this got to do with Shanti's marriage?"

"Manickam, I'm only saying my heart is weak. I can't keep the house in the state I used to."

"But the house is always spotless ..."

"The house is clean because Shanti is doing everything. She's helping me every day – cleaning, washing, putting everything in the right place. I can't do it on my own any more. Without Shanti, this place would look like the monsoons came."

I picture my father's perplexed face as he tries to understand where my mother is heading with this.

"Without Shanti, the house would be filthy, Manickam. The vegetable garden wouldn't be hoed or watered. The clothes wouldn't be washed. You would have nothing to eat when you came home. She's doing everything. She's tired, but she's not complaining. Manickam, I can't survive this without her. All I'm asking is, please, give me some time. I will rest. Shanti will take over my work and I will try to get well."

"Meena, I'm not a hard man – you know me. But you've been to the healer, he has given you special herbs, and your health seems to be improving. You really want to put off Shanti's marriage? That girl's going to turn fifteen, then sixteen years old, and she'll still be living here. What will our neighbours and friends say?"

"Manickam, it's just for now. The neighbours, all our friends – they know I'm sick. They are worried about my health, too. I've already told them Shanti is going to marry Muthan. But we don't have to rush to get it done. I'll tell them I'm struggling with the housework and Shanti is delaying her marriage to help me. They will understand."

"They may *say* they understand, Meena, but they'll be gossiping behind our backs. Stop it now! Stop complaining about this sickness. My poor mother was blind, but she worked until the day she died – and she never complained! Meena, life is not easy. Every day, I also wake up before the sun. I wash the filthy clothes of rich people until my skin comes off! I have no choice! What happens if I stop working? We starve! Meena, I've got my work outside, you've got your work in the house. You're my wife. You must find the strength to keep going for as long as you can, and ..."

"What are you saying, Manickam?" My mother was becoming hysterical. "Don't you see this is serious? I'm sick! I'm dying! I only open my eyes in the morning for you and Shanti. Sometimes, I want to close them for good because I'm so tired. You ... you've got no heart, Manickam. Have I ever worried you for anything since we've been married? I came to this humble home and I took everything you gave me with thanks. I have always been willing to work hard! But now, when I can't work as hard as before, you treat me like I'm a lazy woman? You are a selfish man! One day you will come home and find me lying dead on the ground. Then you will cry because you had the chance to save my life, but you never took it. Do you want that, Manickam? Do you want to kill your wife? At least my child shows some love and care for her mother. She wants to delay her marriage to save my life. But who do you care about? Only yourself ..."

At the sound of my mother's sobbing, I pull myself up and go over to them. "*Apa*, please. Stop this!"

I run to my mother and hold her gently in my arms. Her bony shoulders dig into my flesh.

"Shanti," my father shouts and shoves his finger in my face, his eyes bulging. "You're the cause of this trouble! You put this stupid idea in her head. Now she's speaking like a fool. Like she's gone mad!"

"*Apa*, why do you say these things? You've upset *Ama* now. It's enough."

"You come here, and this is how you talk to me? You've got no respect for your father, girl!" He lashes out with his right hand, but I lean back and avoid the blow.

"*Apa*, you do not see what I see because I am with *Ama* every day. She has waited on us. She's served us all. And she's never complained once about the heap of demands we pile on her head. Look at *Ama*. She's grown old. We have made her old, *Apa*! Do you not see the paleness of her skin? How thin she has become? *Apa*, you cannot let her die on her knees serving us!"

I cannot believe I have allowed myself to raise my voice and address my father in this tone. His mouth twists, but he says nothing more. My mother's weeping has died down to a moan. She lies crumpled in my arms. My father looks at her, mystified, as though her shadow has suddenly taken on a discernible form and she is visible to him after all these years. He seems shaken by the palpability of her.

But he is also wounded by the gust of pain and anger that has blown through his house. He shrinks into himself. For an instant I picture him as he appeared out of that swirl of dust to scoop me up when I had fallen off the Brahmin bull – heroic and strong. He is no longer that man. Tonight, he appears the smallest of the three of us. He searches for more angry words, but can find none. My mother has decided my marriage will be postponed, and that is the final word. My father glares at us both one last time before he turns his back to us and goes to sleep.

CHAPTER 6

THE FIRST FEW DAYS I walked in my mother's shoes, I learnt how strenuous her tasks had been, and what little reward they offered. I had to ensure the smooth running of our household, getting up before sunrise to begin preparing my father's breakfast, usually a meal of roti accompanied by braised potatoes or lentils. My father ate in silence and rarely thanked me. But it didn't matter.

I washed the clothes, cleaned the floors, cooked and cared for my mother, who needed a good deal of attention. I made sure she woke each day to a pristine home. Day after day she opened her eyes and managed a feeble smile, trying to reassure me that she felt better than the day before. But there was no visible change in her condition. She truly appreciated my presence, though, and it gave me a new sense of fulfilment to assist with bathing her, getting her dressed, and cooking a meal for her. I doused her hair with *amla* oil to restore its blackness, washing and brushing it until it gleamed in the sunlight. She tired easily, so I would have to pause at intervals to give her a few moments to catch her breath. If I found it frustrating at first, at least I was learning patience.

My mother and I grew closer. I could see she no longer thought me the incorrigible child I once had been. My sisters had done much in our home, but they'd had no occasion to care for our mother so intimately, and I began to see it as a privilege. I wanted to please my mother, but, equally, I could not fail because neither of us wanted to test my father.

I'd not had occasion to visit my friends for weeks. But Thirna would frequently arrive for a short visit. Sanisha was often on our minds, and we'd hoped that all these months later, she would have settled into her new life and found some happiness in her husband's home. I had broken my promise to go back and see her, and decided it was time I visited her again.

I set off one afternoon after all my housework was complete. As I neared Sanisha's house, I saw a small figure outside, beating the dust from a mat. And when I got closer, I realised it was her. All I wanted was to run up and embrace her. But there was a foreignness about her that held me back. I hid behind the trunk of a tree and heard her grunt as she flogged that mat with all the hatred she could muster: every limb, every muscle tense, her legs braced as though she were standing her ground against an enemy. When she turned her face, I saw a scowl so bitter, she looked as if her life tasted of gall. I wondered whose face she saw in that mat when she beat it? When she was finished, she staggered slightly, out of breath, picked up a corner of the mat with both hands and dragged it indoors like a dead weight. I waited a moment, then turned and walked home.

When my mother asked me how Sanisha was, I shrugged my shoulders. "I don't know, *Ama*. I couldn't find her there," I said. And I knew I would never go back. A few months later, Sanisha put on a white sari dappled with cheerful pink hibiscuses and hanged herself with the sash. When her mother-in-law came upon her that morning, the breeze was twirling Sanisha from side to side as if she were dancing.

We were all sick at heart, but for different reasons. I had lost a friend who hadn't deserved to live and die like that, and I had failed her. Her parents were sorry they had not taken her back when she had pleaded, because it was not the done thing in Vākkuruti. Her husband and her mother-in-law were disappointed that she had been too brittle to withstand the beatings, and she hadn't even borne them a child. Their expectations for a girl won in a game of dice were high.

I didn't go to the cremation. I told my mother that although our grief was new, in truth, Sanisha had vacated her body long before she exited this life. What would I have done in her situation? Sanisha had always been a mild-mannered girl, but I was nothing like her. I wasn't sure I could tame my tongue if I'd been wronged the way she had. Her death reminded me that violence was everywhere, and marriage was sometimes a direct path to it.

The hours trickled into days which flowed into weeks and months. Seasons passed in a blur while I rose, toiled, and slept exhausted each night. I missed my lessons with Aunty Saras. I had spent a good part of nearly five summers under her tutelage, and now there was no hope of even stealing a moment to visit her. Caring for my mother had also changed me. I no longer felt like a child, or craved the childish joys I had known when I was younger.

Meanwhile, Vākkuruti was changing too. The energy that once infused our village was no longer there. That summer, no rains came. We were all sick with worry. We looked to the sky and took offerings to the temple, but not a single cloud formed. The ground cracked beneath our feet, and the animals began to die as the sun scorched our crops. The lakes and wells dried up, and I was forced to walk long distances to fetch water, stumbling across the carcasses of animals on the outskirts of our village. On those draining walks, I often recited the poems Aunty Saras and I had read together.

Hunger began to prey on the people of Vākku̱ruti. The laughter of children descended into the wails of their parents as famine ripped the little ones from their families. The older folk curved like brittle walking sticks. People walked wide-eyed, gathering dry stalks to light funeral pyres. We wondered what we had done to disappoint the gods. Some whispered that Vākku̱ruti was cursed. Many of our friends packed up their meagre belongings and went in search of prosperity elsewhere. Among the marching masses was my dearest friend, Thirna, who had lost her grandmother. Thirna came to say goodbye to me as night fell, promising me that even if our paths never crossed again, she would always remember the seasons when the village was lush and we suckled from her as newborn calves from their mothers. She was still mourning her grandmother. "My *Ava* shrivelled, Shanti, until she just disappeared. My father is so angry. He says the British made him grow crops we cannot eat, so they can sell them. He has sworn he will not see one more day in Vākku̱ruti."

"Where are you going, Thirna?" I asked.

"We are going to Madras. My father says it is a big city that sits on the lip of the Bay of Bengal. Food and water will be plentiful there, and we hope not to struggle any more."

I had heard that the situation was not much better in Madras, but I couldn't bear to tell Thirna that. "My dear friend, I wish you life's best – fertile lands and clear water … and one day a wonderful husband and many beautiful children. Perhaps I will come to Madras and find you there one day," I told her. "Do not forget me." I choked back tears when we embraced. Thirna had been my most devoted childhood friend. And when she left, I knew with certainty those days of juvenile happiness had ended.

Those of us who remained had to make do with little. My father called me aside one day and asked me to ration our meals. "Give your mother the most," he said. "You and I are still healthy and

53

can do without large portions. But your mother cannot while she is sick. I trust you will know how to make the food last."

"Yes, *Apa*, I will do as you say," I replied.

Most days, there was only enough food for two adults. I often pretended I had already eaten my portion, and divided my share between my parents. There were nights when I swallowed my saliva to trick my body into believing I had eaten. I would fall asleep, but the hunger pangs would attack me in the middle of the night. I found that curling myself tightly into a ball was the best way to keep them at bay.

Even the wealthiest of Vākkuṟuti's people were affected by the famine. I wondered how Aunty Saras was coping. The last time I had seen her, a few months previously, she had looked thinner, and her complexion had dulled. When I asked her why, she brushed it aside. "Old age, Shanti!" she laughed, and coughed. I wasn't convinced, but I didn't want to pry. I promised myself that when I went back to fetch water from one of the distant wells in the next few days, I would make a short stop at her house to find out if her health was improving.

A week later, as I was cooking our evening meal, my mother returned from a short visit to one of the neighbours. I was relieved she was spending more time outdoors. Her periods of rest were becoming slightly shorter, and her appetite was improving. But that day, she returned looking gravely worried.

"*Ama*, are you feeling all right? What is wrong?"

She mopped her brow as she sat down. "Shanti, we never know when it is our time. That's why I feel very fortunate to be alive."

"*Ama*, what are you talking about?"

"You know that snooty Saras whose house you used to clean? Always in her fancy saris, looking so well-fed while everyone else starves. Can you believe it – they found her dead in her kitchen this morning!" She clicked her tongue. "Imagine! Just imagine dying alone like that while he was at the temple. Poor thing! No children to look after her."

The pot tumbled from my hands, and its contents cascaded onto the floor. As the ground hurtled towards me, I thrust my wrist out to break the fall, twisting it as I landed in a heap.

My mother rushed over to me. "Shanti! Shanti, are you hurt? Shanti, say something!"

Her eyes were wide. She grabbed me around my jaw and began shaking me. "Look at me, Shanti! I'm here!"

She sat on the floor, put my head in her lap and began to stroke my face. The room spun around me.

"Shanti, are you all right? Talk to me, girl!"

"*Ama*, I am all right ..." I stammered.

"Breathe. You must take deep breaths. Deeper!" she said urgently.

And I tried. But it seemed such an effort. "It is just a shock to me because I knew her, *Ama*. This talk of death is too much for me."

"Oh, sorry my child! You're right. One moment you were in her house, and the next moment she's gone. But I know you've also been sad since Thirna left. I know you're struggling to get over it."

She lifted me up gently. "Did you hurt yourself badly? Are you in pain?"

"No, *Ama*," I said. "I am fine, thank you. I just hurt my wrist a bit."

She massaged it as I pulled myself up into a sitting position.

"Shanti, why you don't go and lie down for a while?" she said, rubbing my back. "I am feeling better today. I'll carry on with the cooking. You go and rest."

"Thank you, *Ama*," I said. "I'm sorry to give you this work. Just let me clean up here before I go."

I mopped the floor without a word and went to lie on my mat. I cried quietly, burying my face in the folds of my sari. 'Aunty Saras, why have you left me?' I wept. I lay there trying to conjure up her last moments. I wondered if she had been afraid or in pain. I was devastated that she had died all alone. In my imagination, I saved her a hundred times. I took her to the temple healer and she recovered, and we went back to the way everything had been. But the sounds of my mother banging pots at the fire outside sucked me back to reality. Aunty Saras was gone, and I had been nowhere near when she needed me.

As was the custom, we all attended her cremation. I stood at the back weeping, surprised at how tiny she looked on the pyre. I wished to touch her for the last time. But no low-caste person could taint the dead. The rites were performed. A man paid a subdued tribute to her, saying she was a good *Brahmin* woman who kept her house immaculate and respected her husband. The gods were appeased with offerings and the flame was lit. Her flesh submitted willingly. I wanted to run up to the pyre and shout out that it was wrong for us to send her off so passively – that she was so much more than people thought. She was a heroine who bent the rules and loved to read and write. She fell in love with a Christian once and consorted with a low-caste girl she considered her daughter. But no one would listen. *This is Vākkuṛuti, where all the heroes are men, and I am nobody until I become Muthan the railway worker's wife.*

The sorrow of Aunty Saras's passing never left me. She was always there in my mind's eye, chatting and laughing, haunting me as I tried to put on a brave face. A week after her funeral two men arrived at our door, each of them with a heavy sack on their backs. It was clear from their attire that they were temple devotees.

"*Vanakum*," the taller man said. "We're looking for Manickam and Meenatchee …"

"Yes, Uncle, this is their home. I am their daughter, Shanti."

"Ah, yes. Well, Shanti, you must know of the passing of our priest's dear wife, Saras."

"Yes," I responded. "It is so sad."

"Oh, it was a shock to many. Not everyone knew she was ill. In any case, you know she was a kind woman. She often gave alms to the poor. And she asked that soon after her death, your family be given these two sacks of rice and beans."

"Thank you, Uncle. I do not know what to say. These have been hard times."

They laid the sacks at the door.

"A bit heavy. Perhaps your father can take them inside," the shorter man said, turning away. "*Vanakum.*"

"Thank you. *Vanakum.*"

I was taken aback, but I shouldn't have been. Aunty Saras had shown me great generosity in life, and continued to help me after her passing. I gazed at the two sacks. They were a reminder of my shame. She deserved more from the girl she had risked so much for.

When my mother awoke, she was delighted to find the donation. "Ah, she was a good woman indeed," she said, wiping her eyes. But when my father arrived, he looked at the bags in disdain and muttered about how he hated rich people's charity. My mother scoffed, "Well, who are we going to send this back to, Manickam? The woman who sent it to us is gone!"

We feasted on the beans and rice for weeks. One morning, as I was scooping another handful of beans to throw into the pot, the old enamel cup in my hand struck something hard. I put the cup aside, plunged both my arms elbow-deep into the bag, and began sifting through the beans. My left hand brushed against the corner of something that felt like metal. What could the temple workers possibly have put into this sack? I peered in. There, toward the bottom, lay a rectangular metal box. I reached in, pulled it out, and headed for my mat.

Whatever the contents were, they were not very heavy. I shook the container gently, holding it to my ear to see if I could guess what might be inside. The box was shiny and caught the light. I brushed off some of the husks and blew off the remaining dust. I tugged at the clasp until it opened. My nostrils were immediately filled with the scent of the sandalwood incense that Aunty Saras used to burn in her house. I closed my eyes and drew in a slow, deep breath.

Inside the box lay a saffron envelope addressed to "Shanti" in Aunty Saras's handwriting. I picked it up delicately. Beneath the letter, she had placed some plain white paper, a quill and ink, another treasured book of love poetry, and an ornate bead-encrusted book covered in flowing hand-painted designs and decorated with the feathers of a peacock.

I jumped up and peered out to make sure that my mother was still at the neighbour's before I returned to my mat and slowly tore the envelope open. It contained a letter.

My dear Shanti,

If you are reading this, then my life has run its course. I hope that I have not left you in great sorrow. I thought of contacting you many times in my last days but I wondered how you might react if you saw me. I decided I would prefer you to remember me in the best of health.

I have known for some time that I am ill. A few moons ago, I too consulted Jairam the healer at the temple and discovered that, unlike your mother, I had no chance of recovery. At first, I searched for a cure at every turn and consumed every possible herb and tea! But it was not my fate to be cured, and when I accepted this, my last days became much less anxious. The physicality of this body is often out of our hands. I had to learn that through the pain, my body was signalling to me that its time had expired, and my spirit must soon go in search of another plane. I said to the divine power, "I am ready. Do what you will."

But reflecting on this life, it is true – I have married well. I have lived well. I have learnt surprising things, and I have had a child without having to bear her. This is the best of everything this life could give me, Shanti.

Forgive me for leaving you this way. I understand you may be angry or feel that I deserted you during an arduous time in your life. Let me assure you that you were the one person who kept me alive for longer than I should have been. My deep affection for you and our afternoons together revitalised me. But there are many mistakes I have made during this life, Shanti. I must beg your forgiveness for keeping you holed up in my backroom to learn, and the lie I devised to explain our relationship. I am sorry that when we met in public, I never embraced you. I hid you as though you were a source of shame, and I am truly sorry. Now, in my last days, I do not care any more about the repulsive stares of people or their razor-edged words.

You may believe that I have been your teacher for several years now. But you have been mine, too. You brought the freshness of your innocence and a keen mind into my home. You put challenging questions to me about the choices I had made and sometimes even made me rethink them! There comes a time when the teacher must say to the student, "I have taught you all that I can. It is time for you to move on to greater things." Shanti, I have taught you to read and write, to add and subtract. I have taught you a bit about life and the way others see it. But there is so much I cannot teach you. There are lessons that life itself must teach you. Some are more pleasant to learn than others. During times of difficulty, do not be despondent! Remember this – you are a store of innate knowledge. You have already lived a thousand lives and the sum of that is vested in you. The struggles of your ancestors are sewn into you. Their joys are wound into your sinews. The secrets of love already circulate in the chambers of your heart.

In the box are my last gifts to you. Use this paper I have saved for you to practise your writing. Do not let your sharpness of mind falter, and take this gift of love poetry that may be a guide to you in matters of the heart. The most important thing I give you, though, is the book that lines the bottom of this box. Treat it with care because its rich and beautiful story will soon come to life.

Now go, Shanti! Dry your tears. Reach for courage and remember that the bonds of true kinship extend beyond the boundaries of life and death.

Joy, love and peace always, my beloved Shanti.
Your Aunty Saras

She had been an extraordinary woman. I pored over her gifts and smiled at the craftiness with which she'd conceived of this little scheme. Outside my house, Vākkuṟuti remained gloomy, but I felt as though I had been lit from within. I returned the letter to its envelope and took the box outside to bury it in a corner of the vegetable garden for safekeeping. The sun was marching swiftly across the sky and my mother would soon return. But just before I lowered the box into the hole I dug, I wanted to have one quick peek at the contents of the peacock-feather book. I opened it to read the first page.

It was blank.

CHAPTER 7

IT WAS DIFFICULT COMING TO terms with the grief of Aunty Saras's passing. I found that housework, though mundane, soon became a welcome escape for me. I also began to cook more adventurously, and fell into the routine of buying spices from the local shopkeeper, Ramdeen. His rotund stomach and bulbous nose would come into view first as he rounded the corner, followed by the rest of his bulk. He bound it, and his nether regions, in a skimpy yellow *dhoti*. A constant itch must have emanated from below, because he often reached down to scratch it in full view of his customers, and would examine his nails afterwards. His hair was an oil slick that crept down like ivy around his double chin.

Ramdeen sat sprawled like an emperor behind his makeshift counter. He passed many hours picking on his young assistant, Bilal, and chewing on betel nut that browned his teeth and turned his breath rancid. Thankfully, there was some respite in the aroma his spices gave off – aniseed, cardamom, turmeric, ginger, garlic – all overflowing from sacks squatting on the ground.

I was relieved one morning to find Ramdeen absent and Bilal in charge. He was a funny-looking fellow with his shock of spiky black hair, his sharp nose and broad smile. Ramdeen had taken Bilal in as his assistant years ago, supposedly as a favour to Bilal's parents. Bilal's father, who has been crippled and has begged ever since I can remember, cannot work. My mother often scratches together whatever we can find for their family, and I take it to their home. Bilal's mother, Raheema, slight and ancient-looking, is always grateful. The scarf she wears hides almost her entire face. "God's blessings on your mother," she says. "She is a good friend to me."

I know it breaks Aunty Raheema's heart that Bilal had to start working at the age of five. She told my mother she took Bilal to Ramdeen's shop and pinched him hard on the arm to make him cry. Ramdeen eventually felt sorry for the boy and said Bilal could help him at the shop if he behaved well. Now Bilal is a twelve-year-old boy who still amuses himself by jumping from one sack of grain into the other to pass the time when Ramdeen is not there.

Today, Bilal was behaving like Shah Jehan in his Taj Mahal because Ramdeen had not been seen for days, and Bilal had been in full charge. The famine meant the shop was looking sparse, and the sacks would soon be empty.

"Bilal, where's Ramdeen today?" I asked.

"That fat bastard, Shanti? He's not here! He's gone out to do some *big business*!" he said mockingly. He mimicked Ramdeen's waddling gait and scratched an imaginary crotch.

"Bilal, stop playing the fool and gather some provisions for me," I laughed. I had brought some of Aunty Saras's beans to barter for split peas, cardamom and chillies.

"Shanti, but seriously!" He lowered his voice. "That fat bastard is hardly here these days. He's doing another business now, dealing with all these people leaving Vākkuruti."

"Ah, yes. My best friend, Thirna, and her family have also left for Madras."

"Madras?" he asked, then shook his head. "No – these people are not going to Madras. They're on their way to the Colony of Natal."

"The Colony of Natal? Where is that?"

"Shanti, have you never heard of this place? Are you living in a hole? Everyone has heard about the Colony of Natal!" he teased. "Ramdeen says it is the most beautiful place on earth." He grew wide-eyed. "There's enough food and water for everyone. It's as green as that vein throbbing in Ramdeen's temple when he gets angry! I have heard it is the closest thing to *Nirvana* on this earth."

"But Bilal, where is this place?"

"From what I understand, nowhere near here. You have to get on a ship to go there and it takes a while to reach. There are many wild animals in that place, and I'm told it's on the sea."

"Who is going to this place, Bilal?"

"Oh, all kinds of people. I know some people from Vākkuṟuti who've gone with their whole families. Lots of young men go. They say as long as you are fit and healthy, you can go."

"But what do the people do when they get there?"

"They grow sugarcane for the British."

"Are you playing a trick on me, Bilal?" I asked.

"No, Shanti, I swear I'm not! The Colony of Natal is a real place. That pig Ramdeen talks about it all the time – how people who have been starving in Vākkuṟuti have gone there and they are living so well, growing their sugarcane and swimming in the sea while the rest of us are sitting with empty stomachs here!"

"But what's Ramdeen's connection to the Colony of Natal?" I asked.

"He's an agent for the British – an *arkati*, they call him. He finds Indians who are willing to go to Africa to work there. He's told me many times the British depend on him, because he only takes the best. One day I even asked him if I could go. But you know him.

He said, 'No, it's not for stupid idiots! And you how old? Twelve years old? If I send you, the British will think we are all a nation of morons!'"

"I'm sorry, Bilal – Ramdeen can be so unkind. But would you really want to leave your parents to go so far away?"

"Shanti, I work all day in this shop and I still don't have two rupees to rub together for my parents. I always think if I went to the Colony of Natal, I would make a fortune and send it back home. Then all the people who spit upon my father's face will have to treat him like a king!"

I gathered up the spices he had packed for me. "Bilal, if that's what you wish for, then I really hope that one day you will go to the Colony of Natal and make enough money to fill all these sacks a hundred times over!"

"Thanks, Shanti! *In sha'allah*," he grinned as I left the little shop.

By the time I arrived home, my mother had already finished some of the housework and begun cooking.

"*Ama*, why are you not resting? You know you mustn't tire yourself!"

"No, Shanti, this is no bother," she replied. "Don't you see I am feeling better?"

"Yes, *Ama*. You are definitely looking brighter and eating better. But we shouldn't rush your recovery or …"

"Shanti," she cut me off. "My strength is coming back, my child. I am almost back to my old self. Your father has seen it too. He said to me, 'Meena, I can see the light in your eyes again. I'm so happy you've rested. It would be so nice if you could take over from Shanti again.'"

"What did you say, *Ama*? *Apa* is really being too hasty! After all …"

"No, Shanti, we had an agreement. You and your father have done a lot for me and time has gone fast. Last year, I put off your marriage. I stole one year of your life, my child. I have to make up for it now."

"*Ama*, that was nothing."

My mother was moving around the house as she used to, sweeping the floor, and stopping every now and then to stir the food.

"Time is passing, Shanti, and you won't always be young. I am better now, you are older, and Muthan's getting very impatient. I can't spend the whole day talking to the neighbours when I'm in a fit condition to work – it's not right." She looked at me tenderly. "I am so thankful to you. Now, we must move forward with our plans."

I swallowed hard.

"Your wedding – it must take place soon," she said.

How foolish I'd been! I'd imagined my mother's recovery would take many more seasons. Only a year had passed, and here I was facing the same dilemma.

I forced a smile. "All right, *Ama*. Begin the preparations," I said and went outside to gather my thoughts.

That night, and for several nights afterwards, I lay in the dark, wracking my brain to find another way out. Could I fake an illness, or pretend to be possessed by a bad spirit? That would put Muthan off for good! But no, that would not work – I'd be hauled off to the temple and Jairam the healer would find me out. Perhaps I could injure myself in such a way as to put me out of commission for a few months. But clumsy oaf that I was, I might cause myself serious harm and end up like Bilal's father. If I ran off to my sisters, they would both send me packing. The thought of following Thirna to Madras was tempting. But it was too far away, and I had no idea how to track her down in such a big town.

But perhaps running away was not as far-fetched as it sounded. I was reminded of how desperate Bilal was to leave for the Colony of Natal. It sounded pleasant enough. An idea began to germinate. I imagined leaving behind Vākkuṟuti, with its famine, poverty and death, its emptiness without Aunty Saras and Thirna, its reminders of the dreary life I likely faced with Muthan. What if Bilal was right and any able-bodied person could sail across the blue ocean and begin again? But could it really be so simple? That all you had to do was grow a few stalks of sugarcane for the British in exchange for independence and prosperity? I was doubtful, but curious. I decided to find out more. I could not shut the door on anything that might save me from this dreaded marriage.

CHAPTER 8

SLEEP DID NOT COME EASILY for many nights. I was plagued by dreams in which I was trying to save Sanisha: first from her husband, then from suicide. By the time I cut her down, it was too late to revive her, and when I looked more closely, her face was my own. I walked around disorientated, while my parents chattered excitedly about the wedding. Within just a few weeks, Muthan would arrive at my home in his finest *dhoti*, bathed in the most overpowering scents. I would have to sit demurely and smile shyly, until it was time to serve him tea and sweetmeats. He would gaze at me like a doll – my hands, my feet, my face – and decide whether he wanted me without even knowing my heart. I knew that in a few days my mother would take me aside to explain the mechanics of my wedding night and all the expectations the adults had of me. She would find sweet words to mask the unsheathing of the sword Muthan would drive into me.

I decided to go to Ramdeen's shop and see Bilal again. As always, he greeted me with a broad smile. "What are you looking for today, Shanti? I have some fresh cinnamon for you."

"Oh, no thanks, Bilal. I actually came to ask you about something you mentioned the last time we spoke. I have a friend who's interested in finding out more about the Colony of Natal."

"Ah, I don't blame her. Best to speak to Ramdeen – he organises everything."

"But he's hardly ever here these days. When can I see him, Bilal?"

"Oh, that fat shit is always back before sunset to close the shop. Your friend can come here then, Shanti."

"Thank you, Bilal. I will tell her. Have a good day!"

"*Ma'aassalaama,*" he shouted back.

I had to test Bilal's claims with Ramdeen. But it would not be easy to slip off to meet him. My father usually returned home from work at around sunset, and he would want to know where I was when he got home. I would have to come up with an excuse to leave the house at that time of the evening.

It was a few days before I finally went to meet Ramdeen. I rummaged through the spices in the house and hid the chillies I had bought at Ramdeen's shop several days before. And as sunset loomed, I pretended to ransack the house in search of them. "*Ama,* have you seen any chillies here? I was so sure we had enough. Did we really get through them so quickly?"

"Look again, Shanti. There must be chillies there," my mother called back.

I pretended to search the entire area, but find nothing.

"*Ama,* they are definitely finished. Oh, do not say that I will have to go back all that way to get more!"

"Shanti, I don't mind, but you know how your father gets if the food is not spicy! I don't want to upset him. Ramdeen only closes the shop at sunset. Quickly run there and get some before he closes."

"All right, *Ama*. I will go quickly," I said, happy to oblige.

I bounded out of the house. The cool evening air billowed between the folds of my sari. I took gusts of it into my lungs as I ran. As I reached the shop, Bilal was about to leave. I saw him wave goodbye to Ramdeen and start off for home. I stood out of sight until he was well on his way.

I rushed up to Ramdeen, still a little breathless. "Good evening, Uncle."

"Shanti – what you doing here? The shop is closed. Come back tomorrow."

"Yes, Uncle, I know. I'm sorry to disturb you. I just want to ask you a question."

"Come back tomorrow, girl. I have another appointment now."

"Uncle, it is very important … I won't waste any of your time."

He eyed me suspiciously.

"Sorry, Uncle. I heard about the other business you are doing …"

He looked at me, puzzled.

"The Colony of Natal?" I asked, tentatively.

He looked me up and down.

"Ah, so news travels fast to your burning ears, eh? What interest you got in my business?" he asked sharply.

"Uncle, I heard that you are helping people who want to leave Vākkuṟuti to go to the Colony of Natal … and …"

"Yes, you have heard correctly! I am a recruiter, highly recognised by the British for my talent for finding young people who want to make their fortune in the Colony of Natal. All these dropouts in Vākkuṟuti – the starving families, these women whose husbands have died and left them penniless – I help them all!"

"Uncle," I asked, "what is the Colony of Natal like?"

69

"Better than *Nirvana*! Paradise! Green fields everywhere, water, animals. You can't compare Vākkuṟuti with Port Natal!"

"And the people who leave our village to go there – are they happy?"

He laughed heartily, his stomach wobbling. "Oh, Shanti. You are still a baby, hey? Who does not want that quality of life? Free passage to the Colony, an estate waiting to welcome you, good money, regular meals, a nice place to live. You told me once that you do a very good job of looking after your father's vegetable patch. It's like that, but much bigger. I wish I could leave Vākkuṟuti for the Colony myself. But I can only go once my recruitment work is finished – the British are depending on me." He paused. "What's your interest in all of this?"

Time was short and I decided to be honest. "Uncle, I am thinking about my future and ... I do not believe there will be much for me to do here when I am older."

He looked confused. "But aren't you getting married soon, eh? Everyone says your mother and father are marrying you off to your long-lost cousin. It sounds like your future is taken care of."

I felt the blood rushing to my face.

"Uncle – that is not all that I want to do. There are many things people do not know about me. I can do lots of things besides hoe the vegetable patch and do the housework!"

Ramdeen was slightly taken aback. "So, what you saying, Shanti?"

"I am saying that ... I do not want to marry my cousin. I would rather leave Vākkuṟuti. Perhaps even ... go to ... the Colony of ..."

"Out of the question!" he thundered. "You are too young!"

"But I am strong and able-bodied, Uncle! For the last year, I have run the household. I've cared for my sick mother, and I have done it well and never complained. I rise at dawn and begin working until I collapse onto my mat at night. And when the next day comes, I am able to do it all over again. Please Uncle, give me a chance. I can prove my worth!"

"Yes, yes …" He shook his head, unconvinced. "They all come here saying the same thing. But you see, I can't let the British down. They don't even want young girls like you because your kind just goes there and eats and has babies. If I send you there, and you can't work properly, then that's the end for me. How old you are now?"

"I am soon to turn fifteen …"

"Ha! Fifteen?" He threw his head back and guffawed. "Imagine how they will laugh in my face if I tell them I am sending a fifteen-year-old along to Port Natal?"

"But Uncle, I look quite a bit older than that. Many people mistake me for a sixteen-year-old," I lied.

He rubbed his hands across his jowls. "Well, there's some nice unmarried men there. Maybe the British will find a use for you." He turned serious. "What papers you got?"

"Papers? I … I'm not certain …"

"You know – papers, papers, man, you silly girl! Papers to show what your name is, where you were born, how old you are …"

"No, Uncle, I … I do not have any of those papers."

"Oh, damn it! Then how do you expect to go?"

"Uncle, is there a way of getting these papers? If you tell me how, I will try …"

He sighed and looked away. "Look, it can be done. But it will take me a few days to contact the people who can help. It makes things very difficult, but maybe I'll be able to organise some papers for you. But listen, you'll have to change your age on the documents if you want to go."

"Yes, Uncle, I'm prepared to, if I need to. Does that mean you would be able to arrange for me to go to the Colony of Natal?"

"Shanti – wait! What will your parents have to say about all this?"

I fell silent.

"Speak up!" he shouted.

"Uncle … uhm … I have not spoken to them about this."

"Ha! So when the hell are you planning to tell them about your grand plans?"

I shook my head. "I do not plan to tell them," I replied.

He looked surprised, then smirked. "Hmmm … you're one crafty little thing, eh? Oh well, that's up to you – I don't get involved in family business. But listen, you sure you want to do this?"

"Uncle, I think I want to …"

"What rubbish is this? Don't come here with 'I think', 'I may', 'I'm not sure'. Make up your damn mind, girl! Don't waste my time!"

I thought about it for a few moments longer while Ramdeen huffed in the background.

"Yes," I nodded. "I want to go ahead with it."

"You sure, girl?"

"Yes, Uncle. I'm quite sure."

"You're not going to make me go through all this trouble of getting the papers and everything and you back out of this agreement?"

"No, Uncle. I promise. You have my word."

"Listen to me, Shanti." He leaned forward and stuck a finger in my face. "I got a good name in Vākkuṟuti because I am a serious businessman, and I don't tolerate nonsense! You don't mention a word of this to anyone, you understand? You don't tell your friends or your family at the last moment. Most important – you do not change your mind! You don't want to get on the wrong side of me. I'm not your uncle. You must call me Mr Ramdeen from now on."

I felt a wave of fear as I looked him in the eye. "No, Unc— Mr Ramdeen. I will not let you down," I said.

"Okay, come back here in four days and I'll tell you if I got your papers."

"Thank you," I said.

"Get out of here now. People mustn't see me talking to you."

I nodded my head, turned and ran off, just in time to meet my father as he returned from work. I slapped the chillies into my mother's hand, and she stirred them into the pot. I watched the flames lick the sides of the pot until the *dhal* inside was bubbling.

I was intimidated by my initial meeting with Ramdeen. His loud voice and brash ways had frightened me. And I began to believe that I was making a mistake, one I would come to regret. But when I weighed this up against the alternative, I concluded that Ramdeen was simply a jagged stepping stone to something much better, whereas I risked a lifetime of unhappiness with Muthan. Four days later, on the evening I was to meet Ramdeen, I told my mother I was going for a short walk and would be back before my father was home. She didn't mind in the least. Again, I approached Ramdeen's shop out of breath. He turned around sharply.

"Oh, it's you! Good thing you came, girl. You very lucky – we got the papers," he said. He went into the shop and came back with some slightly crumpled papers. I could read some of what was printed on them, but pretended I couldn't. They were in a complicated form of English. "These are your papers, but they'll stay with me for safekeeping. We leaving in three nights."

"Three nights?" I gasped.

"Why you sounding so shocked? You said you wanted to go! Now you want to stay here?"

"No, Mr Ramdeen, no! I *am* going. I just thought it would take a bit longer …"

"Eh, when I organise, I organise properly, all right? You still going? You sure?"

"Yes, sir. I am going. I'll be here, I promise you." I tried to sound as convincing as possible.

"Right, now this is how it works. You won't be the only one going. We leave in a group at night because it's not so hot. You'll meet me not far from here, under that clump of trees near the dry riverbed." He pointed to some dense growth across what used to be a rushing river. "I'm taking a new group that night. You slip quietly out of your house. No one must see you! We travel together to a holding facility where all my new recruits are taken to prepare for the boat trip. We look after you while you there, then you take a short walk to get on the ship in Madras and the adventure begins. But I hold on to your papers throughout. You just mark an 'x' on the papers to tell me you understood everything and it's settled."

"Mr Ramdeen, how long do I have to stay there before I come back home?"

"Shanti," he said. "You must think about this for the long term. No use going all that way and crying for *Ama*! You'll have everything there and you'll still earn money for the work you do – it's not like looking after your mother like a slave and not getting one rupee for it! You can come back if you want after, say, three years. But I recommend you go for five years. Most people who go there never want to come back to Vākkuṟuti because life is so much better in Africa!"

He went on speaking for a while about life in the Colony, which I found reassuring. But I had to cut him short and excuse myself so I'd get back home before my father. I thanked Ramdeen for helping me. He promised I would not regret my decision.

But who would not regret leaving home and the only family you have ever known? I walked away from Ramdeen's shop with a sombre new perspective. Minutes before, I had imagined I'd be meeting Ramdeen to find out whether it was possible to secure documentation for the trip. But the course of our conversation had taken such a sharp turn that I had actually committed myself to leaving my home and my family imminently. These three precious days would be the last with my parents until I returned in five years. I would not even be able to say goodbye to my sisters. I took a little time to walk through Vākkuṟuti and record her scenery in my mind. I passed Aunty Saras's house and visited the lake on either side. Vākkuṟuti was not at her most beautiful at that time, but it didn't matter to me. I believed that once this terrible period was over and the droughts had ended, she would return to her former glory. Perhaps I would return in time to enjoy that.

For the next three days, I went out of my way to help my mother and father. Nothing they asked of me was too much, and they seemed to appreciate it. They must have believed I was changing, becoming more compliant in preparation for my marriage, mistaking the excitement that was beginning to brim inside me for my willingness to become Muthan's wife.

The last night we spent together as a family, we fed my father first as always, and my mother and I sat and ate in silence afterwards. I longed to tell my mother the truth, but I couldn't. I was privy to a secret that would drastically change all of our lives. I quietly studied my mother as she hungrily ate that humble meal with gratitude. At that moment, much like when I watched her sleeping, she seemed to me the most vulnerable human being on earth.

That night, doubt rose up inside me. Sleep did not come. Soon I would be leaving Vākkuṟuti – the place of my birth, my childhood play, my learning, my parents and sisters. I went to stand outside and breathe in the dawn air. I never wanted to forget that scent of jasmine – the first fragrance of the day. I dug my feet hard into the soil, trying to imprint them there, as the sun breathed its warmth onto Vākkuṟuti.

It was a day both momentous and banal. My work still had to

be done to keep up the pretence. Clothes were washed, the house swept clean, the food cooked. I thought there should have been something more – some divine portent to mark my final day there. But no such sign came. My mother chatted happily, and I tried to respond warmly. At every opportunity I gazed at her, studied her. I wanted to remember every dimple, every strand of hair, press a whole store of her into my mind and revise it every day ahead. But a day is a short time. It passed so quickly. The sun set. My father came home. We ate. I held them close when we said goodnight.

My father noticed nothing. But my mother looked at me as though she knew something was amiss, but couldn't quite pin-point it.

"*Ama*, you are a wonderful mother to me. Thank you," I said. "I am sorry for the times I have let you down … and for the times in the future when I may do the same."

"Make peace with your mistakes, my Shanti," she said. She walked a few steps away, then turned back. "A mother should not say this, but you are the most treasured of my children."

The sincerity of those words gored me, made me hate myself for what I was about to do. I sat on my mat and cried. I fought time, desperately trying to wind it back for just one more night in this dilapidated house with its broken people.

I stood outside where my parents were sleeping that warm night, listening to their slow breathing and watching Vākkuṟuti drizzle its moonlight over them. I saw them take me in their arms as a crying child, coax me down from fruit trees when I got stuck, and craft the simplest of toys that had brought me so much pleas-ure. I loved them so much. But I could not stay. Aunty Saras had changed me, Sanisha's death had marked me, and Bilal's dream had become mine.

I hurriedly packed a few things for my journey – some clothes and my metal box. Guilt cast a shadow over me, forcing hurtful thoughts into my head – how I had begged Aunty Saras for a 'temporary' solution. How I had deceitfully convinced my trusting parents that I would marry Muthan, and how sincerely they had believed me.

Time raced. Night fell with a clang. I stepped out of my home, turned my back on all I loved, and when my feet smudged the path, I did not look back. I left, a girl running breathlessly toward a destiny carved out of deceit. What had I to be proud of? I had broken my promises to the living and the dead.

CHAPTER 9

VĀKKURUTI'S DRY GROUND, TREES AND ramshackle homes passed in a blur as I sprinted to the copse near the riverbed. My heart was pounding. I rubbed the sweat from my palms onto the sides of my sari. Awkwardly fastened, it was slowing me down. Ramdeen was a dark, imposing figure against the branches. "Get in!" he shouted. "You are late!"

I scrambled into the bullock cart, apologising, catching my feet in the folds of my sari, dropping one sandal on the ground, which Ramdeen hurled into the cart in annoyance. So clumsy, so stupid. What did these people think of me, panting, tears streaming down my face, clutching my small handwoven basket with its metal box and worn clothes inside?

The bullock seemed unwilling to begin the trip, no doubt tired from carrying load after load of Vākkuruti's cowards fleeing their lives. I tried to make out the faces of the people. The moonlight was slowly sketching their features for me when Ramdeen flung a smelly canvas over us and told us to shut up.

I tried to manoeuvre my body into a comfortable position to

create space between the moist body of the strange man I was pressed against and the stench of his sweat. At least I was sitting at the end, so I could occasionally raise the edge of the canvas and let in the smallest chink of moonlight and a whiff of air. The ground was raw and uneven. We bounced, swayed and slapped against one other. There was a child in here, crying from fear, wetting himself with panic, the odour of urine staining the journey. Whenever we were tempted to speak, Ramdeen flew into a rage. "I said, shut up!" he bellowed. "If we are caught, it's over for all of us! Bloody peasants!" he cursed. The man driving our cart did not say a word.

But the violent rocking was not enough to keep sleep from luring me. And I drifted away from our passage into a dark space where my mind was black and blank.

"Wake up! Wake up, you lazy girl! It's time to get off!"

Sleep ruptured. My eyelids flickered open. It could not still be night. A faded light was playing at the edge of the sky. Dawn was about to break. Ramdeen was standing over me, shaking me and shouting. I sat up and the blood rushed to my head.

"Where are we – is this Madras?" I asked.

"No, we are only about halfway there. Hurry up now!" Ramdeen said. "We have to get you out of here before daylight."

I climbed out and looked around to see who else was there. There seemed to be fewer people than when we left Vākkuṟuti, but we still numbered about eight. Their faces were vaguely familiar. I had probably passed them in the streets and greeted them, but I did not know anyone by name. They, too, had just been woken and were kneading the sleep from their eyes. The only passenger still enjoying his slumber was the child, whose father was holding him

79

tightly. I noticed for the first time the protruding belly of the man's wife. She already appeared worn out.

A short, rodent-like little man emerged from a building nearby. The structure looked run-down. Ramdeen threw his arms around the man and the two embraced for a moment. This was Rathilal, who was middle-aged, thin and slightly hunched, which gave him a sinister air. He kept his body perfectly still while moving his head rapidly in all directions, much like an owl. He had cultivated a moustache that almost looked as though it had been drawn on. From the black staining his temples, I guessed that he dyed his hair. Like Ramdeen, his hair had been slicked back with a generous lashing of coconut oil. He parted his teeth to reveal a rattish smile.

"Rathilal, my cousin-brother – how you keeping?"

"Ah, Ramdeen, so well I am. So nice to see you again."

"You fully recovered now?" Ramdeen asked, no doubt referring to his cousin's slight limp.

"Oh, Ramdeen, I'm in the very best of health. Very happy to be back at my business!" Rathilal looked around and did a rough headcount. "Why you so late? I was expecting you early."

"We had some trouble along the way – two of them got away. But nothing to worry about."

Rathilal looked at Ramdeen nervously. His voice dropped to an audible whisper. "You better go back and make sure they don't talk, eh?"

"No, don't worry – you know I can handle them!" Ramdeen laughed, self-assured as ever.

"Bring them in!" Rathilal bellowed, and Ramdeen began shepherding us towards the building.

"All right!" Ramdeen said as we were walking, "I told you this was going to be a process. You don't get on the ship and wave byebye. No – it's an *official* process. This place is called the sub-depot."

He pronounced it with a resounding "t". "My capable friend here, Mr Rathilal, is a licensed recruiter. He, too, works very closely with the British. He has all the *credentials*."

The thin-legged man behind me cut in in a reedy voice. "Credentials?" he asked respectfully. "What does that mean, Mr Ramdeen?"

"Credentials, credentials! You don't know what credentials are, boy? Papers, man! He got papers to prove he's working with the British! Listen, if you don't understand, just keep quiet – don't show everyone what a fool you are!"

The young man looked embarrassed.

Rathilal lined us up outside the building as if to carry out an inspection. "Do not worry, my dear people," he said, with an attempt at reassurance. "I know you are far from home and afraid. Look, I'll be honest with you. This place is not like home, but it's also not as comfortable as Port Natal. It is just a transit place. What does that mean? It means that you wait here for a little while until we receive word from Madras that they are ready for you to come."

The man with the child raised his hand. "Uncle … how long before we get to Madras?"

Rathilal cleared his throat. "My dear fellow – call me Mr Rathilal, hey – you will be staying here as my guests for two weeks."

"Mr Rathilal, why so long? We are keen to get to Natal." It was the strained voice of the child's mother.

"Now, that may seem like a long time, my lady. But we are busy with all sorts of things throughout your stay. We make sure that you have not caught any illnesses on the way, that you are well rested before you get onto the ship, and so forth and so on. Look, let's not get caught up in all this right now. We have enough time to speak about it later. Come inside …"

We were led into a building that resembled an old warehouse.

The rafters were high, and the walls, now coated with grime and the scribbles of children, looked as though they were once painted a starchy white. People who had arrived before us had already settled in. Many lay stretched out on their mattresses, chatting. Some sat up to look at us and whisper among themselves. The air inside was much cooler than outside, and the interior smelt damp. Thin mattresses lined the floor in two rows, and there were only a few small windows that reluctantly let the light in. I thought of how much brighter it would be if the windows were cleaned. The two large double doors behind us were shut. I looked at the faces of the guards all around us. They stared straight ahead without acknowledging us.

Rathilal limped around, showing us our "quarters", which were effectively just the mattresses where we would lay our heads. "Not to worry!" he said. He walked over to the sleeping child who'd been laid out on the mattress he was to share with his mother. Rathilal bent and stroked the child's head. "We'll look after you. Everything will be fine. Oh, that reminds me – I have something for you." He turned and shouted something at one of his assistants. The man fetched a box.

"Look at what we got for you!" Rathilal said, as though he was handing out sweets to children. He gave each of us a bowl and a shawl. "Here, take your *lotah* and *dopattah*. These will be very useful to you for eating, drinking, bathing. And, of course, the shawl will keep you warm when the temperatures drop here at night. Everything else is found!"

I watched him walk away, looking smug. I sat on my mattress and felt an uneasiness creep into me. Everything that was happening here seemed so much bigger than me. I wasn't sure what I had expected but I had not realised there were so many stages to this trip before our arrival in Port Natal. I hadn't asked Ramdeen the right questions. And, unlike those travelling with families, I was all alone. I already missed my family desperately.

When the sun rose, my parents would've woken and found me gone. They would have found the note I had written them, which they would not be able to read. My mother would've taken it to the temple and asked someone there to read it to her. And that stranger would tell her that I was gone. That I could not face my marriage to Muthan, and that I was travelling far across the seas to find my life in another country. Five summers, I promised them – I would return in five summers. That seemed so far into the future now. I began to see the vastness of this new word I had heard – "indenture" – and I felt like an ant in its enormous hands.

The days passed without much to do at the sub-depot. The previous arrivals kept to themselves. But for greeting each other, we never really spoke. Most people seemed to be travelling in groups of friends or families. There was only one other child in the first group, but she was too attached to her parents to break away and play with the little boy who had travelled with us. We passed the time keeping our quarters tidy, and I assisted with the cleaning of the floors – but that hardly took half a day. The food was bland. It comprised mostly *dhal* and rice. But we were grateful for it. It was more than many of us had eaten for months. The mothers were finally able to promise their children a meal, and know they wouldn't have to disappoint them. We ate like animals, immune to Rathilal's gaze.

After a few days, I grew close to the family of four who had left Vākkuṟuti with me. Munisami and Latchmi were a humble, friendly couple who shared snippets of their life in Vākkuṟuti with me. They did not mind that I said little about my life in response. I discovered that the man with the reedy voice was Munisami's brother, Rajandran, a mild-mannered fellow with little to say. He was most at ease with his young nephew, Selvaraj, who soon became my favourite companion. I spent many hours teaching him

83

new games, counting with him, and trying to get him to learn the Tamil alphabet – although he was perhaps a little too young for this. But he was highly intelligent and full of questions. He asked me all about Madras and the Colony of Natal. At times, I felt a bit foolish because I simply did not know the answers.

His mother, Latchmi, was quiet when we first met. But as the days wore on, I began to see her in a different light. She had a certain strength. It had been her desire to leave Vākkuṟuti, and Munisami had agreed to it because she insisted it would yield a better life for them. I grew to respect him too, because unlike many men in our village, he always gave Latchmi a fair hearing. They made many decisions together regarding the wellbeing of little Selvaraj. Latchmi also showed great kindness to her brother-in-law, Rajandran, who revered her. She seemed to understand that he was living in his elder brother's shadow. More than once, I caught Rajandran looking at Latchmi with such tenderness that I thought he would gladly trade places with his brother.

A few days after our arrival, Latchmi became anxious.

"Are you struggling with the pregnancy?" I asked, as we sat chatting on our mattresses.

"Well, Shanti, it is never easy to leave your home when you are nearly eight months pregnant. But it's more than that. Since we've been here, I've been waiting and watching. And I don't have a good feeling about this place. I feel like they are not telling us everything. Like they're keeping things from us. Do you see how shifty Rathilal is when you ask him questions about the journey? He doesn't want to give us any honest answers."

"Perhaps he's waiting for instructions from Madras or the British who are recruiting us," I said.

"No, Shanti. It is more than that. Each time we question him about the details of this trip, do you see how vague his answers are? He must have done this several times already if we are the last group to arrive, and people are leaving here all the time. Those people in the corner there ..." She pointed to the left. "They left early this morning. So how is it he does not know what lies ahead? And where are we right now? Why is no one telling us, except to say we are halfway to Madras? Surely this place has a name!"

She was right, and her concerns fed into my doubts.

"Shanti, don't you remember what happened on the way here?"

"Well, I recall the first part of our journey, but I was so tired that night, I fell into a deep sleep soon after we left. Then I woke to Ramdeen's shouting and we were here ..."

"Hmmm. Well, there was something important that you missed. Two of the passengers on that cart with us – I think they were a married couple – were frightened by something, and they tore a hole in the canvas and got away."

"Ah, is that what Ramdeen and Rathilal were talking about on the morning we got here?"

"Yes, exactly. And before they ran for it, Shanti, I caught little bits and pieces of what they were saying. It sounded like they were following some family members to Port Natal, and the wife was talking about mistreatment of some kind. I'm not sure if they were speaking of these people being mistreated in Natal, or if they were talking about their own mistreatment in Vākkuṟuti. But that's been worrying me for days."

"What did Ramdeen do when he saw they were missing?"

"Well, he heard them jump and fall out of the cart. There was quite a thud when they hit the ground. But then they ran for dear life."

"Didn't Ramdeen give chase?"

"Oh, he tried. It was such a funny sight, Shanti – that portly man trying to run after two agile young people in the night. But it was too dark – he looked around for a while, and he couldn't find them. But he didn't call out for them either. He didn't want anyone to know we were there. He eventually climbed back onto the cart and we carried on. That's why we got here late."

"But why would they keep information from us, Latchmi?"

"I don't know. Maybe the promises they made are false. Maybe Port Natal is all one big lie. Maybe we're being taken somewhere else. How would we know? We have never been there."

"But Latchmi, do you understand what kind of deception this would be? Do you really think the Indian government would allow us to be taken without knowing where we were going?"

"Shanti, do you think Indian officials even care about us? They are probably treating this as a money-making deal between themselves and the British, without any thought of how we might end up."

"Then what are we going to do?"

"Well, this is what I am thinking of, Shanti. I have not discussed it with Munisami yet, but if he agrees, I want us to go to Rathilal and tell him we have made a mistake coming here, and we want to go home ..."

"But you have already come so far! What if everything is fine on the other side and your suspicions are wrong? What if you are throwing away a real chance at a new life – especially for little Selvaraj?"

"Shanti, sometimes, as bad as things are, it is safer to stay with what you know. Yes, things are terrible in Vākkuṟuti, and we were starving there. But at least I know Vākkuṟuti. Port Natal? It is a foreign land run by foreign people, and I know nothing about what life will be like there. What if all our lives are ruined because I forced our family to go there? I can't bear the blame, Shanti, or the thought of what will happen to little Selva. No. I've made up my mind about turning back. I'll persuade Munisami that this is the best thing for us to do. I don't know your reasons for leaving Vākkuṟuti and wanting to go to the Colony of Natal. But it's up to you. You may join us when we talk to Rathilal – if you wish."

I thought about it hard, but there was no way I could turn back. By now, Muthan and his family would have been notified that I had run away. My parents would have been disgraced, and they would surely turn their backs on me if I returned. I could understand why some of the events of the last few days had aroused Latchmi's suspicions, but I had to err on the side of optimism. "Thank you, Latchmi," I said to her. "But I have no choice. I cannot turn back now. I wish you and Munisami only the best."

For most of that afternoon, the couple sat together and spoke intensely in hushed tones. I entertained Selvaraj with a few games while they conversed. When they had made a final decision, they called Rajandran over to discuss it with him. He seemed to favour Latchmi's stance. Meal time was approaching, and Latchmi came and put her hand on my shoulder.

"Shanti," she whispered, "we will do it tonight. While the others are having their supper, Munisami and I will ask Rathilal if we can have a word with him. We will tell him that we wish to return to Vākkuṟuti."

"As long as you are sure that is the best way for you, Latchmi. I hope Rathilal is understanding."

Selvaraj sat on my lap and ate his supper while I picked at mine. I understood why Latchmi had to act. Rajandran had no wife and no children. But any decision Munisami and Latchmi made would have profound repercussions for Selvaraj's future. I saw Rathilal courteously welcome them into his office at the far end of the warehouse. Selvaraj was finishing his plate of rice when I looked up and saw his parents returning. Munisami looked downcast and Latchmi was using the sash of her sari to wipe away tears.

"*Ama*, what's wrong? Why you crying?" Selvaraj began to ask. "Why is *Ama* crying, Shanti?"

"Selva, go and play with Uncle Rajandran," I told him. As he ambled away, I approached Latchmi who was now beginning to sway from the weight of her stomach.

"What's wrong, Latchmi? What did Rathilal say?"

"Shanti, that bastard of a man threatened to take away everything he has given us if we turn back!"

"Latchmi, speak softly!" Munisami said. "People are looking at us."

But Latchmi was undeterred. "Shanti, he is demanding money. He wants money for the trip here and for all he has fed us. He wants to take the clothes off our child's back to pay for it! He knows we have no way of getting back to Vākkuruti, and we have no money. He doesn't even care about how I will manage the journey to Madras in my state, the heartless bastard!"

"Shhh … sit down, Latchmi," I tried to console her. "Don't let Selvaraj see you cry – it will upset him. Now tell me what else Rathilal had to say."

"He won't hear of it, Shanti. He thinks we are cattle to be bought and sold! We will have to go to Port Natal. We have no choice. Munisami and I will be taken against our will."

I could not stop her tears. "Listen, Latchmi," I said, "I know that what lies ahead will not be easy for you, but if you have to go, I'll be there to help you. I won't let you down."

She nodded vigorously and wiped her eyes.

"Now, when did Rathilal say the transport is arriving to take us to Madras?" I asked her.

She looked at me, shaking her head. "Transport? What transport, Shanti? That is the worst of it. That wicked man expects us to make the journey of forty miles on foot!"

CHAPTER 10

THE HUMAN BODY'S ABILITY TO survive is astounding. I look down at my own wiry frame and cannot believe my feet have carried me this far. We are a snaking row of travellers, shuffling to Madras in thin sandals, grateful for the worn soles that protect our feet from the boiling soil beneath us. The sun smoulders above our heads. There were cries of discomfort at first, but they have waned. The chatter has died down. The wind has blown sand into our mouths and dried up our words. We are sleepwalkers now, counting the steps to Madras, visited every now and then by the ghosts of those we have left behind.

Each day I witness the heaving of Latchmi's body, which is fighting the urge to collapse. I feel her mass against my own as she leans on me. The friction chafes us both. But I must keep my word.

Latchmi's belly causes her to stumble sometimes, but she straps her hands underneath it and trudges on. She says it feels as if her stomach will tear open at any moment. I link my arm through hers to bear some of that burden.

I look at the stream of souls ahead of us. Many of them began the journey behind us, but we have been overtaken because we cannot rush Latchmi. Little Selvaraj is also a poor traveller. He splays his limbs across his father's body. His gangly legs have not been able to carry him, so Munisami and Rajandran take turns to balance him on their shoulders. We are all praying for a shower of cold rain that will turn the sand into a soothing squelch of mud under our feet. But relief will not come – we are in a time of drought.

Over one stretch of horizon unfolds another, and yet another. We envy Rathilal as he passes by in his shaded cart. He tries to motivate us with his promises about the wonders of the Colony of Natal. None of us can see it. None of us can bear the grating of his voice against our ears.

At night we camp out in the open, and cover ourselves with the *dopattahs* he gave us. This is the time of day that Latchmi cherishes. Her mind remains stronger than her body – for now. But the goal of Port Natal is too far away. She survives from one sunset to another, when she can rest and allow her stomach to sag. By this time of day, she is too tired to eat or speak. She falls into a coma-like sleep until we wake her in the morning to continue the journey.

It worries me when her mouth hangs open and the words fall out in a slur. "Shanti, how many miles … have we walked?"

"I don't know, Latchmi. But we are nearing the halfway mark."

We pass villages where people stand outside their dung homes looking at us in pity. Some shake their heads in confusion.

"Shanti, what is the name of this place?" Latchmi asks.

"I do not know," I say. I could ask a villager, but I do not want to know. I eventually stop answering her questions because I am afraid of what I will say. I suspect we have lost our way. I have also lost count of the days we have been travelling. I am so disorientated that I only recognise east at sunrise and west at sunset. But I can say none of those things to a woman who needs the comfort of informed words.

One night, as we are setting up camp, I ask Rathilal if I may speak to him.

"What is it?" he asks, eyeing me suspiciously.

"Mr Rathilal." I bow my head. "I am helping my friend Latchmi on this journey – the wife of Munisami. Sir, as you know, she is heavily pregnant and she is struggling more every day to walk these long distances. Would you please respectfully consider allowing Latchmi to travel some of the way in your cart?"

He laughs in my face. "Am I the Ministry of Transport, girl? You want me to carry that low-caste woman in my cart?" he spits.

"Mr Rathilal," I continue, "she is only a few weeks away from giving birth. I am afraid this walking will cause her to go into labour early. It could be dangerous for her and for the baby ..."

He snaps at me. "You want me to show pity to the same woman who tried to desert me after all I did for her – bringing her to my depot, giving her new belongings, feeding her, providing her and that child with a place to sleep? How's that for ingratitude? That woman must learn a lesson! Now leave me in peace!"

There was nothing more I could do. Latchmi would have to soldier on to Madras. Once we were there, I hoped she could give birth in better conditions. I didn't tell her I had asked Rathilal for that favour. She would probably have been upset because she had a certain pride, and would rather press on than accept the help of the man she called a slave trader. But just two days later, I could see she was in distress. As sunset neared, she began to moan and cry out in pain.

"We do not have much longer to go, Latchmi. Keep resting your weight on me. I'll find a spot for you to lie as soon as Rathilal gives us the signal to stop for the day."

"Shanti, I'm not sure I can wait till then. Something is

happening to me … it feels like the baby could be coming now—"

Her breath was coming in short spurts as she hunched over. I mopped her face with my sari sash, feeling helpless. Munisami put Selvaraj down, and he and Rajandran rushed to support Latchmi while I took Selva's hand. Latchmi began to wail, and this attracted the attention of the large group of people ahead of us. I found my shawl and tossed it onto the sand while Munisami and Rajandran eased her down onto it. A gush of fluid wet her sari and streaked the sand.

Munisami recognised the signs and ran into the crowd ahead. "Is there a *doulha* here? My wife is giving birth … *please!*"

I was praying there was a midwife somewhere who could help us. If not, I would be forced to help deliver Latchmi's baby. She read my mind: "Shanti, you'll help me, won't you? If there's no one else who can … you'll help me?"

"Y-yes …" I found myself stuttering, although I knew nothing of childbirth. I had never even carried a baby, never mind delivered a newborn. "Perhaps I should go and try to get help from one of the elders," I said.

"No! Don't leave me," she cried, clutching my hand.

Munisami's hand was on my arm. "Wait here. Don't leave her, Shanti. I think I have found someone to help." And he disappeared back into the throng.

Rathilal and his cart appeared from behind me. "What's all this commotion about?"

"Mr Rathilal, Latchmi is having her baby …"

"What? Here? No – she can't have the baby here! She must wait!"

"What would you have her do?" I shouted. "Should she carry on walking until the baby falls out from between her legs? Or should she die giving birth while she is walking? Mr Rathilal – she is your commodity. You have paid to bring her this far, and you wouldn't let her turn back! If you abuse her, she will die! And what good is a dead labourer to you?"

Rathilal looked shocked. But I no longer cared. I would accept my punishment later. He nudged his driver, and they moved on.

Munisami emerged from the crowd with a middle-aged woman in tow. "Latchmi – look, I have found someone to help."

There was warmth in the woman's eyes. She got down on her haunches and took Latchmi's hand. "Don't worry, my child. I am Sarojini. I am a *doulha*. I have brought many babies into this world."

"Thank you, Aunty," Latchmi said between clenched teeth, fighting the pain. "My friend is here, Aunty … please let her help." Sarojini looked at me. "Of course, child." She turned to me. "What is your name?"

"Shanti …"

"Shanti, will you help me bring Latchmi's baby into the world?"

I hesitated.

"Do not be afraid, Shanti. Your friend has asked you to be a part of this miracle. It is a gift to bring a human being into new life. You cannot refuse," she smiled.

"Show me, Aunty," I said.

And there, among the sands and scrag, with the *doulha's* gentle guidance and Latchmi's relentless pushing, time stopped and cast in our direction one perfect moment of raw joy that momentarily blotted out the anguish of previous days. I held my friend's hand and let her squeeze her pain into me. And I whispered to her how strong and brave she was, and told her to push and goad that tiny soul into the world. After a time, a little girl slipped into my hands, head-first, screaming the way we had all longed to on that journey. We gathered round her, reminded that miracles could sometimes live alongside misery. Some cheered and clapped while others wet the dry sands with their tears.

"Sandhya," said the *doulha*, looking up at the sky to mark the time the baby was born. "Twilight. It is the most beautiful time of day, with its subtle light."

"Sandhya," repeated Munisami as he cradled his daughter and gazed at his wife. "Latchmi, I believe that is a good name for her."

CHAPTER 11

MADRAS PULSATED WITH THE EXCITEMENT of people heading off to a new life. The imposing port gave way to an expanse of water that seemed to touch infinity. Dock workers scurried about purposefully, readying the fleet of ships that appeared as specks on the horizon, arriving empty to dock and ingest the next mouthful of emigrants.

We came upon the city a day after Sandhya's birth. It had changed us, somehow restoring the hope we had lost along the way. We took to that dusty road reminded that another life lay ahead of us. We found our words again. Even Rathilal's hard heart softened. He allowed the new mother and her baby to ride the rest of the way in his cart. Then without warning, as we rounded a corner, Rathilal called out, "We are here! Look! It's the city of Madras!"

We screamed, we ran! We fell to the ground to rub Madras's soil through our hands. We had laboured hard to reach it, and it was going to lead us to another world. There were people waiting for us there, preparing for our coming. They called out to us as we approached the docks, and a facility not far off which resembled barracks. They seemed to understand our hardship and welcomed us. For the first time, I saw the fear in Latchmi's eyes break. She smiled at me. Perhaps our suspicions had been unfounded after all.

How different Madras was to Vākkuṟuti! There were signs of progress all around us – machinery that appeared so advanced, I could not fathom what it might be used for. I felt a little ashamed to be from a village as rural as my own. I thought of Thirna: I was standing under the same patch of sky as my best friend. If only she knew.

We found ourselves outside a large compound, a residential structure.

"It looks as though we have stepped out of one century into another!" Munisami said. "Who could have imagined Vākkuṟuti was so backward?"

Rathilal conferred with some officials before asking us to gather around him. He took his place on a crate and surveyed us all. We were impatient to hear what he had to say, but he seemed overcome.

"Like a father who must say goodbye to his grown children, so I must say goodbye to you who have become like my children." He sniffed, dramatically. "Forgive me for the times when I have been hard on you, as a loving parent is with a child. Understand, it was all for your own good. It was so I could bring you here to this wonderful place where the greatest adventure of your lives will truly begin. May God go with you."

And he cast his eyes downward, dabbing them with a creased handkerchief he'd wrenched out of his pocket. After a moment's silence, he concluded, "I now leave you in the capable hands of my emigration colleagues." He took a large, well-calculated step off the crate, and handed over to a man of medium height, who spoke in monotonous tones.

"Welcome to you all. My name is Mr Raman. I am in charge of ensuring that you fulfil all the necessary requirements to make this sea voyage. I am sure you are all keen to set off immediately, but you have just arrived and need to be adequately prepared for the journey ahead." He placed a pair of spectacles on the edge of his nose and briefly consulted his notes. It was easy to tell this was an educated man. There was still a good deal of talking among the crowd. I could hear some people muttering in broken Tamil that Raman was using too many big words. But no one wanted to appear foolish, so no one interrupted.

"I am having a bit of trouble communicating here," said Raman with a frown. "Can you please be quiet while I speak? If you have any questions, address them to me afterwards."

He cleared his throat. "Right. This is the procedure. You will be living in these barracks to your left for a short while. How long, you may ask. Well, that is difficult to ascertain. It depends on how long it will take to fill any one ship. Cast your eye to that ship over there, for example."

He extended a bony arm toward a large vessel docked alongside the quay, swaying gently on the water. The name *John Allen* was painted in large letters across its bow. "That ship carries over two hundred people. I cannot allow it to leave the harbour half-empty. It makes no sense. I will exercise the same logic with the vessel on which you travel."

He paused to blink deliberately. "I must wait until I have enough candidates to fill it. Perhaps it will take a week. Perhaps it will take six weeks. But I will wait as long as it takes to ensure that this ship, and every other one that docks here, is full before it leaves the shores of Madras."

A murmur rose from the crowd. Many of us had envisaged an overnight stay before boarding the ship. Raman raised his skinny hand to silence us.

"There is also the matter of processing. And that takes time. It is our job to ensure your wellbeing." Raman removed his spectacles and gestured with them. "Will we put you on that ship if you are too weak or sick to make the journey? No. Will we put you on that ship without your official consent? No. That means our well-trained doctors will examine you to ensure that you are free of all disease and that you are strong enough to make the journey.

"Furthermore, we do not want you to be forced into this voyage. As of this year, we have appointed a British magistrate. You will appear before him and give your final consent to go before your immigration contract is finalised. But bear in mind the rules here. The men among you must be no older than thirty-five years of age. The women must be no older than thirty years of age unless they are travelling with their families. If you have already broken these rules and somehow slipped through the system, now would be the time to confess."

At that moment, I felt relieved that Ramdeen had altered the age on my papers. I was among the first three groups of people who had to line up for a process of registration in the reception shed. Rathilal had seemingly handed our documentation over to them, but they still recorded details like our names, and the date of our arrival and admittance to the Madras depot. Guards swarmed around us. When I reached the front of the queue, I came face to face with a young, well-built man with a thick moustache. He made a note of my details and asked me if I knew my age.

"Yes, sir," I replied. "I am sixteen years old."

"Our recruits are looking more youthful by the day," he said to the colleague next to him.

"Why are there so many guards here?" I asked the man.

"Those are *chowkidars*. They are watchmen who make sure you do not run away," he replied. He stamped my papers. "See this enclosure next to us? That's where you'll go next. A medic will be waiting there to do your first check-up."

"Thank you," I said.

I entered slowly, looking around to make sure I had gone to the right tent. The medic was a young British man. I soon discovered that I would have to disrobe.

"Do I have to?"

"That is the way we do it here," he replied.

I swallowed hard and slowly began to unravel my sari. Alongside him were other doctors at work processing all the new recruits. None of them seemed to work with care or sensitivity. There were masses of us and the clock was ticking. The doctor prodded my ribs and said something to one of his co-workers in English. He spoke so fast that I could not understand what he said. They both chuckled and continued to chat while I was weighed and jabbed to determine whether I was fit to travel to the colony. The doctor muttered something to himself as he recorded my information. It was later explained to me that I was allowed to go to Port Natal because I had no apparent deformities, nor could they find any trace of contagious diseases or heart defects.

But the most humiliating examination was still to come. "Stand with your legs apart," the doctor instructed, motioning for me to stand astride. I shook my head.

"It's all part of the exam. If you do not agree, you do not go to Port Natal." He glared at me. I slowly separated my legs and looked away from the shame. I felt the iciness of the steel on my thigh and suddenly it was being plunged into me. I gasped at the pain and jerked away. "Never mind," he said. "Virgin – no venereal disease," he mouthed as he wrote it down. I wanted to cry as I put my clothes back on. When I was done, the doctor grabbed me by the wrists and turned my hands palm up. He had a good look at them. He nodded in approval and shouted at me to move along while he scribbled a quick note on my file before he began examining the next person.

I walked gingerly out of the tent, feeling a dull ache from my internal examination, and met Latchmi, Munisami and Selvaraj, who were still to undergo their tests. Latchmi asked me to hold Sandhya as the family queued. Munisami seemed to take the check-up in his stride, but Selvaraj did not take to it kindly, and cried loudly enough for the doctor to curtail his check-up and hastily record a few notes on the irritable child's health.

There were notices in Tamil and Hindi posted everywhere for our attention. They were headed: "Notice to *Coolies* intending to emigrate to Natal". Listed there were the exact conditions of our indenture. We were promised that once we arrived at the depot, we would be well fed and properly lodged until the ship sailed. There were further pledges of good clothing once the ship was ready to leave, medicines, food and other appliances of good quality on board. The journey would take up to two months, and upon arriving in the colony, there would be a Protector of Immigrants appointed especially to offer advice and assist in placing us on estates, where there would always be a physician on hand.

The posters further promised that in no way would our religious practices be interfered with, regardless of whether we were "Hindoo or Mahomedans". They painted a picture of how we would be joining an existing community of thousands of our fellow countrymen over there, all living in rent-free houses with gardens to cultivate at our leisure amid a healthy climate and an abundance of good water, fruit and vegetables. Bilal had been right after all.

Our duties included cultivating sugarcane, and making sugar, rum and molasses. But other varieties of work would also be available. We would be expected to work "for five years, six days in the week, for nine hours, between sunrise and sunset – all Sundays and public holidays excepted". It seemed a far less gruelling schedule than the one in my own household.

The notices went on to list the schedule of payments. I was

dismayed to see that the women would receive only half the men's earnings, although we would be expected to execute almost the same tasks. This meant that my earnings for the first year would amount to two and a half rupees a month, and in the last year of my indenture, I would take home three and a half rupees while my male counterparts were pocketing seven. But the advantages were that our passage back to India would be covered in full when our period of indenture ended, and while we were in Port Natal we would be allocated rations like *dhal*, saltfish, *ghee* or oil, and salt on a weekly basis. I worked out that this would allow me to save a good deal of money for my parents and my upkeep after returning to India. I imagined they would be much more forgiving if I returned a prosperous woman.

I was pondering this when Latchmi returned from her medical examination, visibly upset. "Shanti, have you ever experienced anything so humiliating?" she said.

She was adjusting her sari skirt as she approached. "I have just given birth. I am not even allowing my husband under my sari, but now I have a strange white man putting his hands in there! I tried to tell the idiot that I have just given birth, but he carried on as though I'm hiding some disease under my clothes!"

"Yes, I had to go through it too."

Latchmi shook her head and clicked her tongue. "They must realise we are not like British women."

Just then Munisami walked over to us, scowling.

"What is wrong?" Latchmi asked.

He threw his hands up. "You will not believe what these British bastards have done! They say Rajandran will not be allowed to board the ship ..."

"But why?" Latchmi interrupted. "He is in good health."

"I don't understand what kind of doctors these are, Latchmi! They told him they are looking for men with strong chests and calloused hands. Those doctors laughed at him and asked him if he'd ever hoed the fields a day in his life. Raj may look thin, but he's a strong man. We have done years of labour in the fields together. I went over there and asked for help from the translator. And I spoke through him to persuade them that Raj is a hard worker, but they told me it was none of my business and asked me to leave."

I felt terrible for Rajandran. He had endured the difficulties of our trip with minimal complaint, but he had come all this way for nothing. Now he was standing in the line of "feeble" candidates who'd been turned away. But he was not alone. He stood clutching Selvaraj's hand and stroking the boy's cheek.

"What happens to Rajandran now, Munisami?" I asked.

"Well, now that he has failed the medical check-up, our family will have to split up here. Latchmi, Selvaraj, the baby and I will enter this compound and prepare for the voyage, like you. But Raj will have to make that long journey back on foot until he reaches Rathilal's sub-depot. And from there, I suppose he will have to find his way back to Vākkuṟuti." Munisami's voice broke. "He's my baby brother, Shanti – his return will cause such shame and disgrace. My father has always been hard on him. He's always told Raj he's weaker than the rest of us. When my brother goes back now, it will only prove my father right. I am sure they'll marry Raj off to the first woman they can find. And he'll just have to accept it. You know, he was hoping to have some money by the time he got married so he could support a wife and child. I don't know what he's going to do now."

It was sadder still to watch Selvaraj being torn from his uncle. Rajandran held the boy in his arms and dried his tears. He clasped his brother and sister-in-law and told them he'd be waiting for them in India. Then he turned and walked away, disappearing among the crowd that would have to go back home. Selvaraj cried for days, believing that Rajandran was playing a game with him, and would soon return. But when his uncle did not come back, the child became quiet and withdrawn.

If we had thought Rathilal's warehouse was inhospitable, our new environment was several times worse. It stank of bleach when we first moved in. But once we poured into the building in our numbers, which swelled to a thousand within days as new recruits arrived, a stifling clamminess grew. Each of us was allocated a tiny space which we occupied jealously. Being squashed together like that, I feared it would not be long before disease took hold. Fights over territory were common, but they were rapidly broken up by the vigilant *chowkidars*.

I tried to find some comfort in the predictability of routine. We awoke every day at six and weeded the gardens inside the compound for two hours. I reminded myself that all work is love, and although there was no opportunity to plant a flower or water it, I took pride even in the job of uprooting stubborn weeds. Afterwards, we were offered a feast of *dhal* and rice for breakfast. We were encouraged to pass the hours by playing games so as to keep our spirits up, but many fell slowly into depression. Time was passing and we were all uncertain of when we would be able to leave.

Munisami, Latchmi and I filled those days with hours of chatter and jokes. We took it in turns to care for Sandhya and play with Selvaraj. I became quite skilled at the card game *Thunee* under Munisami's instruction. Although I had my books with me, it was not advisable to be seen reading them, so I merely lay on my mattress in my quiet time with my eyes closed and recited all the poetry I had committed to heart.

At about five o'clock in the evening, we were given another meal and allowed a bit more leisure time afterwards. But at eight o'clock, all activity had to promptly end so we could go to sleep.

We had been there for three weeks when I was roughly woken

one morning by one of the officials and told to gather up my belongings.

"You – girl! Get your things together and get ready to move to the accommodation depot."

The man stood there as I scrambled off my mattress and reached out to shake Latchmi.

"Wake up!" I called to her. "We have to go. They're moving us to another depot."

The official cut in. "No, no. She's not coming with you. You are going with that group over there."

He pointed to a row of people in the far corner.

"But ... I think you are making a mistake. I am travelling with these people ..."

"Are you related to them?" he asked.

"No. But we are close friends. We are from the same village."

He laughed. "No, girlie. That's not how it works here! You're lucky you came this far with them. Sometimes even families get separated. Say your goodbyes quickly now! We have to go."

I threw my belongings to the floor and took Selvaraj in my arms. "Be a good boy," I said. "Be strong for your *Apa* and *Ama* and protect Sandhya always. I love you."

The child was bewildered. "But where are you going?" he asked. "You promised you would not leave me!"

I squeezed his hand. "Selva, I am just going to Port Natal ahead of you – to make sure it is a good place for you. But you must stay behind to look after your family for me. And pray hard that we will meet when you get there."

"All right," he said. But he still seemed thoroughly confused, and ran to his father and clutched his hand.

I threw my arms around Latchmi. "Take care of yourselves," I told her.

"Shanti. You have been a great source of strength to me. Thank you for everything! I know the gods will go with you. And we'll see you there."

I hugged Munisami and gave Sandhya a tender kiss on her forehead. Then I grabbed my belongings and rushed towards the door. I was ushered into a smaller hall, not far from the main barracks, where I was again allocated a place to sleep. I put my things down, trying to orientate myself and take in what had just happened.

It wasn't long before Raman's head began to bob above the crowd. He entered the hall and stood in front of us, officious as ever. "Good morning. I welcome all of you to the accommodation depot. Do not be surprised by this sudden relocation. The good news is that you will be leaving for Port Natal in a matter of seven days."

There were some cheers from the people behind me. Raman ignored their response. "During this week, you will undergo your final preparations for the sea voyage. That means you will have one final medical examination, and the doctors will hopefully confirm that you are fit to board the vessel. You must have come across the Protector at some point during your stay here. He will further confirm your readiness to travel. During this week, you will also appear before a magistrate to give your consent to embark on this journey. I wish you all the best."

Some people shouted questions at him, but he left as abruptly as he'd entered.

That last week might have been as long as a day in my memory. I felt time accelerate recklessly. Strangely, I was energised by this progress. The yearning for my friends was always there, but I tried to put it aside and focus on the new life that was waiting for me. I underwent another medical examination at the hands of the same doctor, and passed another probe with the Protector in attendance. But something in me had changed. When I undressed in front of each of them, I looked them in the eye. The Protector averted his gaze, and the doctor carried out his examination in silence.

A few days later, I was hauled before a magistrate, my contract of service in hand. True to his word, Ramdeen had recorded my age as sixteen. All the details had been filled in for me on the assumption that I could not write. The magistrate was an ageing man whose spectacles sat at the end of his bulbous nose. A Tamil translator was on hand to assist him.

"Shanti, you have agreed to enter into the system of indenture for a period of three years, which may be extended to five, after which you may choose to accept free passage back to India. Do you understand the conditions of your indenture?" I was asked.

I nodded. "Yes, sir. I do understand the conditions."

"You are a very slight young woman. Do you understand the nature of the work you will be expected to perform?"

"Sir," I held up my calloused palms, "I am well accustomed to hard work."

He gave a strained smile. "You understand that no one below the age of sixteen qualifies for indenture. Are you quite sure you are sixteen years of age?"

"Yes, sir, I am," I lied.

"And you are not doing this under duress?"

"No, sir. It is my choice."

"Well, then there is no reason for me to stop you. Do you agree to place your mark in the bottom right-hand corner of the contract you have been given?"

"I do, sir."

There, printed on the document was my name and the date, November, 1874. Though I had grown used to signing my name, I merely placed an "x" next to it on the form. A girl who could read and write might attract unnecessary attention.

On that final day in Madras, I ate my last meal before the sun shrank from the sky and the moon planted itself just outside the barracks. I thought about my life and wondered how it was possible I could be so conflicted – I had been Thirna's most trusted friend, and I had deceived her; Aunty Saras's beloved protégée, and I had abandoned her; Sanisha's confessor who had failed to save her; the ungrateful daughter who was yet my mother's most treasured child; the coward who had connived with Ramdeen, but who was Latchmi's faithful friend.

That night I drifted, half-suspended on the breaths of a thousand people exhaling their anticipation, towards the sea. It was calling, and tomorrow I would come.

CHAPTER 12

WE FOUND OURSELVES IN THE middle of the ocean, floating on a massive ship called the *James Owen*. Earlier that evening, as night fell, we had gathered like a huge herd of unruly cows, preparing to board the ship. The chatter was deafening. I had looked at the bewildered faces around me before we embarked. Some were setting out on their own. Others were following family members who had already reached Natal safely, and had sent word for them to come. I regretted that my parents would know nothing of where I was now, as we prepared to lift anchor at one in the morning. Yet I was elated, even though I'd heard stories of ships lost at sea. Other labourers had been shipwrecked or burnt alive when their ships caught alight. But I chose to believe in the sturdiness of this ship, and the stories I'd heard at the depot, telling that the *James Owen* was faithful.

I realised too, as we stood on the pier waiting, that my fellow travellers came from a range of India's religious, cultural, language groups and castes. And here we all were, about to board the same ship. The thought brought a smile to my face. Prostitutes stood among devotees. Single men and women lined up alongside families. The high-caste Hindu stood behind the detested *Pariah*. The Mohammedan rubbed shoulders with the Christian. We were the same and yet so different. As they prepared the rigging, I heard the ship's men call us "*coolies*" from the Tamil word *kuli* – the payments made to the poorest of us for manual work in India. We were told that the *sirdars*, Indian men who'd been recruited as overseers, would be in charge of us on that journey. They would stay with us throughout our indenture and teach us to respond to the name "*coolie*" as we worked in the cane fields.

The movement around the ship was frenetic. A man was pacing back and forth on the gangplank shouting instructions at us in two or three Indian languages as we gathered in a thick crowd.

"Does everyone have their tin ticket? Is there anyone without a tin ticket? Raise your hands!"

A few people responded.

"Uncle, over here – no one gave us one of those." A young man in a worn *dhoti* pointed to the disc hanging around the neck of another passenger.

The official rushed towards him and took him by the arm. "Come with me! Without that, you not going anywhere! You need that for identification purposes," he said, leading the man off. He screeched across to a man who was shuffling papers at a desk set up on the pier, "Hey, Dhasra, this chap's got no tin ticket. You people having problems there, or what?"

Dhasra shouted back, "No. Maybe a couple got through without their tin tickets. Bring him back, I'll sort him out."

Then another voice amid the din. "Stay in the line where you are! No pushing and shoving, you understand?" The voice belonged to a short, squat middle-aged man who appeared through a parting in the crowd. He held a finger up as a warning. "Everyone is getting a parcel, so there's no need to push to get in there before your friend. You hear me?" he shouted.

A man behind him was cursing, carrying a large box and fighting his way through the forest of bodies. The stocky man began to reach in and distribute what was inside. The men were given *dhotis* and what appeared to be jackets, caps and a blanket. They would need these extra items for a sea voyage, as the *dhotis* were particularly flimsy. When it was my turn, the man shoved a bundle of two saris, a flannel jacket and a blanket in my direction. I was glad to add these to my possessions. They were still measly compared to what some women had, who had brought jewellery, pots, fabric and medicines.

When the clothing distributor was done with his task, he began to usher people onto the ship. But nothing could've prepared any of us for that transition. We had never been on a ship before, and that final step from land onto the rocking vessel under our feet induced a new feeling of instability.

Once we were all on deck, we were made to line up in an orderly way. "Single women and children, line up here. You see the outer edges of this ship?" The official pointed. "That's where you'll be staying. Families, I want you to make a nice queue here. You will stay in between these women and children." He guided them towards their quarters.

Most of the adults managed to keep their anxiety in check, but the children not so. It was late, and their sleep had been disrupted. They found the throng of unfamiliar faces around them unsettling.

We were soon told to sit. A register was then taken. The ship's hands cried out to each other. The anchor was hoisted upwards and we felt the *James Owen* heave and lurch forward through the midnight waters, tracing a foamy trail in its wake. Amid the crying of babies, I twisted my body and turned my head to take one last look back at Madras, at India. But my view was obscured by the bodies around me. I closed my eyes and imagined the land slowly disappearing in my mind's eye.

We sat unmoving on those filthy decks for hours, aliens propped shoulder to shoulder, eyes wide, staring at the sooty sky. Time passed. The air grew chilly. Our limbs lapsed into numbness. Only the families spoke, feeding each other words of comfort. Occasionally the strains of a song would rise above the murmuring waves as a mother sang to pacify her restless child. It was going to be difficult to communicate on this journey. Many of us were not able to speak the same language. I tilted my head back and strained my nostrils to draw a stream of cold air into my lungs. I dared not stand and peer overboard. We were all truly afraid of the sea and the stories about how the dreaded *paglaa samundar* – the mad ocean – would try to claim our spirits.

Eventually, morning seeped across the sky. Some time during the night, I had fallen asleep. Now the sun kissed my face and prised my eyelids open. We came face to face with one other and our crew again. How different people looked in the sunlight. Our crew were tall, brawny men with sinewy muscles. Their skins were red and raw from long hours of exposure to the sun. They spoke a loud, guttural English, coughing up their words like phlegm in their thick throats.

The captain, Jones, saw us as a herd of animals. He pointed in our direction and gave his crew instructions. With my rudimentary English, I understood his words to mean it was morning, and it was time to wake the *coolies* up.

The ship's doctor, a man called Rawlings, came up to stand on the deck. He was a formidable man who towered above us and left a whiff of acidic-smelling sweat as he passed. I learnt that he was tasked with keeping us in good health, handing out rations, and preventing an outbreak of disease on the ship. But after watching him for only a few hours, I noticed the interest he took in the female passengers. And I later heard that he was in the habit of taking some of them to his hospital quarters for "entertainment".

Jones spat, then barked more orders at one of his men. The sailor disappeared briefly, then reappeared with a group carrying buckets. Some of the other passengers had just woken up and were still trying to get their bearings when Jones shouted for us to line up. Those of us who understood English stood first, and the rest followed our lead, scrambling up and shuffling into a row as quickly as they could. Jones grabbed some passengers by the scruff of their necks if they moved too slowly.

The sailors stood in front of us with their buckets, and without any warning, we were splashed from head to toe with lime. As soon as the initial stab of cold on my skin disappeared, a burning sensation gripped my eyes and flesh. The children cried aloud while the doctor shouted in their faces, telling them to shut up.

After we had been "cleaned", we changed into our new clothing. Our brightly coloured clothes now made way for uniformity. A day later, they issued us with tobacco and soap for the first time. The women were as delighted with their soap as the men were with their tobacco. We were promised we would receive oil, soap and tobacco on a weekly basis after that. But Jones often fought with Rawlings over supplies, so we learnt to become frugal and to stretch out those rations to last us as many weeks as possible.

Most humiliating were the daily medical examinations at the hospital section. Rawlings looked forward to them – an opportunity to see us at our most vulnerable. We peeled away our clothes, and the older women in particular tried to hide their shame while he peered into their private spaces. In time, his examinations became a more brutal game of steel and flesh. Many women were deeply offended, but even those with husbands on the ship could not call on them for protection for fear their men would be beaten and shackled.

It was Rawlings's duty to maintain hygiene on board and to ensure all the passengers bathed every day. One day, he publicly punished one of us for breaking the rules.

Nagamah was a frail, dark-skinned, mouse-like woman who kept to herself. But Rawlings lashed her with a cane several times, often for failing to bathe. She hated having to clean herself in the open area where the ship's men leered at us. The beatings became more frequent, and Nagamah became wracked with nervousness and anxiety. She began to wake in the middle of the night saturated in a pool of her own urine.

As we queued for our medical check-ups one morning, we heard her screams coming from the deck below. Rawlings emerged a moment later, roughly dragging Nagamah up the steps behind him. She was begging him in Tamil to stop. But his clenched teeth betrayed his determination. For a moment no one recognised Nagamah. Her face had been splashed white with the paint used to coat the ship. Some of it had dripped down onto her bare shoulders and matted her mangled hair. Her hands were tied tightly behind her back. Her limp breasts were exposed, and on her bare chest was painted the face of a pig. We stood there, stunned, as Rawlings paraded Nagamah around the deck for us all to see.

"Disgusting pig!" he jeered, poking her in the back. "Bloody pig!"

"What's he saying?" some people were asking. Those of us who understood whispered to the others, horrified. Rawlings grabbed Nagamah by the hair and pulled her over to one of the children, who looked up in confusion. "Hey, you, boy! Look up here! Look at the face of a fucking pig who wets her bed every night!" And he cackled raucously as the other sailors joined in.

Nagamah hung her head while the tears coursed down her cheeks. None of us could look at her. It would only have humiliated her more. That day, I felt a seed of hatred germinate in me. I saw what Rawlings was doing. He wanted us to participate in the degradation of one of our own. And in that act, he not only debased Nagamah – he humiliated all of us. In all the time I had lived in the Madras Presidency, I had never witnessed or heard of anything so shocking. The British soldiers were everywhere, but there were boundaries. They could not possibly shame one of us in that way. When I shared my thoughts with some of the other women, one of them said, "You are speaking of a village in the Madras Presidency, my dear. Now we are on their ship, going to their colony. From now on, they will do with us what they want."

It wasn't long before disease broke out on the decks because our living conditions and sleeping quarters were filthy. Some of us tried to observe the rules of hygiene, but others would not. Very few of us had even seen a seafaring vessel before, let alone travelled on one. Seasickness took hold. The sounds of retching and the sour stench of vomit became a backdrop to our journey. Many on board complained of stomach ailments from the poor quality of the rice. Some contracted illnesses we had never heard of before, like the mumps. People were overcome with high fevers. They had strange visions and whispered mangled words that no one understood. Rawlings came around with sharp needles, pricking our skin and declaring this would prevent the rest of us from getting the mumps. But some of us still did. Chickenpox, venereal disease, dysentery and diarrhoea were everywhere. And more often than not, soap was only issued to us if we grew restless and demanded it.

Despite this, we fell into the routine of our sea lives because there was no other choice. We dutifully woke at six, tidied our bedding, and made our dry breakfast. While the women cooked, the men fetched water for us. The food was truly of a poor quality. On some days we were given dry food, on others cooked rice and *dhal*. Potatoes were for special occasions. Those among us who ate meat – and there were many – were promised a sheep to feast on every other week. But I heard them complain that the carcasses were bony, and the size of these animals was insufficient to feed so many.

The cleaning of the rice was one of the most difficult tasks allotted to the women on this voyage. The rice was dotted with gravel and small stones that would have made the meals inedible had we not spent hours painstakingly sifting through almost every grain on the side of the deck where the wind gusted at us. The captain refused to allocate a safe space for us, or allow us to do this between decks. So we were forced to lay out our bags of rice close to the ship's hospital or the sailors' quarters where we worked under the hungry gaze of the men.

At times, as a clean mound of rice mushroomed before our eyes, the clouds would gather in a threatening swarm. If we were agile enough, we could gather up the cleaned rice and flee to a sheltered part of the boat fast enough for the rice to escape a soaking. But if we were too slow, the rain lashed down, scattering the grains, so all our work came to naught.

It rained often during that voyage, and our captain usually forced us to eat our meals exposed to the elements. When hunger is scraping at your stomach, you are immune to the rain. Still there were men who behaved stubbornly when our food was served, finding fault with everything.

"This bloody rice is too sandy!" they hissed at us and the compounder who served our meals. "And these portions are too small. Do you expect grown men like us to survive on children's portions?"

More than once, I saw them toss their food overboard, hours of our hard work swallowed by the sea.

There were other dangers on the ship we had not anticipated. Certain areas were not safe to enter. The ship's doctor complained that the area where fires were lit for cooking was a hazard, and the cooks could be scalded if the ship banked unexpectedly. The memory of another ship that had set sail for Mauritius was fresh in our minds. A fire on board had burnt virtually every occupant alive, leaving only one survivor. When the winds picked up, it was not uncommon for our vessel to sway from side to side. Anything that was not fixed to the deck slid dangerously close to the rails, with some of it falling overboard. Children often played there unattended, and it worried me that they might lose their footing and be flung into the water.

But there were also subtle changes afoot. The *James Owen's* swaying had begun to loosen the drawstrings that had kept our social norms in place. *Brahmin* men were forced to accept more menial roles for the first time in their lives. The *Pariahs*, on the other hand, strutted around with a newfound sense of pride. On one occasion, I overheard an altercation between a *Pariah* and a *Brahmin* over the cleaning of the ship's heads.

"I will simply not do this," the *Brahmin* spat. "This is not a job fit for one of my standing. Cleaning latrines is the job of an untouchable!"

The *Pariah* hit back: "You forget one thing, high-minded *Brahmin*! We are on a ship floating in the middle of the ocean. We are no longer in India. There is nothing forcing me to clean up your shit any more. I no longer take orders from *Brahmins*!"

Violence became commonplace on the ship. The ship's hands were constantly repairing sails on the deck, so there was no place for us to sit. Many passengers were forced to go down to the decks below, where fights would break out. *Brahmins* and *Dalits* hated being thrust together. But there were also many other castes in between who did not get along or understand each other. At times, it was very difficult to communicate because we all spoke different languages. Vegetarians were upset about being forced to eat meals prepared alongside meat. There were arguments about what kind of meat certain passengers should consume – some would not eat beef, and others would not touch pork. What made the British think we were the same? We were no more similar than they were. And yet the divisions between us confused them, although they'd already carried shiploads of us to Port Natal.

The passengers began to whisper about the ocean's appetite for sacrifice. During that voyage, a group of women passing the hospital quarters before sunset heard the pained cries of a woman. They knocked at the door, but were chased away. Yet they knew something was wrong. They discovered that behind those doors was a heavily pregnant woman in the throes of labour. But days on, there was no news of a baby. Her husband would not speak. And when she emerged from the hospital quarters a couple of days later, she was pale, weak and alone.

Her husband admitted that their baby had been stillborn. "I think the stress of this journey was too much," he said. "Our baby did not survive, but my wife still had to labour for over twelve hours to deliver him. I visited my wife there, but she was bleeding heavily and she was very weak, so she could not come back with me. I told her she should rest and I would come back the next day. But the crew – they waited until nightfall when we were sleeping. Then they took our baby's body and they threw it overboard! When I got there the following morning to prepare our child for burial rites, they said, 'Sorry – you've come too late. For reasons of hygiene, we couldn't keep a dead baby on board.' My wife almost fainted. She put her head on my chest and she cried. She said, 'Arjuna – these people have thrown our child overboard before we even had a chance to name him. Our boy has left this life without a name.' I am not sure my wife will ever get over this."

I remember that woman clearly. I used to see her standing on deck talking to herself, entranced by the blueness below. I wondered if she pictured that solitary little frame sinking, and whether it drew her to the depths below. She used to whisper his name again and again so his soul could find its way home.

Women were especially vulnerable on that ship. There were so few rules, so few safe places where we could hide. It wasn't just the beatings, being drenched in cold water, or pelted with rubbish. It was also the feeling at every turn that there was a pair of eyes hunting us. Whether they were Indian labourers or British men, they all posed an equal threat to us on the ship.

I made acquaintance with a skittish young woman called Muniyamma who hardly spoke at all, mostly sitting in silence on her own. She once nodded at me as I sat among a group of women cleaning rice on the deck. The following day, I claimed a spot next to her, because I was not much in the mood to talk either. I picked through a pile of rice, greeting her and introducing myself. After that, we greeted each other every day.

It soon became a habit for me to sit next to her while we worked in silence. Some of the other women from the same village spoke about how Muniyamma had married quite young, as was the norm, and had enjoyed a good relationship with her husband. They had been married for a year and were hoping to start a family. But while crossing a rushing river one day, he was swept up in the current and drowned. He was missing for three days until a villager fishing downstream found his corpse floating close to the bank where the water was shallower. Muniyamma had lost the man she loved and her place in society. His family disinherited her, and her name was expunged from all official records. Her own family refused to take her back, and she discovered what it meant to be an invisible woman without a home. So when she heard many people were leaving India for a place where no one would care about her bad fortune, Muniyamma made up her mind to go and begin her life again.

Muniyamma often cursed the storms that battered our ship,

and said how much they reminded her of the monsoon rains. We were growing close when one day she sat away from all of us and wouldn't say a word. I tried to speak to her, asking if I'd somehow offended her. She shook her head. "It's not you. I wish to be alone." Though I felt hurt, I respected her wish. I was learning that nothing about relationships in this new environment was predictable.

Almost two weeks later, Muniyamma threw herself overboard. And then it came out: it was her last act of protest against the man who had paid one of our overseers to find him a young woman from below decks while the rest of us slept. For that small sum, the *sirdar* went below, grabbed Muniyamma and dragged her upstairs. She was too afraid to scream after seeing other women being chained on the decks for less. And there, awaiting his prize above, was the chief officer, who led her to his quarters and raped her until his violence was spent. The women who helped Muniyamma that morning said she'd returned with a vacant stare in her eyes. They had mopped up the fluids that dripped from her, cleaned her body as best they could, and laid her down to rest. But the following morning, she awoke and commanded the sea to take her.

I was haunted by her death. I often pictured her small body suspended above the ocean, luring her to the same watery grave as her husband. She was only seventeen when she leapt into those hypnotic waters. I began to wonder – were we bewitched the moment we stepped onto that vessel? After all that happened there – the violence, the fear, the unravelling of everything we had taken for granted in India – I found myself peering over the side of the ship, watching the angry waves lash the boat and imagining what it would be like to join Muniyamma on her serene seabed below. But on nights when violent storms rocked the boat, I would clasp my hands together and pray in short gasps that I would be spared to reach the shores of Port Natal. And in the morning, it would all be over, the ship rocking gently over tranquil seas, and I would rebuke myself for being so foolish as to allow a storm to defeat me.

At that time, both life and death frightened me equally. But I had to press on. "Show no weakness," I said to myself. People were dying all around me, but something told me I had survived this long for a purpose.

CHAPTER 13

ALMOST TWO MONTHS TO THE day we set off, Port Natal rose from the mists like a dream. It could not have pierced the haze in a manner more mysterious or beautiful. It was as Bilal had described – a mass of green beyond the water. And I had lived to see it. Many embraced each other in that moment, relieved that the *kala pani*, the black waters, had not swallowed us. India felt as distant in that moment as if I had only glimpsed it in a photograph. I was elated at what lay ahead, glad I had found the courage to turn my back on a marriage I did not want.

We had changed along that journey. So many beliefs we had held dear in India about caste, religion, the roles of women, had simply fallen away. I wondered whether, when we landed, people would fight to restore them. But I had a feeling that there would be more freedom to choose in Port Natal.

We were transferred from the *James Owen* onto smaller boats, and rowed toward the shore.

Though overcome, we were somewhat more subdued than the day we had arrived in Madras on foot. Perhaps we wanted to impress our colonial masters, some of them lined up along the shore to watch our arrival. *Brahmins* and beggars, warriors and washermen, we whispered about this new land in our myriad tongues, stepping onto its soil for the first time.

When I gathered up my possessions and stepped onto solid earth for the first time after that long journey, the steadiness of land felt strange. We walked along a nearby railway line, and there stood our temporary homes – a series of barracks with high walls. Even now, there were too many deserters among us who would not think twice of fleeing.

We lined up and our names were recorded in a register of sorts. We came to know it as the Immigrants' Register: it contained details of the estates on which we were to be employed, the names of our masters, and important details surrounding events in our lives.

The British had made their mark on what looked like virgin land. The buildings had been painted a stark white, and the style of these structures was long and rectangular. Cerise bougainvillea blooms splashed their petals across bushes in the distance while the sun fought to staunch clouds. A fine drizzle soon turned the air clammy, and the heat stayed close as we walked up the gentle rise. There were birds nesting in the branches of huge trees above us. "This is the Bluff," someone was saying in Tamil. I turned to glance at the sea and take in the expanse that now lay between my family and me.

We were ushered into the *coolie* barracks, all exact replicas built of stone, where at night the chill would bite us to the bone. The guards kept us in check as we crushed together in those cramped quarters. We had not been there for very long when infections began to take root and spread. Afraid of becoming ill, I kept entirely to myself, talking to almost no one and guarding my small corner selfishly. Sadly, the first to go were the children. Their parents sobbed while outside the barracks, the mosquitoes skated in pools of stagnant water.

There were further medical processes to undergo. But we had grown so inured to the shame of these that we unquestioningly undid our clothes, showed the medical officers all they wanted to see, and let them prod us. Even after this arduous journey of home to sub-depot, sub-depot to depot, depot to ship, and ship to barracks, some were still told they were not fit to be employed in the Colony of Natal. So they faced a painful reversal of the journey – barracks to ship, ship to depot, depot to sub-depot, and sub-depot back home, with the assumption they could slip seamlessly back into their old lives.

Shortly after our arrival at the Bluff, another ship arrived. Many of us wondered whether we'd be forced to share these already overcrowded quarters with another three hundred people. But we soon discovered that cholera had broken out on that ship, and the moment the passengers stepped off it, they were quarantined. They were made to pitch tents at the side of the bay for shelter, and had to watch while a bonfire was made of their clothing and bedding.

Despite the circumstances, I tried to find humour in everything I could. At the time, it mostly came in the form of our *Coolie* Immigration agent, a bearded, greying and unkempt man named Donald Grisham. Overwhelmed by the sheer numbers of people who stepped off the boats, he was prone to outbursts. He complained that his superiors had failed to provide him with the tools to do his job. Each time a new ship docked, he scrambled for quill and paper to record the details of his new charges. Any piece of furniture in the vicinity served as a desk. When his paperwork was done, he tore about the shore on a truculent horse poised to cast him off its back at any moment.

But Grisham certainly took his administration duties seriously. And cursed was the fool who interrupted him while he was in the throes of paperwork.

"How many hands do you think the Good Lord has given me?"

he'd snarl, spit flying. "Do you know what I am doing, young man?" he'd ask, his pitch rising. "I am currently trying to effect the disbursement of funds for this man who has travelled thousands of miles across the Indian Ocean to take up employment here, because there is an estate owner whose patience is fast running out as he waits to take this man into his employ! Can't your request wait?" he'd yell.

"Yes, sir!" The official would go scurrying away.

Grisham would turn his attention to the labourer seated in front of him, throwing his hands up. "These people have no idea of the complexities of this work! Each day it mushrooms, task upon task upon task. Disbursements, marriages, births and deaths to be registered, travelling to estates to ensure that all is well, reconciling planters with their disgruntled workers. What more, I ask you? What more can possibly be expected of me? I am a competent human, but only human, after all. They see my competence and say to themselves, 'That Grisham, he is capable of supernatural feats!' But what support do they offer? None!" The *coolie* sitting in front of Grisham would pretend to find his monologue absorbing. He nodded in approval at times, frowned at others, and screwed up his mouth in disgust as Grisham's words grew more impassioned. It was a pity the man was Gujarati and had managed to acquire only a smattering of English words during the voyage. After hearing Grisham out, the *coolie* respectfully put his hands together, bowed his head, and said in a most impassioned tone, "Good morning."

But Grisham was undeterred. He would complain to anything with ears. The morning I appeared before him, he fired a barrage of grievances at me. He raised his voice, he paused for emphasis, he even banged the furniture and gesticulated with his hands high in the air. I started, nodded vigorously and clicked my tongue in feigned annoyance. He filled in my immigration certificate, then raised his voice and over-enunciated his words as though I were deaf. "In seven days, you will proceed to the sugarcane plantation of Master Edmund Wilson in Tongaat, where you will take up your employ. Master Wilson will be unable to fetch you, so you must walk there. Do you understand?" He held up seven fingers to which I pointed individually, counting loudly in Tamil. He was delighted, believing he had broken the barriers to communication. I could not help myself – I bowed low with my hands together and said in heavily accented English, "Good night."

He closed his eyes and shook his head in disgust. "Robert!" he called out.

A nervous young man skidded in. "Get one of the *sirdars* to explain to this woman what's expected of her," Grisham said, and closed my file.

We were divided into small groups of approximately fifty people, each of whom would fall under one Indian *sirdar*. Those in my group were mostly Tamil or Telegu-speaking, and I assumed that we'd been allocated to this group because our *sirdar* would also act as an interpreter for those of us who couldn't understand or speak English. While I understood the basics, I wasn't confident about speaking English – I'd had very little opportunity to speak it at home.

Our *sirdar*'s name was Rangasammy, a tall, dark-skinned, strapping man who strutted around like a peacock in mating season. He was clean-shaven, kept his curly hair closely cropped, and rarely allowed a smile to cross his face. His eyes were deep set, his nose occupied a large portion of his face, and his lips were small, too thin to correspond with the rest of his features. His large head and thick neck flowed into a stocky body.

He was Tamil too, which meant he'd also come from the south of India. I was amazed that he appeared so well fed compared to the rest of us from there. He perspired easily and mopped his brow often. Rangassamy was the same as us, yet different. He didn't cower like us, or avert his gaze when the British addressed him. He made no apology for who he was. He also addressed us as disrespectfully as the British, and as many *sirdars* had done on the ship, he didn't think twice about beating anyone who would not take instructions.

Rangassamy called me to his desk in a corner of the barracks to explain what would happen in the next few weeks. He wore a crisp white Western-style shirt over his *dhoti*, which was rare to see. It looked odd, but he seemed proud of it, rolling up his shirt-sleeves and adjusting his collar. I could see he was trying to recall what he had to tell me. Although my file was lying in front of him, he gave no indication that he could read it. I greeted him, but he didn't respond. "Your name is?"

"Shanti, sir."

"Shanti, you have only a week left in this place." His accent revealed that he came from a rural area of the Madras Presidency. "In a week's time," he continued, "I will be leading you and the rest of this group on foot to Master Wilson's farm in Tongaat. I can't tell you what you'll be doing there. Master Wilson will decide what kind of work will suit you best. I see you are not travelling with any family members."

"No, sir. I am alone."

He shook his head, sighed and leaned in closer. "Look, it doesn't matter that you are not a man. You must still work like a man, you understand? Many plantation owners don't want you women here. They don't need crying babies to feed. Most of them refuse to pay women. But you are very lucky – Master Wilson is a good man, so he makes an exception for young women. But don't think it's going to be easy for you, eh. Planting and harvesting sugarcane is hard work. Your hours will be very long."

"Yes, sir, thank you." I nodded earnestly.

"Good, then! You don't cause any trouble, you work hard, you keep your mouth shut, you'll be fine! The British are strict but fair."

My short conversation with Rangassamy told me that we could hope for no loyalty from him. I already knew he was capable of violence. I would have to feign compliance, never speaking my mind or letting on that I was literate. Rangassamy would never approve of an educated Tamil girl working under him.

The walk to Tongaat was long. People came out to look at us along the way. I looked back at them, fascinated. The men and women had roughly the same complexions as us Tamils, the women being of similar height. But the men were far taller than the males in our group. Their hair grew in tight screws close to their heads. They were scantily dressed, and I heard them talking in a language that was full of clicks. I assumed they were the original people from here, because I had never seen anyone in India who looked like them. I wondered whether it had been the same for them – whether they had grown up with the British living on their land, or whether they had just woken one day to the sight of a ship full of white men with big rifles strapped across their bodies. One of the labourers asked Rangassamy who these people were. "Just ignore them!" he said gruffly. "They are *kafirs*. The British found them here when they came here. You'll see some of them on the plantations. But they are not your friends! You were brought here because they're too lazy to work."

I paid little attention to what Rangassamy was saying. I was reflecting on my journey and my stay at the barracks. Both had demonstrated that despite the promises of an entirely pleasurable life on these shores, I should not be naïve. I had witnessed moments of real cruelty that the British had hidden from us until the sea voyage began. I would have to steel myself for whatever hardships lay ahead on the plantation. I would work hard during the day and spend some time writing once the sun set. It would require focus and a certain emotional distance from others. I wanted no sorrow, no love, no pity. I hoped to cultivate strength, endurance, independence, and a sum of money that would enable me to return to India and proudly show my parents the fruits of my labour. Each step to Tongaat was one step closer to a future I could determine.

Port Natal's breezes were soft and set the leaves susurrating in the canopy above my head. The soil smelt rich and moist. I stopped to rub some of it through my hands and inhale it. I felt a charge enter me. We were here now, gazing up at Wilson's farm – a sky of stalks titillating the horizon. And in that moment, it came alive in my mouth – I could distinctly taste the sweetness of sugarcane.

PART 2

COLONY OF NATAL

September 1876

CHAPTER 14

I AM SITTING IN THE DAMP, my knees pulled up close to my chest, my arms clamped around them. There is something comforting about this posture. Aunty Saras showed it to me when my first flow of menstrual blood came. "Rock from side to side gently," she said. "That will relieve the pain."

But I doubt there is any cure for the pain that now lives in the marrow of my bones. My God! Has it really been two full years since I set foot on Wilson's farm? I remember how I stood at the Port of Madras like a fool, ingesting all their promises. How we have all been duped – thousands of us jostling to make it to the gilded shores of Port Natal, where our dignity, our freedom, and sometimes even the breath from our bodies would be taken. On that first day, we squatted obediently in our groups under the gaze of our masters, while they decided where they would put these *coolie* machines to work.

Now we labour hard each day, then return to the row of *coolie* lines we call home. Our tiny water-logged shacks, our *logies*, are mashed together out of corrugated-iron sheeting or grass and cane-stalks. They are punctured with holes that invite in the rain and wind. There isn't the smallest window to let in the light. Our *logies* are built on lower ground, so each time it rains, the muddy water floods them and makes us ill.

Inside, the wooden dividers do not reach the ceilings. This is where we eat, sleep, cook, fornicate, dry our wet clothes, store our firewood and dishes. Many have died from fires in their shanties, or had their children scalded by cooking pots. Some suffer from night blindness caused by prolonged exposure to the smoke from fires lit indoors. There are no latrines or places to bathe. We relieve ourselves not far from our shacks and our waste washes into the river. We drink, cook and bathe in that water. At the end of a long day in the fields, we crouch beside our huts and scrub ourselves clean out in the open. From here, there is a clear view of the master's mansion with its hot water and crisp linen. I imagine his family sitting down to a sumptuous meal, the scraps thrown to the dogs.

My contract says I must work for nine hours a day, but I often work for twelve or thirteen. Rangassamy storms into my living quarters on a Sunday morning, bellowing, "The master wishes you to work today." I put down my pots, pick up my scythe and head for the fields. Disobeying Rangassamy would result in a severe beating, but no woman here has the courage to defy an order from Wilson. He never forgets. One day, when his family is away, you'll be summoned to his mansion. And when he is done with you, you'll have to be carried out. So rather this mind-numbing cycle of hoeing, planting, watering, harvesting, burning; hoeing, planting, watering, harvesting, burning that eats up days and months and years.

I never question Rangassamy. The memory of my first beating is still too fresh. Shortly after I came here, he scolded me for not ful-filling my daily quota.

"But *Sirdar*," I responded, in full view of my fellow workers, "look how much I have done."

He exploded, grabbed me by my hair and dragged me into the closest building – a shed full of the smell of fresh stalks. "Unhook your sari blouse," he shouted, removing the *sjambok* from his belt. It was a raw piece of hide modified with hooks at the end. "Hold onto this cart!" he raged.

I was trying to say I meant no disrespect when his instrument collided with my back. The sharpness of the blow jolted me, throwing me forward so that my head smashed into the cart. I screamed. "Please stop, *Sirdar*! I am sorry, *Sirdar*!" I turned to see his gritted teeth. He was smiling. And when I turned back, the shadow of his raised arm was drawn on the cart. The blows came in a barrage. My eyes clenched shut. I held my breath, I braced for more. I pleaded, "Stop! Please! I am begging you!" But his force redoubled, shoving the air out of my lungs, the hooks mincing my skin. I slumped against the cart and fell to the ground, sobbing. The rush of blood down my back invited a soothing numbness.

"Never, ever question me, you cheeky little bitch!" he roared.

There was the stabbing splash of salt water on my back as I lapsed into a welcome unconsciousness.

For six days out of seven in the last year, I have gone out to work every day except for the day after that beating – when Rangassamy deducted money from my wages for absenteeism. Since then, I've been struck a few times but never with such force as the first time; which, I suppose, means I'm in a better position than most on Wilson's farm. The public humiliation of a first flogging inspires so much anger, such longing for vengeance. But soon enough, I found it replaced by the kind of quiet acceptance that my mother encouraged me to seek. I cover my ears each time he drags someone into the shed. We show each other our backs when we are washing, and our scars give rise to a strange sisterhood.

I think of how I once longed to be independent. But on the plantation, friendship is key to survival. There are times when you are so badly beaten, you'd bleed to death alone in your hut if no one came to your rescue. Sometimes, when wages owed to you are unpaid, or food rations promised to you are denied or rotten, you would starve were it not for the generous souls who share the little they have with you. There are friendships you would never have fostered at home that flourish here because you try never to sit in judgement of others. You live peacefully with your neighbours, you seek their protection while you pledge them yours, and you become allied. Together, you survive. And sometimes, you share your happiness, even if it is scarce and short-lived. Most of all, you are bonded by hostility toward your common enemy.

I have been blessed with a close friend and confidante, Devarakshanam. She is a young Telegu woman whom I affectionately call "Devi" – the Tamil abbreviation of her name. The first time I laid eyes on her, as I came to after that terrible whipping, I thought I might have been staring into a looking glass, barring her slightly lighter skin. Those who don't know us well think us twins. She came to the colony as a married woman, but she is alone now. When I asked why she left her husband, she simply said, "I do not need my own *sirdar*, Shanti," and I left it there.

Devi has a way with words even though she's had no formal education. When she learnt I could read and write, she begged me to teach her. "No – I am too impatient a teacher, Devi, and in truth, I only know the basics," I said. "Why don't you ask one of the missionaries for help?"

"Because I have *you!*" she retorted.

I gave in, if only to put an end to her pestering. "But don't tell anyone!" I warned her. "I can't have others hounding me for lessons after I've been on the plantation for thirteen hours!"

"Oh no – you have my word," she pledged. "And I promise not to tire you out. There's a nation of Britons depending on you to keep their tea sweet!"

Were it not for Devi's friendship, I'm not sure I would have survived the past two years on this farm. We invent reasons to laugh,
and share our most private fears and desires. Here in Port Natal,
she has become my family – a great comfort to me in a place where
so many of us are isolated from our kin.

There are others who are more fortunate than Devi and me,
who have travelled to Port Natal with many of their relatives. Of
course, seeing an entire brood together sometimes evokes pain in
us, but we have almost been adopted by Mariam and Baboo, whom
we see as extended family. They are our neighbours – a Moslem
couple, who came to the Colony with their children. Mariam is a
large, loud and effervescent woman and although Baboo is quieter
and more contemplative, they are well-suited. Their children are
respectful and polite, but the four-year-old twins often try their
mother. "Were I not Moslem, they would drive me to drink!" she
exclaims. Mariam complains that the strain of looking after them
is second only to the ardour of harvesting sugarcane, and our
peace is often broken by her yelling as she comes upon yet another
mess the two have made. Their elder sister lovingly shields them
from a thumping by sometimes hiding the evidence of wrongdoing
from their parents.

Thankfully, although we were separated for the voyage, I have
managed to re-establish contact with Latchmi, Munisami, little
Selvaraj, and Sandhya, who is now a toddler. They live on a neighbouring plantation within walking distance of Wilson's farm.
Although I do not see them as often as I would like, they visit me
occasionally and my time with the children is always a joy.

Devi and I are not the only single women here. Among our
group is very possibly the most beautiful young woman any of us
has ever seen. Indentured men are more than willing to put a dent
in their paltry savings for a few celestial minutes with Angammah.
Unable to subdue the stirrings in their loins, they blame her for

casting a spell on them. While the rest of us now appear ragged from farming, Angammah still glides into the cane fields each day, slashing the stalks with elegance. The Indian women call her "loose", and the British authorities jail her from time to time as a "woman procured for immoral services" although they never prosecute the men who consort with her.

I was also a bit disdainful of Angammah at first. But Devi took me aside one day. "She is no prostitute from India, Shanti. Angammah came out of a respectable marriage and had two little girls. I heard that one child was about seven, and the other, three. But her husband used to beat them, so she left and took the girls with her."

"But where are they now, Devi?"

"The British who processed them decided the children were old enough to work, so they took them away from her. They sent Angammah here, the seven-year-old to a different estate, and they passed the three-year-old on to someone else to become an apprentice."

"What? What work could a three-year-old possibly do?"

"Oh, perhaps they thought they could teach her some sort of trade." She paused. "So Angammah has spent all these years hunting for the girls. All these men she has been with – masters, *sirdars* and labourers – it wasn't for fun. She asks them questions. She pays some for information. But she still hasn't found her girls."

Among Angammah's customers was Dilip, whose *logie* was close to Devi's and mine. A mild-mannered fellow, it was hard to imagine he had once been a soldier who'd seen a fair amount of violence and brutality. He'd been part of the Indian Mutiny of 1857. Of course, we'd heard the rumblings of it in Vākkuṟuti, but because most of the rebellion had been focused in the central region of the country, we knew little about it.

I broached the subject with Dilip one day, after chatting about the goings-on on the plantation. "You were in the mutiny, were you not, Dilip?"

"Indeed I was," he replied.

"I can't imagine what it must have been like to be caught up in something so … momentous."

"I will certainly not forget it – or my part in it – easily, Shanti."

"What was it like to stand up to the British? We've all dreamt about it, but you're the only one among us who's actually done it."

Dilip was leaning against his hut, bearded and muscular, chewing on a piece of straw. He flexed his shoulders and rubbed the back of his neck.

"Well, Shanti, you know we were employed by the East India Company as the Bengal Army. It was our job to fight alongside the British, but from day one they considered us inferior – turned their noses up at us. It was all rubbish! We were strong and brave. We were strategic. Not to mention, many, like myself were … *are* … high-caste *Brahmins*. If anything, we had to lower *our* standards to fight with them. For a time, we tolerated their arrogance – some of us even grew to accept it. But then our patience ran out."

"So what did you do?"

"Well, it started with a rumour. We heard that some of the rifle cartridges that Moslem and Hindu soldiers were being told to use were greased with the lard of pigs and cows to make for smoother loading into their weapons. The British knew it was offensive to us, but they didn't deny it. They knew exactly why we could not touch those contaminated things, but they just didn't care! Our men in Meerut refused to use the cartridges. But the British just laughed at them! So our fighters rebelled."

"I heard they locked up a group of them for that."

"They did. But what did they think? That we were going to let them rot in gaol? Not a chance! We stormed the place! We rescued them, but by then we were so full of rage, we went into the town and we shot every British person we laid eyes on."

"You just mowed them down … British people?" I was open-mouthed.

"We did. Remember, at the time, I was young and hot-headed – like many of my colleagues. Our actions set off a whole lot of other mutinies. Made the British shiver in their boots. Delhi fell next, and on and on it went. Fortunately for us, there were only about thirty-five thousand British soldiers on the entire sub-continent and they were scattered far and wide, so it took a very long time for their reinforcements to arrive. We kept the rebellion going for over a year until the British put an end to it in Gwalior."

"But if you had such an advantage from the start, how did they defeat you?"

"Ah, we were stupid, Shanti. We didn't present a united front. The company also had armies in Madras and Bombay. Some of those *sepoys* simply didn't support our rebellion, and others even worked with the British to re-take Delhi."

I paused a moment to take it in. "Did they not try to punish you, Dilip – imprison you for your part in the mutiny?"

"Oh, they tried – and they succeeded in capturing many of us. Those who did not actually commit murder were offered an amnesty. But that did not apply to me. I went on the run until I got tired of living like an outlaw. When I heard about indenture, I decided Africa sounded like a better option than most. I gave them a false name and papers, and climbed on a ship. That's how I came here several years ago."

"What was it like, Dilip … to kill all those people?"

"War is a funny thing, Shanti. You start off with the best intentions. You hope to be a hero, but at some point you lose yourself. You start to think like the oppressor and behave like him. You find yourself with a uniform and a gun, and all of a sudden, you think you have a licence to act like God. And it is worse when you are in the company of people who think and feel just like you – the same anger, the same frustration. It is all multiplied."

"An orchestra of violence," I said.

He nodded and lowered his eyes. "We walked through the streets of Meerut with such malice. We put an end to all the British men. But once they were dead, we thirsted for still more blood. We started killing women and children, too. And we even mutilated some of the men's bodies."

"Why, Dilip – why would you do that?"

"I don't know," he shrugged. "So that their families would be haunted by the sight of their bodies, maybe? So they would speak about us at every dinner table in the empire, at every funeral. We wanted to live on in the hatred of their survivors, and that was more satisfying than any punishment we could be given. I was once proud of this." He hung his head.

"Dilip, there is something I don't understand about you. If you are capable of doing all you say you have, why do you take punishment from Rangassamy so passively? Why do you never fight back?"

He gave a dry little laugh.

"Shanti, I'm not a common murderer. I am a soldier. Rangassamy is like that Judas who betrayed the Christian god for thirty pieces of silver. His day will come. The wheel is round."

"But think of the grown men beaten to a pulp, the women raped in front of their husbands, the disappeared children, the workers hanging themselves in their shacks. The wheel may be round, but how slowly it turns …"

"That is true." He raised a shoulder again. "But *karma* decides when the time is ripe for action and we are merely her instruments."

He turned from me and shouted across the muddy lines, "Hey, Angammah, when can I come for a cup of tea?"

CHAPTER 15

WHEN I FOUND LIFE ON the plantation particularly difficult, I would escape to the edges of Wilson's farm, where I'd stumbled upon a quaint wooden building that sat within a wide circle of tall trees. The wind moaned between the tree trunks and I was drawn to its song. The building was probably not for our use. But I loved it nonetheless, because it was always empty, and inside I found complete peace.

I entered through a small door and walked toward the front where I sat on a wooden bench. There were many of them lined up in rows, all neatly polished. I turned my eyes to the very front where I saw the Christian god prominently displayed on his cross, his head sagging, a trickle of blood escaping from under the thorns on his head. I thought of some of our Hindu gods, pictured playing the flute or dancing. Why did the Christians want to depict their god this way? I could not bear to look at him, so bloodied and shamed.

I had come upon this building shortly after Rangassamy had stripped and beaten me, and the memory still haunted me. I knew what it was like to feel helpless, to have none of the powerful take pity on you, even though they knew they had wronged you. I wished I could unwrite the Christian book and give this Jesus a happier ending – one where he would not have to be crucified and die. One where he could return home to his mother and father, and they could be an ordinary family again.

I was dabbing the trickle from my eyes when I heard a man's voice behind me. "*Vanakum.*" The Tamil greeting. I put my hands together to return the greeting, but when I turned, I only saw a British man – a priest, dressed in black, wearing his cleric's collar. I did not want to show my fear at being discovered here, so I merely greeted him back. I wondered how he knew to address me in my native tongue. He asked me in Tamil, "Are you all right?"

I was shocked. "You speak Tamil?" I asked him.

"Yes," he replied. "Madras born and bred. Father John Davies, at your service." He extended his hand. I slowly lifted my hand and shook his. It felt strange to touch his warm, white hand. He was an elderly man and walked with the aid of a stick.

"Shanti. That is my name," I said.

"Most delighted to make your acquaintance, Shanti. Please don't get up. Sorry if I disturbed you. We don't have many people coming to the chapel – except the Wilsons from time to time, of course."

"It's not for *coolies*?" I asked.

"Oh, dear – that's not what I meant. I meant to say, it's not often that anyone at all comes here. We haven't held a proper service here in a long time. But I live at the rectory not far away, and I still come here to pray from time to time. I enjoy the solitude."

"I have only been here a few times myself," I said. "It is very peaceful."

"You are welcome at any time, my dear. There are no restrictions. We leave it open. This is my rule – and, I believe, God's rule

– so I enforce it very strictly indeed!" he laughed.

This brought a smile to my face.

"Ah, a smile at last," he said. "When I walked in, I sensed you were sad."

"I … I don't know why," I stammered. "I am just always so taken aback to see that poor man hanging on the wall. Why do you put him there? It's so shameful that everyone should stare at his pain."

"Ah, that's a long story indeed, my dear, but a very good observation on your part. You know, in all the years I have been in the priesthood – and that numbers several decades now – I have never heard a Christian express that thought. I suppose we are all so used to seeing it. From the moment we're held over the baptismal font and splashed, that is what we see: Christ on the cross. Common as anything. And we never question it."

I waited a moment before I continued, feeling bolder.

"Also, Father, I look at this Christ and I think if he were alive, he would understand how I feel about my life as it is now. I know he lived a long time ago, but I feel … almost like I know a little bit of what he went through, carrying that heavy cross and being whipped. I wish I could tell him I'm sorry he suffered when he was only trying to do what was right."

"Quite right, my dear. Quite right. Shanti, I must prepare for evening prayers now. But I should very much like to talk to you again. Would you be so kind as to visit me – and Christ here, who I am sure would love a bit of companionship – when you have time?" he asked.

"When time allows, Father, I will come back," I said.

When I told Devi about my encounter with the priest, she was very upset. "Don't you understand, Shanti? It doesn't matter whether it's a priest or plantation owner – they are all British! Perhaps he will report you to Wilson and say you spoke out of turn, and Rangassamy will give you another beating! What were you thinking criticising the statues in their temple? It's none of your business! Don't ever go there again."

"Devi, he was not offended by what I said – I could tell. But, more importantly, how many of them do you know who've bothered to learn our language or address us respectfully? There was something different about this man."

"Of course there was something different – he is most likely a missionary, and you know that's how they work. Offering our children places at their schools so they can convert them to Christianity. It's all about how many of us they can turn, how many of us they can convince to forget where we came from and what we have always believed in. If you go back there, I don't want to know about it!"

I understood why Devi was upset. There were several mission schools dotted around the plantations, and the children attending these schools had greatly benefitted from the education they were receiving, but many of them had also begun to adopt the Christian religion and rituals. They spoke of Jesus Christ and the saints, and some had gone so far as to tell their parents they no longer wanted to be raised as "heathens". But I was not in their position. For starters, I was not a young child, and I was not searching for new gods. The ones I had always believed in had abandoned me since I had come here. And the only reason I went to the chapel was because when I set foot in there, it felt as though the plantation was miles away. I could not allow anyone to deprive me of that small piece of serenity.

So I returned whenever time allowed, sitting there quietly, contemplating my life and what I would need to do to stay focused on my goal of returning to India in three years. I worried about my parents and their health. I thought of my sisters, and hoped I'd become an aunt several times over. At other times, I would hear the slow footsteps of the old priest behind me, and we would chat at length.

I began to look forward to our conversations. He had an excellent command of Tamil, and picked up very quickly that I was not speaking a dialect. "Where did you learn to speak this Tamil?" he asked me. I was hesitant to tell the truth. Only Devi knew my secret. But I grew to trust Father John and eventually relented. He listened to the many stories I told him about my childhood in Vākkuṟuti and shared a few of his own about the difficulties he'd faced as a youngster who chose to join the priesthood, much to his father's disappointment. "I think it is safe to say we both disappointed our parents, Shanti – you and I. My only hope is that when you return to India a self-made woman, your parents will understand and forgive you." I developed a deep fondness for Father John, and appreciated that he never tried to preach to me.

One day after several of our talks, I found the courage to ask him for help with something important. "Father, please do not think I'm taking advantage of your kindness."

"Not at all. Go ahead, ask me what you will, Shanti."

"When I hear Wilson and his men, and all the British people who come to the farm, speaking English, I feel so lost because I only understand the basics, and can only snatch a word here or there. I feel they are making decisions about my life, my future and that of everyone around me, and yet I hardly understand a word."

"Yes, my dear. I quite understand how alienating that could be. I was very fortunate to learn Tamil from a scholar my father hired to teach me when I was just a boy. And I thoroughly enjoyed it. My father worked for the East India Company, handling the trade of cotton cloth from India to Britain. He was able to learn just enough Tamil to get by in his dealings. But he had hopes that I would succeed him in the business, and I suppose that was why he set me to work studying the language. But knowing Tamil has proven greatly advantageous to me, so I understand how you feel."

"I have long wanted to advance my learning of English, Father. But I don't know anyone who can teach me. I cannot attend the missionary school because of my work. I know this is much to ask, but ... would you help me to learn the language properly? Please?"

"Me, Shanti? Oh, my dear! No, you are addressing this request to the wrong person. I am a most irascible teacher."

"But I am a good student, Father. I am hungry to learn. If you'd asked my Aunty Saras, she would've told you how dedicated a student I am. If I set my mind to it, I could learn quickly. I would use all my free time to study."

He began tugging at his beard. "Shanti – I am no expert at this, although English is my mother tongue. I would hate to commit myself to—"

"I know you're not an English teacher by profession, Father. But you have taught at a seminary, yes?"

"Well, yes, but—"

"Please, this is all I ask of you. I lost my only chance at further education when Aunty Saras died. And what a bitter disappointment it's been to come to Port Natal and see that there is no prospect of continuing my learning. Father, I slave in those fields the whole day but although my body is working hard, my mind is mostly idle. Please help me."

Father John sat silent, mulling it over. "Well, I suppose it is possible. If you are able to find the time. Of course, we would be governed by your plantation schedule. But I suppose if we spent this time more productively, I could teach you here, possibly teach you at the rectory ..."

I almost threw my arms around him. "Thank you, Father John!" I clasped my hands together. "I am forever in your debt!"

"Oh, no. No, don't thank me, Shanti. You may soon rue the day you asked me to teach you. I am forgetful and cantankerous at times, as I have warned you. But I suppose teaching you English will force me to exercise this ageing brain of mine. Of course, it won't be easy. You'll have to be prepared. I'll put you through your paces. I was a taskmaster at the seminary – don't expect an easy time."

"No, Father – I'm prepared for all of it."

"Good, then. You have a good command of Tamil, Shanti, and I see how easily it comes to you – this poetic language you speak. Once you have conquered English, you will be able to hold the British to account in their mother tongue!" he laughed.

"Father, you think too much of me. But thank you – thank you ever so much for agreeing to do this."

I leapt out of there, longing to tell Devi the good news. It took me back to when I was a little girl playing outside the temple and Aunty Saras had found me. I still remembered the excitement I felt at being invited to her house; this felt the same.

But when I spoke to Devi, she was disturbed about this development.

"I cannot believe you asked him to do this. What if word gets out that he has been giving you private lessons? What on earth would people think?"

"Why shouldn't I have asked him, Devi? This is my one chance to master their language! Why should I not grab it with both hands?"

"Well, because ..." she sighed. "I have no reason, Shanti. Now that you have got to know him better, he does seem to be a nice man, I will concede. Perhaps I'm just envious. But ... wouldn't it be wonderful if I could come too?"

"Come too? A moment ago, you were scolding me, telling me what a terrible idea this was and now ..."

"I've changed my mind." She sniffed. "Speak to your Father John. Tell him I'm coming too."

And so it was that I managed to persuade the elderly Anglican priest to take us both under his wing. Once he'd got over the shock of having to teach two ebullient young women, he agreed. Surprisingly, he and Devi struck up a firm friendship once he had won her trust. He was mostly a forbearing teacher, but as time was of the essence, he challenged us often, pressed us to learn hard, to take books home hidden in our saris, and to try to decipher them even when this was beyond our ability.

Sometimes his young assistant, Father Connor, would pop his head in during our lessons. "Stop driving them so hard, Father John," he would say. "Surely that's enough learning for one day." Father John would shoot his assistant a withering look, which sent him scurrying away. Candle after candle was burnt poring over those books, listening to one another read aloud, testing each other, repeating the sounds to ourselves day and night until they began to grow more familiar, smoother and less ragged in our mouths.

English took on a new life for me. "You must split the language off from its people in order to succeed," Father John told me. "If you detest the people whose mother tongue it is, you will never learn their language properly." So instead of thinking of all the British people who had caused me harm, I thought of Father John, and in time, my mouth began to negotiate the foreignness of those words. I learnt to chew them down and form them almost in the same way I did my own language, realising there was an affinity there. Father John delighted in our progress, and when Devi threw her arms up, frustrated, at times, he'd reassure her: "No need to speak like the queen, Devi. It is quite all right to intone India when you speak English."

"Thank you," Devi said to me on the way home from a particularly trying lesson. "This is a real gift – to be able to get into the minds of the British through their language and see how they see us."

I squeezed her hand. "And isn't it interesting to hear their stories and poems, Devi? This John Donne fellow writing about how, although he is separated from his loved ones, their ties stretch so far, like beaten gold. I sometimes see them sweeping across the night sky, connecting me to my family across the distance."

"Shanti, I hope you are starting to see this take form – this dream you have had for so long to be a woman of letters. Isn't it amazing that in India and here, you have somehow crossed paths with people who are making it possible: first Aunty Saras, now Father John? This indenture: it is a mere distraction for you, and one day you will realise what you truly want to be. I know you detest this work as much as I do. I know better than anyone how you have suffered under Rangassamy. But one day, when you become who you were meant to be, you will see these people are all building the monument you will become. And it will truly be a sight when it is finished."

Devi's words gave me joy. I began to see how Father John was moulding me, and although the misery of my days on the plantation never went away, I imagined them to be a kiln – scorching, but solidifying me. I worked harder than ever. I stayed true to my learning and progressed faster. My long period of deep despair had come to an end, as I lay in my *logie* at night, full of hope that I was edging closer to my destiny.

CHAPTER 16

THERE CAME A TIME OF year when, in our thousands, we would break out of our cages on the plantations. We waited for the sighting of the moon in October, and when she disrobed, the plantations erupted, spilling all of us onto the streets of Durban, in a cacophonous throng. It was easier to breathe the air. And for ten exhilarating days, the rules no longer applied. Work and the troubles of indentured life were forgotten. The internal strains from home died down to a murmur, and we were united in our common identity beyond caste and religion. Muharram, once an Islamic festival, came to belong to all of us.

For days before we gathered, the men were hard at work on the plantations building their gaudy *thaziyahs*. These structures were meant to resemble the mausoleum of Imam Husain, a martyred Moslem religious leader. But in recent years, they'd grown to look more like the Christmas trees in our masters' mansions. Although three tiers high, they needed to be light enough to wheel through the streets of Durban. Most *thaziyah* builders began with a light bamboo or wooden frame that formed the skeleton. The less ambitious builders aimed for a height of about fifteen feet, while the more daring ventured a good ten feet higher. Then it would be garbed in the most eye-catching materials – flowing muslins, silks and tinsel – anything that might lure the sunlight out to play.

There was always great rivalry among the builders, who competed to outdo one another in size, height and décor. Fathers treated the building of the *thaziyah* as a sacred duty that needed to be passed on to their sons. And there was always the presence of an *imambada* nearby, where the faithful could worship during the ten-day ceremony. Some believed any family that failed to observe this tradition would fall victim to tragedy. Each group of builders also made a bright *panja*, shaped as a hand, wrapped in fabric of green and adorned in a garland of flowers, believing it had the power to bring healing. *Panjas* symbolised the right hand of Imam Husain, raised high as he was about to go into battle.

As the *thaziyah* builders set off in a huge procession, they were led by a group of savage-looking mascots we called tigers. Many of them were champion wrestlers wearing traditional fabric costumes enhanced with brightly coloured paint. These men were revered on the plantations for their strength and ability to crush their opponents in the district wrestling competitions we called *kushti*. The tigers were equally admired and feared as they pretended to attack the crowds, much like their feline counterparts in India.

Cloaked in clouds of incense, we marched from one district to another, the stream of *thaziyahs* in tow. We sang with gusto, hypnotised by beating drums that revived the songs of home. Food and alcohol flowed freely, and onlookers gathered round to watch the brave and foolhardy challenge each other to stick-fighting duels in the heat. Devi and I favoured the swarthy men with bushy chests who defeated their opponents with a couple of well-placed blows. We would shout and cheer as the weakling hit the ground and the victor summoned his next competitor.

Our masters called Muharram the *"Coolie* Christmas". But it was no mere carnival. For this short time, the British could not tell us what to do. We banged our tom-toms into the night. Our rhythms frightened them. We sang and danced so riotously, it was as if they had never made us suffer. We reminded them that the longing for our freedom had never left our minds or bodies.

That year, the first day was the most memorable for me. The rest passed in a haze, although each one was demanding, exhausting. I lost all sense of what day it was, how many times the sun had risen and set, how many times the moon had lit our way. We celebrated feverishly, barely pausing to rest. Our voices were hoarse, our bodies spent from all the dancing.

On the second-to-last day, we again moved forward in a crush of people. Devi had her arm linked in mine and was singing at the top of her voice. My softer song began to trail off. Something had caught my attention. There, among the clump of entangled bodies, something was mysteriously forming – the eyes of a stranger. A swatch of lightly toasted skin. A strong nose. A sensuous sliver of mouth. Soot-coloured hair. I was searching now for another shard of that face in the bobbing ocean of revellers. Hoping I could swim to the surface for one more glimpse of those shining eyes, one more piece of the puzzle. Who was he? As we stepped into a clearing, I was blinded by the gaudy muslin of a *thaziyah*. But I saw him still: my mosaic man.

"Devi!" I said, tapping her on the arm. "Stop your raucous singing for a moment!"

She clicked her tongue. "What's wrong with you, Shanti? It's almost over. Just enjoy this last day!"

"Devi – this is important!" I leaned closer to her. "Turn your head to the right – slowly, though. Do not make it obvious we're looking at him ..." I said furtively.

"Who? Who are we looking for?"

"I'm not sure. A pair of eyes. Broad smile. Wavy black hair …"

She looked at me, incredulous. "That describes more than half the men here!"

"Devi, just believe me. There's a man in the crowd staring at me!"

"Are you sure he's looking at you, not me?" she cackled, but earned a glare in response.

"Right!" she said, determined. "Let's track this mysterious Maharajah down!" She narrowed her eyes. "Is that the one?" she pointed. "Why, Shanti, you devil! His *thaziyah* is huge!"

I burst out laughing. "No! That's not him."

"Do not be discouraged," she said. "I hide it well, but I am skilled in the art of courtship."

"No, you're not," I hit back.

"So little you know." She shook her head. "Do not give up hope, my friend. There is still one more day to go. On the morrow, we march to the Umzinto River to watch these *thaziyah* builders toss their creations into the water. I'm convinced that your mysterious Maharajah will show himself before the celebrations are over."

I nodded, but as night fell, I had little hope that this would happen.

The sun and Devi rose with equal vigour the next day. I was thirsty and exhausted, in no mood for another day of merrymaking. But Devi yanked me along to enjoy the final day's entertainment. The only reason I didn't pass up the opportunity was that the very next day, we would return to our treacherous plantations, and who could refuse the gift of a precious last day of pleasure?

The morning passed sluggishly, and the sun clambered high into the sky. I felt Devi's hand on my shoulder.

"Devi, I am not made of the same stern stuff as you. I think I'd rather …" I turned and stopped dead.

I was staring into the face of a smiling man – all the fragments of the features I had glimpsed yesterday, merging into this whole – my mosaic man. I tried to hide the shock of seeing him right there in front of me, although my wide eyes and gaping mouth betrayed me. He was slightly older than me: tall, well-built, and he moved confidently. He had unusually light-brown eyes and a fair skin crowned with curly black hair.

I took a second to study his face – not a face of individually perfect features, but one in which those elements were so expertly composed that he was truly an attractive creature to gaze upon. I was grateful for my dark skin that hid the rush of blood to my face.

"Excuse me." He spoke English. "Would you and your friend like to walk to the river with us?" He paused. "I thought, after my hard work on this *thaziyah*, at least one or two more should admire it before I drown it in the river."

I was both paralysed and speechless.

Devi jumped in. "Of course," she said. "We would love to see … your *thaziyah*. Shanti is very fond of men's *thaziyahs*. I, too, am fond of them. Yours is very … nice." I regained movement in my limbs and nudged her.

He smiled shyly. "This is my friend, Faizal," he pointed to the man standing next to him, "and my name is Mustafa. Come, walk with us."

"Pleased to meet you," I answered, relieved that my powers of speech were restored. I could not have been happier for our English lessons. "I am Shanti, and this is Devi."

"Forgive me for speaking English," he said. "Sindhi is my home language. I overheard you speaking English."

"Yes, Devi and I can speak a bit of English," I said. "Sometimes it is just easier – Devi is Telegu, and I am Tamil-speaking."

"Oh, are you one of the passenger Indians who came here to teach?"

"No." I bowed my head. "I am just a labourer on the Wilson plantation."

"Well then, Shanti, you are being wasted in the fields! Your English is very good. Shall we go down to the river?"

I nodded.

"Faizal speaks English too," Mustafa added.

"How lovely!" said Devi.

As usual, she provided uninterrupted commentary on the proceedings, declaring some *thaziyahs* superior and others hopelessly flawed. Faizal clearly found her entertaining. But my mind was elsewhere as Mustafa's *thaziyah* left the dry earth to be cast unceremoniously into the water. He was proud of his construction, and thrilled when I complimented him. As the crowds fell back, he gingerly took my hand and guided me to a more secluded part of the riverbank. We sat there, finding some relief in the breeze that broke the afternoon heat.

"That's much better," I said, as we settled down. "I think I've had enough of all these festivities for one year."

"Yes, the celebrations do take it out of you. And I must tell you, it's quite heart-breaking pitching your beloved *thaziyah* into the river after all that hard work!" he laughed. The words came easily after that, although I was conscious that this was not the ideal way to meet a man I would have liked to impress. I was dishevelled, and we were both grimy and sweaty. But that also lent the moment a raw honesty. He warmed me with his gaze and said my name, smooth as the sound of a sitar, while I saw myself reflected in his eyes.

We held hands and spoke for hours about his life and mine until the day faded into dusk. "Teach me your favourite poem before I go," he said.

"But it's getting dark, Mustafa. I have to go soon."

"A short one, then … please."

"All right," I relented. "It is written in the *Subhāṣitāvalī* of Vallabhadeva," I said.

I recited it, and he began to repeat every line, eyes closed, his voice melding with mine.

> Although I conquer all the earth,
> Yet for me there is only one city.
> In that city there is for me only one house;
> And in that house, one room only;
> And in that room a bed.
> And one woman sleeps there,
> The shining joy and jewel of all my kingdom.

"Come — repeat it one last time so I am certain I have learnt it properly," he said. And I did, until the words were fixed on his lips.

"I will say it every night until I see you again, Shanti. And if you say it too, it will become a pledge that we'll see each other again."

It was hard to let go of his hand. But eventually I said goodbye and found my way back to Devi, grinning like an idiot. I told her all about him on the way back to Wilson's farm. "I am so happy for you, my friend," she said, beaming.

We passed many people who lay like shipwrecks in the streets after all those days of revelry. But I felt renewed. I thought of how I'd leaned my head against his chest, and when I lifted it, our lips had brushed lightly. I knew he would keep his promise and come to Wilson's farm to find me.

Every day after that, I ached for him a little more. At night, I recited our verse, falling asleep to those words, knowing he was saying them too. It had become more than just a poem. It was a promise.

CHAPTER 17

MY FIRST YEAR WITH MUSTAFA fed my soul. I still spent long hours in the fields, but even as I laboured there, I felt the slow drip of happiness. Sometimes, an unexpected smile played on my lips. The feeling had become so alien, I wrestled against it. Devi lectured me: "It is all right to allow yourself to feel human again, Shanti. The things that have happened here have hardened you, as they have all of us. But you cannot love with a heart made of thunder. Give it a chance."

So I tried to put down my emotional weapons and stop fighting. I felt battle-weary, having been born a poor and low-caste girl in the Madras Presidency, fighting for the right to learn, fighting against my arranged marriage, fighting for a better life across the seas, and arriving here to a renewed fight for survival. By the time I met Mustafa, I was already half-spent. I wished he had known that vivacious girl in Vākkuṟuti who'd loved climbing trees and swimming in lakes. The woman he met at Muharram was a poor imitation. But how restorative love can be. Although on the plantation, I was a mere number, Mustafa seemed to paint me back into being. His strokes mirrored parts of me I had forgotten and chased my inner ugliness away. I saw how elevated I was in his eyes, desired, cherished even. And that made waking every morning more bearable.

The Saturday that Mustafa first came to Wilson's farm, I had returned from a frenetic day in the fields. The sounds of Mariam's children were ringing in my ears. I walked straight to my *logie* and slumped next to the door. And then I saw him approaching, a smile breaking out as he approached me. I got to my feet, my heart banging in my chest as we embraced and he kissed my forehead.

We agreed to go walking together, finding a spot to sit on the outskirts of the farm, leaning against a large branch that had fallen from a tree. He confessed that thoughts of me at Muharram had not left his mind, and he had suffered from our parting. I told him how our meeting had sustained me. We spoke almost until the sun went down, and when I asked him whether he intended to make the journey back so late, he asked, "Is it possible for me to stay?"

I nodded, and we returned to my *logie* where I made a simple meal of *dhal* and rice, which we shared with Devi. She took her leave early, and I fell asleep that night in his arms. He told me he expected nothing but to hold me close. It was the first night since I'd left my home in Vākkuṟuti that I felt completely safe.

We awoke to the tolling of a bell on Sunday morning. The Christians were worshipping, their hymns rising above us in melodic strains. We ate with Devi and drank strong tea. She wanted to know the details of the night before, a gleam of mischief in her eye, and was disappointed to hear that I had merely fallen asleep next to him. "Yes – I'm quite sure that's what your Maharajah came all this way for – to hear his Maharani snoring in his arms." I shot her a dirty look and turned to see Mustafa chuckling quietly.

Rangassamy did not always allow us free time on the weekends. But when he did, Mustafa would come, bringing happiness with him. He was in the habit of picking wild flowers on the way to Wilson's farm, and parting them into two neat bunches for Devi and me. "This is the perfect man for me!" Devi would laugh. "No cooking for him, no tidying after him, but he still brings me flowers!"

One afternoon, after we had eaten our fill and chatted a while, I suggested the three of us walk to the beach. "No, no – I have eaten too much to walk so far – a team of wild horses would break their backs trying to drag me there," Devi complained.

"Fine. You stay here," I said to her. "But you" – I pointed to Mustafa – "up on your feet. Let us go!"

Mustafa pulled himself up, groaning.

Devi shook her head. "*Aiyo*, Mustafa, this is what you get for courting someone who was very likely a British soldier in her past life," she cackled.

Mustafa and I covered many miles that day, talking about his job at the rum factory on Macleod's farm. "Sorry for not coming more regularly," he said. "The factory is always busy. It is not always easy for me to get away if we have fallen behind."

"Ah, but it sounds so much better than working in the fields. It's pure hell with the sun beating down on you all day."

"Oh, I haven't forgotten, Shanti – remember, that's where I started. But I don't know what is worse – killing myself in the fields, or working in this *haram* rum factory which no honourable Moslem should be doing. But what does Macleod care?" He laughed. "Did I ever think I would be faced with a choice like that? Compromise my body or compromise my soul? To think, I was expecting to pick gold from brinjal bushes in Port Natal!" He grinned.

"Do you miss home, Musta?"

"Oh, Shanti," he sighed. "Sometimes. When I allow myself to. You know how it is when you get here. You can't stop thinking about your family and you keep wishing you could go back. But after a while you get so caught up in this life that you start forgetting about the one you had before."

"I have the same feeling these days, Musta. These two years have made my life in Vākkuṟuti seem like someone else's. My connection to India is definitely fading."

"But if you feel that way, why do you want to go back, Shanti?"

"Well, that was the idea from the start – that I'd save my money and go back to my parents when I'm done and ..." I trailed off.

"And do what in Vākkuṟuti, my love?"

I kept quiet.

"How much money have you saved, Shanti?" he asked.

"Hardly any." I shook my head. "I work so hard, Musta. But we women earn so little. And sometimes they deduct from our wages for no good reason."

"But what will you do with so little when you go back to your village? You won't be able to support your parents. You don't even know what their reaction will be when they see you."

"No, I don't – I don't know, Musta! But the way I left them – running away like a coward – I have to make up for it. Of all the things I regret in my life, it is how I let my mother down. She will not have many years left in this world. If I don't get back as soon as my indenture is over, she'll spend her last days yearning for me."

"What about your father?"

"He would blame my mother for what I did. I can only imagine how he has been treating her since I left."

"You torture yourself with thoughts of your family, Shanti. But think of this. What would've happened if you had stayed? They left you no choice."

I nodded.

"Shanti, I, too, imagined returning to India as soon as my indenture ended. But now I am not sure any more. I have a more decent income than most, working at the factory. I send a fair amount home to my father. And that is of great help to him. My siblings are working the land with him. You know, when the British took over Sindh and tried to kick us out and give the land to Hindu *Brahmins*, my family was almost made homeless."

"What did your father do?"

"Well, he refused to leave the land – stubborn old man that he is. He borrowed money from a group of moneylenders from Bombay – the *Banias*. But the interest on their lending rates is so high, you end up paying about four times what the land is actually worth."

"So your father is still paying off that loan?"

"Oh, yes. My siblings sell the produce they grow there. But it's a pittance, really. The money I send home is of more help than if I went back myself."

"Don't you miss them, though?"

"Of course I do. I just try not to think too much about my old life in Thatta. My past and my family are all in one little chest in my head that I am purposely leaving locked for now."

He rested my head on his shoulder. "But you – I think about you all the time. And you have changed everything."

"What do you mean?" I asked.

"Since we met and our ... relationship became more serious, I have thought about staying in Port Natal."

I was surprised. "You mean re-indenturing and staying longer?"

He swallowed. "I mean staying for good ... so we can perhaps start a life together."

I drew in a breath. "I can't, Musta – this is not what I had planned."

"Shanti, none of this is what any of us planned. Did you have any idea when you signed up that you'd be slaving like this on a plantation? I spent the first few years here trying to wake from this nightmare. And now, some good fortune has finally been visited upon me. Faizal and I worked harder than anyone else, and Macleod noticed us. And now we work in the factory. Macleod's got a hard side to him, but he's a little less monstrous than the other sugar barons. And it's a better deal than most of us are getting."

"But is that really enough to keep you from going back home?"

"Yes – now that I've met you. I think about it all the time. You know, it's possible for us both to stay here; for me to ask Macleod to keep me on after my contract ends. You could do the same. We could put our savings together and start a market garden, or try our hands at fishing – there are good opportunities here."

"But this is not our home, Musta …"

"No, it's not. And you'll never think of it as a place that could become your home one day because you think home is only where your parents are, and you think of this land in the same way you think of the British. This is not their land! They came and took it the way they took ours. But it doesn't belong to them: they do not own the people in it, or the rains that fall upon this soil, or the animals that roam it, or this roaring ocean. It all existed before they came here. It is separate from them. Once you realise that, you will learn to love this place as much I do. Think about it – about staying here with me."

"Give me time," I said. "I can't rush an answer on such a serious matter."

He agreed.

"When will I see you again, Musta?"

A look of uncertainty crossed his face. "I am sorry, Shanti, I don't know. If you do not see me next weekend or the next, please understand that it is not because I have lost interest or forgotten about you. Macleod is sometimes unreasonable. I also do not expect you to come all the way to his farm – the distance is too great for you to travel on foot. But I will come back, as I always do."

We had reached the shore, the surf licking at us teasingly. The wind had picked up and billowed beneath my sari sash, raising it into the air like a large bird. I closed my eyes and reached out as though my arms were wings. In that moment, I felt such freedom, as though we could be swept away from here – Mustafa and I, taken to a different shore where we could love each other away from this plantation life and its limitations.

I opened my eyes and he was staring at me. "Come with me," I said. He held my hand and allowed me to guide him towards the cove where Devi and I took shelter when it rained. I recalled the fineness of the sand there, the echoing emptiness of the large hollow that had protected us from the storm. Mustafa and I entered its dark coolness, and I drew him in. I kissed him and felt him unfurl my sari until it fell like liquid around my feet. I spread it on the ground and pulled him down toward me. I fixed my eyes on the silhouette of his face, then closed my eyes and caressed the contours of his features. As I ran my fingertips over his eyes, his mouth, my hands through his hair, I remembered the fragments of my mosaic man and felt a rush at the weight of his completeness on top of me. We fell into an embrace so fluid, so molten, it was as though I had known him this way for a thousand years.

My body was no longer that of the immature child who'd stood in front of the cracked looking glass at home, begging her mother to preserve her innocence. I was a woman now, fully formed, unashamed of my nakedness. My body came to life, awakened by his gentle hands. Like milk and water we merged, Mustafa and I. And while the sea waited and the gulls cried, I knew there was to be a deviation in my path.

CHAPTER 18

IN THE WEEKS THAT FOLLOWED, Mustafa was not often able to visit me. Rum production at the factory was being increased in the run-up to Christmas, and Macleod was hoping to make a small fortune. But once the year ended, Mustafa was given a bit of breathing room as the demand for alcohol lessened, and that meant he did not have to work every Sunday. This gave us all, neighbours and friends, something to look forward to, because we had begun to meet in a larger group for a Sunday meal. When Mustafa came these days, he often arrived with his friends in tow.

Faizal too became a close friend of ours. He had an agreeable temperament and was always full of good humour. Because he was fairly accident-prone, the standing joke was that when he was coming to visit, anything of value, easily broken, or that could cause him harm, had to be put away in safety. "I must be royalty," he said. "It is customary when one of blue blood is arriving to make the necessary preparations well in advance." We grew used to him jumping up in the middle of a gathering, unrolling his mat and facing Mecca to pray. Mustafa said he did it five times a day, no matter where he was.

I developed such a fondness for Faizal, and I hoped that a romance would blossom between him and Devi. They were very good friends, their temperaments well matched, and they sometimes fought as if they were an old married couple. But Devi had her reservations.

"Faizal is the loveliest, kindest soul, Devi. I can't imagine why, when you two get on so well, you won't consider allowing him to court you."

"Oh, Shanti. What is this English proverb Father John taught us? Once bitten, forever shy!"

"Once bitten, *twice* shy," I corrected her.

"Yes, yes – you know what I mean. No more talk of this Faizal nonsense now! He is my friend, nothing more."

As Mustafa and Faizal got to know my friends better, they brought another friend of theirs to join us on their visits. He was a short, clean-shaven, sprite-like man called Chiniah. I was able to have long, involved conversations with him because he spoke Tamil. Chiniah proved to be an entertaining character, highly competitive in nature and a firm atheist, which was strange for someone from the Madras Presidency. He loved to play games, and was skilled at everything from card games to puzzles. On a Sunday when we were all looking for some escapism, we would pack a communal lunch, harvest some banana leaves to eat off (as we had done in India on special occasions), and find a clearing not far off where we could flee the dampness of our *logies* and play our games. Mariam and Baboo liked to join us too, while their children ran around and played close by. We also regularly invited Angammah out on our Sunday jaunts, although she sometimes had visitors of her own and politely declined. The only neighbour who kept his distance was Dilip. I had sensed some tension between him and Mustafa, and assumed it had something to do with the historical antagonism between their people in India, so I did not interfere.

Latchmi and Munisami often made the journey from their neighbouring plantation to join us, Selvaraj and little Sandhya in tow.

"Shanti, we are here!" Selvaraj would declare. "Listen, Sandhya is learning new words."

"That is wonderful, Selva!"

Faizal would interject. "All right, all right, who wants a ride?" The children would throng around him, clamouring for a turn, and Faizal would elevate each of them on his shoulders, prancing around like a horse while they shrieked in delight.

"*Ama*, I can see the whole world from Uncle Faizal's shoulders!" Selva would cry. "That's because Uncle Faizal is as tall as a tree! Give your sister and the others a chance now – they also want a ride," Latchmi would say.

When that game expired, Faizal would throw a dishcloth over his head and pretend to be a ghost, chasing the children around until they all collapsed from happy fatigue. That gave us enough time to lay out all the food we had brought to share.

When lunch was over, the children occupied themselves or dozed while the adults played their games. My favourite was the card game *Thunee*. I had played it so often in the barracks with Latchmi and Munisami that I had become fairly good at it. Devi did better at *Pachisi*, which was played with cowry shells that were moved about on an ornate piece of cloth shaped like a cross. The object was to see who could reach the middle of the cloth first.

We would sit in a circle, place the cloth in the centre and play *Pachisi* for hours, cheering and cursing as luck favoured or deserted us. Faizal was always the most unfortunate of us. He'd slap his leg and look downcast. "Why do I always lose?"

"It's just luck," I'd say, while Devi rubbed his arm and comforted him. I often partnered with him to try to put victory within his reach. But he wasn't a very good strategist, and Chiniah easily outsmarted him. Faizal truly had the innocence of a child, and all his words and actions seemed filtered through a clean heart. He reminded me of what the rest of us had lost along the way.

"Don't worry, Faizal!" Devi would say. "We will have another round and I'm sure you will do better this time."

But he was sometimes inconsolable. "You know why I lost, Devi? Because Chiniah cheated me!" We generally knew this to be true. Chiniah rarely won without cheating. But he would put up a strong defence. "I cheated you? Are you mad? Just admit it – you're no good at this game!"

"But you cheated, Chiniah! God knows – you're a proper *Pachisi* cheat!"

"Yes, Faizal, God knows, God knows … what does God know? God is keeping such careful count of our game, that he's lost count of all our people dying in the fields!"

"Chiniah – what a blasphemer you are! Never mind, the day will come when you'll have to answer for your idle talk."

This was how we passed our Sundays. Our conversations ranged from stories of home and our colourful childhoods, to our adventures on the way to the colony. Mustafa, Faizal and Chiniah loved to do impersonations of the *sirdars* and our masters. At times, they were so funny, the children rolled about clutching their stomachs, tears pouring from their eyes. We were fond of a cup of tea in the afternoon, although Devi complained that Faizal drank too much tea, and had almost finished her supply in just two visits.

"Do you know why they put you in the rum factory instead of a tea plantation, Faizal?" she would ask.

Faizal would look at her lovingly. "No, Devi."

"Because you would bankrupt your master, drinking his crop. All the tea in Ceylon could not quench your thirst!"

He would laugh and shrug.

There came a week when Mustafa sent word that he would see us again the following Sunday. We liked to know when to expect him, so we could all ready ourselves for an outing. We had much to celebrate that Sunday. We had heard during the week that our *sirdar*, Rangassamy, was leaving the plantation for good to start a business.

"Where would he have found the money to open up his own store, Devi?" I asked.

"Where do you think, Shanti? Every time our wages get docked or Wilson doesn't pay us on time, the workers with families get desperate. They go to Rangassamy and ask for help and he lends them money – at ridiculously high interest. They have to pay him back or they know he'll beat the living daylights out of them. With all the profits he's collected over the years, I'm not surprised he's made a pile of money."

That Sunday, we rose early, waiting for our friends to arrive. But as the morning wore on, it seemed they were no longer coming. They usually arrived early because it was a long journey back to Macleod's farm in the afternoon. We were all disappointed, especially the children, who'd been told they were now old enough to take part in our games. I began to worry. It was unlike Mustafa to promise they were coming and not arrive.

Devi tried to console me. "I wouldn't worry if I were you, Shanti. You know how Macleod can be. Perhaps he needed them to do some extra work today."

"You may be right, Devi," I said, and tried to focus on other tasks. But just before midday, Ravi came running up to our shacks. He was a boy who earned a bit of extra money delivering messages between plantations.

"Ravi, how are you?" I went to meet him.

"Aunty, there is trouble at the Macleod farm ..."

"What trouble?"

He was completely out of breath and leaned against my *logie* to steady himself.

"Is it Mustafa? Is something wrong?"

He swallowed hard and asked for water, which Devi dashed off to get. "No, Aunty. It's not him. It's his friend, Uncle Faizal – he's dead!"

I heard Devi's enamel cup clang to the ground behind me.

"What? What do you mean ... dead?" I grabbed the boy by his shoulders. "Are you sure? What happened? Did he have an accident?"

"No, all I know is that he made the *sirdar* angry and the *sirdar* beat him. Uncle Mustafa says you must come now!"

"Go back and tell him I'm leaving now."

The others began to swarm around us. Devi was paralysed by the shock of what she'd just heard. Mariam and Baboo began asking questions, while Angammah rushed out with a cup of sugar water for Devi. Dilip stood outside his *logie*, watching us.

"I don't know what happened, friends. Ravi's just told us Faizal is ... dead." I managed to squeeze out the words. "I'll have to go to Macleod's farm and find out. It sounds like Mustafa needs me. Please take care of Devi."

"No! I am coming with you, Shanti. Faizal was my friend."

I didn't have time to argue. "Grab your shawl and some water, Devi – we have a long way to go."

On that lengthy journey, Faizal loomed large – his smiling face, his innocence, his pleas when he lost a game. Could it really be true? Faizal had meant a lot to us all, but Devi had loved him more than any of us. And I could see she was struggling to keep her emotions in check as we rushed toward Macleod's farm. "Devi, perhaps we should not think the worst – perhaps Ravi misunderstood ..."

"No, Shanti, he is a clever boy. I do not think he would make such a mistake – not about something so serious." She was wiping her eyes. "Also, Shanti … I do not feel Faizal's presence any more."

I slowed down and took her hand. "What do you mean, Devi?"

"I had a special bond with him, Shanti."

"Devi, I do not think you should speak as if he's already …"

"But he is. Listen to me – he is. We had a connection, even if we never acted on it, the way you and Mustafa did. Faizal was the gentlest man I knew."

"But if you cared for each other so much, why wouldn't you …?"

"Because marriage can ruin beautiful relationships, Shanti. I wanted our friendship to remain the way it was – pure and perfect. I never wanted us to fight. I never wanted a harsh word to pass between us."

We travelled the rest of the way in silence. When we arrived at Macleod's farm, it was just as Ravi had said: the smell of death was in the air. Mustafa emerged from Faizal's hut, his face twisted in anguish. He fell to his knees on the ground before me and I rushed to him, knelt and took him in my arms. He buried his face in my neck and I let him cry, felt his sobs near my heart, told him it was all right to mourn Faizal this way.

"I will kill him!" he shouted. "I will kill the man who did this to my *kapal karay*!" I was reminded that Mustafa and Faizal had been "boat friends" – a bond that could only be understood by those of us who'd travelled across those treacherous seas together.

I waited until some of Mustafa's anger subsided. Then I took his face in my hands. "Musta, what happened? What happened, my love?"

"Shanti," he murmured, "you know how harmless Faizal was. He could never hurt anyone …"

"But Musta, tell me. How did it happen? Did he have an accident?"

"No, Shanti! It was no accident! Our *sirdar* Visvanathan killed him. He beat him to death."

I gasped. "Are you sure? Did you see it happen?"

Devi stepped forward and put her hands on Mustafa's shoulders. "Let's take him inside, Shanti. If his words reach the *sirdar's* ears, he may be in trouble, too. Let us take him inside his *logie* and make him some sweet tea to help with the shock."

Once inside the darkness of his home, Mustafa seemed to regain some of his composure. "Did you know that Faizal had a weak heart?" he asked.

"No, this is the first I've heard of it," I said. Devi also shook her head.

"Well, he arrived in the colony strong and healthy, but while he was at the barracks, he contracted measles and it weakened his heart. When Macleod found out, he gave Faizal a job in the factory because he knew he was a hard worker, but he struggled with the manual labour on the plantation. Our *sirdar*, Visvanathan, was very unhappy about this. He'd always picked on Faizal, called him lazy for not being able to work like the others in the fields. When Macleod told Visvanathan he was moving Faizal to the factory, Visvanathan tried to change Macleod's mind. But Macleod wouldn't listen, so Faizal and I ended up working together in the factory."

Mustafa took a gulp of his tea. "But Visvanathan wanted to have the final say. He's always in the habit of getting his way, even if it takes time. We were getting ready to visit you this morning. But when we woke up, there was such a din outside. There was apparently a backlog, so Visvanathan decided he would put some of us to work to sort it out. He dragged one of these poor men out of bed, but then realised he was injured and wasn't in a position to work. So he tossed him on the ground. He looked at me and just ignored me. But then he turned to Faizal."

Mustafa sighed and rubbed his eyes.

"Mustafa, if this is too hard, you do not have to tell us now," Devi said gently.

"No, Devi. It is better that you know what happened because I witnessed it, and if anything happens to me, then at least you will know the truth of how it unfolded."

I felt disquiet settle over me.

"Faizal reminded the *sirdar* that he could not do that kind of labour because of his heart, but the man would not hear of it. He kept on calling my friend a lazy bastard. 'I'm not Macleod,' Visvanathan said. 'I won't let this weakling get away with shirking his duties.'"

Mustafa looked up at me. "Shanti, Visvanathan dragged Faizal to the fields – dragged him along the ground. He showed him this long stretch of cane that he wanted cut. Then he told Faizal he had to carry all that cane and pile it onto the cane cart by himself. I stepped in. I offered to help, and said it would go so much quicker if the two of us were working together. Chiniah also came to help. But that swine sneered at all of us. 'You've got nothing to prove. But this lazy one – he must show me he's a man and he can do a man's work,' he told us."

"Did Faizal refuse, Musta?" I asked him.

He shook his head. "Shanti, since you have known Faizal, has he ever refused to do anything? Even if he was asked to drive pigs, he would gladly do it, although it would be an abomination. No, he took up the challenge. He worked quietly for hours. But because he stopped to catch his breath a few times, his progress was very slow. The *sirdar* came back to see how much Faizal had done, and when he saw that he was not even halfway through, Visvanathan lost his temper. He started shouting at Faizal, telling him he was pathetic, saying no wonder he was unmarried – what woman would want a man who could not even cut down a few stalks of sugarcane in half a day? He pulled out his *sjambok* and started beating Faizal."

There were tears in Mustafa's eyes now and I could feel the sting of tears in mine too. "If only I had got there in time! We didn't hear Faizal's cries from the fields because our *logies* are too far away. But a bit later, Chiniah and I went out to see how Faizal was coping. I don't know how long Visvanathan had been hitting Faizal by the time we got there. The blood seemed to be pouring from everywhere. His face was badly disfigured – it looked like he had been punched again and again. He could hardly stand and he was making a rasping sound, like he was struggling to breathe. Chiniah and I didn't care about Visvanathan. We started running towards Faizal, shouting for the *sirdar* to stop. But when he realised we were coming, he called some of the African workers over and screamed at them to hold us back."

Mustafa was speaking through gritted teeth now. "We fought them so hard, trying to defend Faizal. But they outnumbered us. They forced us onto our knees and made us watch what Visvanathan was doing to our friend. It wasn't enough that he had already beaten Faizal half to death. He tied Faizal's hands together, grabbed him by his hair, dragged him along the ground and tied him to the wheel of a sugarcane cart that was standing nearby. Then he flogged him some more, Shanti – the way I have never seen a man flogged before. Faizal begged until he could speak no more. Visvanathan kept on shouting, 'You Mohammedans are troublemakers! I should tie a rope around your neck and march you to the police station!' He spat at Faizal and mocked him and lashed him until Faizal just went limp. Once he had passed out, the *sirdar* told the Africans to take him back to his hut and leave him there. But they still held us back. We were not allowed to help our friend. I should've fought harder, Shanti. I should've punched those guys holding us down. I could've …"

"No. You couldn't have." I stilled him. "There were too many of them and only two of you. Visvanathan had a *sjambok* and who knows what else? There was no way for you to intervene."

"When did they let you go, Mustafa?" Devi asked him, her voice cracking.

"They waited until he died before they let us go to him."

"Where is Chiniah now?" I asked.

"He's with Faizal, Shanti. He has not been able to leave him."

"Take me there," Devi said. "I want to see Faizal."

"No, Devi – don't go in there!" Mustafa warned.

"Mustafa," she responded firmly, "Faizal was my friend. I wish to see him."

Mustafa looked at me and then at Devi. Then he got up and silently led us into Faizal's *logie*. The smell of dried blood filled our nostrils. And there our friend lay on the ground, so horribly disfigured, I couldn't even recognise him.

Chiniah turned to look at me with swollen eyes. "We had it all planned. We were looking forward to playing *Pachisi* today. He made me promise I wouldn't cheat. I was going to let him win today ..."

Devi pointed at Faizal's body, his hands still bound.

"Bring me something to cut this rope with, Mustafa, and some cleaning cloths and water, please."

"Devi, you don't have to—"

"Please. Do as I ask," she said. "If there are any religious rites to be observed, then carry them out while I clean him. But I cannot allow him to pass into the next state unclean."

Mustafa gave in, and we watched Devi lovingly tend Faizal's broken body, the pail of water at her feet reddening as she bathed him from head to toe.

When she was done, she turned to Mustafa. "It is as you said, Mustafa. When a Moslem dies, all the parts of his being must give account and speak for themselves. Now his body is clean. Every part will speak clearly and attest to the innocence of his heart."

Chiniah went out and dug his friend's grave while Mustafa bound Faizal's body. How frail and anonymous his form looked under that white sheet. Just before sunset, Mustafa lowered him into the ground and placed him facing Mecca while we stood around his grave.

"Go to your *Jannah*, my friend," Mustafa said. "Only the finest shall be reserved for you."

We stood there, enveloped in the afternoon's stillness, trying to understand what had happened. Chiniah grabbed a shovel and began to toss one spadeful of soil after another into the grave until the white of Faizal's shroud had disappeared under the clods of red earth.

As thunder rumbled above us and the skies opened, Chiniah raised his shovel, looked up into the sky and yelled in Tamil, "I hope you are counting! If you are real ... *if* you are real, I hope you count this man among the best we have lost."

He hurled the shovel onto the ground and stormed off.

CHAPTER 19

MUSTAFA NOW ENTERED THE MOST painful period of his life since he had arrived in Port Natal. He was given no time to mourn Faizal. Macleod quickly replaced him. And Mustafa simply had to grow accustomed to living and working on the plantation without Faizal at his side. Chiniah also struggled to regain some semblance of his old jovial self. He drank all the time, and began to make a fool of himself in public. The more he was punished for it, the more he misbehaved.

"Try to keep him away from the bottle," I advised Mustafa.

"After what he has seen, Shanti, who can blame him? If my religion allowed it, I would drink too."

But Mustafa and Chiniah were not over the worst of it yet. There was to be an enquiry into Faizal's death. His body would have to be exhumed, and a court case would ensue. Both friends would be called upon to testify. Mustafa hardly slept. Each time I saw him, the circles under his eyes grew darker.

"Musta, you are working with dangerous machinery in the factory. You cannot go to work exhausted every day."

"Shanti," he said, "I feel like I am on the verge of collapsing, but every time I close my eyes, I see Faizal – not the Faizal we knew, but that disfigured man, staggering towards me in all my dreams ..."

"Musta, I know it haunts you. But your head must be clear now. The Protector is going to look into this matter soon. You and Chiniah will be expected to testify, and we cannot depend on Chiniah to provide reliable testimony any more. If the judge sees there's a problem with you two, he will just dismiss the murder charges against Visvanathan."

"I don't care, Shanti. Faizal is gone. It makes no difference."

"But what about justice for Faizal, my love? I know you are wracked with guilt that you could not help him. But if your testimony is convincing and the judge finds your *sirdar* guilty, he will go to prison. He may even be hanged for Faizal's killing. Do you want to risk another man losing his life on your plantation because you are not interested in giving evidence?"

He sighed, heavily. "I suppose you're right, Shanti. If I can do nothing for the dead, perhaps I can try to do something for the living."

The hearing began about two weeks days later, and owing to the seriousness of the charges brought against Visvanathan, Macleod permitted Mustafa and Chiniah to leave the plantation so that they could testify in the court case. But he wasn't happy about it, complaining to Mustafa that production in the factory would be affected by his absence. I could not go to the court proceedings as I would've liked. But I waited anxiously to hear the outcome from Mustafa, who decided to stay with me until the case was concluded, as the court building was located closer to Wilson's farm than Macleod's.

The case would be heard before a Magistrate Johnson. Mustafa, Chiniah, Devi and I had scraped together some money to engage the services of a lawyer who could act on behalf of Faizal. The lawyer was a severe-looking man with a pointy moustache. He warned Mustafa and Chiniah from the outset that he could not guarantee a satisfactory outcome, as the justice system was skewed against labourers like us.

"The magistrate is working from the assumption that all of us Indians are by our very nature liars. So, when you enter the courtroom, tell the truth as you remember it. Do not add or embellish anything. Any discrepancies will count against you," he told them.

Mustafa chose to testify in Sindhi to ensure he did not make any errors in English that might jeopardise the case. Chiniah would give evidence in Tamil.

On the day the case was to begin, Mustafa rose early, washed, dressed neatly, and made his way to the court. But when I returned home that evening, I was surprised to see him waiting for me there.

"I didn't expect you to be back so soon – how did the case go?" I asked him.

"The magistrate wasn't there." He shook his head. "We will try again tomorrow."

The following day, the case did get underway. It began with Mustafa's testimony. But it didn't go as he had planned.

"Shanti," he said, "I went there so well prepared. The lawyer and I went through everything so many times. When we got there, we told the court we wanted a Sindhi interpreter – then there was a delay while they found one. I assumed the man understood every word I was saying. But soon after I started speaking and he began interpreting, I realised this man was not translating what I was saying accurately."

"So what did you do?"

177

"I started speaking to the magistrate in English. I said, 'Excuse me, my Lord – I asked for a Sindhi interpreter. This man is not doing a good job of translating what I am saying.' The magistrate seemed shocked that I could speak English. He started shouting at me. 'Do you know how many cases are coming before this court today? We are inundated and you want to waste the court's valuable time by first asking for an interpreter, then telling us that you do actually speak English and you don't need one after all?' I tried to explain to him that I cannot speak English perfectly, and I did not want to make a mistake that might upset the quality of the evidence I was giving in court. He said, 'We've brought this interpreter here to assist you and you *will* make use of his services and continue with your testimony in Sindhi. You are not to address me directly from now on. Only address the court through your interpreter.'"

"But when you gave evidence about the actual murder, did the interpreter manage to capture it?"

Mustafa shook his head again. "Shanti – that man did not really understand Sindhi. Look, I am sure he is from somewhere close to where I come from, but he was definitely not Sindhi-speaking, and even when he interpreted what I had said in English, he spoke broken English."

"Were the facts all there, though, Musta?"

"No, Shanti, not really."

"So, what happened after that?"

"Well, the magistrate sent us home and told us to come back tomorrow to hear Chiniah's testimony."

"Did the lawyer say anything afterwards?"

"He only said it had been unwise of me to question the interpreter's translation. He said those court interpreters may appear to be just like the rest of us, but now that they are part of the justice system, they have a much higher status than we do. If we question them, we question the whole justice system. It seems I would've done better to keep my mouth shut."

The final day of court proceedings began with Chiniah being called to the stand. According to Mustafa, Chiniah did a good job of concealing the fact that he'd been drinking. They offered him a Telegu translator, which was not ideal, but at least Tamil and Telegu are related, so the interpreter could understand Chiniah's evidence.

Then Visvanathan appeared in his own defence with a Hindi-speaking interpreter translating his account – the court having finally managed to pair a translator accurately with a mother-tongue speaker. Mustafa and Chiniah were outraged by Visvanathan's denials of culpability. But when they objected to the evidence being given, the magistrate threatened to expel them from the courtroom. Magistrate Johnson made notes as Visvanathan spoke, then went into his chambers for a short break before he returned with his verdict.

Mustafa and Chiniah sat anxiously as he began handing down his findings. "There is some confusion in this case as to what actually happened on that fateful morning the deceased lost his life. We have only two Mohammedan *coolie* witnesses, whom we know were good friends of the deceased; and then we have the accused *sirdar*, a Mr Visvanathan, who has proven to be a loyal and reliable assistant to the owner of the plantation, Mr Macleod. Now, as you know, it is customary for us to request a statement from the plantation owner as to the character of any of his workers on trial, and Mr Macleod has been kind enough to grant the court's request. Based on what he has said, we have no reason to believe that Mr Visvanathan is a man of violent temperament or prone to victimising workers. He has been in the service of Mr Macleod for many years, and has proven to be dedicated and trustworthy in achieving the planter's objectives.

"But to come to the testimony of Mr Macleod's two factory employees, I am compelled to label it nothing other than exaggerated and contradictory. Our first witness tells us the deceased was tied to the left wheel of a cart of some kind while the flogging took place. Our second witness testifies under oath that the deceased was in fact tied to the *right* wheel of a *wagon* as he remembers it. Neither can tell us with any certainty whether the deceased was already dead when he was removed from 'the vehicle' they describe, or whether he died in his living quarters shortly thereafter. This therefore leads me to the conclusion that despite examinations carried out by health inspectors before the indentured are shipped to the Colony of Natal, the deceased managed to slip through unnoticed despite the heart ailment that eventually caused his demise. But the fact that he knowingly chose to enter the system suggests to me he must have been aware of the occupational hazards involved. Therefore, it is my considered opinion that no one is to blame for the death of the deceased. The cause of death on his death certificate shall bear the words 'natural causes'. You are free to go, Mr Visvanathan. This case is dismissed!"

And with the pounding of his gavel, Mustafa and Chiniah watched their last chance to achieve justice for Faizal slip away.

Mustafa turned to me for succour, Chiniah to the bottom of a bottle. That night, Mustafa lay in my arms while I spoke words of comfort to him. "Musta, you did your best for Faizal. You could do no more."

"But I failed, Shanti. Faizal deserved justice."

"This system is much bigger than us, Musta, but divine laws always win over man-made laws. Perhaps there will come a day when Faizal will be avenged." I said the words, but I was no longer sure if I believed them myself. It took Mustafa many hours to fall asleep, and I hoped that when the next day dawned, he could begin the slow process of putting Faizal's death behind him. But before sunrise, I awoke to sounds of panic outside. Mustafa was in a deep sleep, so I slid out of his embrace, wrapped my clothes around me, and went to see what the commotion was about.

"Rangassamy is dead!" Devi called out as I emerged from my *logie*.

"What? How?"

"Sounds like he fell off a cart and broke his neck. They found him this morning. Can you believe it, Shanti? Just going off to start a new life and this happens …"

I thought about this for a moment. "Devi, there are still a few minutes left before we start work. Go ahead without me. I will catch up with you. I just need to make sure Mustafa is all right before I leave."

She nodded. "But don't be late – we don't know the new *sirdar*. You don't want to get off on the wrong foot."

Devi was right, but when she set off, I didn't go back to check on Mustafa. My thoughts were racing. Rangassamy regularly rode on a cart. And even if he'd fallen off from that height, he might have been injured – broken a leg, or similar – but he certainly wouldn't have died.

I knocked on Dilip's door. He'd taken to smoking a strange concoction of tobacco, opium, hemp and brown sugar that was becoming popular on the plantations. They called it *ganja*. Dilip invited me in. A cloud of smoke wafted around his head. He looked at me through drooping eyelids.

"Dilip, have you heard Rangassamy is dead?"

"Yes, I did hear something of that nature," he slurred.

"You know because you heard or because you were there?"

"Oh, Shanti. You sound so … accusatory. Were you not the one standing here just a few years ago asking why the wheels of justice turn so slowly?"

"Were you not the one who told me *karma* had her own timing, and could not be rushed, Dilip?"

He inhaled deeply and blew out a stream of smoke. I had to cover my nose and mouth to keep from coughing. "Shanti, perhaps I am an instrument of *karma* who does her bidding. Perhaps she let loose the savage beast you know lurks within me."

"But why now, Dilip? Why not all the times he humiliated you?"

"Simple. The system takes Faizal. One is taken from the system. Go and tell your Mustafa that justice has been done. His friend's death has been avenged."

CHAPTER 20

I HAD WITNESSED THE STAIN tragedy had left on many indentured men. It was like a dark spot of ink that spread and eventually eclipsed them. They grew either sullen and withdrawn or violent, until the system claimed them too. I thought this might be the case with Mustafa. Perhaps his heart would harden and a distance would form between us in the wake of Faizal's death. But this didn't happen. If anything, it opened his eyes to the reality that tragedy always played like an unobtrusive child on the fringes of our lives. And we should be prepared for the moments when it moved into the centre, before going back to the edges.

If Mustafa had been somewhat sheltered from this reality before, he was now awake to the delicate balance of life in Port Natal – the reality that we were all caught up in a game with fate to stay alive, in which any of us could be eliminated without warning. But amid the sadness, something sensitive and beautiful began to burgeon in Mustafa. He found a renewed appreciation for those he loved. He responded more readily to my needs and emotions, and was much more mindful of the preciousness of our stolen time together.

He was on hand as much as he could be, offering help and support, not just to me, but to my friends as well. No request was a chore for him. He sprang the gentlest surprises on me: a vibrant flower planted in the blackness of my hair, a walk in a stretch of virgin wood under darkening skies, a modest picnic on the vastness of the shoreline. Where did Mustafa end and I begin? I cannot tell. But this I remember clearly: the soft space between the blade of his shoulder and the expanse of chest where I laid my head. How skin, muscle, bone and heart melted to accommodate me. Gradually, the regrets I felt at leaving my family and traversing an ocean to come to this sometimes brutal place began to leave me.

Before my head did, my heart began to see a future with Mustafa. Devi saw it first: "You are deeply in love with him, my friend."

"I suppose I am."

"Since I have known you, Shanti, I have never seen you quite so fulfilled."

"Devi, I know this sounds quite silly, but it feels as though my life began at Muharram. I don't know how I can have lived this long without the knowledge of him."

"Time is going, Shanti. You now have less than two years of indenture left. And you know you can't take him home with you."

"No, of course I can't. To take a Moslem man home and declare him to be my husband? Well, I might as well never return home if that is my intention."

"So what is your intention then, Shanti? Have you thought about his proposal that you stay and make a life here?"

"I'm still in two minds, Devi. I had this planned so well. I wanted to honour my parents by returning home a wealthy woman and deciding my own future in India. But Mustafa has scuppered everything! I cannot see a life without him."

"That wicked Mustafa – putting paid to your perfectly crafted plans!" We both chuckled.

"Has he ever spoken to you of marriage, Shanti?"

"No, never."

"But would you marry him – if he asked, I mean?"

"There is no simple answer to that, Devi. We are different – culturally. We work on plantations that are far apart. I cannot take him back home with me, and he certainly cannot take me back to Sindh. What kind of wedding would we have?"

"Ah, you are getting caught up in too many details – what Father John would call 'peripheral' details. *Peri-pheral*. Do you know what that means?"

"No, I don't."

"Of course not! Because you are busy studying human anatomy with Mustafa while I am here, studying the Oxford Dictionary. It means that the details you are wasting time thinking about, are not central to your relationship, or a marriage, for that matter. He is Moslem, you are Hindu. For a bit of variation, let's get Father John, an Anglican priest, to marry you two and be done with it!"

"Devi, this is not a joke – be serious."

"I am serious, Shanti. This man wants to make a life with you. But he is probably too afraid to propose because he knows you have an aversion to marriage."

"Not an aversion to marriage, Devi – an objection to a marriage with Muthan!"

"Yes, but can you see how Mustafa might think this a sensitive subject for you – one that is best avoided?"

"Perhaps ..." I said.

"Shanti, you know I believe in this notion of the one great love of your life. It is possible to love many men during one's life. But only one of them is uniquely bonded to your soul. I had a husband. I grew used to his presence in my life. But love, admiration, companionship – I never had any of those things with him. With Faizal, I felt that a little. As if it could grow into that, if I allowed it. But I thought I'd fail again as a wife, so I just left it."

"Do you regret it, Devi?"

"I think enough time has passed for me to say yes, Shanti. I do regret it."

"But you would've been a widow now, Devi."

"Yes, but we would've been committed to each other. I would have loved him the way he deserved to be loved – the way he already loved me. That's how I should've mourned him: as a wife, not a friend who washed his body. Fear holds us back too easily. We choose fear over learning to resist it. Be courageous, Shanti, as is your nature. If Mustafa is what you want, do not let him slip away."

About seven months after Faizal died, a new shipment of migrants arrived on our farm. This was not unusual. Many were leaving indenture, choosing to return to India. But the number of labourers who had arrived with us had also dwindled over the years. Suicides, absconding, violent deaths at the hands of overseers, disease – these were like a great scythe that often swept over the fields, claiming the lives of people who needed to be replaced for the cycle to continue.

One of the new recruits was an attractive young girl called Suraya. We sometimes passed each other in the fields, or greeted as she made her way past my *logie* to reach her own. But there was a language barrier that made it difficult for us to converse. One Sunday when Mustafa was visiting me, I was surprised to see her walk straight up to us, beaming. She greeted us both in turn and began speaking to Mustafa in Sindhi. I gathered they were no strangers to each other.

Mustafa smiled. "How coincidental, Shanti!" he said, turning to me. "Suraya is from my hometown. We have passed each other in the streets many a time."

"That is indeed a coincidence!" I said, feeling a twinge of jealousy. "How astonishing that you've stumbled upon each other after all this time."

After that, Mustafa sometimes visited Suraya when he came to see me. I should have thought nothing of it. She was probably updating him on news from home. I knew he was keen to know about the welfare of his family, and his ageing father's health. He invited me to visit Suraya with him, but I felt there was little point in my going along if I could not understand or participate in their conversation, as Suraya could not speak English. Mustafa joked that he would teach me a few words of Sindhi so I would not feel left out. But those visits disquieted me, which Devi sensed.

"Shanti, they are only friends from home."

"Yes, I know. But does he have to visit her every time he comes to see me? Look at her – she's a vision of beauty!"

"What nonsense! This man has lost his mind over you. What makes you think he could even entertain the thought of another woman? And yes, she is beautiful, but a bit dull in the head, if you ask me – no comparison at all."

"Devi, he's never done this before."

"No, but when last did he meet someone from home? He hasn't spoken his language for months, years, more likely. Don't create problems between yourselves based on unfounded suspicions."

But in time, Devi also began to have doubts. "Shanti," she said one day, "you know how fond I am of Mustafa, and I would never say a bad word about him, but ..."

"But what, Devi?"

She sighed audibly. "I think I am ready to agree that Mustafa is spending too much time with that girl, Suraya."

"But that is what I said months ago!"

"It was too soon then. But this has continued for some time now. Perhaps you should address it with him."

"I don't quite know what to say, Devi. Do I ask him if he is being unfaithful to me?"

"No, I think you should just be honest and tell him you feel he spends too much time there, and that it's starting to bother you. If he is the decent man I believe he is, he'll respond the right way."

But there was no need for that conversation to happen. Mustafa's visits to Suraya became more infrequent as time passed, and I began to notice a slight antagonism towards Mustafa and me emanating from Suraya. When I greeted her, she would ignore me. On one occasion when I went down to the river to wash my clothes alongside her, she muttered something in Sindhi, packed up her washing, and left.

The next time I saw Mustafa, I asked him about it. "Musta, Suraya has been so cold towards me of late. I don't know why – I've done nothing to her. But I sense there's some tension between the two of you. Can you please go to her and resolve this?"

"Shanti," he sighed. "Why do you care whether she greets you or not? She's really just—"

"Musta, I try not to have enemies on this plantation. Something has happened to upset her. I cannot communicate with her, so I'm asking you to do this for me."

Mustafa was clearly annoyed, but got to his feet, tossed his bag down, and walked out. He must have been gone for a good twenty minutes when Devi appeared in my doorway. "Shanti, have you heard the din coming from Suraya's *logie*?"

"No, but I asked Mustafa to go over there."

"Well, I've just walked over the hill, past Suraya's place, and the two of them are going at each other."

I threw my hands up. "Let them sort it out, Devi. She's obviously upset with him, and with me for some reason – God knows why. I sent him over there to clear the air."

"Shanti, maybe we should go over there, and find out what's happening. They're shouting at each other at the top of their voices. You don't need to understand Sindhi to know they're talking about something serious and emotional, perhaps ... even personal."

I threw down my dishcloth.

"I'll come with you," she said.

"No, let me do this, Devi. I need to know for myself what's going on."

As I approached Suyara's *logie*, I began to hear the strains of strident voices. Mustafa's was unmistakeable. It had risen to a roar, and Suraya was yelling back at him. I stood a short distance away and listened. I heard my name being thrown about. Whatever it was, however hurtful, I needed to know the truth. My hands were shaking as I lifted them to pound on the door. But as my fist reached it, Mustafa flung it open. He looked ashen, shocked to see me standing there. He reached out to touch me, but I turned to run homewards. Suraya grabbed at his shoulder, pointing at me and repeatedly shouting something in Sindhi.

He jerked himself from her grip and staggered towards me, shouting back at her, a crazed look in his eyes. The neighbours were all emerging from their *logies*. "What's she saying?" I shouted. "Somebody – can somebody please tell me what she's saying?"

I searched the faces around me. One woman came up to me. "She's saying, 'Stop now! Stop it! I will tell Shanti – I will tell her.'"

The tears came then, and I ran towards my *logie* while he chased after me.

"Shanti, wait! Slow down!" he was shouting. But I didn't. I ran on, crashing into my shack, trying to slam the door behind me. He was too fast, lodging himself in the doorway, holding his head in his hands.

"Musta – I do not want to know. Do not tell me." I was gasping for breath.

"Shanti – I have to tell you—"

"Are you deaf?" I screamed. "I don't want to know, Musta! I am not ready to hear it!"

"Shanti – hate me if you must, but it is better that the truth comes out. I have lied for too long."

"I know already, Musta – deep down, I have known for months about you and Suraya. I have suspected ever since she came here!"

"No, Shanti. That's not it—"

"Then what is it, Musta? Do you imagine that I'm so blind I cannot see what has been going on here?"

"I am not having an affair with Suraya!" His voice diminished to little more than a whisper. "Suraya is related to … the woman I am … married to."

"No. No, Mustafa …" I shook my head. "Married? You, Mustafa? You … are a married man?"

Shame clouded his face. "Yes, Shanti. I have been married … for twelve years."

"You were married before you came here?"

"Yes."

"And what does Suraya have to do with all of this?"

He was quiet.

"Tell me more – I demand to know more!"

"I married a woman called Amarah from my city. That is how I know Suraya. She is Amarah's cousin. She recognised me when she saw me here with you."

It all began to fall into place.

"At first, Suraya thought you knew … and I let her believe it."

"Musta, you let her believe that I was with you even though I knew about your wife in India? What must she have thought of me?"

"Well, she thought nothing of it at first because she assumed Amarah knew about you. Where I come from, men often take more than one wife. But when she found out Amarah knew nothing and had not given her blessing, Suraya got very angry and she threatened to tell you."

"So, you have duped both your wife and me for all this time!"

"Shanti, I have no explanation except that I am in love with you—"

"As you are with your wife?"

"Shanti – it was never my intention to hurt you. You know how deeply I love you. I was afraid that if you knew …"

"I don't care about your supposed feelings for me! Tell me about your wife – the one you neglected to mention when I asked you about your family. You haven't been working to save your father's land! You've been sending money home to her!"

"That's not true – I send money home to my father, and he makes sure she is catered for. But you have to understand, Shanti, it was an arranged marriage – not a love marriage. My parents found her for me, and I went ahead with it because they wanted us to marry."

"Is she beautiful, Mustafa? Does she look like Suraya?"

"What difference does that make?"

"It makes a difference to me!" I screamed. "Is she beautiful and light-skinned, and are you the envy of all the men in Sindh?"

He was silent.

"*Tell me!*"

"She looks like Suraya. But it's irrelevant. I respect her, but I do not love her. I love you. In marrying her, I fulfilled my parents' wishes, not my own."

"Then why do you remain married to her? You are in Port Natal now. You are free to divorce her if you wish."

"It's not so simple, Shanti. There is an added complication."

"What more, Mustafa?"

He stared at me for a moment, then let the words fall from his lips. "There are ... children."

I was stunned.

"You are a father, Mustafa?"

"Yes. I have two girls – eleven-year-old twins."

I launched myself at him. "Liar! You lying bastard! How could you keep this from me? Do you know what you have turned me into? You have turned me into your whore, you filthy, disgusting liar! I hate you! I hate you for what you have done!"

"Please, Shanti – don't say these things!"

"Shut up! Do not tell me what to say! How dare you come here week after week keeping up this lie, pretending to be a man who loves me? How have you been able to live with yourself knowing that you have taken the purest, most sincere love of a woman and thrown it back in her face? I have swallowed your deception like honey. You never deserved my trust! Nor did you ever deserve my love, you deceitful bastard!"

"Shanti—"

I slew his words before they could form. "Do not interrupt me! You had a choice, Mustafa. Do not dare paint yourself as the victim! If you loved me, you would have found a way to break this news to your wife instead of lying to both of us, and hoping your deceit would never be uncovered. You chose to be a coward!"

"Yes, Shanti, you are right!" he suddenly shot back. "I am a coward! Her father was dying. She had nowhere to go. And because I worked for him and he treated me like a son, I made him a stupid promise on his deathbed that I would marry her. It was a promise I regretted the moment I made it. I tried to love her, but I failed. And that's why I ran away – not just to help my father get his land back, but because I couldn't be a proper husband to her. I love my daughters, but even they could sense that I did not love their mother. I left because they are all happier without me."

Mustafa leaned against the wall of my *logie* and sank down. I felt like a small, fractured doll. We sat in silence while I pondered all he had revealed. I could make no sense of it.

"Mustafa," I said, "I want you to leave now. And when you leave this place, remember the Shanti who lay in that soft place on your chest to listen to your heart. Remember the Shanti whose face you wet with your tears when Faizal died. Remember the woman who gave her heart and body to you like a gift. That woman has left. Go with her and never come back. I wish never to set eyes on your face again."

"Shanti – please do not end it like this." He extended his hand towards me.

"Love and betrayal should be strangers to each other, Mustafa. When your time here is done, go back to your family. They need you. I do not. I set off on this journey intending for it to be mine alone. And when I met you, I deviated from everything I had planned. I allowed myself to become caught up in an illusion to alleviate my longing for home. Go, Mustafa. Leave me and never come back. I mean it."

He opened his mouth to speak, but said nothing. He must've seen the resolution in my face, the hardness that was taking hold of my heart. He dragged his bag onto his shoulder, holding onto the doorframe to steady himself before he slipped out. In that moment, he took it all with him: love, light, happiness, my future. I watched him dissolve into the distance. I knew that when I woke up the next day, nothing would be the same. The colour would have drained from everything without Mustafa.

Devi came and put her arms around me while I sobbed.

In the months after that, Mustafa came back so many times, I lost count. He visited, he pleaded, brought flowers and scrawled letters. I didn't have the heart to read them. I floated his flowers on the river and watched the current carry them away. My humiliation was greater than my hurt, worse even than the feeling of shame from all the beatings I'd endured since I'd come here. Mustafa was a thief who had stolen years of my life I could never regain. He had taught me the most bitter lesson of all: love can break you more easily than hate. It wasn't that I didn't mourn him – I pined for him as if he had died. But in time, my heart became calloused. I closed it up, and I made a promise never to let anyone into the chamber where he had lived, ever again.

CHAPTER 21

DEVI SPENT WEEKS, MONTHS EVEN, trying to convince me I had been too hard on Mustafa.

"Shanti, what he did was wrong. He had no right to deceive you. I understand why you are so angry. But some time has passed now. And you are capable of thinking more clearly. He has come here so many times, he has told you how sorry he is. If you gave him another chance, he would spend eternity atoning for what he did."

"Devi, you take his part too easily," I replied. "It was all a deception from the start – who can build a real relationship on that?"

"But Shanti, he was a victim of what all of us have experienced – what you ran away from. Our parents always decide for us, unless we are brave enough to do what you did. But not everyone is. He couldn't face living with his parents' choice and that was why he ran away – to come here and meet the real love of his life. He is still essentially a good man, Shanti. A good man who made a terrible mistake."

"But look at what his mistake has cost me, Devi. He was never mine to begin with. He should never have courted me."

"Ah, Shanti. This ... situation has forced us all to do things we once considered immoral. We don't even know the line between good and bad any more – don't you see how blurred it has become? Think of that before you cast him out for good."

"No. I've made up my mind, Devi. No matter how many times he comes here, or how many times you plead his case, I am not taking him back."

Devi clicked her tongue at me. "You are my best friend, and I love you with all my heart. But you are the most stubborn human being I know. And one day, your stubbornness is going to cost you."

For me, there was no turning back the sundials. Of course, I felt the pain of losing Mustafa deeply – none more so than when I went out into the fields every day without the armour of love that had protected me. But at night, too, the loneliness crept in. At times, I felt like the only human being left in the cosmos, with just the stars for companionship.

But something else changed. And weak as I was at that time, perhaps I attracted it; or perhaps I simply had no strength to resist it.

The first time it happened, I was in such shock that I simply lay inert, unable to understand it. That is all I remember. My memory of it is indistinct as smoke. And yet when I woke the next morning, I knew it had happened – because the evidence was there. Since then, it has happened so often, I have lost count. I routinely drift away in that instant to preserve what is left of me.

I must have been in a state of deep sleep, slipping between dreams when first it slid in, furtive and fierce. The dark invited it. And it came because night promised it the protection of a black veil that hides the sins daylight betrays. My eyes burst open from sleep in panic, and I found myself staring into the blackness of my *logie*

– but I was not alone. There was something in there watching me, waiting for me to move, sensing every breath I drew and exhaled, feeding on the vibrations of my hammering heart. It trailed along the ground, leaving its undulating smudge in the sand, flicking its ticklish tongue against my ankle and hissing all manner of obscenities while it sought the warmth of my blood. It petrified me.

I wanted to fight back, but I remembered I was no longer that bold woman who could once summon a surge of strength to wrestle with the monster, squeeze the life out of it. I am now just pieces of that woman – skin held together with bone, who can do no more than lie sprawled on her mat, paralysed. It slithers faster once it finds no resistance. I have no hope of escape, no Mustafa to protect me. There is only resignation, and me, a spectator in my own body.

The scales graze my skin, the muscular body embraces me too tightly, using my bone to anchor itself, advancing along my leg with a firm grip that establishes its dominance. Its power is infinite. It could drain the life from me if it wanted. On this, the Christian Bible is wrong – I cannot rise up and crush its head under my heel. It is always watching, seeking. It observes us in the fields, seeks out the injured and stalks us while we labour, oblivious to its gaze. It chooses each victim individually, patiently. And in that choosing, it owns us more than ever.

Now, as I lie here, it has explored my body with such diligence and found under my night clothes the perfect spot for its jagged fangs. And once it has pinned me to the dustiness of the ground, the great serpent rises, strikes, punctures with such great force that I recoil. "My God! The pain!" I cry while it deftly injects its venom into my flesh, writhing above me, around me, through me, into me, lost in its trance. My wails are deadened by its expanse. I am gasping for breath. My mind, soaked with its venom, explodes. Unconsciousness rescues me and settles me on a plane where calm returns. I can hear it receding as stealthily as it came in.

But that is only the beginning. Once it has found the path to my door, it visits me often. I am so ashamed, I keep this secret. I am so filthy, I cannot even share it with my best friend. I hide from everyone. And each night, I brace for my serpentine suitor's return. How is it possible that it has not killed me? Perhaps I am a snake charmer, grown immune to its venom, bitten so many times that I live on to make the snake dance for me yet another night. I know the time will come when it will unhinge its jaw and swallow me whole. But before then, there is a night when the moonlight casts one stray beam this way. While it thrusts, I peer upwards to see my predator. Staring back at me are the hateful eyes of my master, Wilson.

CHAPTER 22

AFTER THAT NIGHT, I SAW Wilson's face at every turn. When I toiled, I constantly looked over my shoulder to see if he was watching me. I was afraid to bathe at the river in case he glimpsed me from his house. I never went too far in search of firewood, in case I came upon him among the trees. He was always there, even when he wasn't. Nightfall terrified me most of all. I wanted to run and hide in Devi's shack, but I believed he would find me and punish me – and what if he hurt her, too?

She came to speak to me early one morning, rubbing what little sleep she'd had roughly from her eyes. "Shanti, I know how difficult it's been for you since Mustafa left. But let us speak about it. If your heart is sore, I want to know."

"Devi, I can't …"

"We're becoming strangers to each other. You're quiet and sullen all the time. I don't know what's going on in your head. Tell me!"

"I'm not trying to put distance between us, Devi. Honestly. I just do not have the words to explain what I am feeling."

She nodded. "When you are ready, I am here to listen. You are fading. Do not let what has happened with Mustafa turn you into a ghost."

"It's not Mustafa!" I cut in.

"What then? You can trust me, whatever it is."

I was silent.

"What could be so terrible that you won't tell me?"

"Devi, when the time is right, you will know. Now, let us go to work."

She shook her head and turned away.

How my rapist had changed me. He'd stolen my body, my will, my words. He sucked the air from my lungs and shrank me almost to invisibility. He fed me demeaning words, and I ate them. I had allowed him to chill my deepest friendship and turn my days grey.

Now my body was also changing. The smell of food began to nauseate me. There was a tenderness in my breasts that caused me to loosen my sari blouse. My flat stomach began to take on a subtle roundness. And I felt a strange unlocking of the bones at my pelvis, as though my body was preparing to expand itself. When I worked in the fields, the heat rising from the ground often made me dizzy. If our new *sirdar* wasn't watching, I'd sit down to catch my breath.

I wouldn't be able to keep this a secret for much longer. Soon everyone would know.

A few weeks after I had rebuffed her, Devi came knocking on my door, once again before dawn. I had lit a small fire and was warming my hands at it.

"Come in, Devi," I said, the smoke curling around us. "Close the door. Sit down."

She sat next to me. "Are you ready to tell me, Shanti?"

My voice cracked. "I have wanted to tell you all this time, but I'm so ashamed of what's happened, Devi – of what I invited here, into my *logie* ..."

"Tell me. I'd never judge you, Shanti. Just tell me."

"Devi, have you not seen?" I parted my sari to show her my stomach.

She let out a gasp. "Your courses …" she stuttered, her eyes wide. "Have you not had …?"

"They stopped a while ago."

She grabbed my hand. "But … I don't understand. Mustafa left many months ago."

"It's not Mustafa's, Devi."

"Then … who?" she stared. "I have been at your side. You have been with no one."

"No one you have seen me with, Devi. No one in the daylight hours. He comes at night …"

"He?"

"Our Master Wilson …"

She leapt to her feet and banged her fist against the door.

"No! Damn him! No! That bastard has done it to you, too! I swear to God, if I came in here the night he did this to you and I caught him—"

"Devi – it wasn't just one night. It happened many times. In the early hours of the morning mostly, when I was fast asleep."

"Shanti – I'm sorry. I'm so sorry." She pulled me close. I felt a tremor in her embrace. "Why didn't you scream? Why didn't you call for help? I would've come! Dilip – he would've beaten the life out of Wilson!"

"I don't know what happened to me, Devi. Each time he came, I was frozen. A stupid little girl again. I had no strength to fight back. Something closed my throat and for hours I lay there crippled, until the morning light came, and I had to force myself up for work. I never wanted you to find me in that soiled state. When the first birds began to sing, I would make a fire and boil the water and rub my skin raw. Then I would put on my sari and try to hide the shame underneath. I moved slowly so you would not see I was struggling to walk."

Devi dried my tears with the sash of her sari. "Shanti, this man does not deserve to get away with it! We could report him to the authorities – to the Protector …"

"Devi, it's common knowledge that Wilson tortured women for days in his house while his family was away. If he knew I told you, he'd attack you too. And what will the Protector do? Help me lay a charge? From there, it'll go to court where I'll be humiliated as a loose woman who seduced him, while all his powerful friends come to sing his praises. Devi, you saw what happened with Faizal – I don't stand a chance against Wilson in court."

She sank down. "You didn't deserve this. This shame you are carrying – it is not right, Shanti. This is *his* shame." She looked me in the eye. "I don't want you to be afraid any more. Now that you have told me, we can handle this together."

Speaking to Devi brought me great relief. I felt foolish for not having told her earlier. She began nursing me back to health, and ensured I was hardly ever alone. At times, recalling how Wilson had defiled me, I would break into a panic, and Devi was always there to calm and reassure me. "Get it out of your head that you invited him in, Shanti – you and all the other women he's done this to. Since when is cutting cane an invitation for rape?"

We agreed I would sleep in her *logie* at night until I felt brave enough to return to mine.

"Devi," I confessed one night, "I am supposed to be preparing to be a mother. But I can't stop thinking that my body has become a home for this wicked man's child. Sometimes I wish I could cut it out of me!"

"Shanti, you cannot be blamed for feeling this way. This is not how children are meant to be conceived. But give it some time. The baby's father may be the vilest human being for miles around, but babies are innocent beings. They do not choose how they come into this life. Try to sleep now."

In the coming weeks, as my belly rose, I saw some of the other women eyeing me with pity. Many of their pregnancies had also been Wilson's doing. Most of them worked up till the day they gave birth, and returned to the fields shortly afterwards, or their pay was docked. Some wrapped their infants up and brought them to the fields, placing the little ones on the ground close to where they were working. And that was how they grew up, like rats between the stalks, crawling about, grabbing clumps of dirt in their chubby fists. If the *sirdar* didn't mind, they could teeth on a small piece of cane they clutched jealously, oblivious to the life into which they'd been born. Children of sugarcane, robbed of their juvenile joys, conditioned to cry quietly, to embrace their inheritance of poverty and labour. Adults-too-soon in small bodies that would be put to work as soon as Wilson desired it – many of them straddling his bloodline and ours. But how their mothers loved them, doted on them. I too loved the child growing inside me, but most of all, I was afraid for him.

One particularly hot day while Devi was taking her lunch rations, I stayed in the field and found a tree to sit under. I had no desire to eat despite Devi's insistence that I keep my strength up. As I settled down, I saw a slender young woman approaching me. She could not have been more than twenty years old. Her skin was dark and her hair was neatly tied in a bun.

"*Vanakum*," she said, putting her hands together. I replied with the same greeting.

"Why are you not eating?" she asked.

"I am not hungry," I replied.

"Nor am I – too hot today," she said. "My name is Kamla." She sat beside me, crossing her legs.

"I am Shanti."

"Shanti. A very beautiful name," she said. "You are from the Madras Presidency?"

"Yes, Vākkuṟuti – close to Madras."

"Ah, I am from Madras myself." She paused, her eyes flitting over my swollen belly. "How are you feeling these days?"

"I suppose I am coping … under the circumstances."

"When is your baby due?"

"In about four months …" I paused. "Why are you asking me these questions?"

"I am sorry – I don't mean to be rude. I was just trying to … it's just that I have so many friends this has happened to," she said. "It was the last thing they wanted, but …"

I was slightly taken aback by her boldness. But I decided to be honest. "Yes, it is difficult. It can never be easy having a child in a place like this. But it's done now – there is no reversing it."

She smiled. "Don't worry – with the support of your child's father—"

"There will be no support from my child's father," I cut in.

"No support?" She gazed down at her hands. "Shanti, I did not come here to pry. Some women get through this and they manage to raise their babies in the Colony, difficult as it is. But it is not for everyone. Sometimes the hardship of raising a child here is too much. An extra mouth to feed. To keep free of disease and danger on this plantation."

"What other choice do mothers have, Kamla? It is their duty to keep their children alive and happy."

"That's not true, Shanti!" Kamla realised her words had come out too sharply, and she lowered her voice. "I mean … some women choose not to go through with it. There are ways. It costs a little bit of money. But some think it is the merciful thing to do. You save a young soul from the treachery of these fields. This is no place for children – here in the fields or in the *logies*, where many children spend all day without their parents. Do you see these little ones with their blackened faces crawling about in the dirt? What life can they expect to have? One day, you will be forced to watch while your child is beaten and humiliated before your eyes—"

"Wait, Kamla! What do you mean, some women don't go through with it? How could they possibly undo it?"

"Well, there is no way of undoing it, of course, but there are ways of … ending it. There are special herbs you can take. There are healers who specialise in this. My aunt is a healer. For a small sum, she helps many women in your condition."

"Ah, for a small sum … now I understand. Thank you, Kamla, but I must get back to work. Lunchtime is almost over."

"I wish you the best, Shanti," she said, getting to her feet. "I am sure you will make a wonderful mother." She put her hands together and hurried away.

I slowly pulled myself up and trudged back to the row I had been hoeing. It was obvious Kamla was yet another predator on this plantation, trying to trick me into enriching her aunt.

And yet her words stayed with me. They were both terrifying and comforting. Of course I was capable of loving a child. And as Devi had rightly said, all children were born innocent and could not be blamed for the actions of their fathers. But how would I protect and raise a baby on this plantation? Where would I leave the child when I went out to work? This was the Colony of Natal, where loving someone was not enough to guarantee their protection from the ills of this place.

I thought of one of the women here who had lost her little boy, Siva – a sweet child of about six or seven, who had grown up between the furrows. He had died from catching a chill that became pneumonia while he was being bathed outside in winter, even though his mother had begged for a warm place to bathe him. I used to wash alongside them when she was bathing him, and I remembered his tiny, jutting bones and how he cried when the icy water hit his skin. The balance of life and death was so delicate for little ones in this place.

The more I thought about Siva, the more Kamla's words began to take root in my mind. I didn't say a word to Devi about this. I wanted to think about it at length before I made any decision. I spent night after night wide awake, tortured by the thought of my unborn baby and the uncertain future facing us both. I kept asking myself: what is the right thing, the moral thing to do? But when I searched for the answer, I realised morality had long deserted us on the plantations.

Devi remained a great source of comfort to me. But I could tell she was already pre-empting the outcome. She often said how much joy this child would bring me, after all the disappointments in my life. And as we sat in the dusty twilight one chilly evening, she said, "Shanti, how lucky you are. In a very short time, you will be holding a part of you in your arms, nursing him. You will watch him grow and walk and speak and change until he is a young man who can stand on his own. How special that is."

I forced a smile.

"I know he isn't entering this life through the kindest portal," she said. "But you'll see – he will overcome it in time."

"Devi, I'm trying my best to be positive. But I am also thinking of what it'll mean to be the child of a *coolie* in Port Natal. Yes, he will probably have a lighter skin than mine, but no one will care that he's also Wilson's child. He will only be seen as mine. And that will dictate his life – no proper home, no good food, rags for clothes, not even a father to acknowledge him. Is it really fair for me to bring a little human being into the world to suffer? I see no joy in his future. I only see my selfishness in wanting to bring him into the world."

She shook her head. "No, Shanti. Don't think of it in that way. Once he is born, you'll find a way to feed him and clothe him, and make sure he is taken care of. We are all here to help you."

"Thank you – I know I can count on your support, but ultimately it will fall to me as his mother to take responsibility for him. I want to tell you something, Devi, and I'm going to ask that you hear me out even if you don't like what I am saying."

She held still for a moment, then nodded.

"I spoke to Kamla a few weeks ago—"

"Kamla, which Kamla? Oh, don't tell me – the one whose aunt is some kind of—"

"You know her?"

"I have seen her in the fields. I've never spoken to her, but I know she has ... arranged certain things for some women. But—"

"Devi, she spoke to me. She reminded me that this is my choice and—"

"No, Shanti! What are you saying? You actually listened to her? To a stranger who was telling you to put an end to this miracle growing in your body?"

"She didn't tell me to put an end to it, Devi. She just suggested that there are options – choices one can make. This wasn't my choice, Devi. Wilson did this to me. Don't I at least deserve the choice of whether I want to see it through or not?"

"Shanti," she sighed, "it *is* your choice. But have you thought that perhaps this was what God intended? Do you know how many offerings I took to the temple, how many concoctions I drank to be able to have a child when I was married? Nothing worked! It wasn't meant to be. But I believe in my heart that your child is meant to be. Do not do this. Don't even think about it!"

"Devi, please do not speak to me of God. Where was God when Mustafa was lying to me? Where was he when Rangassamy was beating me, or Wilson was raping me? I'd be very surprised if God even remembers who I am."

"It's natural to feel like this, Shanti. I think I would probably feel the same way. But inside your belly is a soul passing through time. He needs to find his way, and you cannot prevent that. You cannot stop him from reincarnating into this body to learn the lessons he is supposed to learn until he reaches *Nirvana*. Shanti, some things are out of our hands."

I knew Devi meant well, but on this matter, we were not of the same mind. I thought of the many children I had encountered on my journey to Port Natal. Beautiful Sandhya, born on the arduous march to Madras. Selvaraj, cruelly separated from his uncle Rajandran. Angammah's children, who were taken from her before I even knew her. And then I thought again of little Siva, who had died on this plantation while his mother risked a beating for staying away from the fields to nurse him until his last wheezing breath. I had been among the gathered crowd when Dilip had lifted Siva's tiny frame onto the pyre and lit the flame. I had been there while the boy lay on that pile of burning sticks, falling to pieces bit by bit – his smile, his glowing eyes and spiky hair, his spindly legs all melting amid his mother's loud wailing, until he was no more than dark ash and gritty bone.

I shook my head. "I cannot do it, Devi. I cannot do it."

Her face fell, but she nodded.

"Shanti, you are right. This is your choice. You must do what you believe is needed, and I will be there to hold your hand," she said, hiding her tears. She rose and walked away.

CHAPTER 23

"PUT ON YOUR SHOES, SHANTI. The road we are travelling is bound to be rough," Devi tells me.

"No, Devi," I say. "No shoes for me."

Devi shakes her head. She thinks I am punishing myself. But I am simply numb, equally immune to Port Natal's drenching rain or the stab of its sun on my face. Today, I long for some small sensation – the jaggedness of stones against my bare soles, the baptism of a cool puddle to reawaken me.

It's a long, unfamiliar road to the mill. Kamla has drawn a rudimentary map and warned us to be there well before dark, because the journey home is potentially treacherous at nightfall, especially for me in my condition. Devi and I avoid conversation. I am past the point of persuasion. She is sapped from trying to convince me to change my mind. And although the shadows of two lonely figures fall on that path, fear is our silent third companion.

Devi surveys the ground before us. She is walking ahead of me because the weight of the baby has made me unsteady on my feet. My breathing becomes heavier as the terrain grows more rugged. I look ahead to the path as it tapers and pierces the distance. How I'd wished this day away when I opened my eyes this morning. But the hours have elongated instead. We stop briefly under the shade of a fever tree for me to catch my breath, and I rest against its trunk, admiring its yellowed bark. Then I see one of its branches hanging withered and blackened while the rest of the tree thrives. Nature knows best of all that sacrifices must sometimes be made for survival.

We rejoin the path and after trudging for what feels like hours, Devi points out the mill.

"I think that's it, Shanti – that building with the brown roof. Let's find another path to get down there," she says, panting.

Devi finds a route, takes my hand and leads me onto it. The grass is flattened from the steady current of footsteps. I imagine the millers hurrying to bake bread, the sinners like me rushing to rid themselves of bad luck and babies. The path becomes stony. There are thorns here. I feel a jab and look down to see a small, smudged trail of scarlet droplets forming where my feet are landing.

Devi pauses to catch her breath. "Shanti, see the settlement just below this hill?" She points to a row of *logies* lined up below us. "She must be there. We are close now." She wipes away the small beads of sweat gathering above her lip and squints into the sun to judge the time of day. She speeds up a little, and I know I should pick up my pace. "It's downhill from here," she says. "But you need to hold onto me. Take extra care where you place your feet. There are many loose stones on this path." As we descend, she first holds my hand, then grabs my arm to steady me. I am surprised by the firmness of her grip. And once we are on even ground, it is still some time before she lets go.

We are so close, I can now feel dread take a hold of me. Part of me wants to ask Devi to turn back. I know she'd gladly agree. But when I think of the alternative, I know this is not an option. Devi is now making enquiries, chatting to labourers standing outside their shacks, passing the time on this Saturday afternoon. Some children are running around, splashing each other with the muddy remnants of the past week's rains. I shut out the sounds of their happy noise. I want this to be over with. I want it to have shrunk into a distant memory. The very act of coming here, of stepping outside our plantation and walking all this way to enlist the aid of a stranger, frightens me.

And then she emerges. Aunty Chinnamah. She is sturdy, slightly corpulent and exudes warmth. Yet beneath her comeliness I see traces of anguish, as if the pain of all who have come here seeking her wisdom has been etched into her. Her greying hair is tied in a loose bun at the nape of her neck. When she says, "Come in," I go obediently. I hold Devi's hand and am led into Chinnamah's *logie*, where the pungent smells of medicine and other strange herbs fill the air.

There is an African man sitting at the back, brewing some strong-smelling tea over a small fire in the corner. He pours some of it into a bowl and brings it to Chinnamah, patiently holding it to her mouth, while she slurps gently. He smiles, satisfied when she has taken the last sip. She seems invigorated by the drink, and smiles back at him.

The smells in here are overpowering. There are bottles everywhere – full of herbs, roots, powders, liquids, of varying colours and consistencies. Her *logie* is bigger than the others around it, but appears chokingly small, filled with all these numinous substances. We women sit on the ground in a triangle. Chinnamah smiles at me, and I ease a little.

Devi leans over. "Shanti, do you want me to tell her?"

"Thanks, Devi. I will speak."

But the old lady overhears us speaking English and responds in the same language, with a heavy Tamil accent. "Tell me 'ow I can 'elp you, child."

"Aunty ... I am in trouble."

"What trouble?" she asks, but I sense she already knows.

"My master – he ..."

"Ah, your master – the one from Wilson's farm, no? 'E has made connection with you."

"Yes, he has been coming into my *logie* at night and ..."

"'E has put baby in you."

I nod vigorously.

Chinnamah looks over at Devi, then turns to me. "Why you left it so late, child? This baby almost ready to be born."

"She wanted to do the right thing, Aunty," Devi says. "It's taken her time to decide."

"So sorry, my child," she says. "This man making connection with everyone. So many girls coming here, same story. 'Ow many times he came to you?"

"Often, Aunty. I don't know for certain. I lost count after three weeks."

"Don't worry. I 'eard he gets tired of one girl easily. Soon he gonna leave you and look for one 'nother girl. And so violent 'e is! My friend was one *ayah* in 'is 'ouse, looking after 'is children. She told me 'e's only scolding 'is children, 'itting 'is wife. Sometimes you see their big 'ouse. You think, so rich they are, so poor I am. But sometimes the wife and children suff'ring same way inside."

Devi and I look at each other. So Wilson hasn't been saving his violence for us alone.

"One thing I must aks you, child. So far you come with your pregnancy. One month or less, you gonna have this baby. You sure, you really sure you wanna do this?"

"Yes, Aunty – I'm sure ..."

"I'm only telling 'cos some girls, they fine after the baby is gone.

They carrying on. But some girls, they only crying, crying after. They wishing they kept the baby and too late it is. That's why I'm telling hall the girls coming 'ere with same problem: babies – they like sugarcane. 'Ow you sweating when you plant that thing and you 'oeing the 'ard ground! Your blood falling in the soil when they beating you. Sometimes rain come, sometimes you watering the cane with your own salty tears. But, when you 'arvesting that sugarcane and the people tasting it, so sweet it is. No one knows 'ow it came way so sweet after all your suff'ring. What it means? It means good can come from hevil." She pauses. "You got no 'usband, child?"

I shake my head.

"Family? No mother, no father?"

"Not here, Aunty. Only my friend, Devi, here."

"Ah, she your friend? I was thinking you two twins." She laughs softly. Then her expression changes to one of seriousness. "Child, this my 'usband, Mzilikazi. He threw bones for you 'cos 'e knew you was coming." She turns to him, and he points to a decorative cloth on which a few small animal bones lie scattered. "'E aksed your ancestors nicely must take the baby back. They told 'im what must do. They saying no 'erbs. Too late it is for that. Only one thing can 'elp you so late. You only take 'erbs after to cleanse."

The old woman pulls herself up and walks over to the doorway of her *logie*. She calls out to one of the children playing outside, and the little boy comes running to her.

"You one big show-off!" she says to him, affectionately pinching his cheek. "Now you must show me and this ladies 'ow brave you gone, now you older. You know that big paw-paw tree on the 'ill? Climb up. Get me one nice green paw-paw from the top. Don't come back with one ripe one, you 'ear? Go quickly now!"

The boy scampers off eagerly.

Chinnamah turns back to us. "You must hunderstand, child,

you taking one chance with this. With some womens, it's working, with other womens, it's not. We only trying, trying, and we 'ope you gonna be o'right. Wait now. 'E's coming."

We sit in silence, listening to the couple speaking an odd, mixed-up language called Fanagalo we occasionally hear on the plantation, and laughing softly.

The boy soon returns, panting. "Aunty, Aunty – I got it! Me and my friend – we were climbing to see who was the fastest and I got here first. I beat him!"

He delivers the fruit into her hands. She turns it over, pleased with him. "Eh, you one clever boy! Now go back and play."

She presents it to me. "I'm giving you one green paw-paw, child. That's all I can do. Skin it and eat at least 'alf. Very bitter it is. I won' lie – you gonna get very sick. Maybe you even gonna get one fever and bad dreams and vomit. But if you eat it, your body gonna struggle to 'old that baby. That baby gonna come out."

Her husband passes her some herbs bound into a large leaf. "Hafter, you must use 'erbs. Mix with water and drink to cleanse you, o'right?"

I nod. "Thank you, Aunty. Uncle, thank you," we say. Devi pulls out a handkerchief into which we have knotted several coins. Chinnamah counts them and thrusts them into her sari blouse.

"Get better, my child," she says as we leave, her husband raising his hand to wave goodbye.

I take the herbs. The paw-paw is surprisingly heavy. Devi takes it from me.

As we walk home, I think about what we – I – have just done. It has been an unearthly experience in that *logie* with the medicine man and woman – a couple dispensing hope, comfort and death, their web of aromatic bottles piled high.

"They are an unusual couple. But it's clear they love each other," I muse.

"True that," says Devi. "I have seen a few like them, but never a married couple."

"I thought it odd at first, Devi, but I suppose they are both healers. Perhaps some mystic force brought them together."

"Did you see how they look at each other, Shanti? He stares directly into her eyes, and she into his. There is no British man telling them how to feel about each other."

I smile ruefully. "They are at least free from the plantations, where our masters shout at the Africans and tell them we are better than them – then call us good-for-nothings, and promise they'll replace us with Africans if we don't work harder."

"The irony is, who do we hate for it, Shanti? Not the British who have done this to us. We have begun to hate one another instead."

This is all the conversation we manage on the way back, the gravity of what we have set in motion weighing heavily on us both. We trudge on until the sun has turned a burnt orange and is sagging low in the sky. When we reach my *logie*, sweating and out of breath, we part ways.

"Thank you," I say to Devi.

"Call me when you need me," she replies.

I take the paw-paw inside, lay it in an enamel bowl, and stare at it for a long time. I run my hands over its surface. It is almost the colour of jade, smooth but for a few blemishes here and there.

I run my hand over my rotund belly. "Baby, I'm sorry. I'm so sorry. I do love you, but I can't care for you. I can't provide for you as a mother should. And as for your father – he is a vicious man who will not even admit you are his. That is why I can't let you grow any bigger inside me. And I can't bring you out into this world. It's too horrible a place for you. There is so much hatred, so much brutality. And if I allow you to grow up here, they will hurt you too. Because I love you, I cannot be your gateway to suffering. I wish to send you to another life where you will be loved and cherished, and the old man assures me my ancestors will take you there. So please – please go gently with them and forgive me for what I am about to do."

I reach for a knife, feeling like an executioner as I skin the large fruit. It glistens, inviting me to take that first bite. I remember the many ripe paw-paws I shared with Thirna as a child, sweet and energising. This fruit in my hands is an instrument of death. I gouge out the first piece and hold it to my lips. I close my eyes and shove it into my mouth. My tongue burns from its acidity. I crush it between my teeth and swallow. It slides down my throat in a slimy trail. I tear off piece after piece with both hands, shoving, choking, swallowing, retching, until I feel it burn my innards.

My stomach begins to churn. I break into a sweat and a wave of nausea hits me. Dizziness takes hold, and although I am grabbing at objects around me, trying to steady myself, the world is spinning and slips out of my grasp. *I must call Devi*, I keep thinking. But something heavy is hammering me into the ground. I feel its full weight now spreading through my chest, into my limbs, paralysing my tongue. Then it tears at my stomach, doubling me over. My legs give way and I collapse, writhing. And then, as the edges of my vision begin to blur, I think I have seen something. Is it Devi coming forward to help me? Is she real or an apparition? I think someone is clutching at me, embracing me, talking to me. But there is a furious rushing in my ears, like the sound of the sea during a storm. And when I try to force my eyes open, it seems I've been beaten and washed onto some strange shore where the gloom presses upon me. There is something invading me, a hand reaching inside to wrench out my entrails. My lungs are so shrunken, I can barely squeeze any breath into them. And when I look up, there is a monster playing on the rocks, like the tigers at Muharram. I try to flee, but it lunges towards me and savages me, eating my intestines. It carries me, bleeding, through a mass of wet foam into the swell, bashing me against those jagged rock formations, and into deep dark waters that burn my nostrils. I flail and kick, but it holds me fast and I know I am about to drown.

"Deviiii!" I screech. "Deviiii, come now!"

But when she comes, it is not my friend. Her face and body appear so large, so distorted that I fight, break free and swim away. Her hands are spindly, liquid tentacles that try to grab me. And when she cannot, she sends the shadows after me. They spiral through the water, racing after me, taunting me, calling to me to come back. Though weakened, I swim hard and suddenly catch sight of the shore. Dilip is there, lighting a fire on the beach. I tread water and call out to him, "Dilip, Dilip, save me – they are after me!" But he seems not to hear me. And as I swim toward the beach and try to crawl out of the water, my cheek chafing against the stinging sand, I see he is building a pyre, and has lain a baby girl on top of it. "Stop!" I scream. "That's my baby! Dilip, stop! I have made a mistake! Don't set it alight!" But he is deaf to me. He lights the flame, sets the pyre alight, and begins walking away. No matter how hard I try to drag myself towards it, every muscle fails me. I claw and claw at the sand until I lie, breathless and spent, the surf lapping at my feet and plumes of smoke dancing in the air above my head. "I am so sorry, baby. I wanted to save you," I whisper again and again. The sky darkens and I feel myself being pulled out to sea and sinking peacefully into the depths.

The morning light wakes me, and birdsong guides me out of my stupor. It takes me a few moments to orientate myself. I open my eyes and draw in deep, slow breaths. Now I remember everything. The long walk to the mill with Devi. Chinnamah and her husband. The green paw-paw.

I use my arms to hoist myself up gingerly and examine the stained, damp ground beneath me. It is done. My baby is blood. I hear footsteps approaching. Perhaps it is the *sirdar* coming to ask me to work on my rest day. But the door of my *logie* creaks open and light falls on Devi's angelic face. She rushes in and throws her arms around me. I fall into them and weep.

CHAPTER 24

IN THE WAKE OF THAT day and night, I could not have been more grateful for the tedium and regularity of plantation life, or its cyclical, predictable nature. There was little variation to the ritual of growing sugarcane; and the repetitiveness of this work, although it made demands on my recovering body, allowed my mind some measure of space to process the painful events of the previous weeks. Mostly, I tried to make sense of my decision, silently arguing with myself like a dogged barrister, reaching the same conclusion each time: I had made the most unselfish choice for my child under the circumstances.

But even as my stomach began to flatten out, I sometimes felt a cavern beneath my heart, where my baby used to be. And there were moments when my hands instinctively searched the dome under which she'd briefly lived before I remembered she was gone. I treasured the silence of the plantation at night, but even that was occasionally broken by the cries of an infant, causing me to sit bolt upright. But I couldn't be sure they were any more real than the fleeting images in my mind's eye of minute limbs I had never touched, or the subtle flutter of a small heart beneath my own.

When I struggled to reconcile my head and heart, I forced myself to think of Devi, who had seen me through a choice she could not herself justify. I wondered what it must have been like to find me in such a state that morning, to put her own hand, like an illusionist, to the work of making everything disappear, erasing the vestiges of what had happened. For hours I had cried, slept and woken in turn, and after nightfall when I gazed over to the side of my *logie*, Devi was still there. Exhaustion had taken her and she was lying on the ground, awkwardly curled, softly snoring, still in the sari she had worn that morning. In that moment, it was impossible to love anyone more than I did her.

In the ensuing days, other friends came to me too, lovingly, reassuringly, sensing what had happened. There was no hiding it in a place like this. They held my hands and told me I would get over it in time. But although I appreciated their sincere words, they brought me little comfort. Instead, I found myself yearning for my family – more than I had ever done since coming to the plantation. Where that longing came from, I do not know. Perhaps I was looking for the consolation of a mother and father, sisters who would hold me close, stroke my hair and remind me of how much they loved me, just enough to sustain me through this precarious life I was leading. These thoughts pulled me back to Vākkuṟuti, reviving strong memories of my life there. I ached for news of my family.

It was only a few months later that it came. One Sunday, as I returned from fetching firewood, I saw a tall figure at my door. I drew closer, looked into the young man's eyes, and immediately recognised the mischievous spark I had last seen many moons ago in Vākkuṟuti's spice shop. I rushed up to him, almost knocking him off his feet. "Bilal, is it you? Is it really you? How glad I am to see you!"

He returned my embrace. His sharp features had remained so,

his nose even pointier than before. He had managed to discipline his spiky hair, but still flashed me that warm smile which had greeted me each time I'd set foot in Ramdeen's shop.

"It was not so long ago that you were wreaking havoc in Ramdeen's shop! Now you've shot up – and you've finally made it to Port Natal, Bilal!"

He nodded shyly. "Yes, Shanti – you should not be so shocked to see me here. You know how long I'd dreamt of this. I pestered Ramdeen every day for years, and now that I'm sixteen-turning-seventeen, I finally persuaded him to send me here!" he laughed.

I offered him something to eat, which he gladly accepted. "Tell me, where are you working?

"On a tea plantation in Verulam."

"Well, then, you have come a long way to visit me!"

He looked slightly guilty. "Shanti, I feel bad. I've already been here a few months, and I put off this visit for too long."

"That doesn't matter Bilal – you're here now. It's so kind of you to visit me."

"It took me a little while to find you, Shanti, but you know, you mention a name here, you pick up a clue there, and you get to know where people are. It was important for me to come and see you."

"I appreciate that, Bilal."

He looked around for a moment. "So, you're all alone. You know, when I got here, I half-expected a man to open the door and knock my teeth out when I asked for you! Are you not married yet?"

I laughed. "No, Bilal! I do not think I'm destined for marriage."

"Then we still have a lot in common," he chuckled.

"How is your family?" I asked.

"Oh, they're as well as one could hope for, Shanti. I send a little bit of money home every month, which helps them – but it's not the same as being there. My mother is getting old and she is struggling to look after my father these days."

"I'm sure you miss them terribly. But how do you find it here?"

"Disappointing, of course. It's nothing like the vision of my twelve-year-old dreams. But before I left, I sat Ramdeen down and I put some serious questions to him about life here. That's how I came to know about some of these hardships before I embarked."

"Ramdeen told you the truth about Port Natal? Many of us wouldn't even be here if he had been honest with us."

"That's true, Shanti. When you left, Ramdeen was at the height of his recruitment success. He was a ruthless bastard back then. But hard as it might be to believe, Ramdeen is not the same man who sent you here. Remember how he used to strut around like an overfed peacock?" We both giggled.

"Well, he's changed a lot, Shanti. You won't believe – he actually fell in love with one of his recruits from a neighbouring village."

My eyes grew wide. "Ramdeen in love?"

"Yes, ma'am! He fell head over heels in love with her and begged her not to go to Port Natal. She finally agreed, and they got married."

"Well, who would've thought a woman could melt that heart of stone?"

"I certainly didn't, Shanti. For years, I hated him. He was so horrible to me. He took advantage of the fact that my father was a cripple and my mother was forced to send me to work. But this woman changed him. She was a nice person, you know. Humble, quiet lady. But he listened to her. He softened a bit. He slowly stopped shouting at me and hitting me, and we parted on fairly good terms."

Bilal finished his first helping of rice, and I offered him another bowl, which he gratefully accepted.

"You know, Shanti," he continued, "for all those years, Ramdeen was just selling people to the British – like spices. And his heart became hard. He didn't think of any of them, even you, as a human being. You were all just his ticket to wealth. I think that when he met his wife, he realised: these are not things. They are people. They are suffering, and maybe I'm partly responsible. And he stopped. He gave up being an *arkati*. He made enough money to expand his shop, and he's back behind that counter selling spices."

"And his wife?"

"Ah, that's the sad part. She was a sickly lady, and she died not so long ago."

"That is sad."

"You know what the older people in the village said, Shanti? They said she was the incarnation of a deity who came to Vākkuṟuti to change Ramdeen, and when her task was complete, she left."

I smiled at that. It had been a long time since I'd heard a story like that from home.

I waited till Bilal had finished his meal, but could hold back no longer. "I am almost too afraid to ask. But every day I think of my parents and sisters. I imagine how angry they are at me for what I did – for the way I left. What happened when they found out I was gone?"

"Shanti, first let me tell you—"

"No, Bilal, please – I need to know how they reacted. What happened right after I left?"

"All right – as you wish." He took a deep breath.

"Well, as I remember it, your parents woke up the following morning to find you missing. They searched everywhere: in the streets, in the neighbours' homes, at the lakes. The search went on for days. The watchmen were called in. Your mother was frantic. She was sure you'd been abducted. But your father kept on saying some of your clothes were gone, and he insisted you must have run away. But he couldn't say why."

"You must've realised, Bilal ..."

"Yes, I knew. I knew immediately. I went over our conversation in my head. I remembered all the questions you'd asked, and I was convinced Ramdeen had arranged for you to go. But I didn't say anything. I was too scared to ask Ramdeen at that time. I thought of telling your mother, but I knew even if I did, she wouldn't listen to me. She insisted someone had taken you in the night. She pointed a finger at Ramdeen. She said there were rumours that he was kidnapping children. And she wanted the watchmen to question him. But you know he always did a good job of covering his tracks. There was no evidence to prove he was involved. Your mother, Shanti – she even went out searching with the watchmen herself, down overgrown paths and old wells, shouting your name. And no matter what your father said, she defended you till the very day she d—"

Bilal stopped in mid-sentence.

"What? She what? She died? She's *dead*? My mother is dead, Bilal?"

He stuttered, "Oh, God, Shanti, I'm sorry ... I didn't mean to ... not that way. I'm so sorry."

"Is my mother *dead*? Tell me, Bilal!"

He put his head down. "Yes, Shanti. It happened about nine months ago. Her heart gave in. And your father ... he was ..."

"My father? He survived?"

"Oh, Shanti – this is so hard. Yes. No! I mean he only survived for a short time, but he pined for her ... and then ..."

"Bilal, no! When I left they were all right! My mother ... she was getting better. My father – my father was in good health. It's not possible ... I don't understand how ..."

"Shanti." He put a hand on my shoulder and guided me to my mat. He settled beside me. "Take a breath. No, breathe deeply, slowly. I know what I have told you has come as a shock." He put his arm around me, as I pressed my head into my hands. "I'm sorry I had to be the one to tell you. I went over and over it in my head – how I would break it to you – but there just didn't seem a right way to do it. I knew you'd struggle to accept it. You just need time to absorb it."

My voice broke. "I imagined they had time, Bilal. I didn't think it would run out so quickly."

"Shanti, it's been almost five years since you left. Now that I am on this side, I realise that each day we are here, our parents are growing older and frailer. We like to remember them as they were when they were young, but time doesn't stand still for any of us."

I didn't respond. I couldn't gather my thoughts into a coherent sentence. We just sat there for a long time – me, emotionless, staring straight ahead, and Bilal with his arm around me – as the slow acceptance of my parents' deaths seeped into me and settled there. After a while, I began to speak again, and he allowed me my tears, my anger with myself, and with my parents for leaving me.

I confessed that I could never forgive myself for certain choices I had made. "Bilal, I made a promise to my mother that I would marry my cousin, Muthan, but I was a coward. I couldn't go through with it. I feared marriage as some fear a deadly disease. That was why I ran away. I went to Ramdeen and I begged him to help me. I didn't even say goodbye to my parents. They had no idea it was my last night under their roof. I crept out while they were sleeping …"

I expected Bilal to judge my choices, but he only said, "Sometimes we are forced to choose, Shanti, even though we may not want to. It seems to me you have been torturing yourself with this since you left. When I came here today, I did not recognise you at first. You look exhausted – so much older than you should. Have you not punished yourself enough, Shanti? Is it not enough suffering for that one mistake that you made? It is time you forgave yourself. Your parents forgave you."

"How do you know, Bilal? How do you know they forgave me?"

"Because your mother had always shown great kindness and generosity to my family. There were many times over the years when we would all have gone hungry if it weren't for her. And when your mother became ill, mine began to visit her often, and they became very close toward the end. She often took me along with her. My mother sat beside your mother almost every day before she died. And your mother poured out her heart. She spoke of you every day. She recalled all sorts of things that had happened to you as a child – the scoldings you got, how you used to tease poor Thirna, how when you started crawling you'd often pick up chillies, suck them, and begin to cry at the top of your voice!"

"That is true!" I laughed through my tears.

"One of her favourite stories was about how you got your name. She said it was not a very common name for a Tamil child. After you were born, the priest apparently told them your name was to begin with the letter 'S'. Your father had a long list of names, but your mother went to the temple to pray one day, and she overheard a woman there praying a most wonderful prayer for peace."

"I think I remember that prayer, Bilal: a Vedic chant she used to make me repeat. *Lead me from the unreal to the real. Lead me from darkness to light. Lead me from death to immortality. May there be peace everywhere. Shanti, shanti aum.* She was a good mother to me, Bilal. She was the gentlest, most passive—"

"Are you sure?" he interjected.

"Of course. My father, he could put up a fight, but not my mother."

"Well, perhaps something changed after you left. I was there on the day, just a few weeks before your *Ama* passed, when Ramdeen arrived at your house, wracked with guilt over what he'd done. He knelt before your mother and he told her the truth. I heard him beg her forgiveness. But your mother screamed at him. She called him a host of terrible names. She cursed his descendants and told him to get out. He got up and left, almost at a run. I'd never seen your mother like that before. Your father couldn't believe it himself, but Ramdeen's confession confirmed his suspicions that you had run away.

"When your mother was a bit calmer, she called mine. 'Raheema,' she said, 'open that box in the corner. You'll find a piece of paper in it. Bring it here please.' She took it from my mother and unfolded it so gently.

"'This is the letter Shanti left for us,' your mother said. Your father was shocked. None of us could read it. But your mother said to him, 'Manickam, this is *our* fault – yours and mine. And this is proof. We drove Shanti from this home by forcing her into a marriage with Muthan. She told me how afraid she was of marrying him, and I still forced her. I am a mother who would not listen to my child's heart, and this is the price I am paying for my deafness!' He took the letter from her, but he could not read it either. He asked her, 'How do you know what it says?' And she said, 'I found it the morning she left when everyone was searching. I took it to Jairam, the temple healer, and he told me what it meant.'

"'But who could she get to write a letter for her, Meena?'

"'Jairam told me she had written it herself.'

"'Impossible! She could never read and write!'

"'That's how little we knew our own child, Manickam. We loved her, but we were strangers to her! I can't imagine how she did it, but she learnt – she learnt somehow. And she never told us. What kind of parents must we have been that she could not share this special gift with us?'

"Your father started to grow angry. He turned to your mother accusatively. 'You knew all this time, Meena? The searches, the watchmen … everyone looking for her. You insisted she must've been taken. You said she'd never run away! You defended her even though you knew ...'

"'I defended her when she was gone because I could not defend her while she was here. I didn't care about the watchmen searching for her. I knew all her favourite places, and I took the watchmen to every place *but* those because I didn't want her to be found. I was so desperate to hold that child in my arms one last time, but part of me wanted her to escape. I wanted her to run – to get as far away from here as she could. I wanted her to have a chance outside this place where everything was already decided for her.'

"Your father was speechless but your mother went on. 'Manickam, you know Shanti was never like Vani or Asa. She was a dreamer, always asking questions we never knew the answers to. She had that rebellion in her eye sometimes, a lust for danger. It frightened me when she was very young, but the older she grew, the more I tried to tame her nature and deny it. We chose the same life for her that we chose for our other girls – but it wasn't what she wanted. Before she left, I had some idea of what Shanti didn't want, but I never took a moment to ask her what she *did* want. I was more interested in being an obedient wife. I got caught up in what the neighbours would say if we didn't marry her off. I fulfilled everyone's wishes but my child's. Stop this anger with her now, Manickam! The years are passing. You have been furious with her since the day she left. It's only you and me now. And we are both close to the end of our lives. Let us take responsibility together for what we did. We love our children, and we tried to do the best we could for them. And we succeeded with Vani and Asa. But we must admit, we failed with Shanti. She was different – a special child. And we failed her. Come and sit here with me, Manickam. Stop your anger now. Wherever Shanti is, I am sure she thinks of us.'"

Bilal paused. "My mother and I slipped out quietly that afternoon. That moment between your parents – it was too intimate to

228

intrude upon. But I know I saw a peace settle over them both, like they had reached an unspoken truce."

"Were they together at the end, Bilal?"

"Yes. It was sad when your mother went, Shanti. My mother cried a lot for her. But they were all there – your father, your sisters, and their naughty children."

"They have children, Bilal? I'm an aunt?"

He smiled. "Of course! Three times over! Vani has one child – a boy – and Asa has two girls. Beautiful children, indeed. After your mother died, your father went to live with Vani and her family. And a few months later, he passed too, in his sleep. He was cremated in the village there."

"And my home, Bilal?"

"Ah, it's very old now, Shanti. It's almost falling apart. I suppose with some work, it would still be possible to live there. But it's abandoned now. No one lives there."

"And Vākkuṟuti? What's become of our village?"

"Oh, there is a bit more development. We survived that terrible famine a few years ago. And the rains came again, and they brought such life with them. It's all come back now – the lushness of it, the energy. I miss it very much."

He sighed. "Shanti, I must go now. The sun will soon set, and it'll take me some time to get back to Verulam. Thank you for the meal."

He held me close. "Take care of yourself, Shanti. I hope we will see each other again soon."

He seemed relieved at having completed his difficult task. He had brought me the saddest news, but he was a kind messenger; also one who had lifted the huge burden of guilt I'd carried all these years.

As Bilal's figure shrank into the distance, I couldn't help but wonder where my parents were now, in what form they had returned, and whether they were finally unconstrained by care: a pair of burgeoning saplings, the first drops of monsoon rain on the faces of thirsty children, or two babes-in-arms teetering on the threshold of youth's ruddy joys again.

It reminded me that while our roots remained in Vākkuṟuti, it could hold none of us. Perhaps it was time I gave in to the subtle beckoning of this continent, which had tried to encircle me from the moment of my landing, despite my resistance. I resolved to no longer be a stranger to Africa. I regarded her with a deeper respect. I invited her potent sun to darken me. I listened harder for her melody in the winds and embraced her rhythmic drumming in the rains. And when I felt I had finally discerned her song, I knelt on her soil and asked her to keep me.

CHAPTER 25

MY COMMITMENT TO A NEW life in Port Natal changed my outlook. Devi said a subtle blush of colour had returned to my cheeks, and I seemed to smile more readily.

"I like it. Also, you no longer grin like an immature girl. Like the cats in those British children's books: che-shyers, I believe! Your smile now has the mysticism of a mature woman," she added.

"Well, I'm glad it meets your approval, Devi! And it's pronounced che-*sher*, as in *Sher*-lock Holmes, by the way," I smirked.

"Now, what for? I swear, they just complicate these names to confuse us, as if colonising us wasn't confusing enough!"

I laughed. I found comfort once again in Devi's humour, and as more of these familiar moments returned, I was reminded of our early days on the plantation before life here had grown so complex.

But there was also some truth to her jesting: I was a woman now. I had left home as an ignorant fourteen-year-old and was now fast approaching nineteen, having survived some truly distressing experiences. It was as if almost ten years' worth of heartache had been piled into five, and both of us knew the toll tragedy had taken on me. I had allowed it to tunnel through me and hollow me out until I'd lost sight of that courageous girl who'd boarded the ship to Natal bent on seizing control of her life and fulfilling her destiny. Now I was determined to search her out, and once I'd found her, reharness her fire and resilience.

This time, however, I was pragmatic enough to understand that my newfound vigour did nothing to change the reality of my situation. Indenture remained brutal, but I would no longer cower at the thought of how it had weakened me in the past, or could still break me in the future. I would find a way to live bravely under its dark canopy, letting the light in wherever I could.

I grew strong, and my resolve cemented; but then came the night when Chinammah's prediction was put to the test. How I had clung to her words when she said Wilson would soon grow tired of me, that I would become invisible to him. I longed for that – for him to look past me, through me, when he surveyed the ripening fields. And yet he did not forget me.

One Saturday night, in a state of intoxication, he still managed to trace his way along that haphazard line of *logies* to where mine stood. Why did he seek me out again when this was not his pattern? Was I easy prey? Had I fought so little that he believed I was easier to subdue than any other woman on his plantation? *Why me?* I wanted to ask, but it is not the question you put to a formidable man when his swaying shadow fills your doorway, and he is already spitting abuse.

So I meekly let him in to re-enact this sadistic dance, one in which he leads and I will suffer if I don't follow.

Time is caught in a web and hangs suspended. The gods watch while I am flung down onto the ground. There is a bestial fumbling and undoing of clothes, my sari clawed at until it falls off me. He brandishes his weapon, breathes his alcoholic vapour all over my face while I lie in the dark – jaw, fists, stomach clenched, pelvis prised open. He whispers a slur of words I don't understand except for *whore*. But I am stoic. I grip my mat and twist a corner of it round my finger until it tears through my skin to distract my body from the friction of his plunging.

How many times has he done this to me? Chinnamah asked me, and I could not answer. But tonight, I am so lucid, my memory so sharp, that every other night lines up like chapters in my head. Fourteen times he has come to me like this. Thirteen times, I have lain here and suffered. But tonight, I shut him out and drift from this dank shack to another time when my heart is happy, the images are crisp and bright, and my feet are small and swift. I am running on the sands of Vākkuṟuti, leaving my footprints imprinted among those warm, soft grains. I am running and I am shouting. I am splashing with my sisters in the lake. I am drinking the creamy milk of a coconut I have punctured until the juice runs down my chin and almost chokes me. I am climbing the mango tree with Thirna like a wild cat, stuffing my pockets with overripe fruit. I am being flung from side to side, holding onto the old bull for dear life, begging him not to throw me off. I am laughing, embracing Aunty Saras.

But suddenly Vākkuṟuti begins to recede, and I am running away from home. I am running to find shelter from a storm. I am running from a *sirdar* who wants to beat me. Running toward a sailor, shouting to stop him from throwing my unborn child overboard. I am running towards Muniyamma as she climbs the ship's rail, calling out to her, 'Do not leave me!' I am choking. I am gasping. I am drowning.

I am whimpering. I am weeping. I reach into the darkness for the shard of broken bottle. My fingers come upon it, and I grasp it firmly. There is a warm wetness in my palm from gripping it too hard. I raise it to his neck. I am plunging, I am thrusting, I am penetrating. His eyes are bulging. He is flailing. He is screaming, he is cursing, he is gushing, he is gurgling.

He is still. He is silent. He is flaccid.

I am breathless. Drenched scarlet. I am pinned down, yet I am levitating.

I roll him off me. He lands with a thud. I smell the dust rising. I pull myself up, and re-shape my damp sari neatly across my body. I am standing in my doorway. The night is cool. His throat is oozing. The stars are beaming. I accept my fate with serenity.

CHAPTER 26

WHEN I WAS LITTLE, THERE was a ritual I relished at the start of each day. "Make *Kolam* – go and scatter the flour for the insects, Shanti," my mother would say. And I would scramble for handfuls of the powdery substance, so fine it slipped through my small, clumsy fingers and made me sneeze if I brought it too close to my face. I would go outside, sit on my haunches and set about drizzling it into the most intricate patterns my young mind could imagine – weaving straight lines and dancing circles. I felt like a giant, watching each tiny ant go to work at this feast I had made for it. At that age, I could muster love even for the smallest of creatures. Yet today, I am imprisoned for the murder of a human being, and I have not yet felt the twinge of remorse.

The night of Wilson's death, Devi was away visiting our friends Latchmi and Munisami. But by the early hours of Sunday morning, the word had spread across the plantation – *Shanti has killed the master!* And although Dilip did his best to fend them off, a throng of faces clogged my door to gasp at the crimson puddle and its smaller rivulets streaking the ground, now congealed. There, just a few feet away, was Master Wilson – a pale shade of blue, an oddly shaped hole in his neck resembling Africa, through which the last remnants of life had trickled out. Some of the onlookers were terrified by the sight of his body. But I had grown inured to death after all the guises in which it had visited me in Port Natal.

At sunrise, the police arrived on horseback with their batons and shackles, the *sirdar* who had stood guard for hours leading them to me. I went willingly with them. I was only sad that Devi would return to find me gone, and curse the day we ever came to Wilson's farm.

I suppose I should have appeared remorseful as they led me away. I wanted to be sorry, but all I could think of was how I'd rid the plantation of the fiend who had ruined the lives of so many women like me. By the time he'd returned to me that night, I had no possibility of forgiveness left in me. I thought if I tallied the death of one man against the misery of all the women he would have gone on to rape, and the suffering of their unborn children, far more was to be gained in pressing that jagged bottle to his throat. But this was a strange ledger in which the courts would see no sense. Of course, many in that moment were shocked by my demeanour, particularly those who thought me loud and forthright. I was quiet and serene as police took me into custody, offending no one, as I inspired no one.

I was chained and thrust onto the back of a cart where I sat obediently, observing the changing landscape once we set off. Wherever we were going, it was a bumpy ride and a distance from Wilson's farm. I nodded off intermittently, waking each time we encountered a particularly lumpy patch of road. After a time, I noticed we were passing fewer farms, and the area was becoming more built up. I soon realised we had entered the Borough of Durban. It was the first time I had been here, although I had heard it spoken of frequently. It was quite beautiful. There were all sorts of interesting structures: administrative buildings, churches and gardens. Some people walked with purpose as if running an errand, while others seemed to be out strolling for leisure. I glimpsed patches of sea in the distance. Eventually, the cart slowed. I turned as it came to a halt outside a formidable stone building, which the signage indicated was Durban Gaol.

Only now did the reality of what I had done begin to hit home. I was soon to be classed as a dangerous criminal. The policemen helped me dismount from the cart as it was difficult to move with my hands and feet chained. Accompanied by the jangle of metal, I took small, deliberate steps toward the cool, inhospitable building. The sunlight pooled in a large patch at the door, but did not reach far into the corners of the reception area, where British men in uniform brushed past me as if I were invisible.

From the rooms beyond, a moustachioed man glanced out of an office, asking his colleagues to begin processing me. "We'll get to you soon enough," one of them told me. "Wait here." He pointed to a wooden bench, where I sat quietly. This spot had the whiff of administration – of busy hands and shuffled papers, inky fountain pens and rubber stamps. But odd sounds seemed to emanate from beyond the open door at the end of the passage. I imagined that was the point where all this bustling order ended and a new world began, where people capable of the most grievous thoughts and actions were holed up together, away from society.

Hours seemed to pass before a man came over to process me. I was asked a number of questions: my indenture number, my name, my age, where I worked. Then another policeman approached me – the one who'd asked his colleagues to process me. He appeared far more senior than the junior officer who had taken my details. This man now nodded brusquely. "Come with me." He seemed irritated that I walked so slowly, although it was impossible for me to increase my pace. He took me into a grey room furnished with a table and two chairs. He pulled out one of them and instructed me to sit, taking his place in the chair across from me, his expression hard.

"I understand you speak English."

"Yes, sir."

"So, we're not going to require an interpreter, I take it. Should you testify in your court case, are you proficient enough to speak English before the court, or will you require an interpreter for … whatever your language is?"

His question threw me slightly. I had not thought as far as a court case. But I suppose, after what had happened with Faizal's case, it would be best for me to speak English in my own defence.

"Tamil is my first language, but if I am called upon to testify, I will speak English," I said.

"Very well! Best to get these niggly details out of the way so this case can go to court as soon as possible. We do not have the luxury of time."

I nodded.

"It is my task to get to the bottom of this heinous crime," he said. "Best you cooperate and answer all my questions honestly. Any attempt to misrepresent the events or your role in them will not be looked upon favourably by the law – understand? You will, of course, be availed of a solicitor to defend you. But even the most … creative of them, shall we say, would be hard pressed to successfully defend a client who killed a man in cold blood."

I was about to respond when we heard a slight commotion outside the room. While my interrogator sprang up and left the room to investigate, I heard snatches of Father John's unmistakeable voice through the door. "I believe … being held here …" and then, more audibly, "I'm quite sure you've made a terrible mistake, sir. This woman is known to me. She is no violent criminal. Surely there is some misunderstanding."

"With due respect to you, Father …"

"John. Father John Davies."

"Father John, Inspector Saunders of the Criminal Investigating Department. I have not yet begun questioning her, but all indications are that the victim's body was found in her shack, and he appears to have been quite defenceless when he met his violent end."

"My good man, I do not wish to interfere in the course of justice, but this woman is a student of mine – a student of the Queen's tongue, in matter of fact. She has been under my tutelage for a number of years now, and has given me no reason whatsoever to believe she is inclined to violence."

"Father John, I am rather pressed for time in this case, and I regret to say, if you persist, you would be impeding my investigation. Will you be providing legal representation for her?"

"I will indeed. Please meet Mr Arjunan, barrister, whom I have asked to accompany me with a view to taking on Miss Shanti's case. Mr Arjunan, meet Inspector Saunders."

I could hear pleasantries being begrudgingly exchanged.

Father John continued, "May I persuade you, Inspector Saunders, to allow Mr Arjunan to converse briefly with his charge, while I impart to you some important information with a direct bearing on this case?"

I heard the inspector grumble about the irregularity of such procedures, but he seemed intrigued by the prospect that Father John might have further information for him.

"Highly irregular," he was now saying to the priest. "But in the interests of expediting justice, I will allow the accused to confer with her lawyer while you divulge all you know about this case."

"Agreed, sir," Father John said.

Mr Arjunan was younger than he sounded. He wore glasses and a brown suit and carried a dark satchel. "Shanti." He shook my hand in lieu of the usual greeting we gave with our hands pressed together. "Father John has enlisted my services to represent you." He sat down and opened his satchel.

"I am grateful that you have come, Mr Arj—"

"We do not have much time," he cut in. "Father John is ... occupying the investigator so that we can make some headway."

I readied myself. "What is it you need to know, Mr Arjunan?"

"I will not beat about the bush," he said in slightly hushed tones. "The question must be asked: did you murder Mr Wilson?"

"Yes, I did."

He let out an audible sigh. "Please enlighten me as to how it happened."

"He came to my *logie*. He raped me. Again."

Mr Arjunan's eyes grew wide. "What do you mean to say?"

"It wasn't the first time, Mr Arjunan. He came there several times – fourteen times in all."

"He attacked you each of those times?"

"Yes."

"Who knew of this? Were there witnesses?"

"No. He always came in the dead of night, often in the early hours of the morning."

"Did you ever attempt to report him?"

"Of course not."

"Now Shanti, I fully understand why it would be difficult to file a report, but did you ever consider perhaps making a formal complaint to the Protector or a local magistrate?"

I scoffed. "Mr Arjunan, you make it sound like a simple matter, which it is not. I am sure you know I would have had to ask Wilson's permission to leave his land to report him to a higher authority, and he would have had to be furnished with my reasons for wanting to leave."

He swallowed. "Did you plan to murder him?"

I shook my head. "Not ... not exactly."

"Shanti, either your crime was premeditated, or it was not. How did you kill him?"

"I stabbed him … in the neck."

"With what? A knife? A kitchen implement?"

"With the shard of a broken bottle."

"A broken … how on earth did that come to be in your possession?"

I was quiet for a moment.

"Where did you get it from?"

"Well, a few weeks ago, I went to collect firewood close to the river, and I found a bottle of clear glass floating there, close to the bank. I picked it up, smashed it against the trunk of a tree and took the sharpest piece with me."

"But why? Why on earth would you have done that?"

"Because I thought … I thought the day might come when I might need to defend myself …"

"Against Wilson?"

"Perhaps."

Arjunan took off his glasses and rubbed his eyes. Then he looked me directly in the eye. "Let me be honest, Shanti. I have great sympathy for you, but this is not going to be an easy case to win. Some would say it's quite impossible. The Crown is bound to argue that you planned this murder well in advance. And if you speak of how you carved that weapon for potential use against your master, the jury will convict you, no doubt."

"The plantation is a dangerous place, Mr Arjunan. There are implications for unmarried women, women who can't defend themselves."

"Yes, I fully understand. But the reality is, not all indentured women end up killing their masters as you have."

"But what should I have done to prevent this happening to me – to so many of us on that plantation? I did not choose to be violated, or fall pregnant. I am merely telling you the truth of what happened, as I will tell the court if you call on me to testify."

"You were pregnant?"

"Yes … but it did not last."

He paused, taking it all in. "You understand, Shanti, if I call you to testify, and you tell the jury what you have just told me, you will likely hang for Wilson's murder."

"I cannot lie, Mr Arjunan – I do not want to die. Of course I don't! Do you think I am not afraid? But I am sick of all the lying and concealment that life here in the Colony demands. Even if I hang for it, let the people know what the British are doing to us. Let word get back to India that this masterful transaction with Queen Victoria they are so proud of is a ruse to abuse us and profit off our pain. Mr Arjunan, I appreciate your agreeing to take on my case, and your desire to win it, but while I was sitting there with Wilson's dead body next to me, I decided that I wanted to stand in the dock and tell my story, no matter the consequences."

Arjunan pursed his lips. "Shanti, you are either exceedingly brave or utterly foolhardy." He looked down at his notes. "I'll confer with Father John. Give me time to consult with others to prepare your defence," he said, closing his satchel. "I'll be in touch."

Inspector Saunders returned shortly after that to take my statement. He questioned me rigorously, often raising his voice and asking me to repeat myself, while he took copious notes. His methods of interrogation were intimidating, but I tried to remain consistent in my retelling, although details of the dates of my master's nocturnal visitations confused me. I realised it was stupid of me not to have kept some written record of the abuse, but when it was happening, I'd had no idea the burden would one day fall on me to convince a court that my master had repeatedly attacked me.

As my interview with Inspector Saunders continued, I found my mind wandering, the fatigue from a sleepless night overcoming me.

Saunders kept it up for hours, but at some point, even he realised I could go no further. He grabbed his papers and stuffed them into a dossier with Master Wilson's name on it. "Fortunate though you are to have a well-respected man of the cloth intervening on your behalf, you have chosen the most inconvenient time of year to commit a capital crime," Saunders told me. "The heaviest rains of the year will come soon and make the court precinct impassable. The jury will be champing at the bit to conclude this case as swiftly as possible. My estimation is that it will begin and end within a week. To put it plainly, that will not necessarily favour your cause. For now, though, I suggest you try to rest. The district surgeon will be here bright and early to assess you." He called on a guard to transfer me to the prison quarters.

The man led me through a series of dark, reeking passages to an overcrowded cell, a place of stone and jagged corners, where I was crammed together with several other loudly chattering women. Some of them were fighting in a corner. I found a small space near the bars, sat on the floor and took in the faces all around me. They surveyed me too. Some women sat hopelessly, staring at the walls. A couple were crying. A few looked decidedly hostile. I averted my eyes. I was seeking neither their attention nor companionship.

Shortly after the district surgeon's visit the next morning, Mr Arjunan came to see me. "How was the examination?" he asked.

"Invasive."

"Well, perhaps it's best to familiarise yourself with Dr Rathbone's methods. He will certainly be back for repeated examinations."

The thought chilled me. "Any news?" I asked.

"Yes, in fact. Your trial is to begin in three days' time."

"Three days? That hardly gives us any time to prepare."

"Well, they cannot have the judge and jury almost drown on the way here if the rains start. These judges sometimes spend ten hours on horseback travelling between courts to ensure justice is dispensed swiftly, and your case will be no different. Your trial will move along rapidly – be prepared for that," he warned me.

Mr Arjunan then proceeded to explain the order of proceedings. Evidence would be led, and the prosecution would present its argument that I intentionally ended the life of a decent man.

"The Crown will find character witnesses who will paint Master Wilson as an exemplary human being. The *sirdars* will bear witness to this. It's also highly likely that Mrs Wilson herself will take the stand."

"Surely not while she is in the process of grieving?" I asked.

"Well, you'd think not. But she seems quite determined to defend her husband's reputation in court. His creditors might be nervous in the wake of his passing. This may compel her to testify."

Mr Arjunan told me he had already confirmed that Father John and Devi would testify on my behalf. Depending on how their testimony proceeded, Latchmi and Munisami might also be called to vouch for me as character witnesses.

"Why get them involved?" I asked. "It cannot be easy for them to leave their young children behind and travel all the way to Durban."

"They have volunteered," he interjected, "and they will make arrangements for the children's care, if needs be. Shanti, I have everything stacked against me as your barrister in this case. Anyone who can testify to your humanity will be a useful weapon in our legal arsenal."

Mr Arjunan went on to say he was looking into one or two other possible witnesses.

But ultimately, as it was my wish to stand in the dock, he had no choice but to respect it.

"Your cross-examination will be harsh and unrelenting," he warned. "We must prepare you for it adequately."

I learnt that once the witnesses had testified and been cross-examined and everyone had presented their closing arguments, the judge would summarise the evidence for the jury, reminding them of the facts of the case and the legal principles they should apply in reaching their verdict. The jury would then go away to deliberate for as long as needed. No unanimous decision was necessary. Only two-thirds of them had to agree on a ruling. We could assume they would find me guilty, as I had confessed to my crime. But they were also compelled to distinguish in their verdict between wilful murder and a killing committed in self-defence. Even if they found me guilty of murder, they could give a recommendation to mercy, to save my life. Failing this, I would go to the gallows for killing Wilson.

Devi visited me later in the day, walking tentatively into the prison quarters where I shuffled out to meet her under the watchful eye of a guard. She said his name was Selvan, and she had bribed him to arrange for us to meet alone. Her eyes were lost in two hollow sockets, and I could see how uneasy these surroundings made her.

She held me tightly. "How are you, Shanti?"

"I am … adapting, Devi. This is not a pleasant place to be. But I am trying to be strong. More importantly, how are things at the farm? How are you all? The children?"

She scowled. "That's what you wish to talk about, Shanti? I have come all this way, and you want to know what the children are doing? Well, they are running around and playing and fighting as they always do, because they do not know their Aunty Shanti's life is hanging in the balance."

"Oh, Devi, I did not mean to be frivolous. It's just that—"

"No! No, Shanti – don't shove me away! We have not spoken

since I left you on Saturday morning. Tell me what happened while I was away. I want to know ..."

I swallowed hard. "He came back. Chinnamah said he wouldn't, but he did. And I don't know what possessed me, Devi, but I knew I could not let him keep on returning."

"But the glass ... what is this thing Arjunan has been saying about a shard of glass? Where did you get that?"

"I found it by the river. I kept thinking, it's just a matter of time before it happens again – before one of them comes for you or me."

"But did you never give a moment's thought to how this could end? We are in the Colony of Natal, for God's sake! When white men kill us, there are hardly ever consequences for them. But if one of them dies at our hands, it is always blood for blood!"

"You're right, Devi – of course you're right. But when Wilson crushed me underneath him this time, I felt the rage of every woman he had ever raped rise up in my own body, and I felt the compulsion to end it for us all. I stole justice for that one night, and it gave me peace."

Devi nodded, tears in her eyes. "I understand." Her voice dropped almost to a whisper. "Have you decided what you're going to say ... in your testimony?"

"Yes. I'm going to tell the truth, Devi."

"But there's another way. You could tell them it was pitch dark. Tell them you didn't know it was Wilson, and you didn't mean to do it. Say you thought a labourer was trying to force himself on you and you defended yourself without thinking. Whatever you do, don't tell them Wilson did it to you before. You can't possibly tell them ... about the baby. You can't, Shanti."

"Devi, no matter what I say, nothing will convince them of my innocence. I killed a white man. I confessed to it. His life had so much value, and mine has almost none. But all I want is to tell my undiluted truth. So many women have suffered, Devi, but we are all eerily silent. The silence is excruciating, like a snake you have swallowed whose fangs bruise you from the inside. On the plantation, I had no voice. But in this court of law, I do, even if it is muted. It doesn't matter whether the jury believes me or not. I will have said it. That is all the justice I can hope for and maybe it will be enough."

Devi shook her head. "You are too young to die! Do you remember what I predicted for you? That you would live an extraordinary life, walk a path that no one else has chosen? It cannot end like this."

"Perhaps this *is* my extraordinary path, Devi. But I am sure, as per your prediction, it is one few in their right minds would choose."

She did not return my attempt at a smile.

"Devi, there is something I must ask of you."

"Anything, Shanti. If it will save your life …"

"This has nothing to do with saving *my* life. But what I am about to propose to you may yet save the lives of many of our children."

She looked at me enquiringly. "You know what joy learning has given me, Devi – what joy it has brought both of us."

"Of course, Shanti. We had such dreams."

"Well, that is precisely why I have this one last wish, a favour to ask of you, Devi."

"That is so final, Shanti. I refuse to believe—"

"If I survive, we shall do this together, but if I don't—"

"What are you asking of me, Shanti?"

"I wish so much for our children to be able to read and write, Devi. I see them labouring on the plantations, despite the *Coolie Commission's* findings that they should go to school, and it breaks my heart. I wish them to learn how to read and think for themselves and argue their point. I know a small number of them go to mission schools. But many will be exactly like their parents – one generation of labourers after another. That cannot be. They must progress! And in order to progress, they require an education – all of them. We cannot hope to stand up to the British as a people one day if our children are illiterate."

"But what is it you wish me to do, Shanti?"

"Not just you – you and Father John. He is a priest, and a British man. He has the means to make a way for our children. And Devi, you read and write English well. Start with a small group of them – all the children on the plantation, no matter what race, caste or language group they come from. Take them under your wing and teach them – teach them to read and write and ask questions, just as we said we might do together one day, if circumstances allowed. One day, our children will have had enough, Devi. They will refuse to be oppressed any more. But it's no use if all they can do is set the sugarcane crops alight in rebellion, or hang themselves in their *logies* to punish their masters. Our children must learn to pit the pen against the sword. There must come a day when the British will not be able to manipulate the law to use against them, because they will be learned. They will rise above all the poverty and shame of our lives, Devi. The British will fear their knowledge."

"Shanti, what you ask for – it is a mammoth task."

"I know. But start with only a small number. Remember, it is possible to set an entire field of sugarcane alight with one small spark."

Devi nodded, still sombre, but I saw a flame ignite in her eye, and in it, something of the hope I had not glimpsed since I had entered this prison.

"Now you must go before your friend Selvan demands another bribe because you have overstayed," I joked.

"Shanti, keep strong. The battle is not over yet," she said, embracing me.

Her visit strengthened me and allowed me to think of a future that might yet hold some potential for the next generation. When Devi put her mind to something, she was a force, and she often got her way without people perceiving how insistent she could be. But I still felt regret that I could not be at her side as she set about her mission.

Hobbling back to my cell, how I wished I could have shed my chains and left that place with her.

CHAPTER 27

THREE DAYS LATER, I WAS led into the courtroom via a side entrance to avoid the chattering throng that had gathered to witness the spectacle. I had given little thought to how much interest my case would generate. We had all heard of domestic hands assaulting their masters in a fit of rage: usually men on the plantations ending the life of an aggressive overseer. But I could not think of one other *coolie* woman who'd killed the owner of her plantation in the act of rape. I imagined how keenly these spectators would turn my story into dinner-table talk, fuelled by the sensational captions the press splashed across their broadsheets. When they stared at me, I did not stare back. I only took in my surroundings – the room full, but tidy, symmetrical in its layout. Yet there was a heaviness there, as if the crushed hopes of all the convicted lingered in this space.

Once seated, I looked up and saw the familiar faces of my friends in the crowd. Father John sat right in front, catching my eye and nodding encouragingly. Next to him sat Devi, alternately wringing her hands and wiping her damp palms on her sari. Towards the back of the room I saw Latchmi and Munisami,

Mariam and Baboo too. And like a shadow at the very back stood Dilip. They should not have been allowed to leave their work on the plantation to come here. But I gleaned that the manner of Wilson's death had frightened our superiors into a small measure of laxity. The anguish in my friends' faces was evident. Devi had spoken of how they hated passing my empty *logie,* exuding its aura of death. And when night fell, they'd argue my case like seasoned men of law who might find one forgotten loophole to free me, until they remembered they were mere plantation workers for whom victory remained unattainable.

A door opened, we all stood, the judge entered, said a few words, and the entire courtroom was seated. For the first time, I noticed Master Wilson's family – his wife and two young children. Mrs Wilson was beautiful, as delicate as china. Fronds of wispy brown hair hung around her small face. I wondered whether it was true that he'd hurt her too, or whether he conserved his violence for women like me. But I also asked myself why she had brought the children to this horrific place, where the details of their father's death would burrow into their little heads and haunt their dreams for years to come. Then I realised how disarming they looked as a family. There was such innocence there, such sorrow in the way they sat with their arms folded in their laps – as if I had robbed them of everything. The jury would need little more than this sad portrait to convict me of Wilson's murder. I compared myself to Mrs Wilson, and saw what everyone else must be seeing. My personal hygiene had fallen away in prison. My sari was crumpled. Clumps of hair had escaped my bun, making me appear slightly depraved. I looked poor and dirty. They would ask themselves why he had craved intercourse with me when his wife was the picture of pristine beauty. They would not understand that he'd wanted to own me wholly.

The judge was talking to the members of the jury, reminding

them of their responsibilities. There were nine of them – all white men. They were dressed in fine tailored suits. The judge handed over to the prosecutor for the Crown, a Mr Derek Grant, who began his opening arguments in dramatic fashion. He bellowed, pointed in my direction, and occasionally whipped his arms through the air, describing me as "uncivilised, violent, a savage". "Members of the jury," he said, "prepare yourselves to hear the tale of a prostitute who lured her master to her shack, shamelessly seduced him in those unsanitary quarters, and murdered him in cold blood. I should like to call upon our first witness, Inspector Edwin Saunders of the Criminal Investigation Bureau."

Inspector Saunders took the stand. Seasoned in courtroom appearances, he addressed the judge directly throughout, and spent some time describing his credentials and extensive experience within the police force. He also alluded to the nature of disputes that generally arose between landowners and members of the indentured workforce, saying these matters seldom required police investigation as they were dealt with efficiently by the Protector of Indian Immigrants.

But he did refer to a few cases in which workers had turned on their employers. "There is something many of these cases have in common, though, m'lord. The offenders were mostly employed in the homes of their masters and mistresses. So they would see to the running of the home, meal preparation, caring for children, and so forth. It is not impossible for disputes to arise when master and servant are confined in such close quarters daily. That does not appear to be true of this case, as the accused was stationed outdoors."

Inspector Saunders then sketched the background to my arrival in Port Natal, my engagement at Wilson's farm, and my record on the plantation. The investigator said he could point to no serious offences, but noted in his conversations with my fellow plantation workers that they had mentioned I had the reputation of speaking out against authority and had been "brought into line" by my overseers on occasion to ensure I adhered to the rules. Mr Grant then led Inspector Saunders into a more detailed explanation of my statement to the police, which they analysed almost line by line. As the details of my allegations of rape arose, the public gallery became restless.

"Halt there a moment, my good man." Mr Grant paused. "Are you saying this loose woman accused a well-respected gentleman of the abhorrent act of rape?"

There was a stir in the courtroom. The judge intervened, lightly banging his gavel. "Quiet, now. Silence, please. I must remind you all that the subject matter of this trial is not for the faint-hearted. In fact, it is my recommendation that women and children in particular be shielded from the harshness of the testimony you are about to hear. Those of a sensitive disposition, I would strongly urge you to leave the courtroom now."

A few people stood, gathered their belongings, and exited.

"You may proceed, Mr Grant."

"Thank you, m'lord. To return to my question, Inspector Saunders, what were the accused's precise allegations against the deceased?"

"Well, sir, she said he had visited her hut on several occasions at night with the intention of sexually violating her."

"Several occasions? Any specific number of times?"

"She said she had initially lost count, but remembered afterward that including the night of the killing, it must have happened about fourteen times."

"Where there ever any witnesses to this?"

"No, there were not."

"Not even on one occasion? She must surely have confided in a friend or relative on the plantation."

"It seems she kept it quiet – until much later, when she claims she became pregnant."

The courtroom erupted, the judge banging his gavel to maintain order.

"Is there any proof of the existence of this infant?" Mr Grant continued.

"Well, there are a number of people who can confirm that she was heavily pregnant at some stage, but she never spoke of having delivered a baby, nor was any infant ever brought to the plantation. She appears to have ... aborted the child."

This time, Mr Grant persisted across the din and the judge's hammering. "The accused admitted to you that she wilfully ended the life of her innocent unborn child, Inspector Saunders – what so many of us cherish as a gift from God?"

"Yes, she did. She said she didn't want to bring it into such a dangerous place as a plantation."

"Yet many other women give birth and raise their children there, happily. What was so special about her child?"

"She spoke of predators on the plantation who might harm the child, and said she was trying to protect the baby from this in the long term."

"Allow me to skip forward to the weapon itself, Inspector. What was the nature of the weapon used?"

"It was the shard of a broken glass bottle."

"Why exactly would she have had such an object as a glass shard, not just in her living quarters, but close enough on hand to be able to stab someone to death with it?"

"She says she kept it there for the purpose of protection."

"Protection from whom?"

"She didn't answer that question directly. She said she kept it there in case anyone tried to attack her or her closest companion."

"So, allow me to understand this, Inspector – she kept this

weapon of choice handy with a view to causing injury or certain death to any man who should cross her path, including her Master Wilson, whom she specifically mentioned by name as a possible danger?"

"Yes, that is correct."

"Thank you, Inspector Saunders. That will be all."

Mr Arjunan stood up to cross-examine.

"Inspector Saunders, you made a very interesting point earlier about the number of murder convictions involving servants who have worked in close proximity to their masters and mistresses ..."

"Yes, I daresay it is a trend."

"What would you say has motivated such murderous intentions in those contexts?"

"Well, in certain cases, it was fuelled by the consumption of narcotics, and – this is not to say it is necessarily true – many servants complained of ill-treatment or actions which they found humiliating, causing them to run amok."

"Ah, so these are personal interactions in which the master or mistress of the house has potentially mistreated a man or maidservant, and the servant has in turn exacted some sort of revenge?"

"So it appears."

"How does this play out on plantations – specifically those where the plantation owner maintains his distance, and delegates discipline to his subordinates such as the overseers? When there is an act of violence, how often is the landowner personally targeted?"

"Well, in such situations, the landowner is never directly targeted. It is always the subordinates who bear the brunt of the labourers' anger. It is not uncommon for those overseers to be severely injured or even killed by vengeful labourers. More often than not, if they want to punish the landowner, they either commit suicide by hanging themselves, to rob him of his expenditure on their travel, board and lodging, or they set the crops alight to sabotage his agricultural business."

"But they never physically attack the farmer directly in that context?"

"Not to my knowledge, no."

"So, when you set about investigating this case, did you ask yourself about Shanti's proximity to Master Wilson? The obvious questions: why she would have personally targeted him if there was never any direct contact between them? Did you ask yourself, under what circumstances they might have personally interacted? Perhaps why he was found dead, not anywhere else on the property, but in her hut?"

Inspector Saunders shifted in the dock. "She did not deny killing him. I had a full confession from her. There was no need to proceed in that direction of enquiry."

"Ah, but sir, it seems to me that there was – because the law distinguishes between wilful murder and self-defence. And if the accused was defending herself against Master Wilson's violent tendencies, that has a direct bearing on how justice is applied, does it not?"

"But she had a weapon – she fashioned a weapon," Inspector Saunders answered.

"Quite right," Mr Arjunan replied. "Are you able, Inspector, to provide me with some information as to how commonly attacks occur against indentured women living on plantations in Port Natal?"

"Well, naturally I do not have the figures on hand, but I would say such attacks are fairly common."

"What is the nature of the attacks against women you have encountered in your distinguished career, Inspector?"

"All sorts. Inebriated men who assault their wives. Men whose wives have abandoned them for rivals who then kill their wives

256

out of jealousy. Men who rape women simply because they are in-clined to violence. There could be a number of motives."

"So, if what you're telling me is true, the plantations do not seem a very safe place for women."

"No – they are not *always* safe."

"Would it therefore be completely unreasonable for a woman to fashion a weapon and keep it with her for protection in case she should encounter a violent man along the way?"

"We do not encourage it, or the plantations would simply de-generate into a morass of violence."

"You do not encourage it, but what police presence is there on plantations to ensure women are not endangered?"

"We rush out to the scene when we are called."

"You mean after the fact?"

Inspector Saunders stared ahead.

"You rush out to the scene *after* a crime has been committed, do you not, Inspector?"

Inspector Saunders nodded grudgingly.

"Let the record show that Inspector Saunders nodded in the affirmative in answer to my last question. A further question, Inspector, about Master Wilson himself. Many are taken aback by the accused's description of her master as a rapist. What evidence were you able to gather on that from other women working on the plantation?"

"What did it matter – the man was already dead."

"Ah, so am I to infer that you went to the plantation, gathered information on the accused's record, interviewed other labourers about whether *she* had committed any serious offences in the past, but did not think to interview anyone about her allegations that Master Wilson had raped her, or whether he might have done the same to other women on the plantation?"

Inspector Saunders reddened. "It is not Mr Wilson who is on

trial here. He is the victim. *If* it happened, she should have reported the matter to the Protector or a local magistrate – that is what the authorities are there for."

"Tell me, Inspector Saunders – have you ever heard anecdotally about plantation owners raping their workers?"

"One or two unfounded rumours may have done the rounds in the past …"

"Has the Protector ever investigated any of these so-called 'rumours'?"

"Not to my knowledge, no."

"What would it take for a woman to report such a crime to the Protector or a magistrate?"

"Well, she would have to obtain permission to leave the plantation to report the allegation."

"And from whom would she require permission to leave the plantation?"

"Usually from the plantation owner."

"And would she have to furnish reasons?"

"Yes, of course. A labourer cannot simply go about loitering without good reason."

"In other words, she would be compelled to say to the plantation owner, for example, 'Master Wilson, please provide me with a discharge to leave the plantation so I may journey to the office of the Protector or the local magistrate to lay a charge of rape against you.'"

"You are making a mockery of the system! It is designed—"

"But Inspector, isn't that how the system is designed to operate? It must be plain to you that reporting an allegation of this nature is no easy task for a plantation worker, is it?"

"Not always, I suppose," Inspector Saunders stuttered.

"Thank you for your concession, Inspector. I am finished here."

A hush fell over the courtroom as Mr Arjunan took his seat.

Perhaps I had mistaken his quiet manner for ineptitude. As Inspector Saunders exited the dock, Mr Grant called his second witness.

"M'lord, I should like to call upon District Surgeon of the Durban Borough, Dr Desmond Rathbone."

Dr Rathbone was a towering man who had spent several hours with me over the previous few mornings, examining my physical and mental state. He stalked over to the stand and took the oath.

Mr Grant picked up. "Dr Rathbone, it is my habit to ask all expert witnesses to detail their experience and expertise, but since you are a regular witness for the state in such cases and a familiar face in this court, I shall curtail that for the sake of brevity. Suffice to say, you have held the position of District Surgeon in this region for the last sixteen years now, and your medical opinion is widely respected."

The doctor nodded politely. "Indeed, sir. I have been in the medical profession for thirty-two years, and have testified in close to forty cases in a range of different courts."

"Let us turn our attention to this case, Doctor. You had occasion to do a full medical examination, physical and mental, of the accused over a period of days – am I correct?"

"That is indeed correct. I arrived over the last three days at Durban Gaol at precisely eight o'clock, entered the facility, and engaged the prisoner for the duration of more than two hours on each occasion."

"Over six hours collectively, then – very thorough from the sound of it. I understand you began with the physical examination, did you not?"

"Indeed, I always find it useful to begin there. The body often offers up tell-tale signs which the subject would not necessarily be willing to divulge."

"Kindly tell me what you uncovered, good sir."

"Well, even after I had introduced myself exceedingly

courteously and explained my purpose, I found the subject somewhat hostile and reluctant to undergo the examination."

"Why was that? Was she anxious?"

"It appeared not. She mentioned she'd undergone a number of these in the past, and made a rather lurid comment to the effect that British men had a penchant for looking up the skirts of indentured women."

"Outrageous, sir!"

"Well, fortunately, I have dealt with many such recalcitrant patients over the years. I simply informed her that it was a requirement of the legal system that I was compelled to carry out the probe. And proceeded with the examination."

"Did you come upon anything unusual, Dr Rathbone?"

"A difficult question to answer." He turned to the judge. "Here, m'lord, I might warn the court that the nature of my findings may be somewhat indelicate for public consumption."

The judge looked up at the gallery. "Well, they have been adequately warned, Dr Rathbone. Anyone who chooses to stay does so at his own peril."

"Very well," Dr Rathbone continued. "Naturally, due to the allegations made against the deceased, it was incumbent upon me to do a full pelvic examination of the accused. I found no presence of venereal disease, but there was an extensive amount of tissue damage to the vagina and perineum."

"What are the implications in layman's terms, Doctor?" Mr Grant asked.

"Simply a confirmation that the accused has recently engaged in sexual intercourse ... shall we say, of a forceful nature."

"Do you mean to say she was raped?"

"No, not necessarily. It is quite possible that the tissue damage occurred either as a result of rape or regular forceful intercourse willingly undertaken."

"Would this attest to the possibility I raised earlier, that she might have prostituted herself regularly?"

"It is certainly not out of the realm of possibility," Dr Rathbone responded. "One more important finding – there is much evidence to suggest she was indeed pregnant in recent months, and induced an abortion post-quickening of the foetus. That is to say, the pregnancy was at a fairly advanced stage when the intervention occurred. I deduce this from the flexibility of the pelvic girdle, which expands as a woman nears delivery. It appears the accused ingested a raw fruit which she revealed to me made her violently ill, and excreted the foetus, or what was left of it, vaginally thereafter. Naturally, as a physician and a Christian man, I took a rather dim view of this. These primitive methods of prophylaxis are both morally repugnant and dangerous. Notably, the accused was quite adamant that the child was Master Wilson's, but naturally there would be no way of proving this."

Mr Grant shook his head gravely. "We are now veering into the accused's mental state, of course, Doctor, but how has she come to terms emotionally with terminating the life of this innocent child?"

"I certainly attempted to probe this matter further, but the accused was highly reticent. If indeed she regrets it, she does a sterling job of concealing her emotion."

"What about her emotions more generally? I mean to say, when you made her acquaintance at first, what was her state of mind – was she fretful, exasperated?"

"Not at all. On the contrary, she was rather calm and settled."

"But sir, would one not expect quite the opposite, given her recent arrest and the charges she was facing?"

"Quite," Dr Rathbone answered. "It struck me as highly unusual that she appeared so composed. My extensive research has shown that Indians are of a far more excitable nature than Europeans, who are widely known to practise better self-control in general. So this demeanour naturally raised my suspicions. Having said that, I had the opportunity to converse briefly with Inspector Saunders, and took note of what he had observed from the reports of the officers who arrested the accused woman. They also described her as quiet and cooperative, even obedient. They denied that she showed any emotional distress to speak of."

"That's rather unusual, surely, Doctor – she had just killed her master and spent the entire night next to his corpse. Surely that would have a material effect on anyone's mental state?"

"It should have, no doubt. That was what betrayed the nature of the crime. Had it been an accident, she would most certainly have displayed both distress and remorse. But a well-planned murder would not have the same emotional outcome. In my mind, something very sinister went into the planning of this killing."

"What of other possible mental deficiencies, though? Signs of insanity, perhaps homicidal mania?"

"Well, let us deal with each of these in turn. It is not uncommon for those who go on murderous rampages to suffer from some kind of epilepsy. The accused, however, exhibits no symptoms of this whatsoever. As for insanity, the woman had a perfectly rational, even vaguely intelligent series of conversations with me. She has a wider knowledge of the world than most of the indentured I've engaged. I also discovered she has been the recipient of advanced English lessons from a local priest. This is not a woman whose wits have deserted her – by no means. And what of your last point – homicidal mania? Well, this often runs in families. Yet there is no record of any of her family members being admitted to an asylum in the Madras Presidency, from where she hails, nor has she herself spent time in any such institution. So no – to put it plainly, I am convinced that there are no mental deficiencies at play here."

262

"But surely the question arose as to what could have possessed her to commit such a heinous crime?"

"Of course. Her answer to that question was frankly chilling. Asked about the act of killing itself, she believes she was wronged, and frames the murder of her master as an act of retribution, as though she were some kind of avenging angel acting, not merely for herself, but for others whom she claims were caught in a similar predicament. But it must be said, she is not delusional. These are the highly organised thoughts of a vengeful woman who neither knows her place in the system, nor has any respect for rules or structure. To believe that she had the right to bypass all the systems in place to report crimes against her and take the law into her own hands is no sign of mental illness, m'lord. It is simply the work of a woman who refuses to accept her station in life and wilfully chose to act outside the rules governing the conduct of an indentured labourer."

"So what is your final conclusion, Dr Rathbone?"

"Sir, there is no mania, no epilepsy, no insanity present. This was indeed a premeditated murder – there is no doubt in my mind whatsoever."

Mr Grant thanked Dr Rathbone and took his seat. I looked across to Mr Arjunan, to gauge his response to Rathbone's testimony. He sat thinking intently for a moment before springing up.

"Dr Rathbone, you mentioned that the accused showed distinct reluctance, even hostility, when you suggested a pelvic examination."

"Indeed. I would have expected her to cooperate with my examination, knowing full well that I was a medical professional, acting on behalf of the court, and any examination I conducted would have a direct bearing on her case."

"Of course. Did you wonder at all what might be behind her reluctance to participate?"

"Well, it would not be uncommon for criminals to exercise defiance in the face of a medical probe which might uncover their deceit. The reason for her obstructionist motive was fairly obvious."

"Dr Rathbone, are you familiar with the mandatory medical examinations indentured labourers undergo before they board the ships departing India for Port Natal, and upon arrival in the Colony?"

"I have some knowledge of them, yes."

"Necessary though they may be, I am sure you can well imagine how the modesty of a sixteen-year-old girl hailing from a conservative culture may be compromised by the invasive methods doctors are sometimes forced to employ. Imagine for a moment a young British woman having to undergo a similar procedure ..."

This roused the courtroom and the judge. "The comparison cannot be made, Mr Arjunan," the judge warned him.

"Apologies, m'lord. I was merely drawing inference between two cultures which equally value the chastity of women."

He turned back to the doctor. "I'm sure you take the point, Dr Rathbone, that given the numerous invasive medical procedures the accused has endured in the past, she might have an aversion to further such processes."

"Perhaps," Rathbone partially conceded.

"Did you rule out rape altogether, Dr Rathbone?"

"Not entirely. There was simply no conclusive proof of it."

"Nor was there conclusive proof otherwise, was there, Doctor?"

"No, there wasn't."

"So, you were not entirely able to disprove the possibility of rape?"

"Not entirely, no."

"Interesting, though, that you found no trace of venereal disease in the accused. Is that not a common feature among women who prostitute themselves?"

"Yes, it often is."

"How probable is it that if legions of men were procuring her services on the plantation, she would be free of venereal disease?"

"Highly improbable."

"So there is little medical evidence to suggest Miss Manickam is a prostitute?"

"I suppose one could infer that."

"A final question about the symptoms of shock, Dr Rathbone. A man as experienced as yourself must have witnessed this in multiple patients who have suffered some form of trauma. Please enlighten us as to what those symptoms are."

"Well, the symptoms tend to vary from patient to patient. I have treated those who yell or run about madly or disgorge the content of their stomachs. Then there are others who sit transfixed, appear disorientated, detached from their surroundings, or exceedingly confused."

"Ah, so it possible that Miss Manickam might have been exhibiting the symptoms of shock when she was arrested, such as disorientation, detachment or transfixion?"

"It is possible, but—"

"Thank you, Dr Rathbone. I appreciate your insights."

Rathbone's expression turned to one of disgust. The court immediately adjourned for lunch, and I was led out to the bleak room where suspects on trial were kept. I revised the testimony of the morning in my head. It was clear Mr Arjunan did not have much latitude, but he had pleasantly surprised me. He soon came to see me, bringing some bread, although I was in no mood to eat.

"Mr Arjunan – thank you. Mr Grant was persuasive, but so were you, I believe. I suppose the difficulty is, they are experts: medical doctors and policemen. We have no experts to call."

"Do not be discouraged, Shanti. We are only hearing one side of the story for now. No one has appeared for you yet, but your story will be told. I will prepare you well. Father John, Devi – they are both reliable witnesses."

"But they are not state authorities, Mr Arjunan."

"Have faith, Shanti. Sometimes the word of a priest goes much further," he said. "Look, there has been another important development of which you must be apprised. The court authorities have received word that a storm is to move over the northern parts of Natal imminently, and may arrive in Durban in the coming days. The Crown is under pressure to reduce its witnesses so the case can be concluded earlier. So are we. I have already learnt your *sirdar* will no longer be testifying. That is good news, but it poses a challenge for us, too. We will have to be strategic about who we choose as our final witness. We are now limited to three witnesses each."

"So who will testify for the Crown this afternoon?"

"Master Wilson's wife."

I gasped. "She will be the final nail in my coffin, Mr Arjunan. They won't need any witnesses after her."

"Well, your testimony will have to form the counterpoint to hers. Eat your bread. You will need some sustenance for what lies ahead."

The recess seemed to last inordinately long. By the time I returned to the courtroom, it was full again and abuzz with talk of the testimony given so far. But the judge put an abrupt end to the noise.

"We are resuming with our last testimony and cross-examination of the day. Mr Grant, is the Crown ready to proceed?"

"That we are, m'lord. I should like to call Mrs Emma Wilson to the dock."

I could sense the collective surprise. People craned their necks to catch a glimpse of Emma Wilson, the woman who had somehow found a way to suspend her grief to carry out this gruelling task on behalf of her husband. She was so petite, the dock seemed to swallow her.

Mr Grant began by paying tribute to her bravery, given the freshness of the tragedy. "I know that it has taken great courage for you and the children to be here today. I wish you to know the court appreciates your sacrifice, Mrs Wilson."

"Thank you." Her voice was light and feathery, tinged with sorrow. She wiped her eyes with a lace handkerchief.

"I am aware it has been an exceedingly emotional day for you, but you are best placed, in the unfortunate absence of your husband, to speak for him. May I ask you to paint the court a picture of the type of man he was?"

"He was a good man, m'lord," she addressed the judge. "We met in England. He came from a well-respected family, and I married him not long after we were formally introduced."

"What motivated you to migrate to the Colony?"

"My husband was a highly enterprising man – very capable too. When he heard of the opportunity to travel to Africa to purchase a property here and transform it into a working plantation, he was immediately intrigued. Many other farmers had failed to cultivate various other crops, but he was confident that sugarcane would do well, particularly in this climate. His father provided him with a loan, and we set off for Port Natal shortly afterwards."

"Would you say your husband's instincts about farming proved correct?"

"Indeed, they did. He bought a beautiful, fertile piece of land fairly close to the coast, he employed a large group of labourers, and from the moment of inception, the enterprise was highly successful."

"What about your family life?"

"Oh, although he worked very hard to ensure the venture was a success, he always made time for me. In the years that followed, I gave birth to our two children. My husband was a committed family man who always provided well for the children and me."

"Mrs Wilson, what sort of relations did your husband enjoy with the workers on the farm?"

"Oh, he was a fair master, and widely loved by them all – or so I thought. It is a pity his main overseer was unable to testify today. He would have attested to this: my husband was firm, but fair. He expected a man to do a hard day's work to earn his wage. I do not believe that to be unreasonable. He trusted his overseers to run the farm as they thought best, and was careful not to undermine their authority."

"Were there ever any incidents of violence on the farm, Mrs Wilson?"

"Sir, plantation life is never without its complications. The labourers are often idle or make excuses for poor work. Some desert. They are always demanding more rations than they are due. But my husband never raised his hand to them. As I said, he left the work of discipline to the overseers who acted on his behalf, and he trusted their discretion in deciding what level of discipline ought to be applied against those who refused to execute their work honestly."

"Madam, today you have heard some frankly lurid testimony no decent woman should ever be forced to hear – allegations that your husband violated an indentured woman who exacted revenge on him. What is your response to those accusations?"

She wiped her eyes and struggled to speak for a moment before the words finally slipped out.

"It is all a deception to taint his good name. My husband was a true gentleman, full of kindness and fidelity. We shared a loving relationship. There was no need for him to seek the comfort of any other woman, least of all a *coolie* woman."

"Madam, what effect has your husband's death had on your family and the labourers at Wilson's farm?"

"I cannot tell you, sir. My children no longer sleep well at night. They are haunted by the thought that they have been partially orphaned. They ask me who has taken their father from them. I have had to put aside my own grief to support them. What makes it worse is that I am a mere woman, and in no position to run a plantation and manage the workers. My duties have always been to take care of the children and run the household. Now everyone's livelihood is threatened. The *coolies* will take advantage without a strong man at the helm. The loss of my husband means my children and I may need to pack up and leave for England, even though my son and daughter know no other home but the Colony."

Her testimony had set off the children, who were now crying quietly. Many in the gallery were gazing down at them sympatheti-cally. Mr Grant offered some final words of comfort before handing over the witness to Mr Arjunan. I realised my lawyer would have to take a particularly sensitive approach to cross-examining Emma Wilson if he hoped to put up a reasonable fight.

"Mrs Wilson," he began. "May I offer my sincere condolences to you and the children for your loss?"

"Thank you," she said, coldly.

"I ask you kindly to bear with me, Mrs Wilson. My intention is not to smear your husband's good name, but merely to assist the Crown in uncovering the truth so that justice may be done. May I respectfully have your permission to proceed with that duty, Mrs Wilson?"

She nodded reluctantly.

"Thank you. Mrs Wilson. May I ask, did your husband ever have occasion to call the overseers to order?"

"Well, hardly. Perhaps once or twice."

"Did you ever witness any such exchanges?"

"My husband liked to keep the business of the plantation separate from the business of the household. But I did perhaps hear him reprimand the overseers a few times – although it happened very seldom."

"What was it that prompted him to do this?"

"Well … at times, there were problems with discipline on the plantation – workers shirking their duties or not meeting the required quotas."

"And how did Mr Wilson urge the *sirdars* to respond to this?"

"He asked them to maintain discipline at all times."

"But what was meant by that, Mrs Wilson? What sort of discipline did your husband have in mind?"

"He did not specify, as I recall."

"But did you have in mind some idea of how the *sirdars* would carry out this instruction?"

"I did not give it much thought."

"But if you had to apply your mind, how would you imagine discipline would be maintained in the fields?"

"Well, I suppose some of the overseers might resort to raising their voices or giving the most idle of labourers an occasional beating – not enough to draw blood, but to ensure they respected their contracts, I suppose."

"Surely, if you know this, your husband would have been aware of it, too."

"Perhaps."

"You mentioned that your husband never intervened in the discipline his overseers carried out in the fields. Did he ever have occasion to witness an overseer beating workers?"

"He would never have done it himself."

"But would he have intervened if he felt an overseer, such as the late Mr Rangassamy, was overzealous in his application of discipline on the plantation?"

"He never wanted to embarrass the overseers in front of their charges. It would render them powerless."

"Do you know of occasions where your husband stopped to watch and take in the more severe beatings which some of the female labourers endured at Mr Rangassamy's hands?"

She swallowed hard. "He mentioned on occasion that he had witnessed something of that nature."

"And did he intervene to put a stop to it?"

"I never asked him."

"Surely he would have mentioned that, Mrs Wilson, particularly given your testimony that he was not a violent man. Did you ever hear him call his overseers to order for beating women too severely on the plantation?"

"I do not recall."

"Mrs Wilson, did your husband ever seek to maintain discipline within your household, using similar methods to his overseers?"

As a look of outrage crossed her face, the judge slammed down his gavel. "Mr Arjunan! I urge you to practise some restraint! This good lady has just lost her husband. I ask you to respect the fact that she is in mourning."

"Yes, m'lord. My apologies to you both. It is just that I have received a disquieting report from a former *ayah* in the Wilson's home who cared for the children. Mrs Wilson, did you ever employ a lady by the name of Ranjeni?"

Mrs Wilson looked pale. "Yes, I remember her well. She stole from us, so I dismissed her."

"How unfortunate. Did the *ayah,* Ranjeni, ever witness incidents of violence in your home?"

"What do you mean to ask? What does he mean by this, m'lord?"

271

"Mr Arjunan! I have already once asked you to rein yourself in!"

"M'lord – my apologies once again. It is possible for me to call the *ayah* as a witness, but time being of the essence, I wish to get to the heart of the matter with Mrs Wilson, if you will allow me just a bit more leeway."

"I warn you, Mr Arjunan – make your point swiftly or I will be forced to curtail this witness's testimony and send her on her way."

"Thank you for your indulgence, m'lord. Madam, forgive me if I am guilty of any callousness in pursuing the truth, but I must press you again. Was there ever an occasion when Mr Wilson raised his hand to you or the children?"

Mrs Wilson covered her mouth with her handkerchief and began to cry. For a split second, the judge grappled with whether he should allow her a moment to regain her composure or dismiss her from the stand. But as her sobs grew louder, he grasped his gavel and before he had even begun to pound it, I knew that would be the end of Emma Wilson's testimony. After he dismissed her, she took a moment to compose herself, then stepped gingerly out of the dock.

I expected to see disappointment in Mr Arjunan's face, but his expression surprised me. In it, I read the resoluteness of a man who knew he had performed the near-impossible task of stretching the law to its limits – as far as it could go for people like him and me. Perhaps he had done enough. Sometimes, in the absence of a clear answer, there was no better instrument than doubt.

CHAPTER 28

THE FIRST DAY IN COURT had left me drained. When the judge adjourned proceedings for the day, I sat with my head in my hands until the cacophony of the dispersing crowd had died down and the guards were ready to return me to prison. Most of all, I craved quiet, hoping I could spend some time digesting the testimony given during the day, perhaps discerning how the jurors might respond to what they had heard. But Mr Arjunan was not finished with me.

"Shanti," he wrenched me from my thoughts, "you'll be transported back to the gaol now, and I will follow. Preparation for your testimony is key."

"Do you mean we will begin work immediately, Mr Arjunan?"

"Why, of course! Mr Grant will do his utmost to trip you up tomorrow. You must remain consistent and confident. Anything that sows doubt in the minds of the jurors may be reason enough to convict you. I would be an utter disgrace to my profession if I did not prepare you adequately," he said. And that was the precursor to what turned out to be hours of planning for my appearance in the dock the next day.

By the time Mr Arjunan left Durban Gaol that evening, I was spent, but at least I felt a little more confident that I could tell my story coherently. Still, that reassurance did not afford me a good night's rest. When daylight came and we were given a few minutes to wash, I took the trouble to scrub my body carefully and make myself look more presentable. I combed my hair, plaited it tightly and neatened my sari as best I could, taking care not to crumple my clothes while being transported to court.

During that journey, I thought about Father John and Devi taking the stand to testify for me. When you are charged with as serious a crime as mine – one to which you have already confessed – there is profound guilt in asking those dearest to you to speak publicly in your defence, especially when you know them to be decent, moral individuals. You worry their very association with you will mark them like a foul odour. I was grateful they had both agreed, but felt ashamed of myself for what I had asked them to do.

Father John, however, was rarely intimidated. I had seen him enter the fray during plantation disputes on a couple of occasions. And he always headed into the eye of the conflict without considering the potential cost to himself. This morning as he nodded to me in court, I saw that familiar gleam of determination in his eye. But I could not discern the mind of Devi, who barely looked at me as I made my way into the courtroom.

After going through the daily ritual of seating the jury and the judge's plea for order as the evidence unfolded, Father John was asked to enter the dock, take the oath, and identify himself.

Mr Arjunan stood up to lead the evidence. "Father John, would you kindly tell me a bit about your appointment to the Wilson plantation?"

"Gladly. I am a member of the Anglican clergy dispatched to the general vicinity under which the Wilson farm falls. In the past, I have served the larger community, but with the growing number of clergymen in the area, I have more recently turned my attentions to the Wilson plantation in a capacity equivalent to local chaplain."

"Ah, so you frequently interact with a range of people living on that farm?"

"Quite correct, sir. I interact with the Wilson family, the staff at the small rectory where I stay, and the labourers on the farm."

"What is your impression of how the Wilson farm is managed?"

"Well, naturally I do not know much about the agricultural processes of the farm. But I infer that it is a successful business operation, not having heard otherwise."

"And from the perspective of a clergyman who interacts directly with employees on the farm who require spiritual support, what would you say is the tone of relations on the farm?"

"There is no simple answer to that, I fear. There are some labourers who find the work arduous, but who endure very little harassment in the fields. There are others who say they have been brutalised and have the scars to show for it. The individual experience tends to vary, especially in relation to whether the *sirdars* find the labourers' toil satisfactory."

"Do you have any experience of what occurs in cases where a worker's labour is found to be unsatisfactory on the Wilson plantation?"

"Workers have told me they are often assaulted, usually by the overseers. I have had incident to witness this."

"Have you ever been required to intervene in any such cases?"

"I have never been asked, but I have intervened twice, the first occasion being shortly after I arrived here, almost six years ago. As I recall, the incidents were a few months apart. One involved an inebriated worker who received a severe beating for insubordination. On the other occasion, a pregnant woman, who was struggling to cope with the demands of work on a particularly scorching day, was quite badly beaten by the previous *sirdar*, a

Mr Rangassamy, who is now deceased."

"Why did you intervene in these cases, when you well knew your intervention was uninvited?"

"Well, in both cases, the people being beaten were quite defenceless. I had been doing my rounds when other labourers called for my help. I could not, with a clear conscience, simply stand there mute, and watch these spectacles unfold."

"How did you intervene?"

"I rushed toward the *sirdar*, raising my voice and asking him to desist on the grounds that his behaviour was cruel and unlawful."

"Did your interventions make any difference?"

"On that first occasion, I believe it forced the *sirdar* to first temper his blows, then halt the beating. Naturally, he did not take kindly to my presence there. But what I found rather more disturbing was that on the second occasion, when the pregnant lady was being beaten and already bleeding profusely, I called out to the *sirdar* to pause his barrage. But this time, he ignored me entirely. I had to physically insinuate myself between him and the woman to impede him, and I bore the full force of his blows before I was able to restrain and calm him. He was lashing her very hard indeed. It was only when I walked away from the fracas that I realised Mr Wilson had been standing some way off, observing the entire incident. I shot a glance at the *sirdar*, who was also staring in Mr Wilson's direction."

"Are you saying Mr Wilson saw this, but didn't himself intervene?"

"No. He simply turned his back and walked away."

"Did you ever address the matter with Mr Wilson, Father John?"

"No, I regret I did not."

"Why not?"

"I had learnt in my dealings with Mr Wilson that I had to be …

prudent about the issues I wished to address, as many of them were of a rather sensitive nature. I did not wish to antagonise him as he was acting as a kind of patron, allowing me almost unfettered access to his property and his labourers. If he felt I was too interfering, he might request that I be transferred away. Our relationship involved a delicate balance. I had to ensure I did not offend Mr Wilson, but at the same time, prevent the workers at Wilson's farm from stepping in harm's way."

"So you never confronted Mr Wilson about concerns you had around 'occurrences' at his plantation?"

"Well, yes, there was an occasion that called for it. I prayed and pondered for many a day as to how to broach the conversation, as it involved a deeply disturbing matter. I had previously heard rumours of … abuse … of an indecent nature doing the rounds on the plantation. But I paid them little heed, until a young woman recounted to me in the confessional, about four years ago, a tale that both shocked and upset me. As you are aware, priests of the Anglican faith are not bound to make use of the confessional, but this young woman requested it as she wished to conceal her identity."

"What did she proceed to tell you in the confessional?"

"She revealed that only a few weeks before, she had been relieving herself in the fields after dark when Mr Wilson came upon her and … violated her."

The court burst into uproar, the judge's voice bellowing above the noise, "Quiet! Silence in the courtroom!" He scanned the benches with beady eyes until the gallery had quietened down before he addressed the cleric. "Father John, I need not impress upon you the serious nature of what you are alleging in this courtroom."

"I am aware of that, m'lord; nor have I forgotten the oath I have sworn on the Holy Bible to tell the whole truth."

The judge nodded. "Proceed, then."

Mr Arjunan stepped in. "Do you mean to say, Father John, that another young woman, apart from the accused, related an allegation of rape to you involving Mr Wilson?"

"Indeed."

"How did you proceed from that point on?"

"I first attempted to establish the truth of what she claimed. She recalled a fair amount of detail. She was quite determined that even in the low light of evening, she had been able to see her master's face. There was no denying that the woman was emotionally distraught and fiercely afraid to continue working on the farm. She also insisted that she was not the only victim."

"Did you believe her, Father John?"

"I was sceptical at first. It is my nature to probe further before I come to any acceptance. But I must confess that by the end of our exchange, I found it difficult to disbelieve her. She was ashamed of what she described as her part in the attack. She repeatedly said it had been foolish of her to relieve herself in that spot – that she should have searched out a more remote place to answer the call of nature. She also regretted not having fought back harder. She cried uncontrollably and her fear seemed genuine. I asked myself, what would she have to gain from accusing her master of such a serious crime? And I could not conceive of a logical answer."

"So, what counsel were you able to give her?"

"I advised her that rape was a crime fully recognised in the law books, even though she railed against the notion that she had played no part in it. But I understood her view to be congruent with her culture's customs around female modesty. Secondly, I asked her who else might have been assailed on the plantation. She said she had heard of others, but did not know them personally. Then I attempted to persuade her to lay an official complaint with the police and the Protector, so that Mr Wilson could be charged if there was any evidence. But she would not hear of it.

She told me her parents, who were both labourers on the farm, would be furious if they found out she'd been speaking to me. When she recounted her experience to them, they'd warned her that if the attack became public knowledge, no one would consent to marry her. She had simply come to the confessional to unburden herself to someone who would listen and show some small measure of sympathy and care. I was rather saddened by that."

"Upsetting indeed, Father John. So, this young woman opted not to lodge a complaint with the Protector or the police. What was your next course of action?"

"I could not go to the police myself. I had no evidence. But I'd had some previous interactions with the Protector, Edmund Tatham, and I thought perhaps I might persuade him to look into the matter in a more generalised way that would not draw attention to this young woman."

"Did he agree?"

"Not at all. I recounted the young woman's tale to Tatham, but he warned me I was stirring up a hornets' nest. I took that to infer this was not the first inkling he'd had of such goings-on. But it was impossible for him to investigate without a formal complaint being lodged – and it would have to be done by the complainant herself. Since there was no chance of that, I left Tatham in peace."

"Did you abandon the matter there?"

"No, in fact I did not. I resolved to address the issue directly with Mr Wilson. I went into a time of prayer, appealing for God's wisdom in how best to proceed, and after a few days, I requested a meeting with Mr Wilson. He agreed to meet me, and I went to visit him at his home, where I was well received by his wife. He was a little less pleased to see me, but was nonetheless civil in his approach. I was offered tea and we retired to a private room away from the bustle of the house. Here, I related to him my very serious concerns about what I had heard. In order to protect the identity of the young woman who had come to me, I spoke in generalised terms about speculation that was doing the rounds on the plantation – that he had made improper advances towards a number of his female workers."

"How did Mr Wilson respond?"

"He was outraged. He demanded to know how I dared enter his house and make such base and untruthful accusations. I explained that part of my pastoral role was to provide succour to the labourers, and that it would have been remiss of me to ignore any grave concerns they raised. He said he was going to write to the diocese to have me removed as chaplain unless I kept my distance. And he added that he and his family would no longer be attending services at the little chapel in the woods so long as I was the celebrant. There was little more I could do in the face of such a strong denial. I gave him my word that I would maintain a measure of distance between us, and he unceremoniously ejected me from his house."

Mr Arjunan took a breath before he changed tack. "Father John, let us move more specifically to speak about the accused, Shanti. When and how did you come into contact with her?"

"It was a few years ago. She began visiting the chapel from time to time, and I sometimes found her when I went to do my meditation there."

"I understand your relationship has developed into a mentorship over a period of time."

"Indeed it has. I am her English teacher. She is quite advanced. I mentor her and her close companion, Devi, whenever time permits."

"What do you know of her?"

"Well, she is a truly delightful young woman – intelligent, widely read, eloquent. She has a wonderful disposition."

"Does she display any violent tendencies?"

"Certainly not! Shanti is undoubtedly passionate, but in battle, she is far more likely to employ words as a weapon."

"And yet she has confessed to killing her master."

"I can only think that something positively horrendous must have driven her to this. It is wholly out of character for her to have behaved this way."

"Is it possible she pulled the wool over your eyes, Father John?"

"She has been my student for the better part of three years – going on four. I have counselled her through some difficult times. I do not believe that she would have committed this crime unprovoked."

The clergyman's comment caused some restlessness in the crowd. But they were still attentive.

"Father John, if the accused shared such pleasant times with you as her mentor, why would she fail to tell you that she had been raped?"

"M'lord, I grew up in Madras in India. I have a fairly good knowledge of many Indian cultures and conventions. Revealing a secret of this nature to a respected elderly gentleman – particularly one with paternal instincts – would be no easy task. Shanti knows I would not judge her. But I believe her feeling of shame was so overwhelming, that it forced her into a very dark space – one in which she had to defend herself in the most violent way possible to counter the aggression she experienced at the hands of her master. None of us would like to admit it, but I believe each one of us in this room is capable of that level of force if we are pushed to the brink."

"Thank you, Father John."

The gavel came down just as Mr Arjunan thanked his witness.

Next, Mr Grant was invited to begin cross-examination. "Father John, you say you were born in Madras. I believe you are fluent in the Tamil tongue."

"Indeed, sir, but for no noble reason other than my preparation to take over the family business – which never came to pass."

"So you were deeply immersed in Indian culture as you grew up?"

"I would say I was more immersed in the language itself than the culture."

"So you wouldn't agree that aspects of the related culture became ingrained in you?"

"Exposure is one thing, but internalisation is quite another. No, I was much exposed to Indian cultures during my younger years, but despite developing a firm respect for them, I continued to live as many other British boys being raised in India."

"But it is quite clear you are drawn to the land and its people."

"Well, it is undoubtedly a fascinating land, or I'm quite sure we would not have colonised it."

"Wouldn't you say that fascination has compromised your objectivity when it comes to your relations with Indian people?"

"I'm not quite sure what you mean, sir."

"Only that some of your relations with Indian people have become unnaturally close. Do you agree that your defence of an intoxicated Indian man and woman shirking their duty on the Wilson Farm was inappropriate given that it came at a cost to Mr Wilson, who had generously paid for their medical examinations, their travels, their rations, and their accommodation on his farm?"

"I am afraid that as a cleric, I cannot concern myself with factors of a mercenary nature. No Christian man ought to witness another being mercilessly beaten without intervening."

"That was an overseer whose violence you witnessed, not that of Mr Wilson, was it, Father John?"

"It was indeed an overseer, but he was evidently acting on his master's instructions."

"Evidently? And what evidence do you have to suggest this? How do you know with certainty that he was acting on his master's instructions, Father John?"

"Well, Mr Wilson seemed to have been standing—"

"He *seemed* to have been standing? You cannot know that! There is nothing to prove Mr Wilson was there from the outset and chose not to intervene when the woman was beaten, is there?"

Father John paused. "No, I suppose there isn't."

"And what of the lady who came into your confessional, Father John? Did you ever get a proper glimpse of her face?"

"No."

"Did you ever meet her on a second occasion to discuss this supposed violation?"

"No, I did not."

"So, I'm point of fact, you still do not even what know what she looks like."

"No, I do not – that is rather the point of a confessional."

"Quite. But the same cannot be said of a legal case, Father John. Should the Protector have been expected to launch the legal case of a faceless woman who would not even come forward to make such a grave accusation in public?"

"No, I don't suppose he could be expected to."

"But despite the law's dictates, you tried to press Edmund Tatham to pursue this investigation based on pure speculation that this had supposedly happened to other women too."

"I did not attempt to press him—"

"You expected Mr Tatham to compromise himself as a favour to you."

"That was not my intention."

"And what of the regular practice of two single young Indian women regularly visiting your rectory almost until nightfall, Father John? You, who by your own estimation, have such a deep understanding of Indian culture, seem wholly unconcerned by the implications of that."

"They are students of mine! To imply otherwise—"

"Do not concern yourself, Father John. I will take your word for it. But it must be said that you have overstepped the mark by over-familiarising yourself with the indentured. You have fostered unrealistic ambitions in them. These women have immigrated to Port Natal as agricultural workers – mere field hands. What use is Shakespeare to them? You have exposed them to an alien world. You have sown a dangerous seed in one of them – some improbable idea of equality, or superiority, even – and that woman stands accused of murder today. I would argue that in so doing, you have inadvertently played a part in the murder of a loving husband and father."

Father John looked stunned. "How could you possibly suggest—"

"Ah, do not take umbrage, Father John. I do not doubt your intentions were good, but this only serves to demonstrate that the education you sought to foist on these labourers was wholly inappropriate for a population so unsophisticated. They revel like wild animals, banging on drums and chanting in strident voices during their version of Christmas. You sought to civilise a savage."

"She is not a savage! You do not know her! She is receptive, she shows a hunger for knowledge. We cannot stop education from taking root among the migrants, sir. The work of the mission schools—"

"Ah, but this woman is no product of a mission school, Father John. The mission schools have a mandate. This woman is the product of your esoteric mentoring. Has she, as a result of exposure to your classes, embraced the Christian faith?"

"No, she has not. I do not think it imperative—"

"What of the works of the great missionaries, Dr Robert Moffat and Dr David Livingstone? I trust these are among the seminal texts you have exposed her to?"

"No, we have not yet touched on—"

"So you have taken on the role of the girl's language tutor, yet you do not care to disseminate some of the most outstanding writing in the English literary canon? Good sir – you are first and foremost a priest. And what is the work of a priest other than to spread the Good News?"

Father John looked angry. "The work of a priest is far more—'

"Father John, do not exert yourself any further. I am quite finished, thank you." Mr Grant turned his back on the priest.

Father John opened his mouth to protest, but although his jaw spasmed, only silence followed. It was the first time I had seen him at a loss for words; but perhaps it was not only words that escaped him. The more I stared at him, the more his power seemed to ebb away. He made a slow, stooped exit from the dock, the judge's eyes following him with pity. I could not imagine it was a common sight for a British man to appear as a character witness for an indentured woman in court. I wondered whether it had ever happened before. I felt rage burning inside me, but I was also wounded by Mr Grant's manhandling of Father John in the dock. Even the judge seemed ambivalent about the Crown discrediting a respected white priest for the sake of destroying an Indian woman. He tapped his gavel. "It has been a taxing morning. I should like to allow the jurors a moment to digest the testimony given. Let us take a short adjournment at this time. We will resume in precisely one hour."

I was led out to the prisoners' room where Mr Arjunan was already waiting for me. He rushed toward me, looking troubled. "Change of plan," he rapped out. "Devi is *not* testifying."

"I don't understand," I said. "You've prepared her to testify—"

"Obviously, Father John's testimony didn't go as planned," he said impatiently. "I'm resorting to the contingency plan before you testify."

"The contingency plan?"

He ignored my question. "I need to speak to the judge so he's aware and can arrange a translator."

And with that, he left. I didn't know how to feel about this development. I was partly relieved because I'd witnessed Devi's extreme stress in the courtroom. I could only assume that Mr Arjunan had asked one of my friends, perhaps Latchmi or Munisami, to testify in Devi's place.

But when proceedings resumed just less than an hour later, it was neither Latchmi nor Munisami he called.

"M'lord, I should like to call Ranjeni Muduliar," Mr Arjunan announced. It was a few moments before I remembered where I had heard that name before. I now realised we were heading into uncharted territory. Mr Arjunan had kept me apprised of his strategy all along the way. He must have good reason for deviating from it now, I thought.

"You may proceed," the judge responded, looking exasperated. I could well imagine the exchange that had preceded this turn of events. Ranjeni rose from the back of the courtroom and hesitantly made her way to the dock. I glimpsed the alarm in Emma Wilson's eyes as she jerked her head around to stare at the woman.

Ranjeni was a sober-looking woman, a good few years older than me. She was dressed in a blue sari with her hair in a low bun. She was sworn in, and a translator was asked to take his place before Mr Arjunan began questioning her.

"Mrs Muduliar, thank you kindly for making yourself available on short notice."

She nodded and gave a half-smile, uncertain of how she should respond. I realised proceedings were going to take considerably longer with the translation required.

"Tell me, in what capacity were you employed by the Wilsons?" Mr Arjunan asked.

"I was employed as an *ayah*, to look after their children. Well, at first there was only one child – the little girl. The boy was born a few years later."

"For how many years did you work for the Wilsons in all?"

"Eight years."

"And what was it like working for them?"

"Fine. I had strict instructions on how to look after the children, and I did my best to follow the *memsahib's* instructions."

"What was your relationship like with Mrs Wilson?"

"The *memsahib* was strict. She liked things done a certain way. I tried my best to do them as she wanted, so she would not get angry with me."

"What sort of things angered her?"

"All sorts of things – like when her children mixed with the others."

"The others?"

"Some of the servants' children would be playing in their quarters, and at times the Wilson children liked to run about and play with them. But the *memsahib* did not like this at all. She was afraid her children would catch a disease from them, so she warned me that they were never to play with the *coolie* children."

"I see. What else angered Mrs Wilson?"

"She wanted me to keep the children away from the *sahib* during the day while he was working. They were not to go near the room he used as his office."

"What would happen if you allowed the children to play there?"

"He would get very angry."

"Do you recall any such incident?"

"Well, once I was bathing the daughter, and the son just didn't listen to me, although I asked him to sit and wait for me. He ran

287

down the stairs, off towards his father's office. I had to pull the little girl out of the bath, throw a towel around her and dash downstairs with her in my arms while I chased her brother. But he was too quick for me. He rushed into the *sahib's* office, bumped the desk and knocked over an ink well. The black ink spread all over the *sahib's* papers, and he was furious. He pulled off his belt and began to lash the boy with it. I begged him to let the boy go, grabbed the child and ran upstairs, pulling him along by his arm. He was still screaming. When I got back to the bathroom and put the little girl down to inspect her brother's body, there were welts coming up all over. The *memsahib* came running in and thought the boy had hurt himself, but when I told her what happened, she flew into a rage and slapped me across the face. She shouted at me, 'This is all your fault! I told you never to let him disturb his father!' She took the boy away to nurse his wounds. I felt terrible. She was right – it was my fault. Since that day, whenever I bathed his sister, I locked the bathroom door and gave the boy a toy to play with so he couldn't run away."

"How did Mrs Wilson address the whipping her husband had given the boy?"

"She didn't speak to the *sahib* about it that I knew of. I helped the cook to serve dinner that evening. The *sahib* came out of his office, washed his hands, and the four of them sat down to dinner as if nothing had happened. Of course, the boy was still a little up-set, but I sensed that his mother had warned him not say anything about it."

"And what about Mr Wilson's relationship with his wife? Would you say they were happily married?"

"It is a bit difficult to answer that. I did not see them together much. The *sahib* was always busy with the work of the plantation, and the *memsahib* was busy with her own work – gardening or crocheting."

"Did they often row?"

"No. I don't believe they fought often, but when they did, it was often of a serious nature. I tried to keep the children away from any conflict. But I do remember that after one fight, the *memsahib* had a broken arm. I felt so sorry for her. Her eyes were red, and a doctor needed to be called to set her arm. She didn't want me to call the doctor at first. I insisted, because I could tell from the way her arm was hanging that it was something that needed to be treated by a proper doctor – not just nursed at home. She was in terrible pain overnight, and agreed to call the doctor in the morning. She told the doctor she had tripped and fallen down the stairs. He put the arm in a sling for her and gave her an ointment to rub on all her bruises. I still recall how she looked that afternoon – like a tiny bird with a broken wing. I noticed they began to sleep in separate bedrooms after that."

"I understand Mrs Wilson also began holidaying with family members more often after that incident – is that correct, Mrs Muduliar?"

"Yes, shortly after that, she and her children returned to England to visit her parents."

"Were your services still required while the children were away?"

"Yes, I just took over other household responsibilities, like cleaning, preparing the tea, assisting with the cooking, and so forth."

"Did Mr Wilson not travel abroad with his family?"

"No."

"Mrs Muduliar, tell me what came to your attention during one of Mrs Wilson's absences."

"One of the cleaners, a friend of mine, was dusting the parlour when the *sahib* brought a young labourer – a woman – in one morning. My friend assumed that she was to work in the kitchen, as there was a shortage of staff there. But the *sahib* took her upstairs and returned without her. It was only when we were cleaning a separate wing of the house that we heard sounds coming from one of the rooms that was hardly ever used unless a guest was visiting. There were thuds, some screaming, and we could hear the *sahib's* voice through the door. This went on for days. When he saw me cleaning outside, the *sahib* warned me to stay away from there. So I did. I was too afraid to go there, or even to just knock at that door once and find out what was happening in there.

"But a few days later, the other staff told me Rangassamy, the *sirdar,* appeared downstairs with another man. They went up to that room and they dragged the girl out and took her back to the fields. The labourers who work in the fields told us this girl had been raped and beaten so many times, it was a miracle she survived. Shortly after that, we were told to clean the guest room, and I found blood on the linen and some of the furnishings. The *memsahib* and children came back a few days later, but they knew nothing because we cleaned up very well."

This testimony should have been too much for Emma Wilson to bear. She had spent much of the trial fighting back tears, sometimes crying openly, but now she seemed shocked, her face frozen, as though the man she had been married to had been a stranger to her all along. I thought she would be tempted to flee the courtroom, but she seemed rooted there, as if she needed to hear more.

"I believe we have heard enough, Mr Arjunan," the judge was saying.

"There is just one more point, if you will indulge me, please, m'lord, and this is in regard to the incident of theft involving Mrs Muduliar."

"Very well, but do be quick about it, Mr Arjunan."

"Yes, m'lord. Mrs Muduliar, I understand you were dismissed for theft."

"That is true," she said, lowering her head.

"What did you steal?"

"I stole some silverware and trinkets from the *memsahib's* jewellery box."

"Why did you do it?"

"I have five children. One of them is an adolescent who was born with general paralysis after I was in labour for several days. She suffers from many maladies. Sometimes I am unable to afford the medicine for her. I stole these items and sold them so I could buy her a tincture."

"You committed a criminal offence, Mrs Muduliar. Why did you not simply ask your mistress for assistance?"

"I had asked her for help before, but she refused. She said I was behaving like a beggar because I had too many children with hungry mouths, and I should see a doctor to make sure I didn't have any more. I decided not to ask the *memsahib* for help again."

"Thank you, Mrs Muduliar – that will be all," Mr Arjunan said.

Mr Grant rose. "Hell hath no fury like a woman scorned, as the adage goes. I put it to you that the reason you are here today is to get back at Mrs Wilson because she dismissed you for theft."

"No, sir," Ranjeni shook her head.

"Are you familiar with the Biblical saying, 'Spare the rod and spoil the child'?" Mr Grant asked.

Ranjeni shook her head again.

"It simply means Mr Wilson was well within his rights to discipline his child as a responsible father. A parent is entitled to that, is he not?"

"I suppose so," Ranjeni replied.

"Tell me – did you actually witness the argument between Mr and Mrs Wilson on the occasion you claim Mrs Wilson emerged with a broken arm?"

"No, I did not see it – I just overheard it."

"So, you are assuming that Mr Wilson was responsible for his wife's broken arm even though you did not see what happened?"

"They were in the same room—"

"So? You and I and hundreds of other people occupy this court-room, but I could still do myself an injury without anyone in this room touching me, could I not?"

"Yes," Ranjeni answered quietly.

"While you were nursing Mrs Wilson's arm, did she at any point tell you – even imply – that Mr Wilson had broken her arm?"

"No, sir."

"Did Mrs Wilson ever intimate at any point to you that Mr Wilson was violent toward her?"

"No, she didn't."

"As for the labourer you claim was brought into the house and kept there for days, were you ever able to interview the young woman to ask what had happened in there?"

"No, I did not speak directly to her."

"Did you ever ask Mr Wilson what had occurred behind closed doors?"

"I did not, sir – it was not my place to—"

"Ah, so we simply have another case of hearsay. The other cleaner told you she saw a young woman entering the house. Were there multiple entrances in and out of the house?"

"Yes, there were several doors leading in and out."

"So, it's possible that the women entered one way and left another."

"It is possible—"

"Then you proceed to go on the word of other staff that the overseer appeared and removed this battered and bruised woman from the room. Did you witness this yourself?"

"No, I did not."

"From whom did you hear it?"

"The other staff."

"By Jove, you have witnessed nothing you are able to corroborate yourself, and worse still, you are a thief! You are quite fortunate that no charges were laid against you. I regret to say, m'lord, that Mr Arjunan has wasted the valuable time of this court, and further smeared the name of Mr Wilson posthumously, by calling this purloining labourer to the stand. Please dismiss the witness."

Ranjeni did not even wait for the translator to finish. She promptly walked out of the dock and almost ran out the court building. The judge seemed appalled that she hadn't even waited to be officially dismissed. Mr Grant had certainly shown skill at discrediting every person who had spoken for me.

It was now my turn to speak, although the previous testimonies did not augur well. I could sense the collective fatigue and listlessness in the room. Yet I could also tell there was a morbid curiosity among those who'd remained behind to witness the spectacle of the murderess testifying in her own defence.

It took me an eternity to reach the dock in my shackles. I heard sniggers. As I stood waiting to take the oath, Devi shot me a glance that held within it one last plea for me to measure my words, especially after Mr Arjunan's dedicated coaching. Yet my heart felt like a *tabla* pounding in my chest.

I took the oath using my father's name as my surname – Manickam – although we had used the name Dhobi in India, my father being of the washermen caste.

The judge turned to me. "You won't require the services of an interpreter, I understand?"

"I will speak English, m'lord," I nodded, hoping my words would carry the weight only English could in the Colony, where other languages were mere barbarian tongues.

Mr Arjunan approached the dock. "Miss Manickam, where were you born?"

"I was born in Vākkuṟuti, in the Madras Presidency, India."

"Why did you come to the Colony of Natal?"

"I wanted to work as an indentured labourer as I felt there were more opportunities for me here than in India."

"How so?"

"I was betrothed to a cousin of mine who was a stranger to me. I felt that I was much too young to get married and preferred to pursue another course."

"But it is the custom of women your age to marry young in India."

"Indeed it is. But I do not believe the custom is appropriate to everyone."

"What was it you feared about marriage?"

"I knew that some marriages succeeded, but many didn't. And I was aware of how difficult life could become if one was unfortunate enough to be promised to a man possessed of an abusive nature."

Out of the corner of my eye, I noticed Emma Wilson draw in a sharp breath.

"But were you directly aware of any such abusive marriages?"

"Yes, I was. A childhood friend of mine, Sanisha, had been married to a most abusive older man who assaulted and violated her frequently. It ruined her life and I decided that I could not take such a chance, so I signed up for indenture."

"What were your thoughts when you arrived in Port Natal and were assigned to the Wilson Farm?"

"I had seen a fair amount of abuse on the ship on my way to Port Natal, but I was much more hopeful when I arrived on land. After all that I had endured to come here, I imagined that this would be a new beginning for me."

"And the first few months were largely pleasant, were they not?"

"Mr Arjunan, indenture is not without many hardships. I was

once beaten by the *sirdar* until I lost consciousness. The accommodation is dangerous, the hours are long, and the rations are often less than promised. But despite this, I managed to settle down and make friends, and that made my situation much more bearable."

"What changed in recent months, Miss Manickam?"

"My plantation owner, Master Wilson, began entering my *logie*, my shack, in the early hours of the morning, in an inebriated and violent state. He would shove me down onto the ground and force himself on me."

"How many times did this occur, and over what period?"

"To the best of my recollection, it occurred fourteen times over a period of just over three months."

"And you kept this entirely to yourself?"

"Yes – I was terrified. I was too afraid to tell anyone, not even my best friend, Devi. I feared if I told anyone, he would victimise us all. But I was also ashamed."

"Why were you ashamed?"

"For a time, I believed it was my fault – that I had somehow drawn him there. Perhaps it was the brightness of the saris I was wearing, or how I draped them. Perhaps too much of my skin was visible. I began covering myself a bit more and trying to blend in with the others when I was working so that he wouldn't notice me when he was doing his field inspections."

"Did that provide a remedy?"

"No. He kept on returning."

"What happened in the wake of those visits, Miss Manickam?"

"I discovered …" My voice began to quiver. "I discovered I was pregnant."

I could hear the gallery stirring but I kept my chin up.

"Did you see the pregnancy through, Miss Manickam?"

"No – I could not. It was not of my choosing, and I feared for my child's safety." I could feel my eyes moistening.

"Why?"

"Plantations are dangerous places, Mr Arjunan. Children are often left to their own devices because there is very little supervision possible. Children have drowned in the river, or caught pneumonia from being washed in cold water, and have been scalded by cooking pots or hurt in fires. I pondered over it for many months, and I eventually knew I could not go ahead with the birth."

"So what did you do?"

"I went to a medicine woman who dispenses Ayurvedic medicines. She and her husband gave me the means to ... to abort the child, and I did it."

"It cannot have been a simple decision to make."

"Yes. It was a very painful decision for me, but I felt I had no other choice."

"Following that procedure, did your master's nocturnal visits end?"

"No, they did not. He returned one last time."

"And that was the very night he died. What actually happened on the night of Mr Wilson's death, Miss Manickam?"

"The master came back to my shack in the early hours of Saturday morning. It was pitch dark. I felt very afraid, more than I had ever been before. He threw me down onto the ground and began raping me again, and calling me a whore. I felt it had become too much to bear – the pain inside and out. I tried to wriggle out from underneath him, but could not free myself from his grip or the weight of his body. All I could do was stretch my arm out – and that was what I did. I reached out with my right arm for a shard of glass I had left in the corner and I locked my fist around it. I pulled it down with all the force I could manage and I ... I stuck it in his neck. He started thrashing about, bleeding profusely – all over me. The blood gushed over my face, into my mouth, my ears, my hair, ran into my eyes. I thought, 'I am going to drown in him.'

So I just shut my eyes tight, and I waited. I counted every second while I waited for him to stop writhing. I could hear the hollowness as his throat gradually emptied and he became quieter. And then his body became still and I knew he had died on top of me."

"Miss Manickam, are you saying you killed Mr Wilson in self-defence?"

"Yes, I did. It was the only way I could fight back."

"You understand you are accused not of culpable homicide, but of *wilful* murder. And that is in large part because of the piece of glass with which you killed your master. Miss Manickam, the Crown would argue that you planned this."

"Planned what, Mr Arjunan? Another rape? Are you saying I hoped my master would come back to rape me so I could kill him? On the contrary, I did all I could to avoid him. But his actions changed me. Before Master Wilson began raping me, I would never have thought of fashioning that weapon. He made me afraid – not just of him, but of all men, even the decent ones. I only did it to protect my friend and myself from *any* of them who should try to hurt us."

"Miss Manickam, do you regret what happened?"

I paused for a moment and thought hard about what answer I should give, knowing exactly what the court wanted to hear.

"I most deeply regret having been assigned to Wilson's farm and ever encountering my master."

Mr Arjunan cleared his throat. "The killing, I mean ..."

"Yes, I do regret it."

Mr Arjunan glared at me. He ended his examination there.

Mr Grant advanced.

"You appear to have been surrounded by abuse, don't you? Abuse at home in India, abuse on the ships, abuse on Wilson's farm. It appears to follow you as closely as your own shadow, does it not?"

Mocking laughter from the gallery.

"I believe abuse abounds everywhere, although the authorities often choose to turn a blind eye to it, sir."

"Tell me more about your education. Has that made much difference to the manner in which you harvest cane?"

More sniggering.

"Mr Grant ..." the judge interjected.

"Apologies, m'lord." Mr Grant turned back to me. "Why do you feel you require education?"

"Sir, I hope not to be an indentured labourer for the rest of my life."

"Ah? What is it you hope for – a Cambridge tenure, perhaps?"

"Sir, I am aware that my options are limited. But I hope one day to open a school where children can be taught literacy and numeracy."

"Good gracious – we have a future educator in our midst, who believes she is more qualified to teach than the missionaries! I know exactly what the *Coolie* Commission has recommended, but why exactly do plantation children require an education?"

"To advance in life."

"Pardon me?"

I coughed nervously. "To advance in life, sir."

"To advance to what station in life?"

"To a station that may be preferable to their current situation, sir."

"Ah, indeed. So, you have an interest in educating children, do you?"

"Yes, sir."

"But none in raising them?"

I bowed my head. "Sir, I have already spoken about the danger facing children on the farms."

"Yes, yes. The court heard your explanation, but I am not

convinced by it. You are aware that the church views abortion as a grievous sin, are you not?"

"Yes, I am aware."

"Do you understand why?"

"I believe I do, sir. Christians believe children are a gift from the Divine."

"Ah, so you understand one cannot simply murder them."

"I did not set out to murder my child, sir."

"But that is ultimately what you did. Strange! I have visited many plantations where Indian families are positively multiplying like rodents, despite the dangers which you claim prohibit child-rearing."

"Indian family structures often assist in raising children, sir. But it is far more difficult for women without a husband, parents, or extended family to find someone to help."

"Ah, so that is the solution! If you cannot find someone to care for a child, simply put an end to the child's existence." He shook his head. "I daresay the Crown has been much too lenient, not charging you with a double murder."

I did not respond to that.

"Having heard your testimony in this courtroom, much of which I believe to be profoundly dubious, I put it to you that had your master raped you, you would have gone straight to Father John Davies to report it."

"I considered this at length, sir, but I could not stand to involve him. Father John's presence in my life is like that of a parent. When I considered revealing this to him, I thought of what it might be like to speak to my father of this. And I could not bring myself to …"

"I am told you enjoy the company of a host of friends on the farm. Is this true?"

"Yes, it is."

"And you never thought to tell a single one of them?"

"Sir, knowing what happened to me would have endangered all of them."

"Enough of these lies! The reason you told no one is because all along, you were plotting the demise of your master. Tell me how he wronged you. Did he leave it to an overseer to beat you for insolence? Did he point out your shoddy work in the fields? What was it that caused this hatred for your master to germinate within you? Was it access to all the literature your indentured mind could not absorb, that gave you fanciful ideas about seducing the master, drawing him to your shack, and thereby one day becoming the lady of the plantation?"

"It was none of that! I had not planned to kill Master Wilson – I had hoped he would leave me alone."

"And yet you still fashioned the weapon that would ultimately end his life?"

"I was frightened. I needed a means to defend myself ..."

"Nonsense! Why did you not go to the police or the Protector if you were so fretful about the master supposedly attacking you again?"

"I have tried to explain, sir. I was not in a position to secure my master's permission to leave the farm. If I risked leaving without permission and I was caught, I would either have been liable for a ten-shilling fine, or faced a week's imprisonment with hard labour. It was exceedingly difficult—"

"Possibly difficult, but never impossible." Mr Grant raised his voice. "This unorthodox education you have received has corrupted your mind!" He stuck a finger in my face. "You elected to take the law into your own hands, to act as some sort of vigilante to end the life of your master ..."

"No sir, I did not."

"You planned it, and you executed it to the last detail!"

"No!" I screamed, grabbing the edge of the dock and pulling myself to my feet. "No, I did not! I am not a murderess! It would have been my word against his – the word of a lying, dirty, poor indentured woman against a powerful white man's. How could I go to the Protector and speak against Wilson without his permission to leave the farm? What should I have said? Should I have bowed low and said, 'Sign this please, Master, so I can go and tell the constabulary and Protector what a violent, alcoholic savage you are, how you raped me and other women on the plantation?' He would have called a *sirdar* to beat me to within an inch of my life or done it with his own fists! You cannot conceive of my life here. The rights you talk about – the rights you believe have been bestowed on us through some commission are rights on paper only. I am *not* my own person. This body does not belong to me! When I put my mark on the paper, I signed all of it away – my freedom, my rights, my body, my life. Wilson came to own it all. And when he wished to remind himself of this, he came to my shack to claim his rights again and again in the middle of the night.

"I hear the way you speak about Wilson as though he was some sort of pillar of your colonial society, a model plantation owner. You wish to believe this of him after all the evidence you have heard? You wish to saint him after you have heard a woman testify as to how he broke his wife's arm and beat his child, and raped another woman who was too afraid to lay a charge? Wilson was a vile, abusive brute! It has happened just as your Holy Book says: Wilson has earned his death through 'an eye for an eye'. What is this feeble attempt you make at uncovering truth in this courtroom? Where is your true commitment to justice? I scoff at you and your system! I no longer care if you hang me! If this court is a place of deception masquerading as a place of truth, you should rather have executed me right away instead of wasting your time with this sham!"

I was shaking. I tried to catch my breath. There was stunned silence as I reached back to steady myself and slowly sank back into my seat. My eyes glided from Mr Grant's face, now burning with anger, deeper into the courtroom. The gallery was hushed. There was shock in the faces of Mrs Wilson and the jurors. And then my eyes alighted on Mr Arjunan, Father John and Devi, who now sat shrunken, any last vestige of hope abandoned.

The judge shook his head and turned to face the jury, addressing them rigidly as an automaton. "Jurors, I believe you have heard all we are going to hear in this case. I urge you to exercise your duty to dispense justice with fairness as you enter your deliberations. Please bear in mind that time is short, so you must inform us the moment you have reached a verdict."

Most of them stared. A few nodded. I was seized by the arm to be transported back to gaol. As I was led out, I stole one more a glance at the jury. Their collective expression confirmed I had sealed my fate.

CHAPTER 29

FATHER JOHN WAS SLOWLY COMING to terms with the injustice of old age. He felt he had somehow missed life's gentle graduation, as though he was first young and then suddenly old, without any transition in between. His hair bleached almost overnight, his skin thinned like onion paper, his fingers curling too willingly into an arthritic arc. Now he limped, leaning hard on his walking stick, driving deep punctures into the soil. These days more than ever before, he felt mortality clinging to him. He could almost smell it beneath his clothes – the lingering perfume of decay that marked him out as a human antique.

There had been a day when his legs carried him swiftly over uneven ground, when he was so sure-footed he could run without stumbling. Oftentimes he had rushed to Durban Gaol, where some innocent soul needed consolation, or convicted criminals called for prayer before overcrowding and disease ate them away. At other times, he found himself among the quiet susurrations of trees surrounding the chapel, where he served Holy Communion to the landowners and their families in their distant, cushioned world.

303

He had alternated between those two worlds in the Colony – that of the powerful and protected, and the underclass of the powerless and discarded. He used to wonder if the rich would have allowed him to bind their hands in marriage or baptise their bawling children if they'd known who he'd laid hands upon in prayer.

At times, he questioned the life he'd chosen. What if he had satisfied his father and become a successful trader? He'd likely be in England now, sipping brandy before a roaring fire and devising how to share his accrued wealth among his descendants. But no. That was not the life destined for him.

He had always been most fascinated by life's joys, sorrows and rituals in equal measure: the births, the baptisms, the confirmations, the marriages, the funerals. The milestones with which human beings mapped their lives to the final point of cadence. But then there were the rapes, the suicides, the murders, which reminded him of how all maps bore perilous contours that every human being hoped never to traverse. He had glimpsed death in all its forms. But there was one manner he had never been able to come to terms with. Every execution he witnessed here in the Colony left him feeling distressed and hopeless. He was unable to reconcile the violence of these hangings with the people who carried them out – British people, like him, who called themselves civilised. He had written to the governor and every other official for miles around about the horrors of the gallows – sent letters to England, even. But no one listened.

He had seen drunk jurors condemn people to death. He had watched the hurried felling of trees and chopping of wood for crude gallows. He had been there as the bell tolled six, the sun waking to the screeching of struggling men whose courage deserted them when the dark hood was pulled over their heads. He almost choked when recalling those final images of a human head threaded through the noose, and its quick tightening. His heart would break to hear the proudest of them beg for mercy. He knew first-hand the incompetence of untrained officials who botched the hangings because they had failed to measure the length of rope properly, or miscalculated the drop. He witnessed men swinging beneath the trapdoor after that loud bang, gurgling, their eyes bulging, the life being squeezed out of them until the final death rattle signalled their end. When he looked back at the British officials who had carried out these executions in their fine suits, he saw only the brutish nature of men who delighted in their own power over life and death.

Father John understood that all human beings would come to the end of their time. He accepted that in this moment, death was standing not far off from him, beckoning. But he was an old man, and that was the nature of things. What he could not witness was one more person in the full bloom of youth die by execution. Most of all, he could not watch the Crown murder Shanti. She did not deserve to die – this vivacious young woman who had become more than a student to him: his friend. A daughter. He had anticipated a damning verdict, and while the jury deliberated, had knocked on doors relentlessly. He had pleaded for a recommendation to mercy. "Do not let her hang," he had begged. "She's a young woman who defended herself in the face of violence and humiliation." But no one would hear him. Her words had unleashed a scandal on this community because to tell the unvarnished truth was to commit a sin in these parts. This was a world of pretence, full of the scent of refinement while the stench of rot bubbled underneath. He suspected that everyone secretly hoped that Shanti's truth would die with her.

Father John knew there was no need to wait for the verdict. It was certain that Shanti's words would bring her death and immortality in the same breath. No one would easily forget who she had revealed her Master Wilson to be. The court record and oral tradition would ensure it. Wilson's widow would wear the stain. His descendants would carry the whiff of the man unmasked as a rapist in court by a humble plantation worker who spoke fierce words in the language of the people who mocked her. And they would remember that she twice felled her attacker; once with her shard of broken glass, and a second time with the words she brandished in their mother tongue.

When Father John visited Shanti at the gaol after her testimony, he saw brief flashes of courage in her. But he also could sense her sadness at knowing she was beyond saving now – the realisation that the end in store for her would likely be a violent one, carried out in the full glare of her enemies.

When he arrived, she was meditating, searching for peace and resolve for what lay ahead. "Do not surrender yet," Father John said. "The jury must still deliberate on your testimony." But both of them could sense the hollowness in his words.

"Thank you for encouraging me, Father," she said. "But I know none of those men will vote to save my life. They are all an incarnation of Master Wilson in some way or another. I saw how they felt for his demure wife, how they admired her delicateness. I am nothing like her. My father hated the boldness in me, and the British hate it too," she said sadly.

"Shanti …" He paused. "If I did not know how stubborn you were, I'd urge you to recant."

"You'd urge me to lie?"

"That is not what I mean to say. Telling the truth is one thing – and that was risky enough. But you called into question the entire system – a system of which the judge and jury are a part. Perhaps even a retraction of that aspect of your testimony would assist your cause."

"You know I would refuse, Father."

"So you will take the full punishment if it is handed down to you?"

"I will have no choice, Father."

He sighed and looked away before reaching into his pocket and rummaging there. "That reminds me, my dear. I have a little gift for you – the work of my own knobbly hands." He smiled and unfolded a starched white handkerchief, revealing a crudely fashioned crucifix made of dark wood at its centre. "I apologise. I was once a very adept woodcarver, but I'm afraid in my old age, I am less dexterous. Forgive the jagged finish."

Shanti reached out to take it and turn it over in her hands. "You made this yourself?" she asked.

"Indeed I did," he said proudly.

"This is very good. Why have you hidden this talent of yours from me?"

"My work allows little time for creative pursuits, I'm afraid. This exercise revealed that I am both severely out of practice, and in need of better tools."

She beamed, examining the crucifix more closely, running her fingers over the detail in the varnished wood. "It reminds me of our first meeting in the chapel, Father – when I spoke about Christ on the cross."

"I thought that might come back to you."

"But wait: why … why have you omitted this … this fabric that ought to hide his nakedness?"

"His loincloth, you mean?"

"Yes – that is it. Where is his loincloth?"

"Ah, my dear, do not be distracted by that. You should know, the loincloth satisfies only the pious puritan's desire to hide the true extent of crucifixion. It was not merely about suffering. It was about humiliation too – why, after all, take the trouble of creating an elaborate crown of thorns to drive into the man's head? It was a tool of ridicule. The Bible tells us, as was the custom at the time, that the soldiers divided His clothes among themselves. It is most likely, my dear, that our revered Christ was crucified completely naked."

"But that doesn't matter. He is your God. It's a question of modesty, Father. Of … using your artistic licence *not* to depict him in such a shameful way."

"Shanti, a god who cannot feel the deepest humiliations of humanity is not worth worshipping. Those images of Jesus Christ in his finest robes, the halo issuing from his crown, have their place. But they mean little to me. I have always been drawn to the image of the Christ who reaches out to the poor and heals the sick and consorts with women condemned for being prostitutes. I ask myself all the time, if He were here right now, where would He be? Would He be dining with the plantation owners in their fine mansions? Plotting with the administrators as to how to put you to death? I cannot bring myself to believe that's who He was. He was the son of a carpenter, a humble boy. And He grew into a man who carried that humility into His adulthood. And when the time came, He found out what it was to be whipped, spat upon and mocked. And He was killed violently while His enemies looked on with pleasure, and His mother watched in agony. In times like these, I do not believe the god of the loincloth is of use to anyone, Shanti."

They sat in silence after that, as Shanti pondered his words and he wondered whether bringing that little icon he had made with so much love and care had been appropriate after all. Perhaps it was too strong a reminder of Shanti's inevitable fate. Before long, the warder called out to Father John that it was time for him to leave. He embraced Shanti and promised he would return to see her again.

But as he left the prison, he was seized by yet another worry.

Devi had come to him last night, wringing her hands, laying out an absurd idea. He had dismissed it out of hand. "No," he'd said abruptly. "I won't entertain it." But of late, Devi had developed an obstinacy that was beginning to resemble Shanti's. And even after he'd turned down Devi's request, he saw a determination in her eyes that told him this wasn't the end of the conversation. Now he feared that if he didn't agree, she would find a way to do it without him – and the last thing he wanted to do was leave her alone in this.

"I want to help," he'd said. "But what you are asking is … impossible."

"Father, for the first time in my life, I look at this and I see no obstacles whatsoever. I've already made up my mind," Devi said. "You cannot change it."

CHAPTER 30

AFTER THE RUSHED TRAVESTY OF Shanti's trial, the threatened storms turned out to be no more than a steady drizzle. Taking their cue from the weather, it was a full week before the jurors returned to hand down their verdict. Soon afterwards, Mr Arjunan prepared to visit Shanti to inform her they would be returning to court to hear the jurors' findings.

The lawyer prided himself on his ability to maintain a reasonable emotional distance from his work. But he had allowed Shanti's case to consume him. From the second Father John had banged on his door, pleading for representation, to the moment Shanti had lost all composure in the courtroom, Mr Arjunan had cycled through a multitude of emotions. He'd been torn as to whether to accept the case in the first place. As a younger lawyer, he'd naïvely believed he could somehow change a justice system skewed against the indentured. At times, he'd been clever enough to manipulate the law to his advantage, but none of his clients had faced the prospect of execution – until now. Mr Arjunan's first instinct had been to turn the priest down, but when Father John offered his life savings toward Shanti's legal fees, Mr Arjunan had softened.

"You are a clergyman," he'd said. "I cannot in good conscience accept this sum from you, appreciative though I am of the gesture. I will represent your friend *pro bono*."

But Mr Arjunan had barely hoisted his satchel onto his shoulder when he began to regret his promise. Of course, it was not impossible for a woman accused of such a crime to be acquitted. But he knew of the unspoken law that *who* she was would doubtless count against her – a parallel system that ran like murky silt beneath the clear blue surface of British justice in the colonies. He also saw in her a certain rebelliousness that perturbed him. The indentured women he'd previously defended had been submissive, subdued. Shanti, by contrast, held herself upright, even in shackles. She spoke in too loud a voice, and seemed to swallow down fear when it rose up in her.

Nonetheless, Mr Arjunan had kept his word and worked tirelessly to ready his defence and prepare his client for the trial. He had anticipated the witness testimony not quite proceeding as he had hoped – Mr Grant was a competent and fierce adversary, after all. But Shanti's testimony had shattered Mr Arjunan, even if it hadn't truly surprised him. In preparing her, he had not prescribed that she deviate from the truth, but he had coached her stringently on the matter of demeanour.

"You have to appear humble and remorseful at all times," he had told her. "Address the judge as m'lord constantly as a sign of respect. Do not speak too vociferously. Keep your head slightly bowed and do not meet Mr Grant, the judge, or the jurors' eyes in the way you are wont to. They will read it as defiance. You must evoke pity in them instead."

Shanti had begun to protest, but Mr Arjunan put an end to that sharply. "Understand this! The entire justice system pivots on their power and your lack thereof. It is bad enough that you speak fluent English and will be addressing the court in their language. You must use other methods to signal at all times that you do not see yourself as equal to any of the British or their charges in that courtroom. Do you understand me, Shanti?"

She had nodded with sincerity, and a sense of relief had washed over him. So long as Shanti understood the dynamics of the justice system, he believed she was intelligent and eloquent enough to play the British at their own game – and possibly win. When she had first taken the stand, it had seemed to Mr Arjunan that everything would be all right. Shanti had struck the right tone. She had avoided argumentation and answered what was put to her as best she could. Even in recounting the terrible rape of that night, Mr Arjunan had sensed that her palpable fear had become real to many listening. But then Mr Grant, sniffing out that small pith of defensiveness, had needled Shanti to the point where her rage had become volcanic. Every British person in that courtroom – civilians and administrators alike – had been scalded by it.

Mr Arjunan berated himself for allowing her to testify. Why had he not, with his years of experience, predicted the outcome? He should have known this was not merely the trial of a woman who'd killed a man, but a trial of indenture and the colonial system itself – of a system that purported to offer justice to all who fell under Queen Victoria's aegis, but that in reality served only the British themselves – the rest of Her Majesty's subjects be damned. Perhaps every now and then, history's tide would sweep in someone of militant character who would challenge the establishment and inspire others to do the same, at great cost to themselves. He sensed he had encountered just that person in Shanti, and felt a measure of reverence for her courage. Still, the consequence was most often martyrdom.

As he made his way to Durban Gaol to tell Shanti of the jury's imminent announcement, Mr Arjunan knew it was also his duty to prepare her for the harshest punishment that could be handed down in a colonial court. It would be incumbent on him, if the court was so inclined, to describe in detail to Shanti what preceded that final walk to her death. He doubted he had the constitution for it.

But Shanti made it considerably easier for him, admitting she'd already acquainted herself with that possibility. She told him she had spent the week pendulating between fear and hope, her spirits lifted only by the regular visits of her friends.

Mr Arjunan spent some time explaining the legal procedure around the announcement of the court's findings, and said he ex- pected the appearance to be fairly concise.

"So, either I will go free tomorrow or I will return here in chains, Mr Arjunan," she said.

"That is the nub of it, Shanti."

"But what if … what if I am condemned to …"

"Let us not speak of that now, shall we? If worst comes to worst, we will deliberate on it. For now, it is best that I inform Father John and Devi to present themselves in court tomorrow morning."

As Mr Arjunan headed from the gaol to the rectory, he became aware of the peace that settled over him as he left the borough behind. As the terrain around him grew more rural, he began to imagine a life outside of law – one that did not involve the aggressive argumentation required by the adversarial system, or pitted the dominant against the disempowered. He had saved enough money to go into business. And although Shanti's case had given him a distinct distaste for plantation life, perhaps there were other options. He had heard tales of the seine netters – those who waded into the rising tide and scooped up the plentiful fruits of the sea to bring back to land and sell there. He thought of the pleasant chill of salt water on his bare feet on days when the sun burnt too hot, the granular scratching of beach sand under his soles. And suddenly he knew his mind was made up. If Shanti were to hang, he would walk away from the courtroom to the sea – which seemed so much more forgiving.

CHAPTER 31

I HAD EXPECTED A RESTLESS NIGHT. But a great peace came over me after Mr Arjunan left, and remained with me as I prepared to arrive at court. The bustle and noise in the courtroom that morning reminded me of the first day I had been brought in there, ignorant of what to expect. But in just a matter of days, I had grown accustomed to the sway of the bumpy cart through Durban's streets, and placing my feet on the path worn smooth by the procession of the accused into the building with its dark-stained furniture, its smells of edict, officialdom and bodies fighting the damp heat.

Among the sea of faces I saw my friends seated in the public gallery. I gave Devi a small half-smile to signal that I was prepared for whatever I was about to hear. She nodded back solemnly but eagerly, which indicated to me that she was not. Emma Wilson sat with her children on either side of her, her arms curled around them both. The jurors were seated, none of them looking directly at me. I wondered about their conversations behind closed doors. Did the passing of seven days indicate that they had fiercely debated my case? How painstakingly had they reviewed the evidence? How many more might have taken pity on me if I had resisted Mr Grant's attempts to anger me?

It wasn't long before the judge entered the courtroom and took his place. In front of him lay a dossier out of which a shuffle of papers came. He ordered them, then began to summarise the facts of the case that the jury had considered before reaching their decision. He recapped the testimony of all the witnesses in turn. I journeyed back over each testimony, from Dr Rathbone's to Ranjeni's, clinging to nuggets of evidence that might have mitigated my parlous position in this battle for my life. But objectively, I knew my own testimony was inflammatory enough to scupper all the evidence that had supported my claims. I heard a stir from the gallery as some of my statements were repeated, and I again realised the gravity of what I had done.

The judge asked me to stand while judgment was passed. I rose. "Miss Manickam, what I am about to say will have no influence on the jury's decision as they have already informed me in writing of the outcome. But before I ask them to reveal their findings to the court, I must simply state that never in my thirty years on the bench have I ever witnessed an outburst of the kind you unleashed on this courtroom. It was not merely an attack on the late Mr Wilson, a man unable to speak in his own defence, but a vitriolic attack on the British justice system – the product of the painstaking efforts of the finest legal minds Her Majesty's legislature boasts. Many would argue that only a depraved mind could so glibly critique this justice system and the system of indenture in as vulgar a manner as you did. Yet Dr Rathbone, after several thorough medical examinations, found you to be of sound mind, which suggests it was pure malice that drove you to slander both your deceased master and the system which afforded you the opportunity to escape your impending marriage in India and partake in a successful agricultural initiative in the Colony of Natal – an opportunity for which you appear to be wholly unappreciative. Respect must always be shown for the proceedings of this courtroom. Officers of the court and witnesses are expected to display decorum within its precinct at all times. Your unbecoming conduct was in direct violation of this code, and I would go so far as to say it made an utter mockery of the legal system. However, your fate is not in my hands. As per the fairness the system affords you as the accused, it is the jurors who must decide. I should like to call on the head juror at this juncture to declare the findings of the jury. Good morning, sir: how find you?"

A burly man stood up. "M'lord, in the case of the killing of Mr Edmund Wilson of Tongaat, we find the accused guilty of wilful murder."

There was spontaneous applause in the courtroom.

"Enough! Enough of that!" the judge intoned. He turned back to the head juror. "What sentence do you believe to be appropriate?"

"Death by hanging, m'lord," came the response. The courtroom once again erupted, the judge's gavel hammering out the finality of those words.

Mr Arjunan jumped to his feet. "M'lord, I would like to request a recommendation to mercy. Miss Manickam is but a young woman who committed a grievous error. Surely she cannot hang for it! I beg you to please temper your justice with mercy."

"Mr Arjunan," the judge replied. "I regret to say that no such measure of mercy was shown to Mr Wilson, his grieving wife or his young children. It is my duty to implement the letter of the law, and that I shall faithfully do today, in view of the clear absence of contrition on the part of the accused. The request for a recommendation to mercy is denied. I suspect you will next request an appeal. But I do not believe any grounds exist for that either. The accused will hang by her neck until she is dead. The execution is scheduled for dawn the day after tomorrow."

I closed my eyes to the stridency around me – the cheering and clapping in the courtroom, the sobbing of Emma Wilson and the children, the strains of Mr Arjunan's continued appeals over the relentless banging of the gavel. I was shocked, more than anything, at the violence of the judge's words. I had expected some sugar-coating – perhaps "execution by hanging" or "death at the gallows". But the image conjured by those naked words, of me hanging by the neck until my last gasp, seemed enough to asphyxiate me. When I opened my eyes, Devi was staring at me across the room – not crying, not protesting, just taking in the jury's words and not allowing herself to capitulate to grief. I appreciated that. It stilled my tears. When I looked at all my friends standing around Devi, I saw it in them too – their stoicism and strength – and I drew deeply from their courage. I did not take my eyes off them as I was led from the courtroom.

On that journey back to Durban Gaol, the echo of those words rang in my ears. Not far from my mind's eye was the silhouette of myself dangling until someone cut me down and gave me a pauper's burial. But I chose not to dwell on that; instead, I looked at my surroundings with very different eyes as we travelled. Knowing this was the last time my gaze would fall on such alluring scenes as the sea, the grass, the trees, knowing that in just over a day, I would shut my eyes to the sunlight and no longer breathe this warm air – that was what moved me.

I found myself deeply grateful for it all: for every moment of my life, even those when I had suffered. I allowed my regrets to resurface, but only momentarily. I thought of my family and my friends, my one love, and everything I had shared with each of them from my birth until this day. And I promised myself forgiveness for all my mistakes. I decided in the last few hours that remained, I would stop punishing myself. I would come to terms with everything I had done – the foolish, the selfish, the shameful and the ignorant. I would not let myself leave this body without that wish fulfilled. And it gave me some small joy to believe that I was almost ready to leave this life unburdened. "I forgive you, Shanti," I whispered under my breath. "I forgive your mistakes." When I closed my eyes again, the morning light played on them and the sunshine warmed my face. As I breathed in, I faintly caught the scent of jasmine in the air.

"So, the die is cast, Devi."

"I believe the die is cast, Shanti."

This was my last afternoon with Devi. A full day had passed since the verdict had been handed down, and the warders had moved me to a new cell – one reserved for those awaiting execution. It was apparently a shorter walk to the gallows. Earlier, several prison officials had come to take my measurements. They laughed and chatted among themselves while they measured me, as though sizing me up for a new outfit for some happy occasion.

Hours later, Devi had entered my cell with a melancholy smile – very different to her countenance in court. She had brought me a parcel, which she placed on the ground before throwing her arms around me. They had kindly allowed her to bring me a final meal, which she had prepared with love. *Dhal*, rice and herbs – a real feast. I should not have had an appetite, but I was starving and ate ravenously.

I saw her watching me eat just the way I had watched my mother on the night I left Vākkuṟuti. "Join me, please," I asked her. "It would mean so much for us to eat together."

Devi only picked at the food. It felt as though she was studying me, trying to memorise all my peculiarities that we used to laugh at, from the way I mixed the rice with the *dhal*, then topped it with

a few strands of herbs, to the noisy way I chewed and swallowed –
once a source of comic irritation.

When she saw that I was aware of her observation, she suddenly turned to chatter. She told me our friends were digesting the
terrible news and sent their deepest love. She said that Bilal had
sent a message to say he would never forget me. She had a long list
of greetings from others on the plantation. This was part of Devi's
last gift to me – a reminder that I was thought of. That I would be
remembered on Wilson's farm once I was no longer there, and
someone else had unceremoniously taken over my *logie*, as if I had
never existed.

I indulged her. We chatted animatedly. We even managed to
laugh a bit, although it was not the hearty laughter we had so
enjoyed on the plantation. Before long, though, we both realised
we could not keep skirting around what was about to happen –
this overwhelming feeling that I was being stalked by a spectre
that would come to claim me before sunrise.

"Devi, you have been more than my friend," I told her. "You
have been my sister – closer to me than Asa and Vani. It is important that I tell you how much I love and admire you ..." That set
her off. She tried to speak, but wept quietly instead. I allowed her
this moment of grief. I imagined her returning alone to the setting
where we had always been together: the paths we had walked, the
fields where we had laboured, the river in which we had bathed,
all engraved with the memory of me and the knowledge that I
would never return. She eventually composed herself, forced a
smile, and looked at me with great tenderness. "The warden will
want me to go now," she said, gazing at the dying afternoon light.
"Shanti, do not stay angry with yourself or the world. Our souls
are bound. We will meet in another life, my friend."

"Do not come tomorrow morning," I asked her. "I do not want
you to see ..."

"Sshhh …" she said. She kissed my hands and held me tightly. "I will be here," she said, determined.

I could not find the will to argue. It would mean so much for her face to be the last sight I cast my eyes upon before the world went black.

Now it has grown dark. And tonight, I am truly alone in the world. I have no family with me, no cherished man to hold my hand, no friends to remind me one last time of the kinship we shared. I have only my journal that I page through to remind me of happy days in Vākkuṟuti with my family, Aunty Saras, my dearest friend, Devi, and the love of my life, Mustafa. It is enough love, I believe, for one human being to carry into eternity with her.

I find myself praying for another extraordinary life. But first, I need to be brave enough to leave this one with dignity and composure. It will be a painful passage, witnessed by many whose hatred for me will only be sated by the sight of my swinging corpse. But it does not matter to me now that I understand Aunty Saras's final words. I, too, now stand on the threshold of that moment when I must leave this place because I can attain nothing here any more. At sunrise, I will make my transition without regret.

CHAPTER 32

WHEN FINALLY I DRIFTED OFF to sleep, I fell into a labyrinth of strange dreams where at every turn my life was threatened. First I was walking the plank and plunging downward into a shaft of icy sea water. Then Chinnamah held me in a tight grip, forcing me to drink some poisonous potion I knew would kill me. And suddenly, Master Wilson was on top of me again, his hand clamped round my throat so hard that I knew he would choke the life out of me. Yet, as I somehow navigated this maze of nightmares, I saw the light at the end. I raced toward it and emerged to find they were all there waiting for me – my executioner with the noose in his hand, the crowd at my feet waiting silently for the hood to be pulled over my head.

I woke with a shock, relieved to be free of these dreams. But once I had orientated myself and realised I was still in my cell, the moon high in the sky, I began to count the hours to my death, torturing myself with the memory of Devi's face as she'd left the evening before – the longing with which she'd stared at me as she disappeared beyond the stone walls of the prison. I began to wish

I'd said more; expressed better what a loyal friend she had been, and what this had meant to me. I should've said sorry one last time for all the difficulty and pain our friendship had caused her. We had shared the happiest of times, but the dark days had scarred her, causing her lasting and deep trauma. And yet she had stayed by my side, never shrinking from the horrors into which my path led her. And now I was about to cause her even more pain.

But that night, nothing played out as I'd expected. Fate was to cast me in a new direction. As I lay in my cell, suspended between restless thoughts and waking dreams, I heard a hiss of low voices. I sat up, thinking something must be amiss. I could hear approaching footsteps, the footfalls softer on the stone than usual – and it sounded as if they were nearing my cell. Could it be morning already? Or were they coming to take me away earlier, to execute me alone before dawn? It made me afraid and angry – I felt entitled to the last few hours of my life.

But suddenly, in the gloom through the grille in my cell door, I thought I saw Devi emerging out of the pall of darkness. I thought I must be delirious: there was no way she would be permitted to enter at night. She saw the confusion in my eyes, and hushed me with her finger across her lips. I began to scramble to my feet. "Devi," I whispered, "can it really be …?" But she stepped back hastily and the door of my cell creaked open, unlocked by a disembodied hand that belonged to Selvan, the guard. Devi rushed at me.

"Why are you here, Devi? Is my execution to take place now?" I whispered, breathless.

"No, Shanti – not now." She was urgent. "You must listen to me! Time is short! Take your sari and your blouse off and give them to me right now. You must wear this old one I have brought you."

"But why, Devi?"

"Shanti!" She raised her voice slightly. "Listen! Just do as I say.

323

There is no time to explain. Father John is waiting outside. You must go before it's too late!"

I could not fathom what wild plan my friends had hatched to secure my freedom. But I felt a rush of gratitude and excitement for what might turn out to be another stolen day and night, and perhaps more to follow. I ripped my dirty sari and blouse off and threw them down, not caring about my nakedness. Devi helped me to hook the other blouse in the dark. I could feel the tips of her cold fingers fumbling against my sweaty skin. I wrenched up the sari skirt she had given me, sucked in a breath and tied it tightly around my waist, knotting it while she began tucking in the fabric, roughly pleating and winding it fast around me. As she threw the sash over my shoulder, she grabbed me tightly and held me close, planting a hard kiss on my cheek. She picked up my diary, shoved it into my hands, then she almost thrust me out of my cell, as I stumbled trying to put my sandals on in that dark passage to freedom. Selvan grabbed me by the arm, running with me. I briefly heard Devi's footsteps behind me as Selvan led me towards the main gate, constantly peering over his shoulder. Devi's voice was low but insistent. "Run, Shanti – there is Father John! There's not much time left – go!"

And I ran! I ran so fast towards Father John that I almost knocked him over as I threw myself into his arms. "Shanti!" he cried. I was so exhilarated, so intoxicated by the rush of that night air – the sudden expanse of space around me, the feel of soft earth underfoot – I filled my lungs almost to bursting.

Father John took my hand, and with surprising determination for a man who was so dependent on his cane, he broke into a slow trot, squeezing my hand as though he feared losing me in this race. I heard his panting above my own, and asked if he wanted to stop to catch his breath. "No!" he shouted back. "We cannot! We must keep moving," he huffed, "or the ship will leave without you. You are going home, Shanti! Home to India."

I was stunned. "How? How did you manage it?" I asked. "It doesn't matter now," he said. "It is done. This is all that matters." At first, it felt as though the very thought of India was invigorating my every step. And then I realised it was only the grasp of freedom propelling me. In my heart, there was a deep sadness about leaving this place. Although I had suffered at the hands of the merciless here, I had grown to love this land, right down to every grain of soil I had nursed, coaxing it to bring forth a sprout of sugarcane. I thought of Port Natal's breezes and the coarseness of its shore, where waves threw themselves with abandon against the rocks, and I knew I would miss it terribly. Tears stung my eyes. I had hoped to stay here and adopt it as my own land, accepting that India had been part of my past, but could no longer be my future. Now, I had to physically tear myself away from Port Natal – from my struggles and my joys here – and prepare myself to trace my way back to my old life in Vākkuṟuti, to that dilapidated home where my mat lay waiting for my body to plant itself there once more.

Father John's grip now became harder, and as we jerked around a bend, there was a horse and cart waiting for us. "Jump in!" he cried, gasping for breath by now. I leapt up, finding my footing and pulling him into the back as the driver's whip fell upon the horse and we took off.

"Wait!" I said. "Where is Devi? She cannot run all that way – it's too far to the harbour!"

"No, Shanti." Father John shook his head. "Devi is not going with you. She is still at the prison paying the bribes. There was no other way of securing your release."

"But I've not said goodbye to her ..."

"There was no time to explain, Shanti! Within the hour, the guard would have led you out to your execution. We could not take that chance." He paused to catch his breath. "All that Devi wishes is for you to board that ship and return home. She was determined that you should not die. She could not take the injustice of it – of you being punished for Wilson's crime. This plan was all of her devising. I had no say in it. Once she had made up her mind, she was resolute."

Ah, Devi, my brave friend. How could I ever thank her?

"But there is something more," he said. "There is something she requires of you in return for your life."

"Yes – anything!"

"Do not commit yourself if you will not keep this promise." He glared at me.

"Of course. I promise. Whatever it is – if Devi has requested it, I will commit to it and keep my word."

"Good, then," he said. "Then there will be no further discussion."

The docks now rose out of the charcoal night as the horse brought the cart to a shuddering standstill. We climbed off, Father John still unsteady on his feet. "Follow me!" he said. We hurried a short way and I caught sight of his assistant, Father Connor. He was holding an infant of just a few months in his arms, gently rocking her. Father John took the baby from Father Connor, placed his hand upon her head, and whispered a quiet blessing. He turned to me. "Shanti, this child … this is …"

But before the words had even left his mouth, I found myself transfixed, reaching out for her. It could not be. I took her from his arms and pressed her to me. Her countenance was so bright, her eyes keen and questioning. I touched her cheek and felt the velvet of it. She was fair-skinned, with a shock of dark hair atop her head. She looked at me and gurgled. And the sound brought a deep happiness to my very core.

"Shanti, there is something you must know. The night you thought you'd lost your baby – you didn't actually. The fruit made you violently ill. It caused you to go into labour and hallucinate.

326

But you were so far along in your pregnancy that your child survived. She was healthy, and Devi saved her. She got Dilip to spirit her off, dodging the plantation guards and risking the dangers of nightfall to run to Munisami and Latchmi, to ask them to look after her for a while. Latchmi agreed because she owed you a debt – the debt of her own child's life – which could only be repaid by caring for yours. Devi always believed, rightly or wrongly, that the day would come when you'd be ready to be this little one's mother. And that time is now."

I gazed upon that bundle in my arms and felt the lightness of her. She seemed so breakable that I held her gingerly. I touched her face again and let her wrap her tight fist around my finger. She was pure perfection – her silken skin, her gentle burbling, the depth of her eyes that seemed to stretch back through time. I adored her in that moment, and was supremely grateful to be able to love this living, breathing child, rather than the dream of her I had loved every day since I'd believed she'd died. I kissed her and held her tight and let my tears flow over her. I thought of Devi and the debt I owed her for the rest of my life, and I was filled with gratitude. And then, the baby began to cry, just soft sounds of discomfort as the crowds began to thicken around us.

"Shanti," Father John said. "I know you will make good. But now you must board this ship." He handed me a bag that Devi had prepared for me. I thrust my diary into it while Father John again took me by the arm, shepherding me toward an official. "Show me the list!" he instructed the man, who thrust it under his face. He put his finger on it to locate my name. "This is her name," he said. "Kavila. The child is to return to India for a naming ceremony."

Then he softened as he turned to me. "Both of you, go with God." He pulled us toward him in a rib-cracking embrace. It was becoming difficult to stand without being shoved by the gathering crowd of passengers, and I was jolted backwards into a knot of bodies, their heat assailing me. But I held my baby close, and protected her from those who rammed at us from all sides. Father John turned as if to go, then swivelled back on his cane. "Shanti! John chapter 15, verse 13. Do not forget it." And he was wiped from my view by the throng swarming the gangplank.

I was swept onto the deck, clutching my baby to my breast, elbowed by all those filled with impatience to see India again. I found a space to occupy and sat down, quietly rocking her, speaking words of comfort. I had expected her to bawl amid this onslaught of sound and smell. But she seemed contented to lie against my skin and listen to my murmurings. I knew then that it was entirely up to me to ensure her survival. She had no father. There was no Devi here, no Latchmi to come to my rescue again. This child who had pushed through me into the light with her refusal to stop breathing: she had demanded to be in the world. I silently pledged to try my best to keep her safe in it.

The anchor was pulled up, and with the slow rocking of the ship, my daughter soon fell into a deep slumber while I lay awake, watching the port recede from me. I thought I saw the frantic waving of Father John's white handkerchief, but it might only have been a dream as I'd allowed the rhythm of the ship's paddles to slowly lull me to sleep for a time. The minutes and the hours fell away as the ship steadily put distance between Port Natal and us. Uncomfortable though it was, I had positioned us between as many bodies as possible so that as temperatures fell, my baby would still be warm. And although I allowed myself to drift into sleep, I was still aware of the precious cargo in my arms, and moulded my body around her like a warm fortress.

I cannot tell how many hours passed before first light fell upon my eyelids. I awoke to find my little one staring intently at me through a pair of dark, enquiring eyes. Her smile seemed to light the sun, and in the early light, I began to take in the details of her features. I saw nothing of Wilson in her. She was mine, as she had been from the moment of conception. I nuzzled her, knowing she would soon be hungry. But Devi had gathered provisions for us, among them, the milk needed for the start of our journey. In time, I would have to barter with the kindly woman sitting nearby, who was nursing her own infant, to feed my child too. For now, I looked down at my daughter and whispered, "Let us go and find the chaplain, my love."

I walked the length of the boat, asking anyone who would listen where I could find the priest, until a small group of people who understood Tamil directed me toward the stern. I saw a man standing there with his back to me, saying his prayers as the sun rose. I waited until he dropped his hands, then addressed him in English.

"Father, I believe you are the chaplain on this boat."

"Yes." He turned to me, adorned in his priest's shirt and collar. "Good morning. How may I assist you?"

"Father, I have a verse in mind, but I can't quite remember what it says."

"Ah, and what verse is that?" he asked.

I had been revising it intermittently in my head since Father John had called it out to me, so that I would not forget it.

"I believe it is John chapter … 15, verse 13."

"Ah, that is a well-known one, indeed – and one of my favourites. *Greater love hath no man than this, that a man lay down his life for his friends.*" I shook my head. For a moment, I could not fathom what it meant – why Father John had been so cryptic in his choice of that verse. But now I saw again the pain etched into his face as he called it out.

And then it dawned on me. I was almost knocked off my feet by the revelation, and willed my legs to hold me upright, especially with the baby in my arms. The priest asked if I was all right, if he could do anything to help. But I found a sudden charge in my feet and fled before he could say anything more. I knew with certainty now what Father John's last words to me had meant.

That very dawn, as I had welcomed the new day and cooed over my baby, Devi had taken her final step toward death – for my sake. It occurred to me how premeditated it had all been – how I'd stripped down to hand her my execution sari while I wound this one round me in the dark, not realising until now, as I gazed more closely at the patterns, that it was hers. When the guards came to seize me in the morning, they would have found me missing – unless my mirror image sat before them, waiting to die in my place. At that moment, they would be taking her down that frightful passage as I safely floated away – her last short journey to the waiting noose and the trapdoor below, the voices of jeering onlookers revelling in her pain, the executioner decrying my crime as though it were her own.

And the British, in the rush to quench their thirst for my blood, would only realise after the fact that they had murdered the wrong woman. Miles away on the Wilson plantation, the *sirdar* would be the first to search for her and raise the alarm when he found her missing. But by then, the horizon would already have swallowed the ship that had borne me away.

How bitterly I cried for Devi, so wild in my tears that my baby also began to wail. But though my heart sat like a stone in my chest, as I knew it would for a long time, I tried hard to comfort my child. "Little Devarakshanam," I said, "do not cry. I know you have had the cruellest introduction to this world – one you did not deserve. But we will begin again, you and I. Aunty Devi loved us both enough to give us a second chance."

I turned around one last time to see if Port Natal was even a blur in the distance. But the wind had been keen, and it had mercifully driven us away from those shores so swiftly that we might have all dreamt up this place called the Colony of Natal – and everyone who inhabited it. I thought of what an enchanting place it was – the landscape so lush, the waters warm and hypnotic, the people born there so tied to the land. How I wished I could take a painter's brush and blot out the British, to return the place to what it had been before they came upon it – before any of us set foot there.

But I do not suppose it is ever possible to undo the past. Wherever we go, we leave our impression, and all the generations that follow are marked by it too. It occurrs to me that the past is neither carved in stone alone, nor recorded singularly by the quill. Perhaps it is etched into the flesh, bones and memory of human beings, and travels silently into the veins of our descendants. Perhaps the only measure of hope lies in the future. For as long as it remains unwritten, it is all we mere mortals have the power to change.

PART 3

VĀKKUṞUTI, MADRAS PRESIDENCY

India 1916

CHAPTER 33

RAKSHA STARED AT THE RAFTERS, contemplating the implosion of her life. Not far from where she lay was the spot where her mother, Shanti, had collapsed just weeks before. The healer had been trying to coax her back from the brink ever since. David was gone. He'd briefly returned even after Raksha had spat her fury at him, and warned him never to come back. Since then, she had answered to no one who came knocking at the door, covering her ears when she heard David's pleas for her to open up, knowing he was too much of a gentleman to enter against her will.

The school was shut. Raksha could not allow the children to see the human cavity she had become, eaten away by all that had come to light in the previous weeks. She had lain in the same position for days, never eating, hardly drinking, her mother's journal lying open next to her, on her chest, under her head.

And yet she could not put it down. It had been left there for her to find, after all. But it was one thing to believe your mother occasionally spoke in half-truths, quite another to learn how deep a repository she was, how many damaging secrets she held. Raksha believed she should have steeled herself better. But there is never a suitable moment to discover your father is not a man your mother loved, or that you are the consequence of rape, or that she tried to abort you.

Raksha realised that no matter your closeness to another human being – whether you shared an umbilical cord or a bed – everyone remained an enigma. There was a part of every human being, a cocoon at their very core, in which secrets lived undiluted. And though we might know altered versions that surfaced over time, we could never fully access the unadulterated truth. Raksha had tip-toed into the most sacred part of her mother's life – her tabernacle, where the mysteries of all she had done and all that had been done to her existed in uneasy dissonance.

Her mother's diary unhinged her; absorbing it had meant pulling on Shanti's skin, breathing into her lungs and allowing Shanti's heart to beat in her. Raksha had wiped her mind clean for Shanti's thoughts to run wild in her head. There were passages that scrambled Raksha and assaulted her, goaded her, made her hate Shanti – cry, curse, scream aloud, lie prostrate and slam her fists against the floor. At times, she'd been enraged enough to invite her mother's death. But although it hurt her, she would not let the truth defeat her. Raksha read and re-read like a daughter, then a scholar – lost in that labyrinth of words, grasping at them for purchase. She repeated passages, memorising them, reciting them aloud; arguing with her mother in her head, condemning and sentencing her. Shanti's words injured and broke her; they patched, emboldened and healed her. They invaded her, drew her close, and comforted her in the same breath.

As Raksha read on, the portrait of Shanti's life began to fill with the nuance of light that distorted black and white, that made all the primary colours run, so nothing was as it seemed. She swung between loving her mother, pitying her, judging her, forgiving her, wanting to save and avenge her. Raksha slowly began to feel the germination of empathy, of understanding, for courageous lives lived in times and places where it was not easy to be the human being you had hoped to be. Finally, as she turned the last page, Raksha found herself able to decipher the words, to distil them into one single reassuring image of how flawed and wounded, how perfectly human her mother was.

How many generations had lived like this in her family, beneath the shade of secrets? They had all, in some way, lived lives of concealment, each keeping their desires hidden, their fears and happiness veiled, their ambitions and remorse buried. Clandestine lives marked by constraint. Now Raksha realised she, too, had repeated history. She had spent long months allowing David to woo her covertly, keeping the relationship from her mother. But if there was one valuable lesson in Shanti's diary, it was that no human being should be compelled to live this way. Raksha would no longer carry the burden of lies and pretence.

What would Shanti's life have been, had she not sacrificed her own happiness in punishing Mustafa for his secrets? All these lost years without the only man she truly loved because he lacked the courage to fight convention and tell the truth. But that was the same crossroads at which Raksha now found herself. Her anger at David had abated in recent days. She could no longer rebuke him for his refusal to keep destructive secrets.

Raksha rose and examined herself in the looking glass in disgust. Her hair was matted stiff from the saltiness of her tears, her face was dirty, her clothes were wrinkled. She decided to build a fire and heat some water. She dipped a cloth into the water and cleaned herself thoroughly, wiping every pore, scorching herself in places with the steaming cloth. It was good to feel something physical, even if it was pain. Then she dried, dressed and perfumed herself, preparing to go and see the two people in the world who loved her, but had hurt her the most. Too much ruin had already been wrought. Surely some of what was damaged could be repaired.

Dear Aunty Devi,

You are no more.

I wrote those four words hours ago, stared at them again and again to internalise their meaning, then walked away from this letter because my mind could not properly absorb the reality. For years, my mother has spoken as if you were alive – simply abandoned in Port Natal. And when Selvaraj's letter came, I imagined the joy of embracing you as you arrived at my home.

But I now understand no such thing is possible. It seems so strange for me to pen this letter, knowing what I do. I have spent weeks digesting the extent of the sacrifice you made, and what courage it must have taken to orchestrate such a sad end to your own life, in tribute to my mother's and mine.

I address this to you because my mother's words in her diary have somehow resurrected you, and you are more alive, more intimately known to me, than ever before. I am convinced that you have transcended this life to live on on another plane, and that putting these words down allows me to somehow reach you wherever you are, even if I cannot touch you in this life.

I want to thank you with all my heart for saving first my life, and then my mother's, and ensuring we were one day reunited. My mother has often said over the years what an extraordinary person you were; only now am I fully able to appreciate what she meant. It saddens me that there is no way to repay our debt to you. But perhaps, if I give you an inkling of the occurrences of recent weeks, you will see that we are trying our very best to honour you in the choices we have made for our future.

Since my mother collapsed, and I confined myself to our home with the singular company of her journal, the revelations that poured forth have profoundly changed me, opening a window into a world I could never have imagined. In reading it, I discovered what it is to love and hate one's only living relative in equal measure. I have given thought to what good people are often compelled to do in predicaments that threaten their very survival. I have come to believe that we are all entitled to our secrets, but those that harm are better exposed to the daylight. I am also learning how one justly holds a loved one to account, but finds the fortitude to forgive them at the same time.

When I was ready, I went to visit my mother at the temple. I had received word a few weeks before that she had made a gradual but steady recovery. But it was not until I had interrogated her every written word that I felt I could go there and face her again. I came to realise that her choice to leave her diary out for me to find was an act of both cowardice and extreme courage. There are private things about their lives, I imagine, no one ever wants to share with their children. And yet, after all her years of secrecy, she bared her soul to me in that book, believing that even after reading it, I would love her as before. It was a demonstration of faith – and one that bore fruit. Truthfully, I love her now with an intensity I have not felt before.

But that did not stop me from questioning my mother when I laid eyes on her for the first time in weeks. She was coping better and had just returned from a short walk around the temple at Jairam the healer's instruction. When she saw me, she reached out to draw me into her arms. But I could not return her embrace – not yet. She sensed that and stepped back, telling me of how, while she had lain inert for so many weeks, Jairam had spoken to her, and with his voice had woven a strong thread she could grasp, one that drew her back as she drifted away from me. And even in that somnambulant state, she had known what Jairam had meant when he'd said, "You cannot leave with regret, with so many affairs unresolved, Shanti. Come back and set everything right with those you love first." Jairam's persuasion had carried her back on a gentle tide to the present world, where she had opened her eyes, longing to see me. It had broken her heart that weeks later, I had still not come to visit her.

I must tell you – I, too, had doubts about how she would receive me. You see, Aunty Devi, I had done something my mother believed was wholly unforgivable. I had fallen in love with a British man who was once a soldier in the service of the Crown. Of course, he is no longer the man who pillaged our villages and sowed terror in the hearts of our people. He has admitted to his atrocities, he is remorseful and penitent, and I have helped him to come to some acceptance of his own violent past.

It was not my intention to fall in love with David. But it happened. And because he chose to share the truth of our re-lationship with my mother, it almost cost her her life. Yet I am now relieved it came to light. I have forgiven him because I know his intention was merely to come to my house like an honourable man, present himself before my mother, and ask for her blessing on our relationship. I was almost too afraid to mention David's name in the presence of *Ama*, knowing her health was still fragile. But, she told me her anger over David had dissipated, that as she lay suspended between life and death, she'd had a revelation of her own – that history would repeat itself if she did not accept my right to choose who to love, as she had hoped to when she was a young woman.

And then I asked her if she had ever really been able to love me; or if, as I had feared, she looked into my face each day and saw in my features my father, Wilson, the rapist.

How my mother wept when I asked her this, Aunty Devi. "You must know I have loved you since the moment I knew you had come to live inside me," she said. "And every moment since then was dedicated to making the best choice I could for you. I only thought of ending my pregnancy because I didn't want to bring you into the world to suffer. Many women abort their babies with good reason, Raksha," she said, "and that is their right. But after I lost you, I felt differently. You were gone, but you remained alive inside me, haunting me every day until I took you in my arms again at the docks."

I listened, but still told her how infuriated I had been with her – how I had judged and condemned her for her betrayal as I read her words and learnt of her deceit. It pained her to hear me say this. After all, she had always known me to be a loving and diligent daughter. But I could see she was learning something surprising about me. I am not the acquiescent young child I used to be. She admitted that she saw something of the rebellion she'd had in her own eyes as a child; and now, instead of censuring me for it, she was slowly coming to terms with my quiet defiance and learning to respect me for it.

She did not try to justify a single action or word. I told her of the demi-goddess she had always been in my mind, and how difficult it had been for me to walk in her footsteps for so long. But I also told her that in reading her journal, I had received the greatest gift she could give me – the knowledge of her flawed humanity, her mistakes, her regrets, her triumphs.

We met as new people, Aunty Devi – broken people, trying to piece ourselves together after a rift so deep, it might have torn our small family apart. I took her hands in mine. "*Ama*, you must stay here a few more days and heal fully, while I visit David and try to mend my relationship with him, if he will have me back. You must make peace with our love for one another. If we behave like the British, who disparage us for who we are, we are no better than them."

There was a softening in her eyes and she nodded. "Raksha, if you have allowed him into your heart, I choose to believe he is a good man. It's true – I have wrestled hard with the idea of your relationship. But that is my struggle, not yours. I have decided that I must accept him. It will not be easy for me at first, and I beg your indulgence. But I will learn. David will come to our humble house. I will welcome him there, and he will sit and eat with us, and in time, I will come to a fuller understanding of your love for each other."

"He is my Mustafa, *Ama*. I know that I will never love another man the way I love David."

"People think that is mere fantasy, my child," she said. "But I have lived it. I know the notion of the one great love of our lives to be true. And that is why you must know something else that I have been keeping from you."

"What, *Ama*?" I asked her.

She told me that about the same time Selvaraj's letter arrived, she had received another letter postmarked Sindh province. And when I heard the name of that province, Aunty Devi, I immediately knew who it had come from. I asked her what the writer had said, and when she told me it comprised nothing but the poem she had shared with her beloved Mustafa, the meaning became clear to me.

"So, is he coming, *Ama*?" I asked her.

"I believe so," she said, the hint of a smile beginning to play at her lips. I allowed her that brief moment of happiness, as she revealed to me that her love for Mustafa had not diminished over the years. I urged her not to judge him for his mistakes or the choices he'd made before he met her, but to find it in her heart to forgive his deception.

"I suppose if we meditate on our collective lost chances, Raksha," she said, "we will see how much we have squandered, and so unnecessarily."

"Enough meditation on the past, *Ama*," I told her. "It is time for new beginnings. We must embrace them with gratitude."

I left for the twin lakes, my head awash with doubt as to how David might receive me. But as I approached in the sweltering heat, he was standing at his fence alongside the lake, looking out expectantly. He disappeared for a moment, then returned with a glass of water. I stopped, reached for it with both hands, and drank it down to the last drop. He led me inside, took me in his arms, and we both wept until we could hardly speak.

We knew it would be only a few days before my mother returned home. David, who is fairly accomplished at artisanry, set about making a few changes in her absence. He reinforced some of the weaknesses in the structure of our house, and gave us a fine wooden table and set of chairs which he had built himself. When my mother returned, she accepted his gift gracefully, and she and David sat at the table, conversing, while I prepared a meal. Though I hovered nervously, worried they might go at each other again, their first interactions were civil, and I trusted that in time they would earn each other's respect. We were all too aware that there was still much to do before Selvaraj's visit. But my mother, David and I set about it with industriousness and excitement, and were soon satisfied that Selvaraj would arrive to a presentable home with enough food to last for many days.

A shadow appeared at our door a week later. We heard the sound of shoes falling gently off his feet. There stood Selvaraj, his hands pressed together – the man my mother had known as a boy. He was full of delight to see us. Selvaraj reminded me that I was once a bawling baby in his mother's arms, and he distinctly remembered the day I had been brought there on your instructions, Aunty Devi. He said he had grown to love me as a little sister, and was quite heartbroken when I was taken away. I felt an instant bond with Selvaraj, although I naturally had no memory of him. He brought a smile to my face, calling me *thangachi*, his little sister.

Selvaraj had brought us gifts from Africa, but the most valuable of them was nestled in a copper urn.

It was you, Aunty Devi. Selvaraj pressed the vessel into my mother's hands. And she took it so protectively, clutching it to her chest as though her own heart could breathe life back into you. She thanked him for keeping you safe across such a long distance, waited a long moment then prised the urn open. Inside, she saw your ashes. And she regretted that so free a spirit should have been contained in the darkness of that urn for so many years. *Ama* opened the box and reached in to touch you – her first contact with you in nearly forty summers, your ashes like powder between her fingers, among them bits of brittle bone that had withstood fire and time. She ran to Selvaraj, and he held her tight until the collar of his shirt drooped with her tears, telling her of how Father John had claimed your body and handed it over to your friends on the plantation for cremation.

And as the evening wore on, you sat among us at that table,

the four of us alternating between tears and laughter, while my *Ama* invoked your memory, your spirit, the fullness of who you were – and you briefly walked among us again. My mother's heart was lifted. Although she'd never see you in the flesh again, at least you were home. It occurred to me, Aunty Devi, that perhaps immortality is not only about living forever. Perhaps it is more about living on in the memories of those who love us and tend those memories with care.

Only yesterday, Selvaraj told us of the docking of a ship from Sindh province at the Port of Madras. The nature of travel to these parts means that only one evening could now separate my mother from the truth of whether the man who once promised her his eternal love was returning to fulfil his pledge. I believe he will come and teach my mother the lesson I myself have learnt about love – the barriers to it are far weaker than the essence of love itself. All that is needed is the will to fight for it. I hope that when my mother and this mysterious Mustafa make their journey to your home, they will stop at the river to scatter your last remnants there, and allow this letter to float away with them. All those years ago, you gave us another chance, but what you cannot know is that your coming to India has again brought the hope of renewal to each of us.

Wherever you are, may you soar eternally, my dearest Aunty Devi.

Love,
Raksha

My dearest Devi, most loving friend,

Tonight, the air has a delicate warmth to it – a tender kiss on a
bare shoulder. The cicadas singing in chorus lend a delicious
frisson to the air. The moon is almost full, but shy, darting behind a cloud now and then, creating an indigo light in the sky.
It is, for me, a night of deep anticipation.

I am girding myself for the coming of the man I loved and
lost so many years ago. It is strange, these feelings that have
resurfaced in recent days. I cannot explain them, except to say
I feel I am a young woman again, falling in love for the first
time. All these days I have raged against the hope brimming
inside me, afraid of yet another disappointment. The pain of
betrayal has never left me. But I have finally grown to understand that, as a young man, Mustafa was also denied the right
to determine his own fate; he simply allowed it to be decided
for him, as tradition dictated. To my more mature mind, this
sin seems so much more forgivable than I found it in the past.

I could not have imagined so heartening a change in fortunes. But I believe Raksha is right: you have brought the
promise of reconciliation and reunion to our house, linking
past so intimately with present. There is a lightness in Raksha's
step since we began walking the path of reconciliation. At
times, there remains an underlying tension, but we are toiling
hard towards a better understanding of each other.

I now concede that she and David are a loving couple. I was
wrong to label their love a short-lived infatuation rather than
genuine commitment. They will soon be married, I believe.
Raksha has confided that David had long wanted to elope, but
that she had stayed because of my precarious health. Since
then, I have encouraged them to go wherever they desire. It
is time my daughter, who suspended her happiness on my

account for so long, allows herself the freedom to enjoy it with my blessing. She and David often speak of Port Natal as a possible destination. I tell them both of its beauty and its violence, but also remind them that their prospects will be so much better than mine. David may easily secure work within the civil service – or Selvaraj's enterprise, as they have struck up a friendship. Raksha may continue her work in the teaching profession. After all, indenture has ended, and there are many young minds full of promise to feed in Port Natal, as you and I had dreamt of doing ourselves.

Many people in this place speak badly of us, Devi. Those who once respected her as a sacred teacher treat Raksha with disdain now that her relationship with David is common knowledge. Matters will only worsen when a stranger from Sindh appears on my doorstep, and I receive him as I have no other man in my entire life. But it is no longer of concern to me. I wish to spurn this convention where crucial decisions are made about our lives based on the opinions of others. To hell with those aspects of culture and custom that prevent us from pursuing truth and happiness.

Earlier this evening, Raksha delighted my heart, coming to sit with me as I dressed and assisting me with my preparations. "*Ama*," she said, as she braided my hair, "there is something about your diary I neglected to say, so caught up was I in the emotion of it. It is truly poetic and lyrical. It moved me. Now I understand what Aunty Saras meant when she said you had the heart of a writer. You *are* a woman of letters, just as you dreamt you would be." When she left, I was so overcome, Devi. That hope I had nursed for so long had been lost in the exertions of my life. Now, all these years later, to hear that assurance from the lips of my daughter gave me more joy than I feel I deserve.

347

Tonight Devi, I am audacious. I dare to hope for more joy. I am heavily perfumed. If my outward appearance does not draw him in, perhaps my scent will! I study myself in the looking glass as I have done for many days now, and I wonder if he will long for my younger self, for the fire that blazed in me, for my firm flesh and fertile mind, or if he will see me as I sometimes see myself now – weakened, a woman inhabiting an ageing body and tired mind.

Sometimes I see pity reflected in Raksha's eyes. It is as if she is watching the unwinding of my soul from my body as it prepares to leave this realm, though neither of us knows exactly when. I think, at times, she too must long for the lustre of my youth – the speed with which I chased her around the lakes, threw her into the air and caught her, her dainty little feet slicing the air.

But you endure differently in our minds, Devi. The sacrifice you made earned you escape from all the indignities of age – regret, confusion, loneliness, the wrinkled skin and coarseness of greying hair, the blue film over the eyes that stops you from seeing the detail in things.

It is a strange thing to contemplate beauty in our old age, precisely when it deserts us. But I wonder how I will perceive Mustafa in the instant my gaze falls upon him. In my mind, he remains that sturdy young man with muscled shoulders, the agility of his arms sweeping me up, laughing, into our cave at the ocean where he gave himself to me time and time again. I try to picture him as he must be now: a smaller man, slightly hunched, perhaps, his gait slower, his footsteps more calculated; a life behind him that he may now wish to forget, a life before him he may yet allow himself to imagine, knowing time is no longer his friend, nor mine.

Time, in its baseness, turns the finest wine to vinegar, flesh to ash, the pride of young men to the shame of their last days. And the journey of my own life has taught me this, Devi: it is only love that defies it, that lies dormant for however long the human heart will keep it asleep. It rises still, energised after hibernation, to teach even the most damaged of us that it is the singular reason we walk this earth. This is what I have finally wrung out of the pungency of my life, Devi – the enduring nature of love in motherhood, friendship, and that of a man who may yet remember why he once loved me.

And I think of you, Devi – in the distant past my closest ally, now the receptacle of my truth and dreams. Tonight, I wondered where the essence of you truly remained. I looked to the sky with its darkening intensity, and an urge impelled me. I rushed in and retrieved your urn, flung it open and seized a handful of you, hurling you, jettisoning you towards the skies. A keen breeze took you, spiralling you upwards and embedding you in the vast night sky. It is you I wish upon tonight, Devi. Defy destiny if you must, and write this love in the stars for us – my Mustafa and me.

Yours in infinite love and eternal friendship,
Shanti.

ACKNOWLEDGEMENTS

IT HAS TAKEN ME NINE years and the indulgence of a very patient family to put this novel together. Several years ago, when I found a photograph of my maternal great-grandmother, Athilatchmy Velu Naiken, on the internet, my curiosity was piqued as to how she came to set foot on African soil. That sent me down a series of rab-bit holes involving my family history, assisted in part by my brother Jeremy, who was equally intrigued.

I discovered some wonderful documentation telling the story of both the indentured and racially mixed side of my maternal family, and the passenger Indians on my paternal side – whose experience of coming to Port Natal must have been quite different in many ways, but convergent in others. This also stirred in me a desire to know more about Indian indenture in the Colony of Natal, and how it played out; not just in the lives of entire Indian families or men who came here, but particularly through the experiences of young women without means who took the leap.

I studied *Inside Indian Indenture*, by Ashwin Desai and Goolam Vahed, like a Bible. What an eye-opener it was; many of the events they relate in their outstanding book have come to find a home in this novel. There are similarly dozens of other academics to whom I am indebted for their extensive research, some of which I was able to include in *Children of Sugarcane*. Their insights, together with my great-grandmother's story, reminded me that although subjugated by a cruel system in which human-rights atrocities were committed, there was something truly heroic about indentured women. I wanted to capture this tragic heroism in a narrative that I hoped would be accessible to 21st-century readers.

Since then, this novel has undergone multiple incarnations. But I must thank the early readers of the clunkiest version – Jeremy Joseph (whom I still picture sprawled on my sofa reading into the wee hours), my parents Andy and May Joseph, who read large portions and convinced me that it was worth finishing, my close friends Paulina French and Matthew Ribnick, who gave me honest feedback on what sections needed re-working, my husband Neil, who fed and watered me during intense periods of writing and stayed up late into the night discussing possible plot twists with me, my daughter Jade, who never once complained about the hours I spent locked away writing and always encouraged me to press on, and brilliant academic and mentor Dr Betty Govinden, who praised me for getting it down.

It is difficult to mould a vast history into an elegant form. I owe my infinite thanks to Dr Helen Moffett, who chiselled it into a more distinct shape a few years ago, and persisted again in the last few months to edit *Children of Sugarcane* with the utmost respect and sensitivity – while emerging from illness. Likewise, historical editor Dr Vashna Jaganarth, while also recovering from compromised health, skilfully raked through this manuscript to address any historical inaccuracies, and gently called into question some modern sensibilities that had crept into the text.

My publisher, Nkanyezi Tshabalala, is a dream, having shown

so much love, enthusiasm and regard for this book. I am ever so grateful for our long literary conversations, her support, and that of the wider Jonathan Ball team, who have treated me with great kindness and poured their time and expertise into birthing this novel.

My sincere thanks to you, the reader, for your willingness to engage with *Children of Sugarcane*. As Angela Carter wrote, "You bring to a novel, anything you read, all your experience of the world. You bring your history and you read it in your own terms," and I am grateful for those interactions, however they play out.

Most of all, I hope *Children of Sugarcane* is able to play some small role in stimulating thinking about how we interpret atrocities of the past, how they have shaped our archetypal perceptions of one another intersectionally, and how we address the intergenerational trauma (conscious or unconscious) that results from our ancestors' pain. It is saddening that over a century and a half later, the majority of South Africans continue to live in the kind of squalor indentured labourers once did. If we begin to think of indenture as part of our shared history, and to explore how deeply stained we all are by our collective colonial past, perhaps we can begin to imagine a shared future in which we work actively towards eradicating the myriad inequalities that currently plague our society.

Joanne Joseph
Johannesburg, October 2021